An author of more than ninet
adults with more than sevent_
Janice Kay Johnson writes about love and family and
pens books of gripping romantic suspense. A *USA Today*
bestselling author and an eight-time finalist for the
Romance Writers of America RITA Award, she won a
RITA Award in 2008. A former librarian, Janice has
raised two daughters in a small town north of Seattle,
Washington.

A *USA Today* bestselling author of over one hundred
novels in twenty languages, **Tara Taylor Quinn** has sold
more than seven million copies. Known for her intense
emotional fiction, Tara's novels have received critical
acclaim in the UK and most recently from Harvard. She
is the recipient of the Readers' Choice Award and has
appeared often on local and national TV, including *CBS
Sunday Morning*. For TTQ offers, news and contests,
visit tarataylorquinn.com

Also by Janice Kay Johnson

Hide the Child
Trusting the Sheriff
Within Range
Brace for Impact
The Hunting Season
The Last Resort
Cold Case Flashbacks
Dead in the Water
Crash Landing
Wilderness Hostage

Also by Tara Taylor Quinn

Sierra's Web
Tracking His Secret Child
Cold Case Sheriff
The Bounty Hunter's Baby Search
On the Run with His Bodyguard
Not Without Her Child
A Firefighter's Hidden Truth
Last Chance Investigation
Danger on the River

Discover more at millsandboon.co.uk

STORING SECRETS

JANICE KAY JOHNSON

HORSE RANCH HIDEOUT

TARA TAYLOR QUINN

MILLS & BOON

All rights reserved including the right of reproduction in whole or in part in any form. This edition is published by arrangement with Harlequin Enterprises ULC.

This is a work of fiction. Names, characters, places, locations and incidents are purely fictional and bear no relationship to any real life individuals, living or dead, or to any actual places, business establishments, locations, events or incidents. Any resemblance is entirely coincidental.

Without limiting the author's and publisher's exclusive rights, any unauthorised use of this publication to train generative artificial intelligence (AI) technologies is expressly prohibited. HarperCollins also exercise their rights under Article 4(3) of the Digital Single Market Directive 2019/790 and expressly reserve this publication from the text and data mining exception.

® and ™ are trademarks owned and used by the trademark owner and/or its licensee. Trademarks marked with ® are registered with the United Kingdom Patent Office and/or the Office for Harmonisation in the Internal Market and in other countries.

First Published in Great Britain 2025
by Mills & Boon, an imprint of HarperCollins*Publishers* Ltd
1 London Bridge Street, London, SE1 9GF

www.harpercollins.co.uk

HarperCollins*Publishers*
Macken House, 39/40 Mayor Street Upper,
Dublin 1, D01 C9W8, Ireland

Storing Secrets © 2025 Janice Kay Johnson
Horse Ranch Hideout © 2025 TTQ Books LLC

ISBN: 978-0-263-39721-5

0725

This book contains FSC™ certified paper and other controlled sources to ensure responsible forest management.

For more information visit: www.harpercollins.co.uk/green

Printed and Bound in the UK using 100% Renewable Electricity at
CPI Group (UK) Ltd, Croydon, CR0 4YY

STORING SECRETS

JANICE KAY JOHNSON

Chapter One

The small cluster of people—four of them in addition to Erin Reed—stared into the packed ten-by-fifteen-foot storage unit. A few feet from Erin, her three-year-old son sat cross-legged on the asphalt, drawing a picture with colored chalk. For a child his age, he was exceptionally patient.

Erin didn't know how she'd have managed if Toby weren't so good at entertaining himself.

Thank goodness Jeremy Conyers, the new owner of this storage facility, didn't seem to mind the chalk. Of course, it would wash off with the next rain, never far away in western Washington. Right now, Jeremy just stood there waiting with his arms crossed. He'd probably conducted enough of these auctions to be able to guess what he'd make for the contents of the units. No doubt he was more excited that whoever won the auction would have to haul all the junk away, allowing him to rent the unit again.

Erin knew that all too often, people spent an awful lot of money to store battered furniture and boxes of used clothing and kitchenware in just decent enough shape to be donated to a thrift shop.

"Three hundred," one guy said without a lot of enthusiasm.

"Three fifty," someone else countered.

Having no intention of bidding this time, Erin pondered why people always deposited their unwanted washers and dryers at the front of a storage unit. Pile a few plastic tubs atop them, and the aging appliances did an excellent job of blocking any view of whatever was stored deeper inside a space that was usually longer than wide.

Erin's livelihood was based on her keen eye. She hit up every garage sale in surrounding towns and judged how high to bid on the contents of storage lockers that went up for auction after the owner quit paying the bills. Her judgment was good enough to support herself and her son without having to pursue Toby's dad through the courts. That might mean actually having to *see* him again.

She knew all of the other bidders here today casually, at least. Two of them sold solely on eBay. One claimed he did, but he usually shied away at the last minute and got outbid, so who knew? She was the only one of the small group who both sold online and had a good-sized booth in an antique mall here in town.

"Four hundred," offered Kevin Hargrave—no, Hargrove, Erin thought.

She kept her mouth shut, and after a few grimaces, so did everyone else. The auction ended there. Kevin and Jeremy huddled for a moment over a clipboard before Jeremy closed the unit door and handed the key to the padlock to Kevin.

As always, Erin crossed her fingers that she hadn't passed up a treasure trove. Her last glance at what she could see reassured her.

A lanky man in his early thirties who'd inherited this independently owned storage facility from an uncle who'd recently died, Jeremy led the group around the end of the cinder-block strip of units to a second one, the contents of which were also up for auction.

Having two in one day was unusual, and Erin hoped

things moved briskly. Toby might have an extraordinary attention span for a boy his age, but it wasn't unlimited. When she smiled and held out her hand, he clutched his chalk and trotted along at her side.

"How come you didn't buy that one?" he asked.

"Just...didn't see anything exciting," she explained.

He nodded. Apparently, he hadn't, either. At least he'd learned that he wasn't allowed to sneak in while the adults were occupied.

Jeremy unlocked this padlock and rolled up the blue door. "Fifteen by twenty-five feet," he told them.

That was about as big as these units came. The contents of an entire *house* could fit into that space.

Erin's attention sharpened, and she wasn't even sure why. The requisite washer and dryer sat in front, although these were in good enough condition they actually might be salable. Nobody was allowed to step into a unit, so they all wandered side to side, craning their necks, even rising on tiptoe. The peculiar shapes under tarps, packing blankets and sheets suggested furniture, although she could see some piles of plastic tubs, too. The most expensive kind, she noted, the ones that wouldn't crumple even if you jumped up and down on them.

A few inches of wood peeked out here and there, and wasn't that the neck of a musical instrument case? A guitar? No, she thought; something larger.

A hum of energy in the air told her she wasn't alone in her interest, although she also wasn't alone in maintaining an expression of skepticism on her face. *Nothing interesting here*, she tried to project. On the plus side, those who sold solely online were less inclined to be interested in furniture, especially large pieces that were hard to store, package and ship.

Bidding started at five hundred but climbed quickly. Erin

prided herself on knowing when to stop, but even when they passed five thousand dollars, she kept going. At eighty-five hundred, her principal competitor, Walt—something ordinary, like Jones or Smith—shook his head and said, "It's all yours. But, damn, I'd like to see what's in there."

She grinned at him. "You and me both. You wouldn't begrudge me a victory dance, would you?"

He laughed. "For that price, you might find yourself weeping, you know."

Unfortunately, that was true.

She signed her name on Jeremy's paperwork and accepted the key, then smiled at Toby. "Let's go get our truck, and we can take some stuff home with us now."

"Yeah!"

The group all walked back to the entrance together. She took the time to write a check to Jeremy and usher Toby to the bathroom before they drove back to unit 417.

After raising the door, she heaved several heavy plastic tubs to the back of her pickup truck, then used her dolly to laboriously move the dryer onto the asphalt surface in front of the storage unit to clear the way. Wiping the sweat from her face with a rag, she grimaced.

Why were the unwanted washers and dryers always at the front? Dumb question. The damn things were heavy and awkward. Why move them an inch farther than you had to? And, hey, if some rainwater seeped under the rolling door, who cared if the dented and/or rusting appliances were further damaged?

Excitement bubbled even as she pressed her hand to her aching lower back and turned to see what treasures she might have acquired.

Toby grabbed a handful of his mother's sweatshirt and didn't move. "Mommy?" He was usually eager to rush in.

Please don't let there be taxidermy elk heads meant to hang on the wall or other horrors.

She looked down to see his attention riveted on the jam-packed interior of the large unit. Her gaze followed his.

The furniture was mostly covered and had more plastic tubs and cardboard boxes piled atop, but…

A sheet had slipped off to reveal the incredibly elaborate top of what had to be a chest of drawers. She'd never seen anything like it outside of a museum. Below a soaring clamshell top were rows of drawers covered with painted—or was that japanning?—animals and even tiny scenes. The leopard seemed to be staring straight back at Toby.

"What is it?" the little boy whispered.

"It's, well, I think it's a chest of drawers, like you have. Except…" Not.

Feeling as if she were dreaming, she squeezed her way past a table that, when she uncovered it, appeared to be cherry or rosewood, every line elegantly curved, the feet perfectly defined claws gripping balls. The chair…yes, there was one…matched. The sage green upholstered seat was covered in plastic and seemed to be in pristine condition.

She banged her shin against a cast-iron stove decorated more elaborately than a wedding cake. More furniture: an astonishing bookcase, a grandfather clock, a china cabinet she thought was from the Eastlake period. At the back stood a wardrobe of dark wood inlaid with flowers.

Despite the packing blankets, sheets and tarps that had been used to protect the furniture, dust lay everywhere. She opened a cracked leather case to find a cello with a bow. Everywhere she turned were antiques, and not common ones, either.

I'm rich, she thought, dazed. Who on earth could have stored nineteenth-and even eighteenth-century pieces of furniture of this quality in an ordinary storage unit in a small town off the highway that led to a Cascade Mountain pass in Washington state? Not exactly the antique hub of the universe, although she did well at the antique mall thanks to the travelers, skiers and hikers who got off the highway for a meal and a search for what they assumed had to be good deals this far off the beaten track.

Blinking, she whirled to look for Toby. He was trustworthy, of course he was, at least for his age, but—

With his small hand, he was gently moving an astonishing painted rocking horse. Oh, heavens...he would want it, and lord only knew how much it was worth. Would there be other toys in here?

"That's pretty, isn't it?" she said.

"Uh-huh. Would it *break* if I got on?"

"I...don't know. Why don't we wait until we get it home?"

He bit his lips but nodded.

She smoothed back his fine, light brown hair that she'd let get too long. "You know what? Let's load up as much as we can get in the pickup truck. I can hardly wait to see what's in all those boxes."

"Can we take this?" He petted the neck of the rocking horse.

"You bet." She smiled down at him, then picked the thing up and carried it out. She spread a packing quilt from the pile she always carried and wrapped the child's horse carefully before positioning it to one side of the bed. Once it was surrounded by boxes, it wouldn't be able to slide around.

Resisting the temptation to peek into some of those boxes was hard, but the sky had taken on an ominous cast. She didn't have a canopy on her truck because she often used it to haul furniture, so she definitely wanted to get home and unload before the rain started.

Toby did do a little poking as she worked, excitedly coming up with some tin toys that looked to be in beautiful condition. Still, he didn't argue when she repacked them and put that box, too, in the bed of the pickup.

Seeing the wonder on his face, she cursed his father for the twenty or thirty thousandth time. How could he have ditched his son as well as her? Did he know what he was missing? Her only consolation was that Toby was a happy kid who didn't throw temper tantrums and enjoyed browsing garage sales with her and figuring out how best to display items in her booth at the antique mall.

After lowering the rolling door, she locked it with a new, sturdier padlock to replace the one that had been on it for years. She buckled Toby into his car seat, although he was almost too big for it, and drove to the storage facility exit, where she input the code Jeremy had given her. Toby chattered during the fifteen-minute trip home, but for once she let a lot of what he said go in one ear and out the other.

Exhilaration still bloomed in her chest, but anxiety coiled around it. The stuff in that unit was too valuable. Who had stored it in the first place? Had somebody died, and heirs didn't know what was in there or that they needed to keep paying the monthly fee for the unit? Legally, Erin thought she was in the clear to start selling its contents, but ethically...she was less certain.

She ought to be gloating.

She was.

It was just that an inconvenient conscience had kicked in.

Mostly, she was unnerved by today's discoveries. Some things were too good to be true. She'd probably find the furniture were all modern reproductions. Worth quite a bit, even so, but that would be disappointing. Still, she wasn't even sure she knew *how* to sell items as fine as those if they were genuine. Did she have room to store them at home? And...what if some of those boxes contained smaller items just as exceptional?

What was more, she had two other storage units to clear out this week, one at the same facility. She'd barely glanced inside it. She was on such a roll, it would be smart to skip other upcoming auctions she'd usually attend in the area.

Right. As if she could resist.

Maybe, though, she should call Jeremy to ask if he'd either try to contact the former owner of this stuff or give her the name so she could get in touch herself.

Yes, that would make her feel better.

TWO WEEKS LATER, Erin was beginning to think she'd gotten in over her head. No, she hadn't been able to resist attending those other auctions. Or winning yet another one that her gut told her would be worthwhile.

She'd had so many units to empty, she needed to hire two local guys to haul everything back to her house. The garage was bulging at the seams. Overflow had long since spilled into her little-used dining room, then the living room. Honestly, she could no longer remember what had come from which unit at what facility—except for the truly extraordinary pieces of furniture from Jeremy's place.

She'd gone so far as to list what she'd decided definitely was a japanned highboy on eBay. Bids had blown her away—until a curator at the J. Paul Getty Museum in southern California messaged her. Erin agreed to let the woman look at the piece. She flew up the next day and bought the dresser for an amount of money that would pay for at least the first year or two of Toby's college education. Erin probably could have gotten more for it from a private collector, the curator was honest enough to tell her, but Erin liked the idea of this handsome piece displayed for the public. In return, the woman offered advice on how to sell a couple of the other pieces. Erin took down the eBay listing and found herself hesitating about the rest of the furniture and the cello.

Her conscience was knocking again. It became especially insistent at bedtime, as did her other worries.

She had to get some—all right, *a lot*—of the stuff from other units sorted and out of the house before she or Toby were buried by a falling tower of boxes.

The trouble was, it took time to research every item, take adequate photographs and write appealing and accurate descriptions. She strove to be transparent as a seller, so that nobody could later complain they'd been misled. If an item had a scratch on it, she described it and showed it in a photo. If the expected maker's mark didn't look quite right, she said so. Either way, she displayed it in a clear photo.

An item as small as a ring or silk scarf took as long as a chest of drawers, which meant that she could spend a day on the contents of a single plastic tub. She wouldn't make a lot of progress at that speed.

She refused to shortchange Toby, either. When he needed her to stop what she was doing and kick a ball in the backyard or read to him, she did. The financial windfall let her send him for a few extra hours a week to daycare, but while he didn't argue when she dropped him off, he wasn't excited, either. Maybe she needed to consider the two larger daycares in town, one part of a chain, one operated by a church. Toby needed more time with kids his age.

After all Erin's brooding that night, she whimpered when her alarm went off the next morning. She had too much to do, but she'd start with going back to the storage facility to talk to Jeremy in person. She couldn't figure out why he was making excuses rather than tracking down whoever had paid rent on that unit for heaven knew how many years. God forbid he give her a name. Didn't he get that she was trying to do the right thing? Why was that a problem for *him*?

Breakfast consisted of frozen waffles, toasted and buttered with no syrup for Toby, butter *and* syrup for her. Super nutritious, but she was too tired to cook this morning, and the waffles were Toby's favorite. He chattered happily between bites.

After swallowing the last of her tea, she said, "I have to go talk to someone this morning. Then I'm taking some stuff to the antique store. Marsha called to say enough has sold to open some room. If you'd rather go play with friends at Mrs. Hall's—"

The three-year-old shook his head. "I don't like Julia. I don't want to play with her."

"But Austin will be there—"

"Uh-uh. *He* said he didn't have to go there anymore."

Austin, not quite a year older than Toby, had been the main draw. Erin hoped Austin hadn't been telling the truth. She'd call Mrs. Hall later to find out. For now...

"Coming with me might be boring," she warned.

"I like going with you best, Mommy," he assured her with his usual heartfelt sincerity.

She grinned at him. "Then let's do it."

Half an hour later, she was waiting while Jeremy Conyers rented a U-Haul truck to an older woman.

"You bought the contents," he growled the minute he stepped foot back inside the office. "What's your problem?"

"I told you! I just can't believe family would have let such beautiful pieces go if they'd known—"

"Uncle Charles sent repeated bills. I sent a final one. They had their chance."

"Will you please check with them? Surely you have a phone number or address?"

He groaned. "Only the mailing address. Uncle Charles's records are a mess. He was getting a little confused toward the end. You know that."

Erin did. "From the layers of dust, I think this stuff's been in the unit for years. Older records—"

The lanky, frustrating young man she was facing yanked at his hair. "I still don't get—"

A familiar tug on the hem of her sweatshirt drew her attention downward to Toby. "I gotta go," he told her.

She summoned a smile. "Okay." She glanced back at Jeremy. "We need to use the restroom."

"You know where it is," he said. It was clear she was beginning to annoy him.

She led Toby to the single bathroom behind the office. Jeremy kept it cleaner than his uncle had. The building also had a garage for maintenance equipment and a golf cart Jeremy used to zip around the facility. Whether he'd wanted to inherit the business or intended to sell it, she had no idea. Whoever was on duty in the office could see people coming and going through the gate, as well as watch security monitors covering the rows of rental units. Out of the corner of her eye, she saw at least three people parked in front of units, either loading or unloading.

A small plastic stool in the bathroom allowed Toby to stand high enough to use the toilet without her lifting him. Once he finished and she let him flush, she moved the stool in front of the sink so he could wash his hands. At home, he handled all this himself, but she wasn't ready to send him off alone in public places. Besides, he would skip handwashing when he could get away with it.

"If I play in my sandbox, I'll get dirty again," he told her as she dried his hands with a paper towel.

She rolled her eyes, opened her mouth...and went still. What was she hearing?

It was coming from the office, only a wall away. Raised voices, metallic slams that must be file cabinet drawers and then a big crash.

She turned off the water and made sure Toby was looking at her and paying attention. "Shush. Stay *right* here. Promise me?"

Looking scared, he nodded.

She felt scared, too, but cracked the bathroom door anyway.

"Where's my stuff?" a man's voice snarled. "Tell me."

Oh, dear God. A black-clad figure who had his back to her was kicking Jeremy, who huddled on the floor among sliding heaps of paperwork and folders. Now the intruder lifted a baseball bat and swung. The distinct *crack* she heard had to be the sound of bones breaking.

"Where? Who has it? You have to know!"

Crack.

Jeremy screamed, then started to babble names. Kevin Hargrove's jumped out at her. Why include him?

"Erin Reed!" Jeremy whimpered.

Erin covered a gasp with her hand. What if he said, *She's here right now. In the bathroom. If you want to ask her about anything.*

The man in black went back to ripping folders from the file cabinets and throwing them around the office, even on top of Jeremy who curled up with his arms protecting his head.

Erin shrank back but had to watch. After seeing what should have been the terrifying man's profile, she realized that he wore a ski mask.

"Mommy?"

She whirled and clapped her hand over his face. Toby's teeth chattered, and after he saw the fierce expression on her face, he started to cry. There was no way out of here except back through the office. If she or Toby caught the attention of this monster, she had a bad feeling they'd both die.

Jeremy wasn't moving anymore. For a moment, the man

stood above him staring down. Then he took something from his pocket and flicked it with a finger.

Already terrified, she didn't see the first lick of flame until papers on the floor caught fire.

Chapter Two

When the black-clad man flung open the door and walked out, the rush of fresh air fed the fire, flames leaping higher.

Shaking all over, Erin made herself stay where she was. She could just see a slice of the parking lot in front of the office through the window. A dark SUV appeared, backing out, swinging in a circle and, an instant later, accelerating too fast onto the two-lane road in front of the storage facility.

She whirled, snatched up Toby and ran with him into the burning office. "Jeremy!"

He whimpered and tried to push himself to his hands and knees but slumped back to the floor. He had to feel the heat of the approaching flames.

"Oh God. Oh God." Erin didn't want to let go of her sobbing little boy, but she couldn't leave Jeremy to burn to death, either. She raced to the exterior door, planted Toby right in front of it, and dodged the fire racing back through the scattered papers to reach Jeremy.

Somehow, she'd never know how, she got her arms around him and began to drag him toward the door. He had to weigh significantly more than she did, but she kept him moving anyway. The heat singed her face and licked at his pants leg.

Toby was distraught, and she probably was, too, by the time she got the door open, pushed the little boy ahead of her, and nearly fell through with Jeremy. She paused to stomp out the fire smoldering on the leg of his chinos, then descended the concrete stairs with his feet bumping behind her.

"Mommy!" Toby whimpered. "Mommy!"

A few more feet. She had to make it a few more feet. The concrete building wouldn't burn, but the roof might.

Then she heard a shout. A car door slammed, and two men ran toward her. One lifted Jeremy and slung him over a shoulder, the other grabbed Toby and took Erin by the hand as they ran a safe distance away.

As Erin collapsed to her butt on the gritty asphalt, reaching for her son, one of her rescuers called 9-1-1.

BY THE TIME Sam McKeige arrived at the storage business on the outskirts of town, the fire was out. An ambulance with flashing lights had passed him, heading for the hospital. The fire truck still sat at an angle in the parking lot. Firefighters were folding up the hose while one looked into the shattered window of what Sam assumed was the office.

The uniformed police officer who had probably been the first responder—or maybe second, the fire station wasn't far away—saw Sam and relief spread on his face.

"Detective," he said, approaching. "One of the victims is on the way to the hospital, but the woman and child are still here. Two other witnesses stayed, too."

Clearly, this had not been an accident.

"What do you know?" Sam asked.

Not much, it developed. The officer hadn't had a chance to ask many questions. The kid had been hanging on his mother crying, and she'd crawled to hover over the injured man until he was loaded into the ambulance.

Sam glanced toward a woman who sat on the asphalt with her back to the post supporting the gate, her body curled around a small boy, her entire focus on him. She was disheveled, dirty, brown hair falling out of a ponytail. A couple of guys, maybe in their thirties, leaned against a pickup truck that sat askew in the parking lot well away from the concrete block building.

Sam decided to take a look inside before talking to anybody and joined the firefighter in the office.

The mess wasn't quite what he'd expected. Several tall, metal file cabinets had been pulled over. File folders and papers spilled out, but it appeared most had fed a bonfire lit right behind the counter. A charred trail led to the heavy door, now propped open.

The firefighter, a man he knew, glanced at Sam. "Doesn't take a marshal to tell us this was arson."

"No. Whoever set this wasn't subtle." Sam scrubbed a hand over his jaw, feeling some rasp. "Guess I'd better hear the story."

He chose the two guys first.

"Detective McKeige." He pushed his twill shirt back to show the badge attached to his belt. "What can you tell me?"

They exchanged glances. "We were just driving past," one said. "Gene here saw smoke coming out of the building, so we pulled in. The woman pushed open the door. Her kid stumbled down the stairs, and she pulled a guy out. He, uh, didn't look so good. Like he'd had a beating. I saw her stamp out fire that had caught on the leg of his pants. I don't know if he was burned otherwise."

"We piled out and ran. I grabbed the guy. I'm a volunteer firefighter in Sultan," the second guy said. "Slung him over my shoulder and took off while Kenneth helped the woman and kid. We were afraid the windows might blow out or the fire might shoot up through the roof." He shrugged. "Called 9-1-1."

"Did you see anybody else around?"

"Before we saw the smoke, an SUV peeled out of the lot here and headed for the highway. Looked like it was really moving. Too far away for me to tell you make or model, much less license plate. Once sirens sounded, a few people who were picking up or dropping off stuff in their units came running. The fire chief told them to go back to what they were doing but not to try to leave until somebody came to talk to them."

"Okay," Sam said. "Let me get your names and phone numbers."

Both handed him driver's licenses; he snapped pictures of them, jotted down phone numbers, thanked them and let them go.

Then he walked toward the woman, whose head lifted before he reached her. The boy twisted in her arms and stared at Sam, too. Sam ignored the familiar squeeze in his chest that resulted from the look. The boy's hair was about the same color as his mother's, but his eyes were a bright blue, even as reddened and puffy as they were right now.

The woman hadn't cried, but he recognized shock when he saw it. He pegged her as late twenties and pretty. Maybe more than that, under better circumstances. High, curving forehead, great cheekbones, chin on the stubborn side and eyes that were…not blue, like her kid's—assuming this was her child—but light. Gray with a hint of green, maybe.

She started to make getting-up motions, and he shook his head. "You're fine where you are. I'll come down to your level."

An attempt at a smile wavered. "Thank you."

Sam lowered himself to one knee and smiled at the boy. "I'm a police officer. My name is Sam McKeige. What's your name?"

"Toby," he whispered.

"Nice to meet you, Toby. I hope you weren't hurt."

The boy shook his head. "I was fast."

Sam grinned. "Good for you." He transferred his gaze to the woman. "I'm hoping you can tell me what happened here. Nobody else seems to know. I wonder if Toby might like to sit in the fire truck while we're talking."

She kissed the top of the boy's head. "What do you say? Would you like to go look at the fire truck? Maybe climb in?"

His eyes widened. "Can I?"

"The police officer says you can."

Sam waved over the firefighter he'd talked to first, who had no trouble coaxing Toby to accompany him for an up-close-and-personal tour of the rig.

Brave kid.

Watching her son walk away, his hand held by the firefighter, the young woman straightened her back and let out a long breath. Sam thought her teeth chattered toward the end.

"It was...weird," she started.

"First, I'm Detective McKeige. Can I get your name?"

"Oh, I'm sorry. I'm Erin Reed."

"Do you rent a unit here?"

"Not right now. Sometimes I have one for a few days." She stopped, apparently realized that sounded odd. "I have a booth in the antique mall right off the highway, and I sell on eBay and I've just started a shop on Etsy. Online," she added, although she must realize that was unnecessary. "I buy stuff where I can get it. Garage sales are good, but mostly I buy the contents of storage units being auctioned off because the previous owner quit paying the rent."

Sam vaguely knew that happened and nodded.

She explained that she'd won the auction on a particular unit at this facility a couple of weeks ago. Actually, on three of them, but she was worried because she'd found some quite valuable antique furniture in the one.

"I can't imagine how it ended up abandoned. I'm trying to convince Jeremy—" She paused. "Jeremy Conyers owns this facility. He's on his way to the hospital."

Sam nodded again, watching the subtle, shifting expressions on her fine-boned face. "I wanted to try to contact the previous owners. There may be heirs who, for some reason, didn't realize their parents had stored such amazing stuff. Or... I don't know. I mean, it's mine legally now, but ethically, I'm not so sure. I sold one piece of furniture for a ton of money and then had an attack of guilt."

His eyebrows climbed. How many people wouldn't seize a trove of valuable stuff and run with it, rather than give even passing thought to returning it to someone who didn't know what they'd lost?

"So, you were here to get the name and contact info from this... Jeremy."

"Right, except I've tried before, and he doesn't want to tell me." Her nose wrinkled. "Either that, or the records here are in such a mess, he doesn't know who rented the unit in the first place. His uncle, who owned the facility forever, died a few months ago. You probably noticed the file cabinets. Records are computerized at most storage facilities."

"Ah." Sam wasn't sure what all this had to do with the fire and what might have been an assault on this Jeremy Conyers, but any background was good. He'd never rented a unit at one of these places in his life and kind of wondered why anyone would unless it was just for a month or so during a move.

He stole a glance toward the fire truck, just in time to see Toby being boosted into the cab to sit behind the wheel. Good; he still had time.

"I doubt any of that has anything to do with what happened," Ms. Reed said, but the uncertainty in her voice caught his attention. "I hadn't gotten an answer from Jeremy, but Toby needed to use the bathroom, so I took him. We were just ready to come out when I heard a man yelling at Jeremy. The man wanted to know where his stuff was. He was…hitting and kicking Jeremy. I…saw him swinging a baseball bat at his rib cage." She shuddered. "He kept demanding answers. He wanted names, but I'm not sure why." Her teeth closed on her lower lip, and she looked almost beseechingly at Sam. "One of the names Jeremy gave him was mine."

Chilled, Sam tried to keep his expression from showing his reaction. "We'll ask him why," he said calmly.

She nodded and kept on with the story. The man had gotten angrier and angrier, throwing over the file cabinets, tossing out anything that would burn, starting a fire almost atop Jeremy. A fire that would have killed a stunned man, if she hadn't been there.

She'd had the sense to wait until the assailant fled, then rushed out, deposited her boy at the door, and somehow dragged Jeremy Conyers to the door, out and down three concrete steps. Adrenaline had helped her accomplish the near-impossible. At that point, the two good Samaritans had hustled them all away from danger.

Ms. Reed couldn't give Sam much of a description of the assailant. He'd dressed in black and worn something like a black ski mask over his head and face.

"I think he was pretty good-sized," she said haltingly. "Not as big as you, but… I don't know, maybe six feet? Strong."

Victims always thought their assailants were bigger and more powerfully built than they turned out to be. But in this case, she was a witness, not the victim, which might give her a little more objectivity. He didn't know.

The SUV she'd seen was black, too, but she hadn't taken in the maker, either. "I'm sorry." She looked chagrined. "I just don't pay that much attention to cars unless I'm shopping for one. I should have tried to see the license plate, but—"

"The building was burning down around you, your son and a man who'd just been beaten."

"Well...yes."

Sam smiled and held out his hand. "Think you can get up?"

She seemed to hesitate for a moment before laying her hand in his. Liking the feel of it, slender but strong, Sam glanced down. Her fingernails were clipped short and unpainted. No rings at all, which was interesting.

He rose to his feet, bringing her with him. She was a little taller than average, maybe five foot seven or eight, and what he could see of her curves intrigued him.

He gave himself a mental slap. Her face was streaked with black, she'd just had a traumatic experience that could have been a lot worse, and he was checking her out as if this encounter was at a bar.

Don't forget the kid, he reminded himself. Even if she was single, even if his scars were as healed as they'd ever be, he wasn't prepared to deal with the boy who was undoubtedly central in Erin Reed's life.

"Do you think the 'stuff' this man was talking about might have been the unexpectedly valuable things that have been worrying you?"

"I..." She flicked a look at Sam as they walked side by side toward the fire truck. "That makes sense, doesn't it?"

"Maybe. It would be ironic considering you've been trying to get in touch."

"Yes. Only... I've won the auctions on the contents of several other storage units in the last couple of months. Three in the past two weeks, a couple of others in the previous month. And it could have been even longer ago that he lost his stuff because of whatever went wrong. So…"

"There's no saying."

"Right. Also, Jeremy gave him at least one other name, too, of someone I know who sells on eBay. He won an auction I was at a couple of weeks ago, and there may have been others."

She was letting him know this wouldn't be simple, Sam concluded. It rarely was, although the tangle of storage facility, valuable antiques and arson as well as a ruthless assailant alarmed him.

"Any chance I can see this furniture you consider valuable?" he asked.

She hesitated. "Yes, although…. I have an awful lot of stuff squeezed in at home. I can't swear what came from that particular lot and what didn't anymore, except for the furniture that stood out."

Her boy came running toward her. Now beaming despite the puffiness that remained around his eyes, he wore a child-size, red plastic firefighter helmet.

"Mommy! Look! I got to almost drive! I want to be a firefighter when I grow up!"

She smoothed his hair with her hand, her smile tender when she looked down at her son. "That's something to think about. We were sure glad to see that fire truck today, weren't we?"

"Uh-*huh*!"

"How come people aren't near as glad to see cops coming?" Sam murmured to her, liking the amusement she didn't try to hide.

"*I* was glad to see you," she said, voice low. "This was scary."

Sam was intrigued to see shyness on her face as she looked away from him.

"It was weird." The bewildered man in the hospital bed didn't look good between the leg in traction, the mummy-like bandages around his head, and the way he gritted his teeth every time he had to take a breath. Looked like he had a couple of burns, too. They glistened from whatever ointment had been supplied, but at least they weren't blistered. His eyes had a glassy look, suggesting he was on heavy-duty drugs.

As for what Jeremy Conyers had said… Wasn't that an exact echo of how Ms. Reed had started?

"Tell me about it." Having pulled a chair up beside the bed, Sam leaned forward, bracing his elbows on his thighs. "Take your time. Let me know if talking hurts too much."

Conyers started to nod, then winced. "Sure. Um. I vaguely noticed someone parking out front, but I was talking to Erin Reed—"

"I've already spoken to her."

He swallowed. "She took her kid off to the bathroom. I guess you know that. But we'd left everything up in the air, so I wasn't paying attention until this man burst in the front door waving a baseball bat. I wanted to shout a warning to her, especially since the boy was with her. But I didn't want to give away the presence of anyone else."

"Smart," Sam said with a nod.

The story offered didn't deviate much from what Erin—Ms. Reed—had told him. The assailant had yelled that he'd learned he'd been locked out of *his* storage unit and his things had been sold at auction, and he wanted to know who had them. The emphasis on *his* was noticeable and undoubtedly mimicry.

The part she hadn't heard was that Conyers asked which unit had been rented to the man. Of course he wouldn't say, since that would have identified him. He'd bellowed something about how the place couldn't get away with stealing many people's possessions, and Jeremy must know who had his things.

"I wish I could have kept my mouth shut," he mumbled. "I *should* have. Only... I thought he was going to kill me."

"You had good reason," Sam said grimly. Seeing Jeremy's increasing distress, either physical or emotional or both, made him feel guilty for pushing, but he had to have answers. "Can you tell me how many names you gave him? And who they are?"

"I think...three or four. He got madder and madder. I could tell he was losing it." Conyers supplied the names. He looked especially chagrined when he said, "Erin."

"You saved her by not telling your assailant she was there in the building."

His Adam's apple bobbed. "Do you think he'll go after her?"

That was exactly what Sam thought—and feared. He had to ask one more question. "Do you have records of more than those four auctions that have taken place in the, oh say, last six months?"

Jeremy's pained gaze met his again. "They were in one of those filing cabinets. I don't know what survived. And... I'm not even sure who won out on the more recent auctions. It's usually the same half a dozen people bidding. None of them stood out to me."

"We'll hope those records didn't go up in flames."

And, oh yeah, no camera pointed at the parking lot in front.

Chapter Three

Shaken as she was, Erin ditched the idea of going to the antique mall. Instead, she made a rare trip through a Mc-Donald's drive-through and bought lunch for herself and Toby, which they ate at their own kitchen table. It was close enough to nap time when they finished eating that Toby didn't object to going down for his nap—although he begged her to sit with him, which he hadn't done in a long time.

Once he was asleep, Erin called the daycare operator, keeping her voice low.

"I'm afraid it's true that Austin won't be coming here anymore," Mrs. Hall confirmed. "If Toby were here full-time, his mother might have kept bringing him to me, but she felt Austin needed more chances to play with boys his age." She sounded sad, and Erin understood. If you'd taken care of a kid eight hours a day, five days a week, potentially for years, it must be hard to say goodbye.

Erin also heard resignation, meaning Mrs. Hall understood the decision—and expected that Erin might make the same one.

She wouldn't right away. Mrs. Hall was flexible, happy to accept Toby if Erin needed a place to take him out of the blue even if only for an hour or two. But eventually…yes.

Probably.

Although she'd have liked to crawl into bed and pull the covers over her head—or maybe suck on her thumb like she had until she was almost Toby's age—Erin made herself use the time while Toby was sleeping to work. She opened a plastic tub almost at random and found it full of costume jewelry, scarves—a few of them silk—and a collection of purses. Oh, and a pair of knee-high boots and some slippers at the bottom.

Some items she placed immediately in an empty box that would go to the thrift store. The slippers had had it. The boots...maybe thrift store. The scarves smelled musty, but she could wash them. A couple had frayed edges, and she put those in the Toss bag. The silk ones, cleaned and pressed, would sell quickly at her booth in the mall. Sorting the jewelry took most of the afternoon. A few decisions were easy, but she had to get out her jeweler's loupe to look for markings and do Google searches on many pieces. Most also went in the thrift store bag, although she packed them in individual sandwich bags. A few were worth listing online, and she managed photos and even write-ups on them before the doorbell rang.

One box down, a few hundred to go.

Erin had a feeling she knew who she'd find on her doorstep. She wasn't sure whether that feeling was apprehension or something else she didn't want to name.

Sure enough, a peek between blinds showed her that Detective Sam McKeige stood waiting, tall, lean and commanding. And yes, as dauntingly handsome as she remembered. However kind he'd been to her, she had a suspicion that his nature was forceful.

The moment she opened the door, warm brown eyes studied her. Although, she backtracked on the *warm* part of that description. His gaze was unnervingly sharp and perceptive. He nodded. "Ms. Reed."

"Detective. Come in." Oh, heavens—he'd be appalled by the overwhelming stacks of boxes and more that had devoured so much of her house. She so seldom had people stop by, she tended to forget how abnormal this was. Her cheeks heated.

Of course, his eyebrows rose as he took in the living room and its five-foot-wide path leading to the kitchen. *Hoarder.* That was what he'd be thinking.

"It's...not usually this bad," she heard herself saying. Apologizing. "I've bought too much lately. I've sworn off storage unit auctions until I whittle this down again."

"Uh-huh."

She sighed and led the way to the kitchen, excruciatingly aware of him close behind her. "Let me check on Toby," she said and whisked down the short hall to the bedrooms.

As far as she could tell, Toby was still sound asleep. Thank goodness.

Returning to find the detective standing in the middle of the kitchen, she asked, "Do you have more questions, or do you mostly want to see the furniture?"

"Let's start with the furniture." He cleared his throat. "If you can find it."

She glared at him and was quite sure his mouth twitched into a half smile. She marched straight to the door leading into the garage, knowing it wouldn't look any better organized to him.

Fortunately, she'd grouped the furniture, keeping every piece wrapped in packing blankets. One by one, she pulled the blankets off, let him study the dining room table and set of chairs, the whimsical woodstove, the grandfather clock, the china cabinet the museum curator had agreed was classic Eastlake and finally the wardrobe with flowers inlaid in mahogany.

"Oh, and look at this rocking horse." She uncovered it in turn. "Needless to say, Toby covets it."

McKeige gently set it to moving. His voice softened. "I can imagine."

"I'd let him have it, except it's worth in the neighborhood of two thousand dollars." She turned, finding what she looked for and opening the case. "There's this cello, too. I'll have to get it appraised, since musical instruments aren't my thing, but my best guess is that it'll go for five thousand dollars or more."

"This was a gold mine for you."

"Yes, and there's a ton of smaller stuff, too. The antique tin toys will go like hotcakes online, and I haven't even *looked* in most of the boxes from that unit. Truthfully, I'm not sure anymore that some of the ones from that unit haven't gotten stacked elsewhere. I had a couple of guys empty three units that day and cram the stuff in wherever it fit."

McKeige rubbed his jaw while he looked around. Erin doubted the stubble was a fashion statement, although she could be wrong. It did accentuate a strong jaw and the hollows beneath his cheekbones. She thought she was seeing weariness, as if he was short of sleep.

"I can see why you're worried. You said you already sold a piece?"

She told him the amount it had brought in and who had bought it.

"Museum quality." He eyed the rest of the furniture with a different expression.

"Yes." Feeling chilled, Erin crossed her arms as if to hug herself. "In one way, it's logical to think this is what that man is after. Except...it's all so beautiful, so well chosen. You can imagine what the home looked like where this furniture came from. He doesn't fit."

"No." There was something electric in the detective's eyes when they met hers. "Unless all of this was stolen."

Horrified, she said, "Oh no! I didn't think of that."

"Makes you wonder why he'd quit paying on the unit, though."

"Unless he was in prison?"

McKeige grunted. "But the bills must have been paid up to, what, three or four months ago?"

"Longer ago than that, but yes." She frowned. "Jeremy's uncle hadn't held an auction in quite a while. I think there was no payment for at least six months, from what Jeremy said. Everything in the unit was covered with dust. I'll bet no one had been inside it in years. That doesn't fit with it being a cache of stolen goods."

He let out a long breath. "No, it doesn't. This is a strange one."

"Do you want to see anything else?"

He shook his head and helped her cover everything before scanning the crowded garage again. "Bet you haven't parked in here in a while."

Erin made a face at him. "You'd win that bet."

"Do you own the house?"

"No." Back in the kitchen, she said, "It's a rental. Thank goodness the landlord doesn't bother with inspections."

The low, rough chuckle gave her goose bumps.

She was disconcerted to find herself so attracted to this man. After Shawn had walked out, reminding her that he'd never wanted to have kids—although the unintended pregnancy was no more her fault than it was his—Erin's ability to trust any man had corroded. Even if she scraped the rust away, there might not be anything solid underneath. She couldn't imagine herself having brief hookups, and certainly not while she had a young child at home. Toby was her focus. He had to come first.

And she had no idea why she was thinking about this, anyway. Sam McKeige hadn't given her the slightest indication that he was interested in her that way.

"Would you like a cup of coffee?" she asked.

"I would, if you have time to explain your business more thoroughly."

"Yes, of course." A chair scraped on the floor behind her as she started the coffee maker. Coming back to the table and sitting across from him, she asked, "What do you want to know?"

"Everything." Creases deepened on his forehead. "How long have you been at this? How did you get started?"

Instinctively defensive, she asked, "What does any of that have to do with what happened today?"

"Nothing. I'm…curious. Also, feeling ignorant about the storage unit business, how auctions go and why anyone wants someone's discarded junk."

She could take mild offense at his dismissive tone but chose not to. Instead, she explained how the auctions worked—specifically, that bidders weren't permitted to so much as step inside the unit before they decided what, if anything, they were willing to spend.

He stared at her. "So you're buying blind."

Erin waggled a hand. "Not always. Sometimes furniture, at least, is in plain sight. There are other ways to judge, too. How carefully was the smaller stuff packed? If everything is in cardboard boxes, were they stacked so high the ones on the bottom are getting squished? That suggests the unit doesn't have anything valuable or even breakable in those boxes. Did they buy heavy-duty plastic tubs to make sure nothing got broken? Good sign. But if they bothered to store a sofa that a cat has been using as a scratching post, I tend to think they probably didn't have anything else that's worth my while."

"So you gamble that you'll happen on a unit like the one with the antiques."

"No. I've never hit on anything like this before. I doubt anyone has, at least in this part of the county."

After a moment, Detective MacKeige nodded. Eastern Snohomish County trended toward rural, dotted with small towns mostly strung along the highways. Real money would be in south county, butting up against Seattle and it's prosperous suburbs.

"Do you ever go to auctions in Shoreline, say?"

"No. I doubt I'd ever have the nerve to bid high enough." She told him what she'd paid for the miraculous contents of the one unit. "That's far and away the highest I've ever gone. I just…had a feeling."

"Got it. So, what do you typically find? How do you sell all this?" He nodded toward the dining room visible from his seat at her small table.

With an ear cocked for Toby's reappearance, Erin did her best to give the detective a tutorial of how she sorted and sold the things she found. She showed him the items she'd taken out of the one tub just before he arrived, explaining her decisions, how she determined a value and whether something would be better sold online or in her booth at the mall.

After she poured them coffee, he questioned why she didn't have her own store. She give him a lesson in that, too, including the fact that she'd then have to spend forty hours a week or more there or pay someone else to do it. "And the mall is big enough, with enough variety, to draw people who maybe would think my own store was too small or that the display in the window wasn't exciting. I wouldn't have time to go to storage unit auctions and garage sales—"

"Or you'd be paying someone else to man the cash register."

"Right. Also, I make a lot more with online sales than I do the local ones."

He was interested in that and why she did both. What sold best where? His questions kept coming.

Finally, she asked, "Does this really have anything to do with a guy who was mad because it hadn't occurred to him that the storage unit would get rid of his stuff if he quit paying the rent?"

He gusted a sigh. "Probably not. It's just... What happens when he finds out some of those possessions have already gone into a dumpster or been sold at a thrift store or on eBay?"

That gave her pause. "He'll be even madder?"

"Yeah. And honestly, what you do once you take possession of other people's things probably *isn't* relevant. I just... like to know the context."

"I understand that." She hesitated. "Would you like another cup of coffee? You look tired."

He grimaced, deepening some of the lines in his face, and ran his fingers through already ruffled brown hair a little darker than hers. "I got called out for what looks like a gang shooting last night that left one guy dead and a woman in critical condition."

"Oh. I suppose you do always have several investigations going at a time."

"'Several' is an understatement. The population in the county has boomed, with a lot of that spilling out of the cities that have their own police forces. We stay busy. Most of those investigations move along slowly, and I concentrate on the latest incidents. In fact, several of us worked last night's shooting, and I'll probably hand off my part in it to focus on today's assault."

Relieved, she bobbed her head. "What do you think will happen next?"

"My gut says this guy isn't going to shrug and say damn, easy come, easy go. There was something in the unit that's important to him."

"That something might be easily recognizable…"

"Or not," he agreed. "Next thing I'll do is warn the other folks Mr. Conyers named. I'd tell you to focus on your more recent acquisitions, except—"

He didn't have to finish. A faint twist of his lips told her what he thought about her jam-packed house.

"It's just Toby and me." That popped out without conscious thought. "We don't need a lot of space. If I stored all this somewhere else, it would eat away at my profits."

McKeige grimaced. "I do see that. If you're really making a living from this—"

"I am. I make more than I would holding any job I qualify for." She pushed back her chair and stood, annoyed that she had to justify her livelihood or any of her decisions. Who was this man to judge her?

The expression on that lean face guarded, he rose to his feet, too. "I apologize if I sounded critical. I didn't intend to. I suppose I always thought those people who hold up the line at the post office are doing the eBay thing part-time."

"Post offices aren't as busy as they used to be. They should be grateful for eBay sellers that use the service."

"They should." Now she'd swear his eyes smiled. "Thank you for your patience." His gaze strayed past her, and he said with unexpected gentleness, "Your future firefighter is awake."

She looked at Toby standing in the door of the kitchen, rubbing his eyes from his nap, then back at McKeige. Was that pain she saw flashing through his eyes? If so, he hid it quickly enough. He clearly didn't intend to linger.

"I need to get moving." He extended a business card to her, undoubtedly identical to the one he'd given her earlier in the day. "I'll be in touch if I learn anything, and you call me if you have any reason to be nervous."

"I will," she agreed, lifted Toby to her hip and led the police officer to the front door. She did not let herself watch as he bounded down the steps and strode toward his unmarked but clearly official SUV. He was an interesting man—okay, sexy—but that didn't have anything to do with her.

Erin just hoped he was good at his job.

JEREMY CONYERS HAD given Sam three names besides Erin Reed's. Sam caught them all at home in the late afternoon. He started with Kevin Hargrove, a thin man who was either balding early or older than Sam's guess of midthirties.

He looked startled when Sam showed his badge but let him in. They sat in the living room—one *not* being used for storage.

Once Sam described what had taken place today, Hargrove stared at him in horror.

"Erin's okay? And her little boy?"

"Yes. She was quite a heroine. Mr. Conyers likely will be hospitalized for a few days, but the outcome would have been much worse if Ms. Reed hadn't heard what was happening and been able to pull him out."

Hargrove said he'd purchased the contents of only one unit in the past month at that particular storage facility. "Maybe even longer than that," he said. "This is part time for me. I can only go to auctions on my days off." He drove for FedEx, he said, then shrugged. "I keep hoping to get lucky, but, uh, it hasn't happened yet."

Sam listened for resentment or bitterness, but didn't hear either.

"This eBay thing is more a hobby for me than anything," the guy continued.

What about the contents of the unit he'd purchased most recently?

"Nothing to get excited about," he said. "I made the most from a big box of Breyer horses, some of them old enough to be really collectible."

Sam knew what Hargrove was talking about, a pleasant change from the rest of his day. His ex had carted around a box of the plastic horses in hopes she'd someday have a child as horse crazy as she'd been. Michael hadn't seemed especially interested—

Long practice let Sam slam the door on the memory.

"I'll make back what I paid for the contents," Hargrove continued. "Plus a few hundred, I'd say. I can show you what's left. I mean, I took a bunch to two different thrift stores, threw some stuff out. I don't have quite everything up online yet. That's time-consuming."

He had everything laid out on long folding tables in his garage, set up to allow him to park in half of it, Sam couldn't help noticing. Sam didn't see anything he could imagine inciting the previous owner to rage, but he had to issue a warning.

"Problem is," Sam said before leaving, "the man who attacked Mr. Conyers had several names, one of which is yours. He doesn't know which one of you bought the contents of the unit that was previously his." He handed over another business card. "Call 9-1-1 if anything at all makes you uneasy. If you see something—say, someone peering in your windows—call me."

"If my place gets broken into, it'll probably be when I'm at work, don't you think?"

"That would make sense, but this guy's behavior wasn't rational this morning," Sam cautioned.

Hargrove gulped, nodded, thanked him and said, "Maybe I'd better hide the stuff I haven't sold yet."

Sam left that decision up to him, since he was confident the creep wasn't after Breyer horses.

The next two visits weren't as clear-cut. The second was to a fortyish woman whose husband was a long-haul truck driver. She was alone in a rambling house on acreage at least half the time.

Like Erin, Larissa Cavender wasn't quite sure what in her detached garage had come from sales at that particular storage facility. She didn't have the accumulation that Erin did, but there was plenty she hadn't examined yet.

"Haven't found anything out of the ordinary," she said, looking worried. "I wish I had."

He issued the same cautions, more uneasy about Ms. Cavender than he was about Kevin Hargrove or Walt Smith, the other man he'd managed to connect with. She was a woman who didn't work daytimes and was, therefore, usually home.

When Sam quit for the day, he went home even though he had a suspicion the pickings for dinner would be slim. Quiet sounded good to him.

Quiet, he realized shortly after getting home, that would allow him to run the events of the day repeatedly in his head and brood. Sam wasn't surprised that his thoughts turned first to Erin—and to her cute little boy. The kid made her even more vulnerable than she'd be on her own. What good had it done to tell her to watch out?

Even knowing the other eBay sellers were at risk, Sam worried most about Erin. He told himself it wasn't only because she drew him as no other woman had in longer than he could remember. Or because of the little boy who didn't look as much like Michael as Sam had first thought…but there was something there that had triggered an ache beneath his breastbone.

Chapter Four

"Oh, Erin!"

Recognizing the voice, Erin turned once she'd finished buckling Toby into his seat in her pickup truck. "Andrea. Hi."

Her neighbor, half of a nice couple whose youngest child had just graduated from high school leaving them empty nesters, wasn't smiling for once. "I wanted to tell you, last night was Darren's poker night, and he didn't get home until almost one o'clock. I'd long since gone to bed."

Erin tensed, almost certain this wasn't going anywhere good. "You and me both."

"The thing is, somebody was walking around your house, even peeking in windows, or that's what it looked like to Darren, anyway. When the headlights hit this person—Darren thinks a man or maybe a teenage boy—he bolted. Darren backed out of the driveway and followed him to the corner, but once he got that far, he didn't see a soul. He didn't call 9-1-1, because there wasn't much use in getting someone out here, but he didn't like what he saw."

Goose bumps rose on Erin's arms. "No, that's creepy. Please, tell him thank you for chasing this guy off. I'd like to think it was just some teenager...but why *my* house?"

"Well, you do have an awful lot in there," Andrea said kindly.

Embarrassed but trying not to show it, Erin said, "Yes, but wouldn't you think that would put off any average burglar? I mean, what's he going to do, sit down and start opening boxes with me asleep down the hall? Wouldn't he want a house where he can grab the newest iPhone or some other electronics?"

Andrea nodded. "You're right, that would make more sense. Maybe he was peeking in windows at all the houses on the block. And doesn't *that* make me shiver since he could have been looking in my bedroom window."

It made Erin shiver, too, because she had reason to fear this hadn't been the "average" burglar. Not given the horrific assault and fire yesterday.

"Thanks for letting me know," she said, starting around to the driver side of her truck. "I think I'll call the police to tell them what Darren saw, in case there are any break-ins here in the future. Or were in the past," she added.

"That's smart." The cheerful woman smiled, waved at Toby and called, "Have a good day," before returning to the front porch of her rambler.

Erin decided to wait until she'd dropped off Toby at daycare before calling Sam. It wasn't as if he could do anything about a prowler who'd made a clean getaway, but she felt sure he'd want to know. Just in case.

Toby seemed more resigned than excited to be left at Mrs. Hall's, which of course made Erin feel guilty. But she confronted the same problems with changing to a larger daycare: primarily, that many didn't accept drop-ins, certainly not on short notice, or insisted on payment for a minimum number of hours even if she only needed to leave him for two. Still, she reminded herself that the recent windfall meant she didn't have to watch her pennies quite as closely, and Toby really needed time spent with other boys near to his age, but frugality was a habit.

Maybe she'd visit other daycares in town and see what she thought. There was no hurry, right?

No hurry to call the detective, either. She'd wait until she got home later. Surely the prowler wouldn't return to the same house a second night in a row.

She drove to the antique mall and parked beside the back door so she could easily unload. She'd brought a nice floor lamp, several decorative pillows, a handsome bedside stand and several boxes of smaller items that she had no doubt would be quickly snapped up.

She apologized to women browsing her booth when she started stacking boxes in front.

"Ooh, did you bring some goodies?"

She smiled. "I did. Let me finish unloading my truck so I can lock up, and you can check out the new stuff once I've had a chance to set it out."

Two of the three women set aside items they'd already decided to buy, with her promise to hold them until they worked their way back to her space.

She always enjoyed restocking. To her eye, some booths were too thinly stocked. Others were crowded, with dinnerware, jewelry, antique tools and a dozen other miscellaneous things shoved onto shelves together whether they belonged together or not. Erin tried to hold to themed sections: kitchen, garments and accessories, jewelry—mostly in a glass case—books, decorative items and so on, all displayed on furniture that was also for sale. Artwork she fit in as she could.

She'd heard gossip that the space next to hers might be vacant soon. The guy who rented it didn't do a good job of stocking it, and a lot of the stuff he had for sale looked more thrift store than antique store to her. She'd already put in her bid to expand into that space, if and when it did become available. Just think! She might be able to have her dining room back.

At the thought, she cringed a little, remembering the way the detective had studied the piles that filled too much of her house. She hadn't exactly seen contempt on his face but possibly disdain.

She shouldn't let that bother her. Who cared what he thought? But she was afraid she did. She'd had to let him see so much of the reality that made up her life. And no, she wouldn't have been a social butterfly even if her home looked like other people's, but she was self-conscious enough to make excuses to avoid inviting anyone into her home.

Fortunately, she'd priced everything last night, because the three women came back and snapped up a surprising amount before she even found a spot to set it down. They were followed by other customers, and she ended up staying longer than she intended to chat with people, get an idea what they were looking for, even arrange to bring a round oak table she had in the garage for someone to look at the next day. By the time she left, she'd collected a large sum at the front counter.

"You're going great guns!" Marsha Van Beek declared as she signed the check with a flourish and handed it over. "This doesn't even include what you've sold in the past couple of hours. I haven't had time to tally it."

"I know you haven't. There's no rush. And it was a good day, wasn't it? I'm having a fabulous run on garage sales and storage unit auctions. I could refill my space here every day and hardly have a dent in what I've piled up at home."

"Well, you're definitely my top seller," the owner of the mall said. "I'd love to see you be able to bring in more furniture."

Erin would love that, too. She told Marsha about the

couple she planned to meet in the morning, with a promise that the mall would get their cut if they purchased the table.

Marsha, a slender woman with hair of constantly changing color cut in a chic bob, had heard about the fire at the storage facility. She hadn't known Erin had been involved, though, and asked avid questions. Erin was a little bit glad to escape.

She let herself out the back door, where the parked cars belonged to proprietors of the various spaces in the large mall—fifty-eight at last count—as well as Marsha and the clerks who worked what hours Marsha couldn't be here or that were especially busy. This was the first time ever that Erin paused, holding the door with one hand, to study the parked cars and look for movement before she let the door lock behind her.

She didn't like the shiver of apprehension that had her hustling to jump into the cab of her truck and lock *that* door before she even inserted the key in the ignition. She was glad she'd been able to park so close.

The fire itself, and hearing Jeremy share her name with the man beating him, had been bad enough, but picturing some dark-clad man circling her house, peering in windows and probably checking whether doors were locked made it all more real. The monster who attacked Jeremy might come after her.

Would telling Detective McKeige what Darren had seen really do any good? Pulling out of the parking lot and flicking on her signal to turn onto the highway, Erin wondered if he had the power to arrange for a patrol officer to pass regularly down her street.

The town council had decided a couple of years ago that they'd save money by firing their police chief and two officers and contract with the county for law enforcement services instead. Until now, she hadn't had an opinion either way, but she'd heard grumbling from people who claimed getting a response after a crime took longer than it used to, and having a deputy driving through town wasn't the same as having officers stationed right here.

Sam had come quickly yesterday, though. No, she shouldn't think of him by his first name. Detective McKeige had arrived in a timely fashion, not that far behind the firefighters coming from the station half a mile away. He must have been in the area. But why? To interview someone about the night's crime? Were those people locals?

Suddenly aware she'd been driving on autopilot, she glanced at the storage facility as she passed, seeing poor Jeremy's SUV parked outside the blackened office. Was he even out of the hospital? Even if he was, she doubted he was in any shape to drive. She didn't envy him the task of cleaning all that up, and especially not of having to sort salvageable papers to try to restore records. She hoped the computer had survived unscathed. She presumed it held the most current records about renters and their payments. If not…oh, that would be disastrous!

She stuck to the speed limit, which didn't seem to be popular. She winced as the latest passer had to cut sharply into the westbound lane inches from her fender because he hadn't allowed enough room to pass. Did he really think he'd get there that much faster than she did? What was more, the line was a double-yellow. If a cop had seen, he'd have earned an expensive ticket.

A few drivers stayed behind her. She must have noticed them unconsciously, because a stir of unease told her the big black SUV had been there, a couple of cars back, since shortly after she turned onto the two-lane highway.

Unfortunately, black was a popular color with men who liked to drive giant vehicles, from a Tahoe or a Durango to a Ford 250 or a Silverado. Just because this one reminded her on a visceral level of the vehicle at the scene of the fire didn't mean every big black truck belonged to the enraged arsonist.

Even so, she found her gaze flicking to the rearview mirror often after that. When she made a left turn into town, squeezed between the highway and the river, the SUV did, too. She briefly relaxed when she lost sight of it—it must have made a turn. But then she was blocks from Mrs. Hall's house when she saw it behind her again...or one that looked similar.

He couldn't be *following* her, could he? If so, if it was him, was he a danger to the kids at Mrs. Hall's home daycare?

No, that didn't make any sense. But Erin knew she didn't like the idea of that masked man knowing where she left Toby sometimes. Or where she lived. She had only a phone number listed in the skinny local directory, but this wasn't a big town. If somebody had asked for directions...

Erin drove by Mrs. Hall's, turned at the next corner, cut through an alley, and parked in front of a stranger's home. Keeping her eye on her mirrors and windshield, she took out her phone, found the card Detective McKeige gave her and dialed.

SAM STRAIGHTENED IN his chair, lifting his feet from his desk to plant them on the floor. "You think you're being followed?" Disquiet—no, alarm—jolted him. "You say you've pulled to the curb? Do you see the vehicle?"

"No-o. Maybe I'm shying at shadows." Erin Reed sounded timid now. "It's just... I don't know why, but I don't want that crud from yesterday knowing where I leave Toby."

"That's understandable."

"I probably wouldn't have called," she admitted, "except my next-door neighbor told me something this morning."

What she told him redoubled his worry. Yeah, break-ins weren't uncommon in any community. But the odds of someone casing this woman's house within two days of the fire and assault at the storage facility? Sam didn't buy it as chance.

"Okay," he said. "Why don't you go to the daycare now and pick up your boy, as long as you don't see the vehicle again. Was it an SUV or a pickup truck?"

"An SUV," she said, only the faintest of tremors in her voice still betraying her nerves. "I'm sure yesterday's was, too."

"The other two witnesses agree. Put me on speed dial. If you see the SUV again, in the neighborhood, behind you on the road or near your house, call me. I was about to call it a day and leave anyway. I'll stop by and talk to your neighbor, see if he can tell me anything he didn't mention to his wife."

"Thank you," Erin said. "I should tell you it can wait until tomorrow, that you deserve to be able to go home, but—I'm scared."

"You have reason to be." He didn't even look up when a detective he often worked with escorted a shambling man who had to be homeless past his desk. "Staying alert is smart."

She thanked him again and hung up. Sam rolled his shoulders to relieve tension he hadn't realized was building, grabbed everything he needed from his desk and stood to go. This satellite office was located in Monroe, one of the largest cities in east county and home to a huge Washington state correctional institution. A fair number of men Sam had arrested resided there. Seeing the walls of the prison when he went by gave him pause.

He hadn't thought to ask which neighbor—right or left—of Erin Reed's house had been the one to see the prowler. He almost made it an excuse to knock on her door before as well as after talking to the neighbor but didn't let himself. He looked up the address and found a Darren Hillyard right next door to Ms. Reed's rental.

The guy was home and happy to talk. He stepped out on the porch and gestured as he described seeing someone dressed in black, or at least dark colors, coming from the back of her house and stopping to look in a window to the garage.

"Erin keeps a bamboo blind pulled down, so I know he couldn't see anything. I don't know about the slider in back or the bedroom or kitchen windows, but it didn't look good. I'd have called 9-1-1 right then, except my headlights glanced right off him as I turned in, and he broke into a dead run. Took me a minute to back out of my driveway and follow." Darren shook his head. "Could have gotten into a car parked at the curb around the corner, or he might just have been hiding in someone's shrubbery or around back of one of the houses."

"Did you happen to notice what vehicles were parked along the street?"

Darren's forehead creased. "I did. I mean, I was trying to see if anyone was sitting in any of the cars. Most everyone in the neighborhood has a garage or a carport, at least, not to mention the driveway. So it's usually the beater some kid's friend drives that you'll see at the curb." He was thinking hard, showing a hint of perplexity.

Sam didn't say a word to interrupt the cogitation.

"There was a big SUV midway down the block. Right before the alley that passes behind Erin's house and mine. Not a crossover." He shook his head. "Wish I knew my cars better."

"What color was it?"

"I want to say black, but there isn't a streetlight right

there, so it could have been, I don't know, dark blue or something like that."

Sam pulled up images of full-size SUVs on his phone and gave Darren plenty of time to scroll through. He ruled a few out and thought what he'd seen was angular, not as rounded and modern as a few of the newest models. But he ended up shaking his head again.

"Could be a Yukon, Suburban, Expedition... I'm sorry. I wish I could be more help."

"You were observant," Sam told him. "I suspect the prowler jumped into his SUV and lay down across the seats, something like that. No reason you'd have gotten out and shone a flashlight in." Seeing Darren's expression, Sam added, "If a situation like this arises again, please *don't* do anything like that. Hang back and call 9-1-1. Or me, if it involves Ms. Reed's house or what appears to be that same vehicle."

They walked back together, and Sam gave him a card with his mobile number on it. Thanking him again, Sam jogged up to Erin's small porch to ring the bell. He wished he could reassure her instead of further frightening her.

AFTER THE DOORBELL RANG, feet thundered through the living room. Fortunately, although Toby could reach the doorknob, the dead bolt was too high.

"Wait up!" she called anyway, following to find him bouncing up and down in impatience. What a surprise—he wore his fireman's hat. He was barely willing to take it off to go to bed.

"It's the 'tective," he declared. "Isn't it, Mom?"

"I don't know who it is." She used the peephole to assure herself that, yes, Detective McKeige was on her doorstep, as tall and daunting as always.

But on my side, she reminded herself, *so why daunting?*

She knew, though; his presence threatened her belief she neither needed nor wanted a man in her life. Right now, she did need him.

"Guess what?" she told her eager son. "You're right! It is Detective McKeige." She unlocked the dead bolt, then smiled at Toby. "Do you want to let him in?"

"Uh-huh!" Turning the doorknob was a two-handed job for him, but he succeeded, tripping and hanging from the knob as he pulled the door open. "Hi! Mommy said *I* could let you in."

The detective smiled, although once again she saw a flicker of something in his eyes. Discomfort? "Thank you. Still planning to become a firefighter, are you?"

"Yes! I liked driving that big red truck."

McKeige laughed. "I thought about becoming a firefighter instead of a police officer, but this suits me more. You may find you're interested in all kinds of jobs before you get old enough to decide."

"What kind of jobs?"

"Oh, I wanted to be an astronaut or a rancher… I have horses and enjoy riding—"

"Uh-oh," Erin mumbled.

McKeige's sharp gaze flicked to her. "That's on his list?"

Toby's blue eyes widened. "You have a horse? Of your *own*?"

"I do. Maybe someday you can, too."

"Can I—?"

Erin cut him off. "We don't ask for favors. Detective McKeige is here to talk to me about the fire and the scary man. We need to let him do that."

Toby reluctantly shuffled back and let McKeige in.

"Why don't we talk in the kitchen?" Erin said. "Toby, you can go back to playing."

His voice rose to a whine. "Can't I…?"

She raised her eyebrows.

He sagged, looked reproachful and trudged down the hall toward his room.

The detective grinned. "You should add 'actor' to his list."

She laughed. "You're right."

He followed her through the stacks of boxes and furniture without comment, agreed he wouldn't mind a cup of coffee and sat at her kitchen table.

"He's a great kid," he said, with restraint.

"Yes, he is." She took mugs from the cupboard, glad coffee was already brewing. She wanted to ask if he had children, but something held her back. Maybe he did have a son, but didn't see him often after a divorce. That would explain what she thought might be pain when he looked at Toby.

They weren't friends. She couldn't expect him to tell her something like that. No, he wanted to talk about a violent, masked man who likely had been looking in her windows last night while she and Toby slept.

Apprehension tightened her throat. "Did you find out anything?"

Chapter Five

Nothing Detective McKeige told her surprised Erin. Instead, her anxiety climbed into the red zone. This was ridiculous. She'd lived a quiet life, her divorce the greatest drama in it—and divorce was an all-too-common drama.

"Why me?" she heard herself say and knew she sounded piteous. She shook her head before he could answer. "I know, I know. It's because Jeremy gave this guy my name. But why wouldn't he tell Jeremy what he's so desperate to get back? Most of us would probably give it to him without even charging him, and at most we'd expect to be reimbursed for what we paid at the auction."

"Which I gather in most cases wouldn't be any more than the several months of payments he must have missed."

"Less!" She wrinkled her nose. "Expect for the big unit full of the exceptional stuff. And even that…"

He offered a crooked smile. "You've been *trying* to find the owners so you can give it all back."

"Well…some of it." At a tilt of his eyebrows, she sighed. "I've already earned way more than I paid for the contents just from the one sale."

"Do you have any idea how rarely I encounter a person who is so determined to do the right thing?"

"I can't be *that* unusual."

"Maybe not." He stretched his arms over his head until she heard cracking sounds, groaned and then dropped them to his sides. "I'll admit, in my line of work I don't often meet the cream of society."

"Unless they're victims," she said ruefully.

His smile might have made her blush. She hoped not.

Before either could say anything else, his phone rang. He took it out, frowned and answered, "Detective McKeige."

All Erin heard was a man on the other end of the call talking quickly.

"Okay," McKeige said, "I'm on my way." He ended the call. "That was Kevin Hargrove. I gather you know him? He came home from work to find the contents of his garage trashed."

"Oh no!" Kevin didn't make an awful lot from his efforts. Erin hoped this didn't discourage him from continuing to try. She'd started with the auctions and garage sales as a way to support herself and Toby without having to put Toby into daycare for long, expensive hours. But she'd discovered what she did was fun, too, and she'd hate to see someone like Kevin give up. Everyone needed to have a dream. "At least he wasn't home."

"That's something," the detective agreed, pushing back his chair.

"I forgot to pour the coffee," she realized.

He chuckled. "I'm fine. I've been mainlining it all day. Before I go, did you have any questions?"

"Is there anything I should do that I'm not already?"

Creases formed on his forehead. "You did put me on speed dial?"

She nodded.

"Let me repeat—if anything at all doesn't seem right, call 9-1-1 and me. Don't hesitate." Muscles flexed in his jaw. "I wish..." A slight shake of his head told her he'd cut himself off. "I'll be in touch."

Her head bobbed, and she followed him to the front door. "Tell Kevin I'm sorry this happened."

"I'll do that." McKeige opened the door and turned to look at her, gaze troubled. "I'm worried about you most of all. You and Toby—" Again he stopped himself. "Reality is, you have the most stuff here. The others are hobbyists in comparison. He may quickly dismiss other names on the list. If this guy realizes how much you have crammed in here, he's going to focus on *you*."

She took an involuntary step back. "But...somebody Jeremy didn't even name could have bought the contents of the unit. I mean, does this guy even know *when* his stuff was sold?"

"That's a good question, and I'll be asking Mr. Conyers. Has he taken a call in the recent past from someone who realized they'd dropped paying for whatever reason? You'd think he would remember, unless it happens too often."

"At the bigger facilities, there usually are several units a month." Although some people just quit bothering to pay because their stuff wasn't that valuable. Even people who couldn't keep up payments normally wouldn't go off the deep end this way. "But Jeremy only inherited something like three months ago. Before that..." She shrugged.

"Yeah." McKeige's frown deepened. "You be careful, Erin."

Were they on a first-name basis now? Or did that go only one way? And what a frivolous thing was that to be thinking about, given the frightening knowledge that she likely did have whatever this nutcase was after...and that he didn't hesitate to hurt anyone who got in his way.

How was she supposed to figure out what he *was* looking for?

WITH THE DOOR left up, afternoon light supplemented the lone bulb overhead in Kevin Hargrove's garage. Was this a major crime? No, but Sam was appalled nonetheless. The rage demonstrated here equaled what he'd seen at the storage facility—there just hadn't been a human being for the intruder to vent his fury on.

Everything so carefully set out on folding tables had been swept to the concrete floor. At a guess, booted feet had trampled on all of it, crushing the breakables. An ax that had presumably hung on the wall with other tools had been used to smash even the tables. The single window was shattered. The ax had been left embedded in a workbench built-in beneath it.

If Hargrove had been home, he'd be dead.

Sam breathed a word he shouldn't have said under his breath. He glanced to see Hargrove staring with shock, even though this wasn't his first sight of the mess.

"Did you touch anything?" Sam asked.

The guy shook his head.

"I'm going to ask you to leave it all as-is behind a closed garage door until I can get a technician out here, probably tomorrow, to dust for fingerprints and search for anything the intruder may have left behind."

Hargrove's head turned slowly, his eyes dazed. "Nothing here was worth that much."

"No, but this has to be the man who battered Jeremy Conyers and set the office on fire, likely hoping he'd die in the fire. He's going to visit everyone else on his list, and my worry is that one of those people will be at home." Larissa Cavender. Erin Reed, made even more vulnerable by her young son. "I'm giving this my all, and I'm including the damage to your property."

Hargrove's prominent Adam's apple bobbed. "Thank you."

Sam retreated from the garage, and the homeowner

pushed a button on the remote he clutched to let the door clatter down.

"I was talking to Ms. Reed when you called," Sam remembered to say. "She was upset that this happened to you and doesn't want this to discourage you from pursuing the storage facility auctions." Had she said that? He didn't know but felt sure that was what she'd meant.

Hargrove tried to smile. "If you see her, tell her thanks. I'd a hundred times rather this—" he paused, struggling with what to call the offender "—monster came here than her house. She's a nice lady, and she has that cute kid. Have you met him?"

"Yes." Sam shared Hargrove's horror. "I've encouraged her to call for help if she hears so much as a creak that doesn't sound normal." He didn't say that he suspected he wouldn't be sleeping well during the nights to come, not when he expected that call from her.

He filled out a quick report for Hargrove to give his insurance company and left, not as glad to be heading home as he should be. He'd intended to cook instead of grabbing takeout but figured he had to have a microwaveable meal in his freezer. He'd lost enthusiasm for the rerun of a Seahawks game he'd missed because of work, too. Honestly, he was tempted to drive back to Erin Reed's neighborhood, park down the street and keep an eye on her house.

Overkill, he told himself and took the turn onto the highway that would lead him east toward Monroe and the old farmhouse he owned on some acreage on the outskirts.

He knew what Toby had wanted to ask him. Even if putting the kid up on one of his horses would bring back memories he tried to block, he should offer.

The turn signal clicked as he grimaced. With luck, they'd stop this scumbag before Sam had to see the hope on Toby's face again.

THE NEXT MORNING, Erin winced at the sight of herself in the mirror. Her eyes looked sunken, and the dark circles below didn't help. That was what sleeplessness did for you.

She mostly planned to work at home, although she'd intended to grocery shop. Forget that. She could scrounge up meals of some kind. Toby would be happy if she fed him grilled cheese sandwiches for lunch and macaroni and cheese for dinner. They'd manage.

Unfortunately, she had promised to haul that round oak table to the antique mall to show it to the couple. She should put on some makeup so she didn't look like one of the walking dead, but that seemed like too much effort.

The couple were delighted by the table, which they claimed was exactly what they wanted to fit in a nook in an old house they'd recently bought. They shifted the item to the back of their truck, and she and Toby walked them in so they could pay for it through the clerk behind the counter. Then she hoisted Toby onto her hip and fled without even checking her booth.

As the day went on, she wished she'd taken Toby to Mrs. Hall's for a few hours. He tried, he really did, but couldn't entertain himself for an entire day while she worked. They kicked a ball out in the backyard for a while, with her making a mental note that she needed to mow, and she played several games with him. Thank goodness he still napped.

She set up to take photos of some of the things she planned to list on eBay or Etsy, a finicky process that required concentration. Those photos had to be crystal clear, appealing...and honest.

Dinner... Well, she'd load up on veggies tomorrow. And just about everything else. She had enough milk for the mac and cheese out of a box, margarine was getting low, and Toby would have to settle for a frozen waffle tomorrow, since no milk meant no cereal.

Her phone hardly rang all day. She called the hospital and learned Jeremy had been released, but he didn't answer his cell phone. Tomorrow would do. He was probably sleeping, the way she wished *she* were.

Detective McKeige neither called nor stopped by. The man presumably had investigations that didn't involve her. As long as nothing happened…

After putting Toby to bed that evening, Erin sat down to pay bills. She gave up after she tried to add an extra thousand dollars onto her rent and was able to delete a few numbers before it was too late.

Tomorrow, she thought for at least the twentieth time today. She was too tired to do anything *but* sleep tonight.

Of course, she checked locks on doors and windows several times. She also picked up a soundly sleeping Toby and carried him into her room to sleep with her, something she rarely allowed. Finally, she set a low stool and one of Toby's toys out in the hall. Hopefully, they would trip anyone who tried to creep in the dark toward their bedrooms.

Feeling like that was the best she could do, she brushed her teeth, crawled into bed and was out as fast as her bedside lamp.

SHE STARTLED AWAKE. What…? Belatedly, Erin realized Toby was in bed with her. Had he kicked her or—? But then she heard a sound she couldn't identify. It wasn't loud, but it didn't *belong*.

She lay there stiffly and strained to listen. Had the sound been here in the house, or was she just hearing something outside? A cat jumping over the fence, making the gate rattle?

A thump came next, quiet enough it might not have awakened her in the first place, and she knew: it was out in the garage.

If anything at all doesn't seem right, call 9-1-1 and me. Don't hesitate.

There'd been enough intensity in Sam's husky voice that Erin groped for her phone on her bedside stand. Her hand shook.

9-1-1 first. Would somebody in the garage be able to hear her? She didn't think so, not if she kept her voice low.

Never mind, she'd call Sam first. She wouldn't have to explain to him. He could call 9-1-1 for her.

His phone rang three times before he came on, sounding wide-awake. "Erin?"

"I think somebody is in the garage. I... Will you call 9-1-1 for me?"

"Yes, and I'm on my way. Don't go out there."

Her breath caught at a scraping sound. The door from the garage into the house was steel. Had some kind of lockpick skated over the door?

Oh God, oh God.

Toby still slept. She sometimes thought he'd sleep through an earthquake. Right now, she could only be grateful. Keeping him quiet might have been impossible.

Still clutching the phone, she slid out of bed and tiptoed into the hall. Sam was saying something, but she didn't try to make it out. Another scratching sound came to her. Her heart beat so hard, it throbbed in her throat as well as her chest. Her breath came short. She barely remembered in time to dodge the obstacles she'd set out herself. What if she'd gone crashing down?

In the doorway to the kitchen, she stopped. The dim light from the window showed that the door into the garage was still closed. Standing still, she waited.

Then the door seemed to quiver, and a low growl sounded like a profanity, or worse, to her.

She yelled, "I've called the police! They'll be here any

minute! And I have a gun, so don't even *think* about trying to come into the house!"

For a moment, nothing happened. Then another curse, and a few thumps rang out. Was that the sound of the side door from the garage? What if the intruder ran by the kitchen window? Erin stepped into the hall.

Finally, she pressed her forehead to the wall and lifted the phone. "Sam?"

No one was there. With her tight clutch, she'd probably ended the call herself.

She stayed where she was, shaking and straining to hear any tiny sound. Had he really fled? And…what would she find in the garage? That was her livelihood out there! What if too much was smashed? And God help her, why had he wanted to come into the house when the garage was stuffed full? The chances were best that whatever this man was determined to find, it was out there.

She couldn't hear the highway from here but did hear a few cars. One maybe a block or two away? And then a siren, distant but gaining in volume rapidly. She hoped with all her being that it was coming here. Probably a patrol officer sent by Sam.

Erin wished it would be him. He made her feel safe, even if she really wasn't. She drew in and let out a shuddery breath. Safe wasn't all she felt when she was with Detective McKeige. He was the sexiest man she'd ever met. More than that, he was large, strongly built, reassuring…and kind.

Flashing lights and a screaming siren were right outside now, probably in her driveway. The whole neighborhood would be awakened. She hurried to the front door to see Sam leaping out of the same SUV he'd driven earlier. He'd turned off the siren but left on the flashing lights. He jogged toward the porch, where she belatedly turned on the light.

His eyes locked on her. "You're all right." His voice was rougher than she remembered.

Hugging herself, she nodded. "I think he's gone."

"Let me circle the house before I come in. Lock the door behind me. Don't open it until I come back."

"Yes. Okay." She did as he asked, becoming aware of another approaching siren.

Just as the next police car pulled to the curb, also cutting off its siren, a rap came on the front door.

She unlocked it, and Sam stepped over the threshold. To her astonishment, he wrapped her in his arms and gave her a hard hug. He didn't let it last long, but he muttered, "You scared me."

Was he supposed to do that? Who cared? She just wanted to stay in the circle of his arms, lay her head against that broad, solid chest. She wanted—

Too much. This was no time for fantasies.

"Detective McKeige?" The voice came from out front. "That you?"

"It's me," McKeige said, still within touching distance. "Looks like the intruder broke in the side door to the garage. I haven't gone out there yet to see what damage has been done. He didn't get in the house?"

At the faint question, she shook her head. "I yelled at him. Said the police were on the way, and I had a gun."

He cocked an eyebrow. "Do you?"

"No." Erin smiled weakly. "Unless there's one in some box I haven't opened yet."

"You might have a whole arsenal out there. Maybe that's what he's mad about. You don't take a man's guns."

"I hope that's facetious."

Under the circumstances, the flash of his grin startled her. "Of course it is." He nudged her backward and made room for the uniformed deputy who stopped on the porch.

"Did you hear a car start, ma'am?"

"I thought I heard one about a block away. The timing would have been about right."

"And how long ago was that?"

"I...don't know." Time felt weird right now. "Um, five minutes? It was before I heard the first siren."

"He'll be long gone then."

Of course. She remembered her one glimpse of the SUV almost rocking onto two wheels as it turned out of the storage facility.

"Please, come in," she said.

"Where's Toby?" Sam asked.

"Still asleep. Well, I'd better take a quick peek."

The two men followed her through the path between boxes and furniture but presumably stopped to talk. She should be embarrassed anew by the hoarder-house look, but she felt too much to allow it entry now.

The small lump under the covers in her bed hadn't moved at all. She stepped closer and whispered, "Toby?" When there was no response, she laid a gentle hand on his back and felt it moving in the natural rhythm of sleep.

When she eased back into the hall, Sam—oh no, she would use his name talking to him if she didn't quit thinking of him that way—was waiting right outside the door.

"He really hasn't woken up?" he murmured.

"Nope. Thank heavens," she added.

"All right." He backed away. "You'd better come with us. You'll have a better idea than we will what damage has been done or if anything seems to be missing."

"Why would he have been trying to get in the house if he found what he's looking for?"

Somebody had turned on the kitchen light, letting her see the sharp attention from the officer. "He tried to get in?"

Her head bobbed. "I think so. I heard scraping on the door. It's steel, you know. It was metal against metal."

"Son of a—" The detective abandoned her in favor of the door. "You have a dead bolt on it."

"Yes, it was already there. I thought it was kind of unusual, but those push-button ones aren't much use."

"No, they aren't, and the typical cheap wood door can be kicked in, no matter what lock secures it."

"I'll have to thank my landlord."

Sam pulled a pair of thin plastic gloves from a pocket, donned them and undid the dead bolt, then opened the door.

Seeing darkness, Erin said, "The light switch is to your right."

He reached, and light flooded the garage.

The first words out of her mouth were, "Oh no."

Chapter Six

It didn't look as bad out here as he'd expected after hearing Erin's exclamation. He wondered if a whole lot more damage would have been done if the intruder hadn't been trying to keep quiet. Boxes and rubber tubs had been tossed, their contents jumbled, one tub broken beneath the mark of a boot print.

Erin exclaimed and rushed into the garage. Picking up an embroidered shawl, she draped it on a box, then reached for a broken lamp with a fancy porcelain base.

Sam felt a chill as he took in the overall scene and thought he knew what that SOB had been thinking. He'd yanked out boxes looking for his own. Were they cardboard or plastic? If plastic, had he been looking for a particular color? This guy had to be short of patience, which didn't come as a surprise. As long as he stayed quiet, he could have taken hours to search out here. Instead, frustration had seized him, and he'd decided that Erin would *tell* him the location of what he wanted.

Sam's initial fear for her had settled once he saw her alive and well. Now it became jagged again. She wouldn't be safe until this creep was behind bars—or dead. He wasn't the giving-up type.

She kept fluttering around, picking things up, then setting them down. He doubted she'd rest easy until she'd restored order out here.

"At least we know one thing," he said.

Her head turned. "What's that?"

"He's probably not after the pricey furniture and boxes from the storage unit you paid so much for."

"How can you—?" But she broke off as she looked around. "You're right. He could have seen some of the furniture. And the rocking horse."

"Exactly."

"The only thing is, I don't know if everything that came from that unit is together out here."

Sam almost groaned. Of course it couldn't be that simple.

Deputy Warren, who had stayed silent until now, spoke up. "Can you tell if anything is missing, ma'am?"

She made a funny sound. "No. How could I? I mean, he could have pocketed some small things from one of the boxes he opened, but…"

"It's not likely he bothered," Sam said.

"No."

"Come on inside," Sam suggested. "I'll walk Deputy Warren out, then come back. We'll want to secure that outside door for the night."

"Oh! Yes. I hadn't even thought of that."

They could push a few heavy boxes against the door. Sam didn't say so, but that would work. The door itself was flimsier than the one leading into the house and would need to be replaced.

She set down the couple of things she was holding as if they were incredibly valuable, then walked toward him.

This was a bad time for him to react to her fine-boned, curvaceous body and tumble of shiny hair. Or maybe he should wonder why he hadn't sooner, given that she wore only a pair of boxer shorts and a snug-fitting tank top. Her breasts swayed when she moved, and he swore he saw the rise of her nipples. Some color rose in her cheeks, and her eyes shied from his. She could probably read his mind.

He backed up clumsily, grateful when the deputy got out of his way. He hoped he was blocking Warren's view of her. She flicked off the light in the garage and slipped by him, letting him pull the door shut.

"I want to talk to you before you go back to bed," he told her, then walked the deputy out.

"I'll file a report," Warren said, pausing on the doorstep, "but I get the feeling there's more to this than just tonight's break-in."

Standing on the porch, Sam summarized what had happened so far. The deputy knew about the storage facility attack and arson, of course, but he hadn't been aware of the relatively minor yet still ominous break-in at Hargrove's place.

"This guy will be back," Warren said, frowning.

"Oh, yeah." Sam rolled his shoulders. "I doubt if he'll take the chance of making a return visit tonight, but I'm going to stay anyway. Ms. Reed has a three-year-old son. If this piece of—" He swallowed the rest of it. "If he gets his hands on the boy, she'd do anything."

"I have a boy about that age myself. I would, too."

So would Sam, who'd have sacrificed anything including his life to save Michael. The jab of pain was duller than it had once been, but still hurt.

They said good-night, and Sam went back inside, locked the door behind himself and returned to the kitchen, where he found Erin sitting at the table. Her back was straight, her gaze fixed on the wall in front of her, her hands clasped on the tabletop in front of her. She was too still.

"Okay," he said, staying on his feet. "I'm going to see what I can do about that door. There's no reason you can't get some more sleep, even though I know that seems unlikely right now."

He hadn't seen her blink in so long, her eyes must be dry, but she did turn her head to look at him.

"You're kidding, right? I won't be able to fall asleep. I'd get started out in the garage, except I'd be too far from Toby."

"With your permission, I'll stay so you *can* sleep," he said, making sure there was no give in his voice. "If I can find my way to your sofa—"

Her face crumpled momentarily before she regained control. "That's asking a lot of you, but...you can sleep in Toby's bed. It's a twin, too small for you, but better than the couch. He doesn't usually sleep with me, but tonight—"

She wanted him close. Sam understood.

"A twin bed is fine," he said gently. "I never sleep deeply. Nobody will get into this house without me knowing."

The sudden sheen of tears in her beautiful eyes tempted him to reach for her, but he didn't dare. He was a cop; she needed him. Later, maybe he could give her a call...if he could get past knowing he wouldn't be able to avoid her boy.

"Thank you," she whispered. "You probably have a family but—"

"No family." If he sounded harsh, he couldn't help it.

"I'm sorry. I mean, it's none of my business. I shouldn't have asked."

She hadn't really. He had no business being sensitive. She'd presumably either gone through a divorce or lost her husband to an accident or illness.

"No, it's okay," he said, quietly. "My wife and son died. It's been a while, but—"

A small hand rested briefly on his arm. "I'm really sorry. Make yourself comfortable. If you want coffee or a bite to eat—"

Immensely relieved she hadn't asked any questions, he said, "No. Once I take care of that door, I'll try to get to sleep, too."

For a lot of reasons, he doubted that would happen.

FEELING ASTONISHINGLY RESTED CONSIDERING, Erin made it all the way through her morning routine in the bathroom and was in the kitchen before she realized... Toby hadn't joined her yet. Uh-oh.

She rushed down the hall. Toby's bedroom door was open, of course. Still in his pajamas, he stood next to the bed staring open-mouthed at the man who lay on his back, hands clasped behind his head, smiling at her son.

"I borrowed your bed," Sam was saying.

"How come?"

Sam's gaze shifted briefly to Erin, frozen in the doorway, before he said, "Your mom had some excitement in the middle of the night. After that, it seemed like I'd get more sleep here than if I went home." He paused. "She can tell you about it later."

"I'm sorry if we woke you up—" Erin began, but he shook his head.

"Just waiting until you were all done in the bathroom."

"Oh. Um." He had slept in the T-shirt he'd worn beneath a jacket last night, thank goodness, because he'd pushed the covers down to just above his waist. She'd have seen that muscular chest and powerful shoulders bare otherwise. Probably best not to have the picture stuck in her mind.

"Toby, come help me with breakfast," she said. "You'll let me feed you, won't you?" she asked Sam.

"I'd appreciate it. I settle for cereal most mornings."

"Well, we're having waffles from scratch today." They'd have settled for frozen if not for him.

Toby joined her in the kitchen, his expression eager.

"What are we gonna do today? Maybe Mr. 'tec...tective can go with us?"

Oh, heavens. It was Saturday, and she'd been thinking they ought to do something fun for Toby, at least for part of the day. Unfortunately, she'd have to call her landlord and hope he didn't want to come out and inspect the damage. Still, Toby came first.

Maybe just lunch, somewhere with bouncy balls... The Evergreen State Fair was going on in Monroe, but it was expensive and really too overwhelming for a child Toby's age. Except money wasn't as tight, she reminded herself, and undoubtedly there would be rides for young children. They could pet some animals, too.

Of course, the ten days of the state fair meant big business at the antique mall, too, as people driving by the sign let themselves be tempted coming or going. Which meant she ought to spend some extra hours there.

"Let me think about it," she said and measured flour into a big bowl.

"Think about what?" Sam asked as he strolled into the kitchen.

She liked the dishevelment of his hair and even the stubble on his jaw. "Oh, we're just making plans for the day."

"Mommy said we could do something fun, but I don't know what," Toby contributed. "Sometimes we take a picnic to the park on the river, an' that's all."

"Hey!" she protested. "You like splashing in the water."

"Yeah, but *today* I wanna—"

"The you-know-what has started," Sam pointed out.

Toby's forehead crinkled, and he opened his mouth to ask questions.

She leveled a look at him. "I said I'd think about it."

Her unexpected guest chuckled. "Can I do anything?"

"The coffee is ready. You can pour yourself some."

He came close enough for his arm to brush her shoulder as he chose one of the mugs she'd set out. She'd put milk on the table—who really kept cream around?—as well as the sugar bowl. He sat down, ignoring both, and took a first sip.

Toby climbed up in his usual place, with the booster seat raising him to an acceptable height. "What are *you* gonna do today?" he asked.

"Probably work for a few hours, then clean my house, maybe?" He frowned thoughtfully, as if considering everything he had to do about her garage break-in.

Toby scrunched his nose. "That's not fun."

"No, it isn't," Sam said apologetically.

Erin added a fourth enormous waffle to the plate she'd kept warm in the oven, then carried it to the table. She wished she had real butter to offer and more than one choice of syrup, but her grocery shopping was strictly limited by the tastes of a preschooler.

As soon as she said, "Help yourself," Sam shifted one of the waffles to his plate, his expression anticipatory. He didn't look picky. She cut a quarter of one of the other waffles for Toby, added margarine and sat down with the rest of that waffle. She probably should have stopped at three. She hardly remembered how much Shawn ate, and anyway he was both thinner and a few inches shorter than Sam.

Toby did most of the talking, his eagerness greater than his appetite. The landlord definitely would have to wait; the hope on her son's face always got to her.

Sam had been watching him, too, even as he was on his second waffle and not yet slowing down. She thought he sighed when he set his fork down on his plate. "As for the something fun, I have two suggestions," he said. "One is the you-know-what. The other is, uh, you two come out to my place. Toby could get up on one of my horses."

Toby stared at him as if he were the Wizard of Oz. Erin felt almost as stunned.

"You mean that?" Toby asked.

A muscle jumped in Sam's jaw. "I wouldn't have said it if I didn't." He resumed eating, but he kept an eye on her and Toby.

"Mommy?"

"I... That sounds fun to me, too," she heard herself say, only a little breathlessly. Maybe Sam wasn't thinking of her as Ms. Reed any more than she thought of him as Detective McKeige.

He smiled, if wryly. "It's settled."

WHAT HAD HE been thinking? Sam watched Toby explode from the back seat with no help from his mom. What he should be doing today was checking up on the other auction buyers, talking to Jeremy Conyers again and sticking with Erin to ensure her landlord bought a steel door with a dead bolt to replace the one that had been ruined last night.

Had it occurred to her yet that if her landlord came by to replace the door he'd take a look in the garage and potentially into the rest of the house, too? Not that she was damaging the house...

"You called your landlord yet?" he asked Erin.

She moaned. "No. I'll do it as soon as I get home. I promised Toby a fun day, and... I'm a coward."

"Tell you what," he said. "I'd be glad to replace the door if he'll pay for it."

"You mean, so he doesn't come to the house at all? You're already doing so much..." But she desperately wanted him to do the one more thing, he could tell.

"I don't mind," he said. "I'm going to be keeping a close eye on you and your place anyway."

How close, he wasn't telling her.

If he didn't insist on being brutally honest with himself, he could use the need to watch over her and Toby as an excuse for inviting them to his place today. Of course, that wasn't it. He was pretty sure he'd succumbed to the expression of dawning hope on Toby's face, the one that had triggered an electric shock to Sam's heart. No, Toby didn't look *that* much like Michael, but there was something.

And then there'd been the temptation to spend time with Erin when she was actually happy.

Toby's eyes widened when he saw the two horses waiting at the paddock fence. "Do they have names?" he asked in a hushed voice.

Sam glanced down at the boy. "Nebula is the gray gelding. Daffy is the palomino."

"For Daffodil?" Erin asked.

He grimaced. "Yeah. They came with their names. I just can't quite spit that one out."

She giggled, a sound that he felt like a touch. Damn it.

"They're *big*!" Toby gazed up at the horses with awe.

"He's only been on a pony before, at another boy's birthday party," Erin murmured. "He's been talking about it ever since."

"I can *really* ride?"

"You really can."

Once Sam had learned that Erin grew up riding, although she hadn't been on a horse for several years, he'd decided to saddle both and take them for a short trail ride. That is, unless Toby freaked out to find out how high off the ground he'd be.

Erin had brought a carrot, and Sam left her showing her son how to safely offer treats to a horse. He carried out bridles, saddles and saddle blankets, and demonstrated for his small and rapt audience how to saddle a horse. Toby thought Sam was being mean when he whacked each horse's side while tightening the girth, and Sam had to explain why he did it.

Erin suggested he take Toby up in front of him and ride around the corral behind the barns.

Once Sam swung himself onto Daffy's back, Erin lifted Toby up to him. The kid was warm and wriggly and felt fragile, and for a sharp instant Sam wished he'd never suggested this. It took him back to a place he didn't want to be, but he knew how to don a mask and did. Toby wouldn't notice his tension, but Erin might.

She led Nebula to the corral and used the fence rail there to get a leg over the gelding's back. As Sam held Daffy to an amble around the corral, he kept an eye on Erin until he was sure she knew what she was doing.

Toby was quiet for the first few rounds, and then he said, "Can I hold the reins?"

Sam guided him, showing him how to position his hands, and then let him have the reins. Not that the palomino noticed. She continued to circle without needing guidance, but Toby was delighted.

"I want to gallop!" he declared, bouncing.

"Not today," Sam told him but couldn't hold back a grin. "Shall we go out on a trail?" he asked Erin.

When she agreed, he unlatched the gate from horseback, took charge of the reins again and urged the mare to stretch her legs into a slightly faster walk.

When he turned his head, he saw mother and son both beaming. That coil in his chest eased. Maybe this hadn't been such a bad idea after all, giving a kid as sweet-natured as Toby a treat while his mom let go of the fear that had to be dogging her nonstop. A break, that was all this was.

Chapter Seven

Erin hated watching Sam drive away later that afternoon. Naturally, she gave a happy wave in case he glanced in his rearview mirror. He'd done so much for them already. How could she beg him not to leave them?

She had to remind herself that there was good reason she hadn't remarried or even wasted time dreaming about meeting the perfect man. Probably because he didn't exist? And after years of building a solid life for herself and her child, she'd hate someone thinking he could make decisions for her.

Okay, just acknowledge it: she was scared. Detective Sam McKeige would come quickly if she called, and that was what she really needed from him. He seemed to genuinely *care*. Giving the time he had to Toby was amazing. She didn't think she'd ever seen Toby more excited than he was when Sam loosened the reins and pushed his gorgeous palomino mare into a lope. Afterward, Toby had grinned, exclaiming, "We galloped! Did you see us, Mommy? Did you?"

Standing in her driveway, feeling bereft for no excusable reason, she smiled at the memory.

And instead of Toby going straight down for his nap when they got home, he thrust out his lower lip and insisted on waiting until Sam reappeared half an hour later and backed into their driveway with a brand new door. It was in the bed of a pickup that must be what Sam drove when he wasn't on the job.

Toby was almost as interested in the construction project as he'd been in the horses. Especially since Sam was nice enough to let him "help."

Sam would be an amazing father. Except…there was something in his eyes that he tried to hide. Pain that she understood in a way she wished she didn't. If Erin lost Toby… She shuddered.

She did her best to put Sam out of her mind and went to work, first using soap and water to clean gray fingerprint powder off the door between the house and garage and numerous plastic tubs that had been dumped. The broken door had been dusted for fingerprints, too, but Sam had tossed it in the bed of his pickup and said he'd "take care of it." She didn't know if that meant throw it away or save it as evidence, but she decided not to worry about it.

Next she went through boxes she'd bought at a recent storage facility auction. She could at least separate those out from garage and yard sale stuff, which she'd boxed herself. Or older purchases that didn't look very exciting and had therefore gotten buried at the back of the garage. She studied, photographed and researched a few pieces of furniture, too, then had to decide which should go to the mall and which be sold online.

Toby was his usual patient self once he woke up and had a snack. She indulged him with a game of hide-and-seek, first in the house with her being the one who hid, then a second round in the garage where there were entirely too many nooks and crannies he could squirm into but she couldn't. They did this often enough she'd gotten to know many of his favorite hidey-holes, but as she shifted furniture and boxes around, adding and taking away, she created new places for him to hide.

Unfortunately, the rocking horse caught his attention again. Given his excitement about horses and galloping, she reluctantly allowed him to ride it.

"We can put it in my room, can't we, Mommy?" he begged, finally getting off.

Dollar signs danced in her eyes, but she recognized true love when she saw it. He'd understand if she said no and explained how much they needed money for rent and groceries and gas for the car—she never mentioned the still tiny savings account she'd started with college for him in mind—but there was something magical about this horse.

It was taller than modern ones she'd seen, carved entirely out of wood with joints so skillfully made, they were hardly visible. The intricate paint job, the genuine leather saddle with stirrups just right for Toby, the leather ears that were getting just a little floppy, combined into something she'd never be able to give him again. It was meant to be an heirloom, she thought. It could be one for her and Toby. She imagined bringing it out of storage for his children and closed her eyes.

"Yes. Okay. It's beautiful, isn't it?"

"Uh-*huh*!" He danced around her and wrapped both arms around her thigh in a hard hug.

She opened her mouth to beg him to be careful with the rocking horse, then managed to make herself shut it again. You couldn't give something wonderful to a three-year-old and then ruin it for them by making them promise never to crash into it with another toy or scratch it or rock so hard those perfect joints started to separate.

She had to let it go. Once she carried it into his room, it would be his. It would still be beautiful when he outgrew it, she convinced herself. *Think how many children have probably already enjoyed it.*

Toby was so happy with the new addition to his room, he let her work in peace for a good hour before he reappeared.

"Can we show it to Sam?" he asked, breaking her train of thought. "He'd like it. Wouldn't he, Mom?"

"We may not see him again," she cautioned. "He was here for special reasons. But yes, I'm sure he'd like it." Seeing his mouth open again, she knew distraction was needed. "Maybe you should name your horse."

"Yeah!"

Of course, he immediately began trying out names, which made it impossible to concentrate on work, so she gave up and put on dinner.

Two days later, Erin opened a cheap plastic tub she'd hauled in from the garage. It was a little grungy, not uncommon when it might have sat in a storage unit for years, and one corner was crumpling as if someone had either piled too much weight on top of it or sat on it before discovering it wasn't sturdy enough.

She'd dropped Toby off at Mrs. Hall's for the morning, giving her much-needed uninterrupted hours to work her way through as much stuff as possible. Something that the black-masked man wanted enough to be willing to set a fire and leave an injured man to die in it was here in her house—well, probably in her house.

She never quite forgot the urgency. It nudged at her, even when she was playing a silly game with Toby or restocking her booth at the mall or standing in line at the post office to mail items people had purchased on eBay.

Sam had called yesterday to check in. His tone had been courteous but not warm. He was sending a message, she assumed, feeling a little hurt but understanding. He hadn't had any intention of getting involved with her and Toby. It was just the middle-of-the-night scare and an apparent weakness for small boys.

She pried the top off the box and set it aside. At first sight, the contents weren't promising. Although that might not be fair, since everything was jumbled together. It might have been packed carefully, once upon a time, but upended a few times since. She first lifted out a scarf and saw that it was cheap polyester. Thrift store, she decided without hesitation. A second equally cheap one was stained. Throw away.

It was really a rather strange conglomeration. No, that wasn't right—everything appeared to have belonged to a woman, but if so, her tastes had varied wildly. Soft and pastel here, loud and vulgar there. Costume jewelry, and some jewelry well worth the time to clean up and sell. A sandwich bag held a pair of earrings that almost had to be emeralds; the setting was certainly fourteen or even eighteen karat gold. Oddly, there was clothing amid the jumble: a pair of stained leggings—why would anyone have put *them* in storage?—a couple of blouses and near the bottom a bra.

She didn't really want to touch that but picked it up gingerly between her index finger and thumb. It was blue satin, slightly discolored as if from sweat. She dropped it in the black trash bag she always had beside her workspace.

Peering at the items that had worked their way to the bottom of the tub, she was tempted to just dump them out. But some of it was jewelry, and she'd have to look closely at that. A few single earrings didn't match any she'd already looked at, and a delicate chain that might be gold had tiny links clogged with...something. Her nose crinkled. Suntan lotion, maybe?

She picked up a yellowing box that probably once held a new watch or the like and removed the lid. Even though she had no idea what she was looking at, she recoiled. It was…organic. She thought. Like flesh but mummified. She reluctantly stuck her nose close to take a whiff but was unable to smell anything except the musty odor held by everything in the tub.

Her skin actually crawled as she studied this downright creepy item someone had thought worthy of saving. It lay on a bed of the cushy white stuff that came in jewelry boxes, only this was stained, too, in an unpleasant rusty color. If she didn't know better, she'd think this was…a tongue.

Erin might have squealed as she shoved her chair back. Later, she was glad no one was there to hear her. She was being ridiculously squeamish, but—

She made herself look again, and her stomach turned.

Sam might think she was making an excuse to get him back here, but she didn't know what else to do but to call him. Even he'd agreed that sooner or later she would likely come across something that would be out of the ordinary… and this certainly was.

SAM HAD BEEN talking to the owner of a rental equipment business in town when his phone rang. A chain-link fence had been cut, and several expensive ride-on mowers as well as a small tractor had been stolen last night. The owner of the business was furious. Sure, he had insurance, but both mowers had been reserved for this weekend, and he might lose good customers when he didn't have the equipment ready when they needed it.

Sam glanced down at his phone, intending to ignore the call, but when he saw Erin's name, he changed his mind.

"Excuse me. I need to take this call," he said. The guy nodded, and Sam walked away. "Erin?"

"I…found something strange. Maybe strange. I can't be sure, but—"

"Whoa. What can be maybe strange, but you don't know?"

"I…" A huff of breath, and then she said more steadily, "I think it might be a tongue. It's all dried up, like mummified or something, and it could be from an animal of some kind. I probably freaked out for no reason, but—"

Feeling grim, he said, "I really doubt you did." She'd taken the horrifying events of the last week better than he'd have expected. Probably because she couldn't afford to break down, not when her son needed her. "Was this… tongue in with other things?"

"Yes, and it was an odd mix. I was already wondering."

"Okay," he said. "Don't touch anything you haven't already. I'm speaking with a business owner who had some equipment stolen last night, but it shouldn't take me long to finish up here. I assume you're home?"

"Yes. I was going to go get Toby, but… I'll call the daycare operator. She'll be fine with me leaving him longer."

Sam finished his report and decided the dollar amount of what had been stolen here justified bringing out a technician to look for fingerprints. There were only a couple of surfaces on padlocks that had been cut and left that could possibly hold a print, but it was worth a try. They'd find fingerprints, but only ones belonging to customers and employees, just as the tech had determined, after getting elimination prints from Erin, that only her prints were on the doors on each side of her garage.

Then he drove barely within the speed limit to Erin's overstuffed ranch-style home. He wanted to use lights and siren to get there faster but knew his sense of urgency wasn't matched by the facts.

Still, he was glad when she opened the door immediately after he rang. Her stress showed, but he also resisted yanking her into his arms the way he had last time. He needed to think about the uncomfortable intensity of emotion he felt for Erin before he acted on it.

"Thank you for coming right away," she said, backing up to let him in. "It's in the dining room."

"I'll want to look at everything that was packed with it."

She nodded.

A small box, maybe four inches each way, sat in front of a chair where she'd probably been working.

Erin gestured at it. "I...didn't want to keep looking at it."

"Was it in this box?"

"Yes."

He pulled some latex gloves from his pocket and donned them before carefully taking the top from the box. Then he stared. She might be right. Yes, it could conceivably be from an animal, but...it looked just the right size for a human tongue that had shriveled as its moisture content dissipated.

Riveted on the sight, she said, "I don't know why it didn't rot."

"He may have kept it in a drier place initially. And it goes to show that the storage unit was solid. No leaks, kept above any rainwater on the asphalt."

He started by taking a couple of photos before carefully restoring the lid to the small box and setting it inside a paper evidence bag. Then he let her show him everything else she'd found in the dirty plastic tub, taking photos as they went.

He agreed with her that the items didn't seem to have belonged to the same woman. The stain on the leggings was highly suggestive. He folded them into a bag, too. He couldn't be sure about the gold chain, but he had a bad feeling that it was skin cells and maybe blood embedded in the tiny links. That one, too, got its own bag. A lot of the rest, he decided to pack back into the original tub, which might still hold fingerprints.

"I'll have to take this with me," he said. "I'll give you

a receipt. You'll have to itemize the things you think may be valuable."

She gazed into the tub, an expression of repulsion on her face, but nodded at last. "There are only a few things. Those earrings, for one."

He nodded. They'd caught his eye, too.

He carried the tub out and locked it in the cargo section of his department SUV, then came back with the form he needed her to fill out. She jotted down only a couple of items and handed the pen back to him.

"Honestly, if I never see any of this again, it's fine. I just…have a really bad feeling about it all."

"I understand," he said. "I'll take the tongue to the medical examiner first and have it identified, then send the rest to the crime lab. I hope they don't take too long."

She was wringing her fine-boned fingers together. Anxiety and horror hadn't made her any less beautiful, even knowing she wasn't the kind of woman who usually turned heads. His had turned the minute he set eyes on her.

Yeah, he had to deal with this. He doubted she'd be interested in a short-lived relationship that required her to sneak away when she could take some time or invite him into her bedroom across the hall from her little boy's. He wouldn't be so drawn to her if she was. Her fierce love for Toby was part of what made her so attractive. Nothing subtle about that.

"Okay," he said. "Where was this box?"

"The living room. I'll show you." She led the way.

He didn't see anything he'd call a gap, and none of the nearby tubs were the same color or as dirty. Nonetheless, still wearing the gloves, he lifted lids on every nearby tub.

Nothing seemed obviously related to either of them.

"I'm sorry," she said. "They all look so much alike, you know."

Having seen the treasure trove in her garage and house, he did know.

"Why would a single box from a unit have been separated from the rest of the contents?"

She crinkled her nose. "When either I or the two guys I hire unload stuff, I don't have any *reason* to keep things from a particular source separate. Furniture sets tend to get put together, but cardboard boxes or plastic tubs?" She shook her head. "It's wherever there's room. And I was thinking today—"

When she broke off, he said, "You were thinking?"

"Well, Toby and I were playing hide-and-seek. He almost always wins when we play in the garage, because there are plenty of tunnels between piles and probably even some mazes out there. But what occurred to me today is that, while I get to know some of his favorite spots, they change regularly. I remove boxes or bigger items, replace them, wedge a tub in someplace without a thought."

"In other words," Sam said, "your maze shifts from day to day."

"Exactly. It never occurred to me it would matter where I put any particular thing. Well, except when I knew it would be valuable, like the furniture I showed you."

"And the rocking horse."

Now, she really looked chagrined. "I succumbed to Toby's begging and let him have it. It's in his room—and has a name."

He raised his eyebrows.

"It's a girl, he says. She's Rosie."

"He doesn't think his buddies will make fun of that?"

"I did hint at that, but… Well, he only has one good friend from his daycare, and Austin has never been here."

"Ah." Did she *ever* invite anyone to her house?

"It's only been this last year that my, um, backlog has

spilled into the house. And… I know it's sort of strange and probably makes me look like a hoarder, so no, I don't like people to see." She was talking faster and faster. "But while I'm not swearing off auctions, I'm resolved to be way pickier so I can catch up enough to make our house livable again."

He laid a hand on her arm. "Erin."

She looked as if she'd braced herself.

"Your house is clean, and you and Toby *don't* need much space. I'm not judging you. I understand why you've accumulated so much. In fact, I admire you for making a solid living from your skill at judging what's valuable or at least will appeal to shoppers. Don't apologize for that."

Her relaxation was subtle, but her smile was pure sunshine. "Thank you." Then she made a face. "I'm always thanking you!"

Amused, he said, "Then knock it off. And remind yourself that I'm doing my job. Mostly," he added but could tell she heard only that he was being paid to help her out.

She squared her shoulders, nodded and smiled again, but only pleasantly. "Will you keep me informed?"

"You know I will. It occurs to me, though, that we may need to get prints from the guys who haul stuff for you."

She shook her head. "They always wear leather work gloves. I've seen them take them off to open a can of pop or when they're driving, but never when they're loading or unloading. Also, I've never seen either of them peel the top off a tub. So if you find fingerprints inside the one you just took, they're either mine or the previous owner's."

"Okay," he said with nod. "You wouldn't have purchased from a unit that consisted of only a few plastic tubs, would you? I'm assuming there are a whole lot of boxes, furniture, whatever, from the same unit."

"That's true," she agreed. "I mean, unless that tub came

from a garage sale where I offered money for the contents of a few boxes they maybe hadn't even set out yet? That happens."

"Is it likely?"

She frowned. "Probably not. Nothing looked that appealing when I opened the tub. I don't remember it, either, which I think I would if I'd bought the stuff individually. Truthfully, I haven't done that kind of thing in a while. I'm doing better with the auctions. Older garage sale stuff I haven't gotten to would likely be in the back in the garage. And anyway…"

Sam grimaced. "We know the man who attacked Jeremy Conyers was after his possessions that had been sold from that particular facility."

"Right."

"Well, not meaning to nag, but I hope you'll try to find the rest of the stuff from the same storage space."

"Of course I will. Here, let me walk you out."

He missed feeling the warmth but told himself it was just as well she'd taken what he said as a warning. Even so, he was as reluctant to leave her as he'd been every other time.

Traffic was heavy enough once he reached the highway to require his concentration, however. He radioed in his intentions so Dispatch knew he wouldn't be immediately available and headed for Everett, where the medical examiner's office was located.

He arrived just as a jet took off from Paine Field, close enough to make him want to duck, and carried the tub in. Given that the day was winding down, he was grateful that an investigator was willing to take a look immediately… and even more grateful when the young woman looked up at him with a faint hint of shock and said, "The medical examiner needs to look at this."

She disappeared for about ten minutes, then returned with the older man who was the current county medical examiner. He nodded, bent close to study the tongue and said, "I'd like to look at this under a microscope."

There was one in the room, not surprisingly, along with equipment Sam didn't recognize. He'd attended autopsies here, but his errand today was unusual.

"It's certainly a tongue," the pathologist agreed, "and I'm almost certain it's human. Given the context… Well."

Sam nodded, then showed them the necklace, too.

Those were definitely human cells trapped in the links, the medical examiner confirmed after studying it under the microscope.

In the end, Sam left both items with them in hopes DNA would give him some answers and took everything else with him, including the items with stains. Fingerprints on anything in the tub—or *on* the tub—would be more helpful right now. DNA results were too slow, even if the medical examiner had agreed that the attacks and break-ins suggested answers were needed *now*…before someone died.

Chapter Eight

Erin was helping Toby buckle into his booster seat when her phone rang. Oh, goody. She didn't much want to deal with *anyone* right now...except Sam McKeige, whose name showed up on the screen.

She closed the car door so Toby wouldn't be able to hear what she said. "Sam?"

"Yeah. I stopped at the medical examiner's office. They're confident the tongue is human and plan to extract DNA and send it off."

Hearing an undertone, she said, "That's what you wanted, isn't it?"

"Except that results will take months. And then if there's no match in any database..."

"Oh." He wasn't telling her anything she didn't already know from the mysteries she read. "Then it's not much help, is it?"

"We may get lucky." He didn't sound convinced. "I've just parked to drop off the other stuff at our evidence unit. Fingerprints could give us a direction a lot sooner." He paused. "Did you have a chance to hunt anymore?"

"No, I had to do a couple of quick errands, then pick up Toby at Mrs. Hall's. I'm standing outside her house right now." Toby had seemed awfully glad to see her. She sighed. "I shouldn't have left him so long."

"At least he's not stuck in daycare full-time."

"No, that's true, but the only boy his age—"

"Austin?"

"What a memory! Austin's mom moved him to a bigger, commercial daycare. I may have to do the same but—" What was she doing? The detective was not her best friend eager to listen to all her confidences. "I'm sorry. Um, thank you for—"

He cleared his throat, and she chuckled.

"For calling."

"Yeah." He was quiet for a minute. "Do you have dinner planned?"

"Not really," she admitted. Was he—?

"What if I pick up a pizza and bring it by? Does Toby like pizza?"

"As long as it's cheese only." She felt a foolish smile spread. "We'd love that."

He wanted to know her preferences, and they came to an agreement. She was still grinning when the call ended. Earlier, she could have sworn he was warning her off, but she had to have misread him. Her giddiness was absurd considering her own determination to be uninterested in Sam anyway.

And then there was the rest of her day so far...and the reason she'd had to call him.

Her smile dwindled. At least Toby would be thrilled.

SAM CALLED IN the order during his drive back across the trestle over the Snohomish River and the wetlands surrounding it. Technically, he'd finished his working day, but for a detective, that meant nothing. He considered a forty-hour workweek to be a vacation.

He'd left a message yesterday for Jeremy Conyers, who apparently wasn't eager to call back. Until now, it seemed…

Sam tapped his phone. "Mr. Conyers?"

"This a bad time?"

"No, I'm driving but have hands-free."

"I went back to work today, but you know what the office looked like." Conyers gusted out a breath. "I'm paying a nephew and a friend of his to help clean up and haul crap out to the dumpster. So far, I've recovered a few records but not many, and none that would interest you."

"Because they're for on-going rentals?"

"Right. I've got the computer in at a shop, but they don't know yet how much they can save. And even if they succeed, I only began using it recently. My uncle's business practices were at least fifty years out of date. I hadn't even started entering the paper records, so I'm not sure how much help I'll be."

"What about records for the units where you auctioned off the contents? Wouldn't that be in the computer? If they were recent?"

"No." Conyers sounded as glum as Sam was starting to feel. "Those units were all ones where nobody had been paying for a while. I don't know if Uncle Charles hadn't noticed—he was kind of losing it—but I could tell we hadn't received payment for six months or more. I still sent off a late bill to each address, including a warning that the contents would be auctioned off. When there was no response or the bill was returned to me, I went ahead. All I did was make a note in each file of how much I received and the check number. Far as I can tell, that all burned."

"You sounded as if you thought there might be old records at your uncle's house," Sam reminded him.

"It's conceivable. What I had for those units was skimpy. If he kept older files, I might find more." After another sigh, Conyers said, "Give me a couple of days, and I'll do some digging at Uncle Charles's house. Man, I haven't even started there. It doesn't look as if he and Aunt Marie ever threw a thing away."

"That's tough." Sam could empathize, but the problem wasn't one he would ever face. His mother was dead, and he and his father were estranged. Sam wasn't even sure he'd hear if or when his dad died. "I hate to keep pushing, but like I said, Ms. Reed had a frightening break-in during the night when the intruder had to know she and her boy were home. She scared him off, but I'm sure he'll be back."

"I'll do my best," Conyers said, about the same time Sam reached the riverfront town of Snohomish.

Once he'd picked up the pizza from his favorite parlor, he headed east along the valley, brooding about his sudden turnaround. He'd resolved to keep some distance, and usually his self-discipline was better than this. The trouble was, he wanted to be close to Erin, not the opposite. If it weren't for her boy—

A car passed him on the two-lane freeway driving way too fast and barely able to make it around his vehicle and back in his lane before an oncoming semi would have flattened it. Sam wanted to turn on the lights and at least ticket the fool, but he was tired and didn't want the pizza to get cold. How did anybody drive this stretch of the highway without seeing all the warnings? Drivers were requested to turn their headlights on even in the daytime. With the highway raised because of frequent flooding, there was nowhere to pull off. More head-on collisions occurred on this stretch of road than anywhere else in the county, but people didn't seem to learn.

Sam's thoughts returned to his unaccountable weakness where Erin was concerned…or maybe it was about her three-year-old son. Or both.

Part of it, he knew, came from the dread that had taken up residence under his breastbone. A hard knot of worry. Jeremy Conyers would be dead…if Erin hadn't intervened. Kevin Hargrove would be dead if he'd happened to arrive home when a stranger was in his garage smashing things to vent frustration. If that same stranger had been able to break in to Erin's home from the garage, *she* might be dead.

Even before her discovery today, Sam had been working this investigation harder than he might normally when it wasn't a murder.

Yet.

Sam knew Erin was at the heart of this ongoing string of crimes. Once this scum eliminated other eBay sellers, he'd circle back to Erin. He'd seen her garage now and possibly guessed that she had more in her house. If she had what he considered his, he probably wouldn't be able to find it without her guidance, something he wouldn't get without threats or the point of a knife or barrel of a gun.

What would happen when he got to her and found out *she* couldn't find what he was looking for? *That* was what scared Sam. Especially since she had a huge vulnerability: that cute little boy.

Sam wondered whether there was an ex-husband who'd be able to take Toby for a few weeks.

After pulling into Erin's driveway and parking beside her pickup truck, setting the brake and killing the engine, he rubbed at the ache in his chest with the heel of his hand. He'd ask her about the boy's dad, but he'd be surprised if the guy was in the picture at all. When she talked about setting out on her new career, Sam had heard the trace of desperation. Monthly payments from the ex would provide a cushion he felt sure she didn't have.

He grabbed the pizza box and got out.

Erin returned from tucking Toby in for the night to find Sam had put the leftover pizza in the fridge and was loading their few dishes after rinsing them.

"Thank you. Can I offer you a cup of coffee?"

"No, I should get home," he said, closing the dishwasher. "I want to talk to you about a couple of things, though."

She stayed on her feet, wary of where the conversation was about to go. "Okay."

"First, I plan to come back in the morning if that works for you and help go through boxes. I may bring in another officer, too."

She opened her mouth, then closed it. "It's important whoever is here is careful."

"That goes without saying."

Did it?

"The tongue was all the way at the bottom of that tub. Would the other stuff have caught your eye? I mean, I often go through one of those tubs wondering why anyone bothered saving a single thing in it. Another one with…with…"

"What might be a serial killer's trophies?"

He hadn't put it that bluntly before, but she'd considered the same possibility, too.

"It won't be that easy to pick out, that's all," she said.

"I get that, Erin." He had a gentle tone that she'd never be able to resist. "Two of us working at a time has to be faster than you going at it alone."

"Yes. Okay."

He shifted, rolling his shoulders in a betrayal of some discomfort. "Something else I wanted to ask. Is Toby's father around? Or any grandparents? I'm thinking someplace he could go stay for a couple of weeks."

Erin shook her head. "Shawn dodges paying child support. He hasn't seen Toby since he was a baby."

Sam no doubt had to hear stories like that all the time, but his mouth tightened anyway.

"My parents were killed in a car accident," she continued. "Missing them was probably one reason I got married too quickly. And Shawn's dad...no."

"All right. Just a thought." There it was again, a note she'd almost call tenderness, especially coupled with the softening of his expression. The expression returned to cop-neutral as if he'd flipped a switch. "Expect me between eight and nine, if that's not too early."

"Nope. Toby is a 6:00 a.m. alarm clock."

He chuckled. "That doesn't surprise me."

Moments later, he was gone, and she was left to study the piles of plastic tubs almost as tall as her that filled the living room. She'd have to follow his example—not waste time evaluating individual items, probably even sorting them. For now, their only goal would be finding anything else that qualified as creepy.

Should she plan to take Toby to Mrs. Hall's tomorrow, maybe for the whole day? He wouldn't like it, but it would free her and Sam—no, *call him the detective*, since he'd be on the job—to concentrate. On the other hand, Toby did entertain himself well, and she could take her usual breaks to play a game.

That was what they'd do, unless Toby bugged Sam too much or got whiny. Those were the moments when she most appreciated Mrs. Hall's open drop-in policy.

She felt a pang as she wondered if she'd ever see Sam again once he succeeded in arresting the horrible man who'd left Jeremy to die in the fire and was now terrorizing her.

She made a face at what amounted to a moment of sheer fantasy. There was only one priority right now: finding out who had broken into her house, thereby ensuring Toby's and her safety.

What were the chances she'd get any sleep tonight, after last night's terrifying interlude?

SAM HADN'T TOLD Erin that he intended to park somewhere on her block to keep an eye on her house that night. He would let himself doze but no more. The sound of a vehicle engine anywhere in the vicinity should awaken him, and how would anybody enter her house silently?

With her front door solid and the door into the garage now steel with a dead bolt, the one vulnerability was the kitchen door leading to the backyard. While it wasn't steel, it had a dead bolt, too. Kicking it in wouldn't happen quietly. Breaking a window seemed logical, and he believed he'd hear that as long as he left his own window cracked.

He'd have rather guarded her and Toby from the inside, but asking to move in seemed over the top. That much closeness held a different kind of risk, too. Now that he knew the skimpiness of the knit boxers and thin tank top that she slept in, he imagined coming face-to-face with her in the middle of the night when she'd just come out of the bathroom. He could keep his hands off her despite temptation...but why set himself up like that?

Best not to put himself in that position.

He went home, showered and ate, then drove back to her block. As her neighbor had pointed out, there weren't many cars parked at the curb versus in driveways. That might make him conspicuous, but he doubted the creep had surveyed the area enough to know which vehicles belonged and which didn't.

He laid his seat back in hopes a casual glance would make his truck look empty, then closed his eyes and tried for the shallow sleep that usually came easily. Not tonight.

He had only two brief alarms during the night. A car crept by so slowly, he came to an instant state of alertness. Not a big black SUV, he noted, watching as it continued onto the next block. The driver was having trouble maintaining a straight line. Drunk seemed likely. Sam's debate about whether he had to pull the car over ended when a garage door opened in the middle of the next block, the car made it in—lucky it was an otherwise empty two-car garage—and the door closed behind it.

The second time, he lifted heavy eyelids to see a flicker of movement in the front yard of a house a couple doors down from Erin's. A dog, he finally realized, a big one. It was sniffing and peeing its way along, presumably an escapee from its own yard.

The pale light of dawn killed any last hopes of more sleep for Sam, who groaned, ran a hand over his face and started the engine. He'd get a breakfast sandwich at a fast-food joint, then come back. Since he'd shaved last evening, he hoped it wouldn't be obvious to Erin that he had done anything but sleep in his own bed.

When Erin let him in half an hour later, she looked even more tired than he felt: puffy eyes with bruised circles under them, her movements slow enough he suspected she was on autopilot. Guilt struck; if he'd slept in her house again, *she* would have slept, too. They'd both be more efficient today.

He'd have to think about that.

"Coffee?" she asked.

He'd had a cup of crap brew from the fast-food restaurant. "Thanks," he said.

She turned without another word and headed for the kitchen. He heard a tuneless form of singing coming from that direction in a high voice.

"Jingle bells, jingle bells, jingle all away."

Amusement improved Sam's mood. "He's ready for Christmas?" It was still months away.

She made a sound in her throat. "A little early. And unfortunately, that's the only part of the song he remembers."

Somewhat imperfectly.

"Jingle bells, jingle bells, jingle... Mommy!" Kneeling on a chair, his elbows planted on the table, Toby grinned. "Sam!"

"Yep. You're bright-eyed and bushy-tailed this morning."

"I don't have a tail! Why'd you say I had a tail?"

Sam let out a sigh he tried to keep soundless, but Erin gave him a sidelong look of sympathy. He didn't know the origin of the saying himself but had heard it had something to do with... "Squirrels. Always bright-eyed and how they flick their tails like they're ready to go at any minute."

"They are fast," Toby conceded.

Erin had shuffled over to the coffeepot and was pouring what he presumed was a second or even third cup for her and one for him.

"Toby staying home today?" Sam asked.

"We'll see how it goes," she said.

"What do you mean, Mom? You *said*—"

Her turn to sigh. Sam grinned.

Two hours later, he still had his audience. Erin had dragged a couple of tubs to the table, one for her to start with, the second for him. Toby had decided Sam was more interesting than his mother and had queried Sam about nearly everything he removed from the tub. Erin eventually squelched that, but Toby still watched with interest. As Sam packed everything back in the third tub he'd dug through, Toby said, "Mommy, can I go ride my horse?"

"Sure you can." She held out an arm. "Hug me first." Once Toby had trotted away down the hall, she said, "Thanks for being so patient. I know he's a lot."

Sam shook his head. "He's a good kid. I haven't heard him whine yet."

"Oh, he's capable, but he doesn't do it a lot. Toby was born cheerful."

"Isn't the first thing a baby does is cry?" As if he didn't know. Hearing Michael's first cry, he would have sworn his heart had doubled in size. Dr. Seuss had gotten that one right.

"Well, yeah, but you know what I mean. When I took him out, he'd grin at every person he saw. He never had the 'stranger danger' phase that most babies and toddlers have."

"I remember that—" He all but bit his tongue, he cut himself off so fast.

She'd quit working and watched him, her eyes compassionate. But she didn't say a word. Obviously, she wasn't going to push.

Maybe that was why he heard himself say, "I had a son. I told you that, didn't I?" He cleared roughness from his voice. "He...was killed when he was four."

"Oh, Sam," she said softly, reaching across the table to touch the back of his hand. "I'm so sorry."

He turned it over and gripped her hand. "It was tough. He...was with his mother. We were separated. She'd been drinking heavily. I never thought she'd drive drunk with him in the car but—" Man, he couldn't find the next words. The real next words were, *I'd have done anything. I* would *do anything.* Meaningless, when you couldn't go back.

"I can't let myself imagine." Her eyes darkened. Then tiny creases formed on her forehead, and she said, "That's why you're worrying so much about Toby and me, isn't it? Because...because of your son."

Of course it was. Partly. "He reminded me of Michael at first, but not so much as I've gotten to know him. You're right. Toby is pure sunshine."

"I will never understand."

He took the same jump she had, to the ex, a guy who'd

walked away from his own child. "I can't either," he agreed. What kind of man did that?

"I tell myself it's his loss." Erin lifted one shoulder. "Except Toby's lost something, too."

"I'm not seeing it. He's happy because he has everything he needs here with you, Erin. He might have questions later, but he's not mourning a father who is not in his life, or you'd know it."

"Look how he latches onto you. That tells me something."

"It may just be that I'm new." For her sake, he hoped that was the case.

Darkness shadowed her eyes for a moment. "I hope it was fast. What happened to your little boy."

"So I was told. Mostly I try not to dwell, but—"

"Toby reminded you. I'm sorry about that, too."

The words that came out of his mouth startled him. "I'm not."

Chapter Nine

He blinked, then frowned. Finally, voice hoarse again, he added, "I've tried not to be around kids. I thought I'd just be punishing myself. But Toby... He's his own person." He shrugged. "At first I thought about Michael. Now, I just see Toby."

"I'm glad," she said.

He shook himself. Time to rebuild his wall. "I'm ready for a new tub. Does it matter which one I grab?"

"Oh...we can probably skip some. I'm done with this one, too."

He waited until she'd put the top back on hers, then took it before she could stand, piled it atop his and lifted both.

"I could have—"

He lifted his brows.

"You know I haul stuff all day, every day."

"Yeah, but I'm here right now."

She rolled her eyes and led the way to the living room, where a small gap showed where they'd pulled out these boxes.

He added the two he carried to a new pile they'd started, then said, "Any two?"

"No, we can skip this one. I glanced in it earlier—it's Christmas ornaments."

The tub itself was bright red with a green top. Out of curiosity, he peeled off the lid to see that cardboard dividers and layers of cardboard protected a large tree's worth of delicate ornaments. "Huh," he said. "I've seen these for sale in the hardware store before Christmas."

She gave him a strange look. "Doesn't everyone pack their ornaments in one of these?"

"I don't usually bother with a tree," he said shortly. He and Ashley had gone to her parents' for the holidays every year, killing a good part of his annual vacation, but it was important to her, and having grandparents mattered to Michael, so Sam had never complained. "Do you have one of these boxes?" he asked, but then wished he hadn't. The topic was irrelevant to their task and to his job. He still hadn't come to terms with the idea of getting too personal with Erin.

"Sure. Last year, I let Toby pick out a new ornament. I thought I'd make it an annual tradition." She shrugged. "The ornaments in there—" she nodded to the bright plastic tub "—look especially high quality. I might keep a few. Otherwise, I'll make a display of Christmas decorations at the antique mall when we get closer to the holidays."

"That makes sense." He looked around. "Do you have any suggestions, or do we need to go through them all?"

"I see others that I packed myself from garage sale purchases, or that I glanced at already, but for now—" She grimaced.

"Got it." He chose two at random, discovering the second was seriously heavy.

"What?" she asked.

"Feels like it's full of bricks."

"Hmm." Erin removed the top, and they both stared in at a couple of concrete figurines. "Garden sculptures. Those'll go fast." She sounded delighted. "Let's put this one by the front door."

He shook his head and hefted it himself. "Why don't you let me load it in your truck?"

"Thank you. I may as well take advantage of your strong back."

She lowered the tailgate, watched him heave the box in, then closed it again.

Inside, they took a couple of more tubs and carried them into the kitchen.

"This one's dirty," he commented.

"Like the one with the tongue." She eyed it when he set it beside his chair. "You're right, but it's not the same color."

"Does anybody buy all matching ones when they decide to store a bunch of their possessions?"

She made a face. "Mostly not. I suspect a lot of people start with a unit when they're moving, then keep adding to it instead of closing it. Or else they buy more plastic tubs when they've filled the first ones, or see a sale."

A grunt expressed his opinion of paying monthly for years to store stuff you didn't need or even want in your home.

She'd had the same thought, of course, given that emptying those units in the end gave her a livelihood. But what a waste for the original owners.

SAM HAD JUST finished his second molasses cookie following the sandwich Erin had fed him for lunch when his phone rang. He'd been surprised to make it undisturbed through the morning.

He answered and walked into the living room for the brief conversation. Deputy Warren had been called to a home that had been burglarized, and he thought Sam might be interested.

Sam didn't have to ask why. It wasn't hard to guess. Sam thanked him and said he'd be right there.

He went back to the kitchen, where Erin was rinsing the plates and Toby crumbled the remains of a cookie he hadn't been able to finish. Both gazes went right to Sam.

"I knew I'd get pulled away sooner or later. I need to talk to my lieutenant about assigning someone else to help you, too. For now, I'll try to get back this afternoon but can't promise."

"I'll just keep on," she said, sounding undaunted—or maybe just determined to remind him that she usually worked alone.

"Okay." He ruffled Toby's hair, then glanced at Erin. "Lock behind me?"

"Oh, sure."

Almost to the front door, she said, "Is this thing you're leaving for related?"

"Probably not, but I have everyone on alert."

She gave him a sturdy nod.

Sam yearned to stay. It was all he could do not to reach for her. To touch her, one way or another. Her eyes widened as he betrayed more than he'd intended, but he made himself nod, open the door and go without looking back.

The address he'd been given wasn't half a mile away. Sam parked at the curb and walked up the driveway.

Ed Warren stuck his head out of the side door into the garage and waved to get his attention. "Thought I heard you."

The moment Sam stepped into the garage, a place of shadows since it was lit by a single bulb dangling from a rafter, he saw why Warren had called him. "Damn," he said softly.

This space wasn't jammed on a scale with Erin's garage, but it was close. His first thought was that the homeowner was also an eBay seller or the like—except as he scanned the contents, it became apparent that furniture took up much of the space in here, along with a washer and dryer not hooked up and of course the ubiquitous plastic tubs along with plenty of packed cardboard boxes.

The tubs and boxes had been dumped, the contents ransacked quite a bit carelessly or otherwise trampled.

"The homeowner have any idea what has been taken?" Sam asked.

"Unfortunately, she doesn't. Her son and daughter-in-law are in Europe—London, where he had a two-year contract position. Mom offered to store their stuff."

Sam winced. "I hope she wasn't home."

"No, thank God. She spent the night in Seattle with her daughter. I don't like to think what would have happened if she'd been home and came out here to see what was going on."

"No." Erin had done the right thing. Sam's guess was that this was a more typical burglary, and the perp might have run rather than attack, but...there was a lot of destruction out here, too. He shook his head. "I don't think this is the same guy that broke into Ms. Reed's garage, but this is a step up from our usual burglaries where someone just grabs some electronics."

"That was my feeling," the deputy agreed.

"I haven't heard of anything else like this," Sam commented. "Have you?"

"I hadn't, but while I was waiting for you, I called Snohomish PD and spoke to a detective there. They had a break-in a couple weeks ago that sounds a lot like this. Didn't come up with a witness or fingerprints, unfortunately."

Which likely meant the sheriff's department wouldn't, either, but they had to try.

"You call for a fingerprint tech?"

"On their way. We're keeping them busy in our little corner of the county," Warren said dryly.

"Yes, we are. Do you need me?"

"No, just wanted you to see it."

Sam took a last, frowning look around. "Keep me informed, would you?"

"Sure thing."

Warren was a good cop. Sam wondered if he'd applied for promotion to the detective division. He might not be interested—but Sam would have to ask him.

Didn't it figure, his phone rang again before he could even get in his vehicle. He wouldn't be making it back to Erin's this afternoon—although he had every intention of spending yet another night parked close by to watch over her house and its occupants.

ERIN HAD THOUGHT everything from the storage unit with the unique and valuable items had been deposited more or less together in her garage. Still, she wasn't surprised when she discovered that wasn't the case.

This tub, she'd found in the living room. Erin had been working her way through everything in this one room to be sure she didn't miss anything. So far, she'd only set a couple of boxes and plastic tubs aside, in both cases because the contents held such obvious appeal she'd want to list them on her eBay site or put them in the antique mall as soon as she had a moment to pursue her actual livelihood.

The moment she pried the top off this tub, she gasped. It was partly filled with books, leather-bound and in beautiful condition. She stroked one of the bindings and handled the books carefully as she lifted them out. Books weren't a specialty of hers; she sold some that she came across, but nothing like this.

Research, she reminded herself.

Carefully rolled in crinkly paper was a scarf with exquisitely detailed birds and flowers embroidered on a cream silk backdrop. Gently laying it out, Erin realized it wasn't intended for a woman to wear, although she certainly could, but rather to lay over the top of an upright piano. Even the fringe was in excellent condition.

She sighed with pleasure and set it aside.

Several more treasures, including a number of other pieces of fabric art: tatted doilies, fringed and lushly decorated scarves that looked designed to cover a small tabletop and so on.

The plastic tub itself looked like some she knew had been piled around the children's rocking horse Toby had so coveted.

Almost to the bottom, she found tied in faded blue ribbon an inch-thick pile of letters. Those she took to the dining room. Even the ink had a different look than was usual now. After untying the ribbon and opening a selection of the letters, she found the handwriting all the same. They also seemed to contain only the first name of the writer and her correspondent. All were addressed to *Dear Kitty*, and signed *With all my love, Winnie*.

She'd have to read the letters with care—the handwriting was sharply slanted and spidery—to hope to find any details about where either woman had lived or a last name. Guiltily, she realized she'd already spent more time on this one plastic tub than she should have. She'd promised Sam to ignore anything that she could be certain didn't have anything to do with the other, odd collection.

Still, she took time to call Jeremy Conyers.

When he answered, he said, "Erin," without a lot of enthusiasm.

"Yes, I just came across some letters in a tub I'm sure is

from that same unit. You know, the one with such beautiful things."

"Which, for reasons I don't get, you want to give *back* to the family that quit paying the storage rent."

"Well, that's not quite true. But there are some things that shouldn't have left the family, and…" She stopped. "Anyway, I came across a possible name, although it's only a first name. Kitty."

"Kitty."

"From the handwriting, I'm guessing the letters are from the 1930s or '40s. Maybe even earlier than that. Anyway, I thought if you happen across that name—"

"Uh-huh. I'll let you know. Although you may have to wait in line behind that detective. He's not letting up, either."

For which she could only give thanks. "Are you okay?" she asked tentatively. "You sound tired."

"Not quite myself, but I'm starting to dig into the boxes my uncle had stored in his garage. I have a feeling I'll be building a big bonfire in the backyard one of these days. Why he kept such old records is a mystery to me."

"But that's exactly where you'd find records for this unit!"

He sighed. "Maybe. Just because it's old stuff doesn't mean it's been sitting in that unit for fifty years. Those plastic tubs looked more modern than that, for one thing."

She blinked and focused on the sturdy tub in front of her. It wasn't new, by any means, but when had such things started being manufactured? People had once used wooden trunks, many with arched lids. Cardboard boxes would have come next.

"You're right," she said. "Still."

"I owe you," he said. "I'll keep looking."

"I couldn't have left you," she protested.

"It would have been smarter for you to grab Toby and

run. You took a risk," he said gruffly. "I'll never be able to thank you enough."

Before she could open her mouth again, he'd cut the connection.

"I HAVE A rookie for you to borrow," Sam's lieutenant said during their latest phone conversation. "Kid broke his ankle tripping on the stairs downtown."

Sam had heard about that one. Twenty-one or -two, the young deputy would never be permitted to forget his clumsiness.

He wouldn't be able to carry full boxes and tubs for Erin, Sam reflected, but otherwise might be a good choice if he had any kind of eye at all. It wasn't like he could be called out, the way Sam so frequently was, or assigned a regular patrol.

"He's better than nothing," Sam said. "Ah...what's his name?"

"Patrick Knapstad."

"Right. Is he available tomorrow?"

"No, he's in some pain and supposed to stay prone with his foot elevated." The lieutenant sounded disgusted at one of his officers taking it that easy but added, "I'll have him there at eight o'clock Tuesday morning."

The day after tomorrow. Sam hoped the kid actually turned out to be useful.

He wanted to stop by Erin's house and see how much she'd accomplished, get himself invited to dinner—or bring a take-out dinner with him again. He'd been involving himself with her and the boy more than he should, though. He needed to focus on their safety, not making friends...or reaching even beyond that.

Instead he headed home, shoveled some manure from the paddocks and turned the horses out to pasture for tonight and tomorrow. Then he showered and turned on a Mariners baseball game while he ate a sizeable helping of chili that he'd frozen the last time he cooked.

His phone stayed silent. Erin would have called if she'd found anything. He convinced himself nobody would attempt a break-in during daylight. Late afternoon and early evening were the least likely times, given that so many neighbors would be arriving home from work.

When dusk deepened the sky he saw through his front window, he turned off the TV, realizing a minute later he couldn't remember the score. He could turn on the radio in his truck...but this was early enough in the MLB season, there was no point getting excited one way or the other. Funny, when once upon a time, he'd been passionate about the sport.

He'd played on a minor league team for a couple of years, but shoulder damage he'd done playing college ball returned in an ache that required alternating ice and heat to treat after games and even practices. He didn't want his body to break down over a sport. He'd never regretted that decision.

His wife did, though; she'd had visions of her husband pitching in the World Series, making the kind of money most people didn't even dream about. He thought now she'd been drinking too much even before he applied to the police academy and then took a job in a mostly rural county sheriff's department north of Seattle, but things were never the same between them after he gave up on his own boyhood dream of stardom. She drank more, which he hated, and by that time he suspected they stuck together only because of Michael.

Erin was right, he thought, as he made the twenty-minute drive to her place half a dozen blocks from the river. He couldn't deny his attraction to her...but he dreaded thinking what it would do to him to see her bright, optimistic little boy dead.

Once this was over, he should probably back off and stick to his vow never to have children, not when he of all people knew you never got over the devastation of losing one.

Right now, though... Yeah, he'd park outside her house, sitting in darkness hour after hour, just to make sure this piece of scum didn't so much as look in their window.

What he hadn't decided was what he'd do if he got called away.

Chapter Ten

Was it possible for sunny good fortune to shine down on you even as a dark cloud hovered? Erin had no idea. She wished the better-than-ever sales balanced out the fire, the break-in and the ever-present anxiety, but it didn't seem to work that way.

Still, she couldn't help feeling good about her day. The owner of the antique mall had called that morning to let her know the booth beside Erin's had been cleaned out.

"Eleanor says she's going to concentrate on eBay from now on," Marsha said. "She's been putting in a lot of overtime at her day job and hasn't been able to pick up much in the way of new items lately."

The booth had looked picked over for quite a while. Whereas Erin could fill it in a heartbeat.

Well, not quite that, since it required her to load furniture and boxes she already had ready to go. She'd have to haul them to the mall, then go back for another load and another—because it turned out she'd had a stellar weekend of sales in her existing booth and needed to restock it, too.

She ought to stay home doing the task Sam had assigned her, but she needed to keep making a living, too. She'd spend a few hours tonight going through boxes at home, she decided. And she'd taken so much stuff out of her house today, she hoped she could consolidate what was left in the house to clear at least some space, if not a room. Now if she could just find time to list more things online...

Knowing how busy she'd be, she'd taken Toby to Mrs. Hall's for the entire day. She'd promised him they would go out for dinner after she picked him up. She felt guilty watching him trudge in the door with an air of resignation instead of the excitement he'd have felt if Austin had still been there for him to play with.

Some kids had to go to daycare forty hours or more a week, she reminded herself. Mrs. Hall read stories and played games with the children in her daycare; she had a swing set and a sturdy climber with a short slide in her fully fenced backyard. Toby would not be suffering.

The proprietor of another of the more successful booths, Steve Boulton, was leaving just as she arrived. He grabbed a brick to hold open the door for her benefit, then said, "Need a hand?"

"I wouldn't mind one," she admitted.

Steve was in his early sixties but lean and strong. A couple of years ago, he'd told her his history: the company he worked with had gone under, and he'd decided to try the antique business rather than job-hunting. His wife's health wasn't good, and he wanted to be home with her rather than always on the road as he had been.

He carried more than a fair share of the heavier items, moving them as she decided where to put what. He had a good eye, she'd already known, and made a few suggestions.

"Bless you," she said as they parted out back. "I'm off to get another load, but thanks to you I have plenty of energy left over."

He laughed. "And no short helper today, either."

"I figured this would be too full a day for him," she conceded.

After she packed the pickup truck and even the passenger

seat beside her as full as she could, Erin made the return trip and unloaded with some help from yet another booth proprietor. Over time, they'd all formed a kind of community that she appreciated. A few months back, she'd caught a browser pocketing jewelry from a booth across from her, and someone else returned the favor for her.

That memory on her mind, she decided to display some especially nice jewelry inside a glass-fronted cabinet that locked. It was a bit of a nuisance for whoever was at the front desk when Erin wasn't here, but she had a price point that separated the small pieces she'd leave unprotected from the items that were worth extra effort. Usually—always on weekends—two people worked the front desk and took turns circulating and helping customers, so it wasn't difficult for a customer to get someone to unlock to show a particular item.

She turned in place, pleased with her effort. Bright pieces of collectible dishware joined quilted placemats and fringed cloth napkins on a table she'd snapped up for next-to-nothing at a yard sale. She'd found a bouquet of silk flowers to display in a tall, distinctive vase she thought completed the effect. Smaller rugs draped over a rack. A beautiful, though worn, Grandmother's Flower Garden quilt lay as if tossed casually over the back of a wing chair, while a copper floor lamp made the corner cozy. Framed prints, porcelain figurines, some antique kitchen tools and more had their spots. She'd even found a place for a lawn mower and for a few yard tools—and one of the two concrete garden sculptures. She didn't expect any of the yard stuff to last through the weekend.

Marsha came by to admire her effort and give her a nice check for the previous week's sales. As a result, Erin was feeling good when she picked up Toby half an hour later.

He waffled on the dinner selection but finally decided on chicken nuggets and fries from Burger King. Fast food wouldn't have been her first choice, but she'd worked hard enough today to feel an ache in her shoulders and back. She wasn't in the mood for cooking.

Of all people, they encountered his friend Austin and Austin's parents at the restaurant. The two boys ate quickly and ran off to play in the pit of plastic balls, giving Erin time to ask how they liked the bigger daycare center.

Austin's mother made a face. "I still have mixed feelings. There's a kid I'd call a bully except he's maybe four years old. Austin has come home crying a few days. At least there *are* other boys his age."

"Don't forget the lice outbreak," her husband said.

"Yes! And lice seem to have defenses against the shampoo you're supposed to use, so I've had to comb and comb and comb." She wrinkled her nose. "And then they came back, either because one of the parents didn't do the job adequately or because the facility didn't clean well enough. Of course, they had to close for a couple of days while this was going on."

Austin's dad grinned at Erin. "Bet you wish you'd moved Toby sooner, huh?"

She had to laugh. "I keep going back and forth. He really misses Austin, but Mrs. Hall is so good about me dropping him for as little as an hour or two at a time. I doubt most places would permit that."

"No, I think there are strict rules about drop-offs," the boy's mother conceded. "But Austin misses Toby."

"I'll visit the place," Erin decided as the boys ran back begging for ice cream cones. Or maybe she'd just check the drop-off limitations and price on the website first. And yes, kids could pick up lice just about anywhere, but the thought made Erin shudder.

"I'll call, and we can plan for Toby to come over on a Saturday or Sunday to play," Austin's mother suggested.

The boys cheered.

On the drive home, Erin said, "Weren't we lucky to see Austin and his parents?"

"Uh-*huh*," Toby agreed. "*He* says he wishes he still went to Mrs. Hall's."

Erin wondered if that was true or whether he'd been momentarily inspired by getting to play with Toby.

"He says a boy there hits him sometimes," he added.

Erin had been keeping a sharp eye on her rearview mirror to be sure they weren't being followed, but what he'd just said had her mouth dropping open. That was more than the preschool version of bullying. How would she feel if she picked up Toby one day and saw a bruise on him courtesy of that brat?

Rationally, she knew the boy might be struggling with hard times—say, his parents had separated. But she was protective of her own son, likely because of the way Shawn had so utterly rejected him. Maybe Toby was bored at Mrs. Hall's, but he was also safe, and it wasn't as if he couldn't play with younger children, even if most of them were girls.

She made herself study her mirrors again as she turned onto their street. Home looked good right now. Thank goodness for the longer days this time of year, because it hadn't even occurred to her to leave on lights. With dusk, it was getting to be a little harder to make out details as she turned into her driveway.

Still, she didn't notice any vehicles in driveways or at the curb that didn't belong. Once she'd helped Toby out of the car, she took another careful look around, then listened as he chattered about a new game they'd played today at Mrs. Hall's. The day couldn't have been *that* dull.

Once she unlocked the front door, Toby slipped past her and ran ahead. She had barely locked up when he screamed.

ERIN HAD NEVER been so glad in her life as she was when she ran to the dining room and saw Toby alone. He wasn't hurt—*thank you, God*—and no stranger had broken in to grab him.

Only then did she let herself see what he had.

His favorite toys were sturdy plastic animals: dinosaurs, a mastodon, elephants, lions, tigers, horses, cows, whales, a hammerhead shark. They bought a new one every time they went to the Seattle zoo. He kept them in a box. Somebody had been in his bedroom, had carried his toys into the dining room, dumped them out—and methodically beheaded every one. That somebody must have used a sharp knife, she couldn't help thinking as she stared in shock.

Her antique sycamore table looked as if an ax had been taken to it.

Finally, she turned slowly to see that, just as in the garage the other night, tubs had been tossed around and dumped on top of each other, and the stuff inside had been trampled.

Terror seized her as if a real tiger strolled toward them, tail twitching, lips pulled away from its long, sharp teeth.

What if whoever had done this was still in the house?

Erin grabbed Toby by the hand, swung him to her hip and ran back the way she came. With her shaking hand, she fumbled with the lock on the door. The moment it gave way, she ran for her truck. She gave one wild glance back but saw no one pursuing, no dark shape visible through the front window. Even so, she unlocked the driver door, all but threw Toby in and clambered in after him before locking the doors again. Finally, she got the key in the ignition, started the engine with a roar and backed out into the street.

Not until they were half a block away did she brake, hearing herself whimpering, and look at her son, who watched her with shock as tears ran down his cheeks.

Sam was just thinking about leaving his house when his phone rang. *Not a call-out, please.* The lack of any decent night's sleep recently was catching up with him. He'd had to work at convincing himself to get moving for another stakeout on Erin's block. A couple of the buyers of the goods auctioned off at the storage facility hadn't had a break-in yet. Why would the guy go back to Erin's until he'd checked out other possibilities?

But Sam knew he also wouldn't be able to sleep worth a damn if he stretched out in his own bed because he'd thought, *nah, the guy won't be back yet.* Those sounded like famous last words to him.

And now Erin's name showed on the screen of his phone. "Erin?"

"Sam?" she whispered, followed by a strange sound. Her teeth chattering?

His alarm jumped into the red zone. "What happened?"

"I've been gone all day." She had obviously gathered her composure. "We...we just got home. Somebody has been in the house. He ransacked a few piles of tubs, but that's not the worst part."

The hair rose on the back of his neck. "What? What's the worst part?"

"He...he got a bunch of toys from Toby's bedroom. Animals. And he..." another chatter of teeth "...cut their heads off."

Sam swore viciously. "Are you still in the house?"

"Nuh...no. We ran out and locked ourselves in the truck. And I'm up the block where I can see the house. I don't think anyone is still there, but..."

"Okay, good. That's smart. I'm on my way." In fact, farther on his way than he'd realized. He shouldn't drive when he was oblivious to what he was doing. "Why don't you stay on the phone?"

"No, that's okay." She was calmer now. "I'm sorry I have to keep calling you like this—"

"Don't be. Haven't I made it clear that I want to hear from you if anything at all feels wrong?"

A meek "yes" tweaked something under his breastbone. What if she'd called 9-1-1 instead of his number, and he'd heard what happened tomorrow? He'd have guessed she hadn't trusted him…or maybe didn't want to bother him? He'd have felt sick about it, that's what.

It wasn't necessary, but when he reached the highway, he slapped on his flashers and accelerated. Drivers moved over to let him race by. He didn't go a lot above the speed limit but enough to cut the time it took him to get to her house by a good ten minutes.

The moment he reached her street, he searched for her truck. There it was, almost to the corner, facing her house so she could watch it. Approaching from the other direction, he swerved right into her driveway and slammed on the brakes.

Pulling his service weapon, he jumped out and ran to her front door, which stood open. He cast a glance to see that she hadn't started back to the house. Good.

"Police!" he called, shouldering the door wide enough open to let him in, then set about clearing the house. Doing that included stepping over Toby's toys, something that would make him sick once he allowed himself to take in the ugly threat aimed at a small boy and his vulnerable mother.

The kitchen window was broken, just enough to allow an arm to reach in and move the latch so the window could be opened. Things had been swept from the kitchen countertop, too, in a flash of temper: stoneware canisters that had held white flour, whole wheat flour and sugar were smashed on the floor along with a bottle of olive oil crushed by a heavy foot. The dish drainer was dumped on the floor, too, some of the dishes broken.

When had the break-in occurred? The intruder had made some noise. Had he known neighbors weren't yet home from work? Or did he not care? He seemed to lack any semblance of self-restraint, which was a big part of what scared Sam.

There was no indication that the burglar had gone into the garage. He could have looked around out there, then locked the door behind himself when he came back in, of course, but so far as Sam could tell, everything stored out there looked as it had after Erin picked up after the last intrusion.

Maybe the guy had just wanted time to look for the possessions he regarded as his in the house—but it was equally possible that terrorizing Erin had been his goal.

If so, he'd succeeded. Sam felt sick looking at those toys. He'd had plastic animals like that himself when he was a kid. So had Michael. To threaten a child to get at his mother... That struck Sam as evil, not a word he could remember using a lot.

He made a quick call for a fingerprint tech, even though he knew the intruder would have worn gloves, then put on latex gloves himself and picked up all the animals and their heads, setting them carefully in their box. He closed the lid. Out of sight, out of mind probably wouldn't work, but Toby didn't need to see this again.

Finally, he called Erin.

He went to meet them at the front door. Toby clung to her, nearly strangling her from the looks of it. Her face had a pinched look he hated to see.

"Hey," he said gently.

"How did he get in?" she asked.

"Kitchen window." He wasn't surprised she hadn't noticed. In fact, he was glad she hadn't hung around trying to figure something like that out. Getting herself and Toby out of the house had been the smartest thing she could do. "Not a big hole. We can tape some cardboard over it, but the window will have to be replaced."

"Mr. Weaver is going to start questioning whether he wants me as a tenant."

"We're having a string of unrelated break-ins in this part of the county," Sam said. "No reason he needs to know that somebody, uh—"

"Has it in for me in particular?" She shuddered, then kissed the top of her little boy's head. "Maybe if I'm lucky he'll upgrade the window from aluminum to vinyl."

She hadn't moved from the porch. He stepped back. "I picked up the toys and put them out of sight. Have you two had dinner yet?"

"Yes, that's why we're getting home so late." She inched inside, shuffled forward a few feet, and then her dilated eyes met his. "Can you tell *when* he was here? Did he wait for us or—?"

"No indication of that." Sam didn't have to say, *No way to tell if he did.* He could have fled out the back when he heard Sam's siren. She had to know that. "I'm hoping you can tell if anything—especially an entire tub—is missing. Looks kind of different in here to me."

Her head turned as she explained what she'd done today, finding room for a significant amount of goods in her now-doubled booth at the antique mall. "That may make it harder for me to tell if something else is missing, but I'll try."

"Okay." He let them pass him and then gently herded them to the kitchen. Gaze falling on the damaged table, he immediately regretted his move, but there wasn't a lot of choice here.

Expression stricken, she said, "I'll put a tablecloth on for now." The set of her mouth firmed. "I loved this table."

Those cuts were deep. Refinishing wasn't going to save it.

"Toby?" she said. "Can I set you down?"

He shook his head hard and tightened his hold.

Sam stepped forward. "Hey, buddy," he said. "Can I hold you? Your mom needs to look around."

Toby sniffled, cast a teary-eyed look at Sam, then nodded. When Sam closed the last distance, the boy almost threw himself into Sam's arms.

Erin looked surprised but also surreptitiously rolled her shoulders. Seeing Sam's expression, she said, "I hauled a lot of stuff today. Toby weighs at least as much as the chest of drawers I carried out to my pickup."

Sam chuckled even though he didn't feel any kind of amusement. The brutal nature of this break-in on top of the last one let him feel as if he didn't dare take his eyes off Erin and Toby. No more assuming they'd be safe during the daytime. What was more, he didn't like imagining her straining to get something as sizable as a dresser out of the house and up into the bed of her truck.

"You have any help on the other end?" he asked.

"Actually, yes. Another proprietor helped carry all the heavy things in from that first load, and then I had a different assistant when I got back with the second load. I really emptied quite a bit of space here."

"Anything from the garage?"

"The dresser, a table and a lamp. Otherwise, I had things I've already researched and priced packed near the front door. I pointed out that pile to you, didn't I?"

She had.

He sat down with Toby, both of them watching as she pretended to ignore the mess on her kitchen floor and instead wandered through the dining room and living room, making little cries now and then. Sam felt sure there was some breakage, which a small entrepreneur could ill afford.

That said, she had plenty of inventory. His mouth actually quirked at that thought.

Finally, she came back and sat down. "I don't know. I can't be sure."

He'd had time to think and said, "My guess is, if he found what he was looking for, he wouldn't have done this other… damage." He tipped his head toward the shards of broken canisters and dishes on the floor as well as toward the box of toys he'd shoved under the table.

Erin followed the direction of his gaze, then lifted her head to meet his eyes. "That…makes sense." She didn't move. "I need to clean up."

"I'll help," he said.

"You don't need—"

He raised his eyebrows, stopping her midsentence.

"Thank you. I feel bad. You must want to get home."

He shook his head. "No. I plan to spend the night right out front of your place. I won't be leaving you two alone again."

Although how he was supposed to accomplish that while continuing to do the rest of his job, he wasn't sure.

But then he remembered: the rookie. What was his name? Patrick… Knapstad. That was it. Young and inexperienced, but he presumably could shoot any scumbag going after Erin and Toby.

Sam guessed he ought to tell Erin about tomorrow's assistant.

Chapter Eleven

Surprised, Erin said, "Wouldn't you rather stay inside? It's not like you haven't done that before. I know the twin bed is too short for you, but..."

Even with him sitting, she was all too aware of his sheer size, both lean and muscular.

"I...didn't mean you to know I was out there." He glanced down at the boy sitting on his lap. "I don't want to put you and Toby to any trouble."

Did he *hear* himself?

Her laugh cracked in the middle. "You come running every time I call. Having Toby sleep with me is no hardship, Sam. Besides, tomorrow I can clear out the living room so you can get to the sofa, which pulls out, assuming you'd prefer that. I feel awful that because of us you can't sleep in your own bed! And that you'll be running back and forth to take care of your horses."

"They're out to pasture." He cleared his throat. "I'd be glad to stay here rather than trying to catch some sleep and keep watch at the same time in my truck."

She almost opened her mouth to ask if he really thought this faceless monster would keep coming back...but she knew better. Of course he would. The man had broken in twice already. She was grateful that she and Toby hadn't been home when he broke that window and let himself in today. What if Toby had been napping in his bedroom? How long would it have taken for her to run down the hall, rouse him, open the window, knock out the screen and climb outside?

Too long. Somebody would have been waiting for them.

She shivered at the knowledge, forcing a smile for Toby at the same time. Eyes wide, he was listening to the adults. She hoped he couldn't read between the lines. Or understand how conflicted she felt.

Depending on herself was important to Erin. She was grateful for kind gestures, like help carrying furniture or heavy boxes into the antique mall from her truck, but she hadn't had anyone to turn to in the big ways since Shawn left. And after he was gone she'd come to realize he hadn't been dependable even before that. She'd had severe morning sickness, and he hadn't changed a single behavior out of concern for her.

Water under the bridge. She shouldn't have to remind herself. Except, for Toby's sake if not her own, she couldn't afford to be too proud to accept help now.

Sam had done more for her in a week than anyone had in a long time. She couldn't let him know how attracted she was to him, or he'd assume she was just clinging out of fear and gratitude. Though, a few times there had been a glint in his eyes that made her wonder...

Well, quit, she ordered herself. If he asked her out after this was all over, that might be different.

Instinct said he wouldn't. Whether he was physically attracted to her or not, however wonderful he'd been with Toby, she couldn't imagine him choosing to get involved with a woman who had a son so close to the age his own son had been when he died. That wasn't something any parent would get over or move past. Losing Toby...

She shied away from even the thought, as if she was swerving to avoid a headlong collision on the highway. No. Just…no.

Toby wasn't the only one watching her, and she had a bad feeling Sam saw at least some of what she needed to hide.

"I'll change Toby's sheets right now," she said. "If you have anything you want to bring in…"

Sam shook his head. "I will move my truck, though. I'd rather it not be obvious you have anyone else staying here."

He was baiting a trap. Understanding what he was saying brought her fear back to the surface. "You want him to break in again."

His eyes darkened. "I do." Lines on his face deepened. "Maybe you and Toby should move to my place while I stay here. I'd like to keep you both out of this."

"This?" she repeated. "But it's all happening because of me. My decisions, what I do for a living."

He half stood, realized he didn't want to dump Toby to the floor and sat again. "You didn't do a thing to deserve being a target." That voice was unyielding. "You're making a living. The decisions on what you should bid for and what to skip, how high to go, are good ones. How could you possibly have anticipated anyone storing a petrified—" The noise he made had to be born of frustration. "I've never heard of anyone finding something like that in a storage unit. Have you?"

"No." She bit her lip. "Not paying the bill wasn't smart."

Toby had been staying unusually quiet, not surprising after discovering his beheaded toys and having her snatch him up and tear out of the house. Of course, now was the moment he asked, in his high, piercing voice, "What's petri…petrified, Mommy?"

Only from long practice was she able to smile. "Dried up." She wrinkled her nose. "You know. Like an orange that rolled to the back of the refrigerator and neither of us saw it for a long time. It would shrink and be wrinkly and hard."

Sam muffled what had to be a laugh.

"Oh," her son said. "But why would it be—?"

She cut him off. "I found something icky in one of the boxes that had been left for way too long. You don't need to know what it was. But somebody who owned the stuff in the box is mad because he forgot to pay to keep storing it, and now he wants it back. If he'd asked nicely, I might have let him take his boxes, but he's broken into our house and scared us instead. He doesn't deserve anymore for me to just say, 'Oh, that's yours? Of course you can have it.'"

Toby reached out and fingered one of the ugly gouges in the table. "I don't like him."

"I don't, either," she said. Her gaze rose almost reluctantly to meet Sam's. "We're really lucky to have Sam here so we don't have to worry so much about him, right?"

"Uh-huh." Toby had been sitting up with his back straight, but now he relaxed to rest his head against Sam's chest in a gesture of pure trust. "I like sleeping with you anyway, Mommy."

She smiled. "I know you do, pumpkin." Pretending she didn't notice the way Sam had stayed still as the little boy snuggled against him, she said, "It's time you brush your teeth, and I'll tuck you into bed before I make sure Sam has something to eat."

"We coulda brought him a hamburger and fries."

"We would have, if we'd known what we would find at home. As it is, *we* had dinner, and Sam hasn't. And your tummy is full, so you don't have to watch Sam eat."

"But..."

She leveled a mom stare at him. Toby sighed, sat up again and slid from Sam's lap. "Will you come say g'night to me?"

he asked the imposing, armed man he'd assumed would be glad to snuggle him. "When I'm ready?"

Her heart almost broke at the stunned expression on Sam's lean face.

"Yeah." He cleared his throat. "Of course I will, buddy."

SAM TRIED TO persuade Erin that she didn't need to feed him, but failed. Unlike Toby, she sat across the table from him and watched him eat a black bean quesadilla she'd put together with amazing speed. Unfortunately, she kept nibbling on her lower lip, which he found distracting.

After clearing his plate, he laid down his fork. "I think I told you earlier that I'd try to find another officer to help go through boxes."

"I remember."

Her clear gray-green eyes held as much trust as her son's bright blue ones had. That kind of trust usually was something he shied away from. A man could fail to live up to it… but he knew in his head, if not his heart, that there'd been nothing he could do to save Michael. Failing Erin and Toby wasn't an option.

"He's not going to be as much use as I'd hoped for," Sam continued. "He's young—a rookie—and wearing a cast because he broke an ankle. I didn't ask, but he's presumably on crutches." Or a walking cast? Did it matter? "Which means he can't haul the heavier stuff for you. But there'd no reason he can't go through tubs as fast as I can, and he's armed."

A flicker of worry—disappointment?—crossed her face. "Will he be here instead of you tomorrow?"

"I should be here, too, for some of the day. I get called out often, though, and I've asked to be notified every time there's a residential break-in." He frowned. "I should have mentioned the antique mall, too."

"I can ask the owner to let you know if anything like that happens."

"Okay."

"I'm sorry I didn't get more done today—"

Sam shook his head. "You can't just drop your job. I understand that. Anyway, opening some space may make our work here go faster."

She offered him a cup of coffee, which he accepted despite his intention to go to bed soon. He didn't expect to sleep deeply anyway.

Bringing a mug to the table, she asked, "Did I mention talking to Jeremy Conyers? I gather he's starting to go through records stored in his uncle's garage?"

"So he tells me. Did he call you?"

"No, I just wanted to remind him to keep an eye out for anything that might be connected to the unit that had such expensive things in it." She mentioned the letters, which didn't sound all that helpful to Sam, but alarmed him in a different way.

"I'd rather you let up for now on trying to find these people," he said. "Probably that box wasn't connected to them, but I've started to wonder whether the guy really had an entire unit filled with his own possessions. What if someone in his family said, 'Sure, you're welcome to store what you need to in our rental'?"

"That would explain why he didn't know the rent wasn't being paid anymore," she said slowly.

"Exactly."

She made a face. "Okay. It's not like tracking those people down is a high priority anyway."

He should have gulped instead of sipped his coffee, then suggest she start for bed while he moved his truck. The need to stretch out in bed was creeping up on him anyway, but mostly he was disturbed by how comfortable he felt in one way with this woman...and how on edge he felt in another way.

He hadn't let himself feel much for anyone in a long time. He'd been conscious that even with close friends, some space had opened to separate them. His grief hadn't let him forge new connections. As for women, he'd gone out a few times and slept with one, but afterward he didn't like himself much. He hadn't especially liked *her*, and going through the mechanics without emotion wasn't him. It never had been, but now, he was best off to keep to himself.

Except, where Erin was concerned, he was having some trouble convincing himself he should. For the first time in a long while, he'd reacted immediately—to her curves, to her fine-boned face and to her courage. That physical attraction had deepened as he found her to be generous, determined, fiercely protective of her boy...and tender. Sam was shocked by how much he wanted some of that for himself.

He let them fall into general conversation that smacked of first-date exchanges. She was so hopelessly behind on what movies were coming out in the theater and streaming, she hardly remembered what she'd liked. Her work and Toby consumed her time. She didn't say a lot about the ex, but Sam already had developed a serious case of hate where he was concerned. Not that it mattered, since she hadn't so much as set eyes on the guy since he'd walked out on her.

"FedEx brought the divorce papers. I signed them and sent them back." She shrugged as if there was no emotional hit anymore to something that had to have been part of the kind of betrayal you never let go of.

He admitted he hadn't been to a movie theater in years but refrained from stating he didn't date. He did watch an occasional show streaming but read more often than he turned on his television.

His mouth quirked. "Except for sports. I follow professional football and especially baseball. I played all the way through college, then in a minor league for a couple years before hanging it up to became a cop."

"Really?" She looked fascinated. "You played professional baseball?"

He laughed. "If you can call it that when the pay is so pitiful, the crowds so small and the amenities so pathetic. If my wife hadn't worked, too—" Whoa! What was he thinking?

"I'll bet she didn't mind. I mean, pro sports always sound glamorous."

He'd walked right into that one. "Yeah. She had a lot more faith than I did that I'd get called up and that fame and fortune would be ours. Truth is, I'd started having shoulder pain before I even signed on, and it got worse for all that I tried to ignore it." He grimaced. "A lot of my teammates were younger—they'd been signed out of high school—and I began to feel like an old man. Got bored, too."

Her head tipped a little as she studied him. "So you didn't quit after a serious injury. Or did you wait until the end of the season?"

"Nope. Threw a pitch in practice, felt grinding pain and walked off the mound. Told the manager I was done, went straight to the locker room—which, by the way, wasn't half as nice as the one at my high school—got dressed and went home."

Where he'd been making dinner when Ashley walked in.

"I hope your wife was supportive." Erin made a face. "I shouldn't have said that. It's none of my business."

"Well, you know the outcome." Something he hadn't shared with anyone in years, even though a few people he worked with knew what had happened. "She threw something at me to express her fury, wanted to know why I hadn't asked her opinion and went out and got drunk with a girlfriend. After that, she started keeping the makings for her favorite drinks on hand."

"You must have been young when you had your son."

"Too young," he said bluntly, "except I fell in love with him in a way I didn't know was possible."

She touched the back of his hand, fingertips gentle. "I know."

Sam knew she did. He saw it on her face every time she looked at Toby. Sam didn't doubt that Ashley had loved Michael, too, but…not the same way. Maybe amid her dreams of that glamorous future, she'd just been too young to commit so intensely to a child who consumed a lot of energy and time.

"Yeah." He heard his own gruffness. "I should move that truck and let you go to bed."

To his regret, Erin snatched her hand back. "You're right. Here I am being nosy when you're just thinking about doing your job."

"No."

In the act of pushing back her chair, she went still. Her eyes searched his.

"You have to know—" His throat felt like it was full of gravel, and his voice sounded as if it was, too. Somehow he was standing.

"Know what?" she whispered, rising to her feet.

"You're more than a job." Oh, that was eloquent.

Eyes wide, she waited.

"I'd like to kiss you."

Her eyes dilated, and she moistened her lips. "I'd like that. Although…"

"Although?"

"I… It's been a long time. I mean…" She gave a funny, one-shoulder shrug. "Except for Toby."

"I haven't been involved with anyone for a while, either."

He might have smiled; he wasn't sure. "I think I remember how to do it."

Erin laughed, which gave him a major bump in his mood and enough impetus to walk around the table, slide a hand around the nape of her neck and drink in the details that made up a face he'd been drawn to at first sight. Then he bent his head and kissed her.

Chapter Twelve

Erin's last thought was, *What if I've forgotten what to do?*

His lips were so gentle, she quit thinking at all, just savored. And then they firmed, which was even better, and he nibbled at her lower lip until she did the same to his. Of course, that let him in, and the slide of his tongue against hers had to be the most erotic thing she'd felt in forever.

She gripped his shirt in both hands and just held on as the kiss deepened, still at an almost leisurely pace. His hand cupped the back of her head now, tilting it to give him the best access. She wanted more and got it when he wrapped his arm around her and pulled her tight against him. Nothing had ever felt better in her life than that long, hard body. She rose on tiptoe, loving the sensations from rubbing against him. She wanted to climb him, discover the warmth of his skin. Maybe this was all instinct. If so, hers was on target.

Sam groaned, freed his mouth from hers to nip her jawline and then her neck. She let her head fall back as he kissed his way down her throat to the hollow at the base, where he startled her with a hot, damp touch of his tongue.

When she jerked in reaction, he lifted his head. His eyes were darker than she'd ever seen them, but blazing, too, if that wasn't a contradiction.

Erin wasn't sure she even breathed as they stared at each other.

Another raw sound escaped him, and he stepped away. Without his support, she swayed before she grabbed the back of a chair to steady herself.

"I didn't mean to take it that far," he said roughly.

"I…" She knew she blinked a couple of times. "I liked it." So dignified: she'd just bared herself!

Only he grinned. "I did, too. We'll have to do it again."

Now would be good.

But he was rolling those broad shoulders and moving his head as if to ease tension in it.

Had he worried that Toby might still be awake? And…she wasn't ready to invite Sam into her bed, was she? She didn't groan, but only because she restrained herself. If he'd kept kissing her like that, she doubted she would've ever paused for a moment of calm decision. As it was, Toby was asleep in her bed, the only one large enough for her and Sam to share. Although they could surely manage on a twin bed…

If her cheeks weren't already red, they must be now from the heat burning her face.

Sam cupped her chin, which rested nicely in his broad palm. His expression was regretful, but even as she gazed up at him, he donned his usual calm mask. Becoming the cop again, because that was what he thought he needed to do? Or stepping back, figuratively if not literally, because he wasn't sure he should have kissed her?

All she could do was rub her cheek against his hand, smile and step back in actuality.

"I should have moved my truck sooner," he said. "There's still enough traffic out there, he's unlikely to be hanging around now. It won't take me long, but you don't have to wait up for me. I'll lock the door behind myself if you want to start getting ready for bed."

However tactfully he'd phrased it—that was an order. He'd prefer she had used the bathroom and disappeared into her bedroom before he returned. That stung, but she had too much pride to let him see that.

"Go," she said, flapping her hand. "Fair warning, Toby is an early riser, which means I am, too."

"I did notice last time. That's fine. Knapstad may be here as early as eight."

She wished him good-night and headed for the hall. Only a minute later, she heard the quiet sound of the front door closing.

THE THUNDER OF small footsteps in the hall brought Sam lurching out of a dream he hadn't been enjoying.

"Mommy!" was followed by a "shh" that came way too late.

Sam groaned, yanked the pillow out from under his head and slapped it over his face. No, he hadn't slept well, for multiple reasons. Nothing like staying alert for any faint sound that didn't belong—a sound made by a killer—along with brooding over a kiss that had been even better than he had imagined...but that also scared him. The happy boy out in the hall being one reason for that.

No clock. He groped blindly for his phone lying on a headboard shelf. It read 6:03 a.m. Glad the pillow would muffle the sound, he groaned again. He'd give a lot for another hour.

Mother and son had moved out to the kitchen. He heard a chair scraping, Toby chattering, the refrigerator door opening and closing. Man, he hoped she didn't mind him using her shower. And that she didn't have a low-flow showerhead.

He emerged twenty minutes later, wishing he'd brought a change of clothes but figuring no one on the job would notice, given that he wore similar getups most days. If his day included an appearance in court, he'd have had to run home, but as it was, he could do that later. Pack a duffel bag, he decided, even if he would still have to go back and forth to take care of the horses.

When he appeared in the kitchen, Erin smiled at him without quite meeting his eyes. Toby beamed, and Sam couldn't resist stopping to ruffle the boy's hair.

"Just in time for breakfast," Erin said and set a big bowl filled with scrambled eggs on the table to join a pile of toast and a plate heaped with bacon. He had to guess this breakfast was much bigger than what she and Toby usually ate.

He pulled out a chair. "This looks amazing. If you went to a lot of extra effort just for me, though—"

"No, Toby and I like to treat ourselves at least once a week. And I'm guessing a bowl of cereal wouldn't hold you long."

No, it wouldn't, but he said, "I don't like adding to your workload."

"I love bacon," she assured him and sat at the third place.

A red-and-white-checked tablecloth covered the deep slices in the wood. Would Toby forget they were there? Sam wondered if any of the tables she had out in the garage would end up here as replacement. Or maybe she'd wait until she saw something she liked better.

He ate with pleasure, even as he watched Erin alternating a bite for herself with tucking a napkin in the neck of Toby's T-shirt, steadying the glass of orange juice that he had to clutch in both hands to get to his mouth, wiping up spills and so on. The familiarity of it felt... Sam couldn't quite decide. He liked seeing Erin helping the little boy without ever getting irritated or making him feel less than capable. The deep ache beneath his breastbone wasn't unexpected. Weirdly, though, Toby reminded Sam of Michael less and less often.

Michael had been quieter and more reserved, even as a toddler. Sam had sometimes worried that Ashley ignored him or grew impatient with him. In the first couple of years he didn't really see that—but he was away a lot, traveling with the team. Later, once Ashley began to drink at home even during the day—

He told himself to knock it off. Why rewind a video that couldn't be edited?

Toby finished eating first, of course, and announced he wanted to play. Only then he said, sadly, "I wish I could play with my animals."

"We'll buy new ones," Erin assured him. "You have plenty of other toys. Why don't you do a puzzle?"

Sam thought he had a box of similar animals up in his attic. Some had been his as a kid. Of course, they'd gone with Michael when Ashley left Sam, but after the accident—

More he didn't want to think about, but the memory of packing everything that had been Michael's flashed whether Sam liked it or not. He'd left Ashley's clothes, jewelry and even the furniture in the small apartment for her mother to deal with. Everything of Michael's, he'd taken, even though his grandmother had loved her grandson.

Why not climb up in the attic later, when he was home? What had he been saving them for? If Michael could know, he'd be glad his favorite toys would be loved.

A sound escaped Sam that he hoped neither Erin nor Toby heard. He rarely let himself get morose. Give the toys to another boy who'd enjoy them. Nothing complicated about that.

He finished eating, thanked Erin again and set to work. Struggling with his focus, he'd gone through four plastic tubs in the living room before a vehicle pulled into the driveway beside Erin's truck. He waved her back to a seat and went to the door to allow the rookie in.

Sam immediately saw the walking cast. Good. Crutches would have gotten in the way. Knapstad was tall with a decent build and a boyish face, especially when he looked eager as he did now.

"Detective. I hope I'm not too early."

"No, we've been at work for a while." Realizing how that sounded, Sam added, "Ms. Reed has a young son who likes to get up with the chickens."

"Oh." Knapstad smiled broadly. "I'm glad to have something useful to do. They've had me planted at the front desk."

Sam introduced the deputy and Erin, then dug in his pocket for latex gloves to hand him before sitting him down with a tub. He detailed as many of the contents from the tub that contained the dried-up tongue as he could recall, hoping that gave a good idea what to watch for.

"Nothing seemed to go together," Erin said from off to the side. "Except they all belonged to women. Well, the tongue, we don't know, but—" She looked sorry she'd let herself rattle on.

"So you think—"

"Trophies," Sam said grimly. "That's our best guess. Our difficulty is that Ms. Reed has been productive lately in purchasing contents of storage units that came up for auction." He paused to let her explain why that was and what she did with the things she bought, then continued, "That means she has more here than usual, and because the house and garage are crowded, the contents of any particular unit didn't end up together. A tub might have been shoved in anywhere it fit."

The rookie was looking around in a certain amount of awe and probably bemusement.

"We can't assume any others from the same unit were the same color or even a plastic tub versus a cardboard box or—" Sam had noted a few stuffed black plastic bags out in the garage "—a sack."

"Sad to say, that's true." Erin smiled at the deputy. "Sam—er, the detective or I will keep dragging boxes over for you to go through. With a lot of them, it's often clear that it's not what we're looking for. You may find ones full of dishes wrapped in newspapers, or pots and pans. Sometimes clothes, but that's less common."

"Because people don't put their clothes in storage."

"Right. They put furniture, knickknacks, toys their kids have outgrown, washers and dryers—" for some reason she made a face at that "—photo albums, books, CDs, framed art. Well, you'll see."

She got Knapstad started, asking him to let her know if he saw anything he suspected was especially valuable or at least easily salable so she could tag that box, then resumed her original spot.

Sam continued with the box he'd been going through— clothes and shoes, but a man's. He continued carefully, just in case their possible serial killer was an equal opportunity offender and had murdered a man or two along the way. When he was done, he said, "I'd recommend thrift store," and took a sticky note and marker from her to affix to the outside.

They had a system now: stuff that looked good for the booth at the mall or potential eBay in one pile, thrift store in another, uncertain or mixed in yet another pile. Because of the room she'd opened up yesterday, they were able to slide boxes around instead of having to wedge them back where they'd come from so as to be able to pull out another one.

Toby popped out every fifteen minutes or so and either watched them or wanted Mommy. She disappeared with him briefly, her eyes always meeting Sam's when she returned. He knew why; she was asking, *Did you find anything?*

He hoped if there was anything else gruesome to be found, it was in one of his boxes, not hers. Every time, he gave a slight shake of his head.

He couldn't say he minded when at about ten o'clock his phone rang. He knew the number: the lab where he'd delivered the tub with everything *but* the tongue.

Sam took his phone out to the porch before he answered the call.

It was the same woman he'd spoken to that day. Her eagerness raised the hair on the back of his neck. "We have hits on several fingerprints on items in that tub you brought us. The outside of it, the lid inside and out, had prints we're assuming belonged to one individual. We found the same fingerprints on items in the box, but also separate prints, not surprisingly."

His heartbeat had quickened. Was it possible it would be this easy?

"Names?" he asked.

"Only forensic hits for the ones on the tub and lid," she said regretfully. "Three of the other prints belong to murder victims."

It was like a gut punch. They'd been right.

"I assume you have contact info for investigators?"

"I do. I'm sure you're not surprised to hear that the ones on the tub are associated with those three crimes...and have shown up at other scenes where the victim was never found or where the fingerprints were assumed to have belonged to a friend or someone else who'd had reason to be in the home or car."

"Why don't I come in?" he said. "That way I can see which fingerprints go with what. Oh—did you hear from the ME? I assume he came up with DNA?"

"He did and sent it off, but reminded me how long it would likely be before we get a response. That said—"

her voice brightened "—now we have good reason to put a rush on it."

"We do indeed. The offender is right here, searching desperately for his goodies."

"And may have his eye on another victim," she added quietly.

Not a thought he liked. Especially since he knew what woman this piece of scum was watching.

SAM HAD GIVEN Erin his okay to go to the antique mall the following day. Call it a hall pass, she thought, her nose wrinkling...except she didn't actually mind his protectiveness.

She was even more frightened now and could tell that he was, too. He didn't like to let her out of his sight. She didn't love going out on her own, either, but Marsha had called to ask her to come by since a gentleman—that was the word she used—had been asking questions about items she had for sale.

In barely more than twenty-four hours, quite a few things from Erin's double booth had already sold, too, so Sam helped her load the bed of her truck before he took off in response to a call about a break-in that he didn't think was linked to the storage facility.

Usually she would have taken Toby with her, but the tension had risen to a point where she felt better having him at Mrs. Hall's for the day. If only she had family she could place him with! Hearing verification that the box had, just as Sam guessed, held trophies from multiple murders had shaken her world. She'd have been shocked to see a mugging; the odds of finding something like this were infinitesimal.

But she didn't know how to do anything but go on.

After dropping off Toby and driving to the mall, she carried a box of miscellaneous items she'd priced some time ago in through the back door. A woman browsed in her booth, smiled vaguely at her but otherwise paid no attention as Erin set down the tub, peeled off the lid and looked around to see where she had gaps that needed filling. The only other person close by was a man hovering in a booth across the aisle, which specialized in antique tools, but he didn't seem interested in them or her. She guessed he might be the woman's husband, bored but trying to entertain himself.

Once she had a better idea what she needed, she let herself out the back again, greeting the proprietor of another booth getting out of her truck even before the door swung shut. Erin pushed it open again, blocked it with a brick they frequently used for the purpose, and they went in together carrying their next load.

By the time Erin had restocked her enlarged area, she was wondering about the man who had been so insistent she come by to talk to him. Well, she needed to see Marsha anyway. She finished stacking several now-empty plastic tubs and was straightening when she almost bumped into someone.

She felt a flare of alarm when she recognized the man she'd noticed earlier. Apparently, not a bored husband. Had he been watching her the entire time? Waiting until she was alone?

She'd like to believe he was only being considerate by waiting until she was free, but he didn't back away when she nearly bumped into him. He leaned toward her, his expression so intense *she* wanted to retreat from him.

Her voice squeaking the tiniest bit, she asked, "May I help you?" She was already cataloguing her impressions. Midthirties to early forties, she guessed, seeing a little gray in the afternoon stubble on his jaw. Brown hair, gray eyes that glittered, a mouth compressed into a thin line and a solid build. Cords stood out in his arms, bared by a V-necked white T-shirt...and his fingers were curled into something close to fists. Several pockets of his cargo pants bulged with unknown items.

"Yeah." He seemed to bite off the word. "What took you so long?"

"I'm not here most of the time. The ladies at the counter in front could have helped you. Anyway, I've been here for probably half an hour. I wouldn't have minded talking as I worked." She sneaked a peek one way, then the other. Was it bad luck that nobody happened to be in sight?

"Where do you get this stuff?" He jerked his head toward a glass-fronted cabinet.

She frequently used that word herself, but his tone belittled her work. Taking a casual step away from him, she said, "Oh, a variety of places. Garage sales—most weekends, I go to any in the area." Except, when had she last been to one? "Even thrift stores, occasionally. When the contents of a storage unit become available because the owner quit paying the rent, I sometimes bid to purchase them. If you're interested in something in particular and care where it came from, I can try to remember."

"That." He pointed at a cut-glass vase.

She frowned at it, finally shaking her head. "I'm afraid I don't recall. I frequently have cut-glass vases and plates. If you're looking for one—"

"What about *that*?" he snapped, this time stabbing his finger toward an unusual pair of wrought-iron bookends.

"I—" She started to shake her head, even though she could picture the plastic tub they had been in.

"You don't know." He sneered. "What kind of business is this, when you don't know anything about this junk you're selling?"

Her temper began to simmer. "I know quite a lot about everything I sell," she snapped in turn. "I research every item, then determine how old it may be and a reasonable value for it." She took offers on occasion, but not one from this guy, if driving down her price was his goal. "If you disagree with my asking price, there are at least forty other booths in this antique mall alone. Feel free to look elsewhere."

"I don't want to look elsewhere. I want to know where you get your things and what else you have that isn't displayed yet."

He was giving her the creeps. Her gaze drifted down to his work boots. Yes, those would be good for trampling.

It occurred to her to try to place him into the frame where the masked man fit who'd beaten Jeremy and lit the fire. She couldn't be sure, but…he was around the same size and bulk.

A ball formed in her stomach, and her instinct begged her to run. Instead, she squared her shoulders. "You're making me uncomfortable. I do have other stock in storage. If you're looking for one thing in particular, ask. Otherwise, you're welcome to browse, but I need to leave."

He took a long stride closer to her. "You're not much on customer service, are you?"

Nerves prickled beneath her skin. "Excuse me."

He grabbed her arm at the same moment voices cut into the bubble they seemed to have occupied.

"Yes, one of our booths has a wonderful collection of vintage quilts and other fabric arts." It was Marsha, and she was in this aisle.

The rumble of a male voice answered, followed by the more excitable voice of a woman.

The hostile man took his hand from Erin's arm and backed away. "I'll be back," he said, low and rough, before he turned and rushed away just before the other three people came in sight.

Shaking, Erin's first thought was to call Sam. Her heart hammered, and she gave herself a minute to calm down. She could be overreacting. They all got unpleasant customers.

She wanted to think he'd left...but she'd find someone to walk her out to her truck to be sure she wasn't alone in the parking lot—and that nobody followed her.

Chapter Thirteen

Sam stayed at his desk at headquarters to make his calls, received with intense interest and cooperation by every investigator he reached. The crimes had occurred over four years, not so long that a detective would have forgotten one that had remained unsolved.

The picture that began to form for Sam was even worse than he'd expected. The crimes linked to the man's fingerprints started with brutal rapes and escalated into rapes followed by murders. The women were in their twenties to early thirties, all pretty, blond to mid-range brown hair. One had been a graduate student at the University of Washington; another an attorney; and a third in sales at Nordstrom. Two had been attacked in their own homes, others snatched somewhere between work or a social engagement and home. Every detective to whom Sam spoke wanted this guy with anger he shared.

The earliest crime, a rape, had happened in Bend, Oregon. That woman had been a ski instructor and lift operator at Bachelor Butte. The first murder the fingerprints pinpointed was in Beaverton, a suburb of Portland, Oregon. The other crimes had been committed in the greater Seattle area, not surprisingly, since the killer's trophy stash had been deposited in a storage unit in Snohomish County, just to the north of King County, which included Seattle.

Neither rape victim that survived had recognized their attacker, because he had never removed the black ski mask he wore over his head, and he'd also battered their faces to the point where their eyes had swollen shut. The closest any of them had to a witness was a woman who had seen a pickup truck pull to the shoulder of a rural road. The driver had gotten out and dragged something out of the bed of his truck and tossed it in the ditch. The woman had been too far away, given the darkness, to make out the license plate or see any more than to believe he wore something black over his head. A hood, she'd assumed at the time. She waited until he was gone before she ran to see what he'd dumped.

She admitted to screaming all the way back to her rural home and locking all the doors and windows before she called 9-1-1.

Some of the women had had an uneasy feeling they were being followed before the assaults. One victim, eventually murdered, had told a friend she'd swear someone had been in her house...but whatever made her uneasy was subliminal. She couldn't say, *That's gone*, or even, *I could tell someone looked through my drawers*.

Investigators looked hard at men in the women's lives: recent dates, boyfriends, coworkers, anyone with whom the women had clashed. They had names—but no two investigators had so much as glanced at an individual who had also come to the attention of a detective looking at another crime. Now, with what Sam was able to tell them, they were all able to eliminate everyone who'd drawn their attention.

"He's a ghost," an older detective said wearily. "Doesn't this guy have to make a living? If he's moving around the Northwest, he sure isn't holding down a job." He paused. "Unless—"

Sam had the same thought. Their perpetrator could be a long-haul trucker, a salesman with a route, who knew? He frowned and made a note to look at what had been happening in each city leading up to the murders. There could have been conferences, fairs, art exhibits. The guy could be a runner who traveled to compete in marathons or even just ten Ks. The possibilities went on and on. Wouldn't another investigator have had the same idea? And reality was, this guy had been lurking in Sam's corner of the county for a couple weeks now.

Because this was home? Or was he renting a place locally because he was determined to recover his trophies? Probably not staying in a hotel or B & B—his comings and goings late at night would stand out, especially if he assaulted another woman and ended up with her blood on him. Everett was a big enough city to have some Airbnb rentals, but Sam doubted the smaller towns like Sultan and Monroe offered much like that. Still, it was an avenue to pursue.

Whether this was the killer's home territory or not, he'd learned that a storage unit he considered his personal vault had been violated and the contents sold off. Had he driven in and found the lock had been replaced—or there was no lock at all, and the unit was vacant? A question to ask Conyers: once the contents of a unit were auctioned, would the code to the gate still have been valid?

If the footage of traffic in and out of the facility had survived the fire, it might be worth taking the time to watch. If someone remained conscious at all times of where cameras were placed, he could keep his face from being seen, but would he bother when he'd come and gone from this facility multiple times in the past?

No matter what, everything had changed for the man now. Rage drove him, rather than his more usual targeting of a particular woman. Unless, of course, he had a dual interest in Erin.

Sam's jaw clenched so hard, his molars ached. He wanted to believe the killer had zeroed in on her house because she was one of the names Jeremy Conyers had thrown out as a possible purchaser of the contents of that particular unit, not because he'd ever set eyes on her.

Sam didn't dare let himself believe that. He thought it was irrelevant anyway. The level of rage and violence demonstrated when that scum attacked Conyers said no one who might be in his path was safe. Beheading a little kid's toy animals? That was sick. Only a monster would do that.

He'd ignored several calls for the past couple of hours, only checking messages now and again, but when Erin's number came up, he answered.

"I hope I'm not interrupting anything important," she said, sounding anxious.

Going for calm reassurance and hoping his fear wasn't leaking into his voice, he said, "No. Right now is good to talk."

"Oh. Well, I thought about calling you earlier, but I didn't want to overreact and waste your time, only I talked to Patrick—you know, Deputy Knapstad—and *he* thought I should let you know about this guy—"

Sam was still tracking her run-on sentence but thought it was time to interrupt, if only so she could catch a breath. "I want you to call me *any* time something worries you."

"Oh." She was quiet for a moment. "You know I went to the mall because a man had some questions for me."

Sam leaned forward, tension crawling up his neck. "And?"

She told him about a strange encounter with a man who hadn't fit any definition of a customer. No, Sam didn't like anything she told him.

"I don't want you there alone again," he said flatly.

"He was really creepy," Erin admitted. "But if he attacked Jeremy and is the one who broke into my house a couple of times, why would he get in my face like that? It doesn't make *sense* that he'd let me see him! What could he possibly have hoped to learn from asking me the questions he did?"

"I don't know. Maybe that vase he asked about came from one of his boxes, or he thought it might have? Or something else?"

"But if he wasn't sure about them—"

"Could he have believed he might be able to intimidate you into letting him in your house to look around?"

"Would any woman in her right mind agree to that?" Erin sounded more spirited now. "Anyway, if that's what he wanted, he'd have gotten further by being nice and interested in what I did and how I picked out what to display in the mall."

All true, but unlike some serial rapists and murderers, he might be antisocial and lack any semblance of charm. He also might be oblivious to how he presented to other people.

"Only…" Erin's tone shifted. "Did I say he grabbed me?"

"He *what*?" Sam shot to his feet. "Did he hurt you?"

"I…may have bruises. He just grabbed my arm, but—" There was a pause. "Ugh." She must have pushed up a sleeve. "I do have bruises."

"Are you with Knapstad right now?" he asked.

"Yes. Well, I'm in the kitchen, and he's in the living room, but I'm sure he can hear me."

"Toby?"

"He's…still at Mrs. Hall's."

"Okay. We'll pick him up later."

"You can tell the bruises are from fingers digging into my arm."

Sam thought a few pungent words but didn't say them. "How did you break his hold?"

"I didn't. I got lucky, because we both heard Marsha coming down the aisle with a couple to look at a booth past mine. He let go, said he'd be back and rushed away."

"Son of a—" Sam stopped himself. "He threatened you. I mean it. You're not going there alone or just with Toby again."

"You can't trail me twenty-four hours a day."

"Watch me."

"Usually the mall is busier than it was today."

Sam dug his fingers into his hair and yanked. "Tell me you didn't go out to your truck alone."

"Of course I didn't!" She sounded annoyed, understandably, considering he was questioning her common sense. "I found a man I know to walk me out. Josh is an ex-marine, and he looks like it."

"All right." Sam forced himself to take an emotional step back. "I'm heading out in a few minutes. I should be there within half an hour."

"Don't hurry if you have something else to do. Patrick *is* here."

"I'll let you know if I get delayed." Sam ended the call.

He wished Erin were a little less gutsy, less certain she could handle anything. Because now he'd seen some crime scene photos that depicted apparently strong, successful women who'd faced a monster and lost.

SHE'D SWEAR SAM had aged a decade in one day. Unless it had been happening so gradually, she hadn't noticed until he reached a tipping point.

He sat at the kitchen table with her and the young deputy, talking about two break-ins he'd just learned about. "One is in Gold Bar. It doesn't sound like it could have anything to do with our problem. The responding deputy is thinking teenagers after the usual, stuff that's easy to sell or pawn."

Patrick nodded, appearing unsurprised.

"The other one was at the home of an antique dealer. Owns one of the stores on First Street in Snohomish." He named it, and Erin nodded.

"I've never met her, but that's a great store."

"She had some stock at home. A neighbor saw a rental truck backed up to her garage and didn't think anything of it since she moved things in and out on a regular basis. In this case, it wasn't her. She admits her security is limited. Thinks the garage door could have been forced. She does buy occasionally from auctions at storage units, but she says it's been awhile." His mouth tightened. "I called Conyers. He didn't recognize her name."

"But somebody might have told this guy that she was a dealer, so he took a look," Patrick suggested.

"That's what I'm thinking." Sam made an odd, rough sound. "I also wonder if we should warn anyone in the area who deals in vintage or antiques. Do you know how many there are?"

Erin understood his dismay. Snohomish was famous for its antique stores coupled with cafés and bakeries. Highway 2 was heavily traveled because of the ski area at the pass and because it continued into eastern Washington. Every small town along the way, including Startup, Gold Bar and Skykomish, had antique stores. And that didn't include the proprietors that clustered together in malls, like the one where she had her booth. They were talking about a staggering number of people. And what could they do to protect themselves anyway?

"But there are a couple of names Jeremy gave you that haven't had break-ins yet," she protested. "Wouldn't they make more sense?"

"Yeah. I think I need to call Ms. Cavender and—who's the other guy?"

"Walt Smith." Erin heard how stifled she sounded. The memory was all too vivid, hearing Jeremy choking out names in the hope he'd survive.

"Right. That's it." Sam rubbed his eyes. "I'll call them both this evening."

She thought he might be done, but instead he said, "Normally I wouldn't share this much detail with you, Erin, but you've already guessed at how bad your discovery was." He went on to talk about what he'd learned today, glancing rarely at the young deputy, mostly watching her. Did he fear he was terrifying her?

Well, he was, but she needed to know what she'd accidentally stumbled into. Who had been less than ten feet away from her and Toby as he battered Jeremy and then trashed and set fire to the office. Who had now broken into her house twice.

So yes, she shuddered but insisted he continue when he broke off.

Finally she asked, "Do you think these are all the women he's attacked?"

"No." Expression grim, Sam said, "I'm guessing he's worn gloves some of the time. Rape survivors don't all report the assaults. There could be women found dumped in a ditch, like the one was, with nothing to tie the body to him. Especially if he also goes for women who live on the fringe of society—prostitutes, teenage runaways—and women who are loners enough that nobody notices when they disappear. He could have left plenty more victims in his wake. That—" his gaze never wavered "—is one reason we need to find the rest of his stash."

"Are we sure—?" Patrick started to ask, but Sam cut him off.

"He doesn't know we found the one box, but what are the odds that was the only one? Did I mention that his fingerprints showed up a few places where there were break-ins but no apparent victim? Or in one case, a woman went missing and has never been located?" Voice as hard and as gritty as granite, Sam said, "We want to nail this guy for *every* woman he terrorized."

Patrick's head bobbed, as Erin was sure hers was, too.

Sam gave himself a shake. "Patrick, why don't you call it a day? We'll see you first thing in the morning. I can make calls from here this evening. I'll be staying nights until we catch this—" He swallowed whatever language he'd started to use.

"I can keep going if you need me," Patrick offered.

Erin managed a smile for him. "My eyes have started crossing, and it must be worse for you when you're not as familiar with what you're looking at. We made real progress today."

They had worked through everything in the living and dining rooms. Tomorrow, they'd start on the garage, the mere thought of which made her want to groan. If only they knew how long ago she'd won the bid on the contents of the one unit! Unfortunately, she'd started spilling over into the living room and the dining room as much as four months ago. Chagrined, she tried to remember. Could it have been longer?

She stayed sitting where she was, hands folded on the tabletop, while Sam walked Patrick out. Because he wanted to share information out of her hearing? Or was he going to collect something from his truck? She had zero interest in moving or thinking about what she could make for dinner or even about fetching Toby.

Her gaze strayed to the clock on the stove. It wasn't even quite four o'clock, nowhere near as late as she'd thought.

Sam walked back into the kitchen without her even having noticed the sound of the front door closing. Erin slowly lifted her head, to find his gaze locked onto her face. His brown eyes weren't warm, they were tumultuous. He chose the chair kitty-corner from hers, then held out his hand. After a moment, she laid her smaller hand in his.

Neither moved until he swore, half stood and pulled her to her feet.

Far from resisting, Erin all but threw herself into his arms, plastering herself against that tall, muscular body. This was what she'd needed as she sat there like a stone, trying to make sense of the violence and threats in a life that had been *peaceful*. Now...oh, she felt too much.

"I needed this," Sam growled against the top of her head. "Just let me hold you."

That wasn't all he wanted. His erection pressed against her belly, firing the nerve ends from her toes to her fingers. It was as if having him would solve everything.

She lifted her head so she could look into his eyes. "Will you...will you kiss me?"

"GOD, YES!"

Stress and fear drove him, part of the brew that made this courageous woman more desirable than anyone he'd ever met. If there weren't so much more mixed in, he'd have tried to make himself back off. But the truth was, he'd wanted her from that first interview.

His mouth closed over hers, the kiss moving past gentle and exploratory to urgent, even desperate, with warp speed. He needed her, and he needed this.

Sam discovered he'd already yanked off her shirt, leaving her hair wildly disheveled—or maybe he'd done that with his hands—and he was fighting with her bra clasp even though they still stood beside the kitchen table.

She'd asked him to kiss her, not strip her and lay her back on the table so he could bury himself in her.

"Erin," he said hoarsely.

She blinked. "Sam?"

"I want you. If you're not ready to go there, we need to bring this to a stop."

More blinks. Her cheeks were rosy, her lips plump, her usually clear gray-green eyes dark.

The wait for her to absorb what he'd said was tortuous.

"I'm ready."

It took him a second, no more. Then he groaned, captured her mouth again and picked her up to stumble blindly down the hall to her bedroom.

There, he got a grip on his hunger. She hadn't gotten close to a man since her scumbag ex had dumped her along with his smart, loving boy. Patience was needed here.

And so he laid her on the bed, kissing, touching, exploring, even as he finished peeling off her clothes. He talked, although he had no idea what he was saying. She was exquisite, long-legged, athletic yet curvy. He kissed and licked and sucked her beautiful, generous breasts with taut nipples.

He paused now and again when she tugged at his clothes. Unlacing his boots was a chore he could have lived without. At last she could explore him, too, the way she so obviously wanted to.

Stroking her wet passage, he moved between her thighs. The first pressure felt better than anything he could remember. It also wrenched him back to awareness.

"Erin." Voice guttural, he was thankful that he could still form words. "Are you on birth control?"

"No! Oh, we can't stop!"

He rested his forehead against hers and took a couple of deep breaths. "I have something. Just…give me a minute."

Sam hadn't thought they'd get here, but impulse had

grabbed him after he filled up with gas a couple of days ago. He'd stuck two of the condoms in his wallet. Which was…in the pocket of his pants, wherever they were… His head turned. Tossed too far away.

But he lifted himself, made it across the room and secured the condoms. He tore one open and donned it one-handed before he reached the bed.

Erin, he found, had pushed herself up and was surveying his naked body with clear pleasure. He grinned, enjoying her blush, before sprawling half beside her, half on top of her, and kissing her until she spread her legs and her hips began moving. Finally, he pushed inside her, bearing his weight on his forearm while gripping her hip to position her.

In mere minutes, they found a rhythm as if they'd done this a thousand times. She made incoherent sounds, dug her fingers into his back and finally cried his name in seeming astonishment.

Only then did he let himself go.

Chapter Fourteen

Erin couldn't understand why she didn't feel more awkward in the aftermath of the most astonishing lovemaking she'd ever experienced. Except really, she didn't have *time*. The deadline for picking up Toby at Mrs. Hall's loomed too close. She had to hustle to get dressed, splash cold water on her face in hopes of countering the glow-in-the-dark pink accented by what might be friction burns from Sam's stubble. Hair combed...check.

Sam insisted on driving her. "Your place should be okay," he said, as if she'd argued. "Plenty of people coming and going."

He was right; she lifted her hand to greet Darren who appeared to be coming home from work.

Appearing preoccupied, Sam didn't say a word until they were almost to the babysitter's, although she saw his gaze flicking to the side mirror and back to the windshield.

"Let's eat out," he said suddenly.

"What?"

"We need the time-out," he surprised her by saying.

From the constant stress? Or did he want to put off any private talk? But she only nodded. If she'd had dinner planned, she couldn't remember what she'd had in mind.

Toby was delighted to see Sam and was chatty enough

to cover any tension between his mother and the detective. Assuming there was any, she thought in chagrin; for all she knew, Sam thought they'd had a good time that he hoped they might repeat someday if the opportunity arose.

She, on the other hand, lacked any semblance of sophistication. She'd slept with only two other men before, her high school boyfriend and Shawn. And truthfully, her own emotions were muddled. She knew that Sam had had mixed feelings about her from the beginning, if only because of Toby.

Despite all that, she enjoyed dinner at the pizza parlor, especially watching Sam continue to charm her son in a relaxed way that betrayed none of his initial discomfort.

She shouldn't have been surprised to feel her muscles tightening the minute she pulled into her driveway. Lights showed through the front window. Had she left those on? She wished she'd approached from the other direction so she could have seen the side door and window into the garage.

Sam gave her a swift look even as he leaned back to unbuckle Toby's seat belt. Then he murmured, "Why don't you let me have your keys?"

"Sure." She handed them over with relief.

By the time she helped Toby hop like a rabbit out of the truck and followed, Sam had disappeared inside. He was just coming back in from the garage when she lifted Toby to her hip and stepped inside.

He gave a slight shake of the head along with a smile, and she puffed out a breath she hadn't known she was holding.

Toby struggled to be let down. "Didn't you hear me, Mommy? Huh?"

"I'm sorry!" Her laugh seemed to fool him, at least. She smacked a kiss on the top of his head before setting him down on his feet. And what did he do but run to Sam, renewing her newest anxiety: was he getting too attached to a man who hadn't promised anything but to protect them in the short term?

She played a few games with Toby, who was disappointed because Sam excused himself to return phone calls. Then she supervised bath time and read a couple of stories to her clean, contented little boy as he snuggled beneath his covers and tried to hold out against the sleepiness that finally overcame him.

When she returned to the kitchen, Sam sat at the table. He was in the act of stretching his arms over his head until she'd swear she heard some popping sounds. Groaning, he lowered his arms before rolling his head one way, then the other. Erin had already known she wasn't the only one feeling tension, but now, with him not having noticed her in the hallway, she saw lines on his forehead she'd swear hadn't been there before.

"Is something wrong?" she asked tentatively.

He made an effort to smooth his expression that wasn't entirely successful. "I just spoke to Larissa Cavender and Deputy Warren. Her place was broken into. She and her husband had driven to the waterfront in Everett for an early dinner. She'd taken some boxes of the nicer things she had into the house and stowed them in a closet in a guest bedroom. Good thing, because the garage was trashed. This guy hasn't developed any patience."

"That's awful!" Erin dropped into her usual chair at the table. "She's a nice lady, and she works hard at bringing in at least a part-time income from eBay sales."

"That was my impression, too." Those furrows carved on Sam's face deepened again. "I'm mostly glad her husband was around when this happened. Probably the guy wouldn't have waited for her to get home, but..."

Erin shuddered. Sam reached over the table to clasp her

hand. She let herself hold on, wondering if he had any idea how grateful she was to have him here.

He sighed. "Is Toby asleep?"

Erin nodded. "I think I'll get started in the garage. I... feel like we're running out of time."

Eyes sharp, Sam didn't even try to dispel her uneasiness. "I want to tell you to take the rest of the evening off but—" He grimaced, then tried to turn it into a grin. "Lead on, Ms. Reed. You're the tour guide."

The awful face she made at him relaxed his smile into something more like the real thing.

He nodded his approval when she propped open the door leading into the garage. She set up a couple of folding card tables and chairs and, with a mental shrug, chose a tower of stacked plastic tote bags of varying vintage and colors for them to start with.

Sam only had to ask her opinion once, when he found a snarl of jewelry, scarves, high heels and what appeared to be a hopelessly snagged wedding veil.

She dug deeper with him hovering over her and came up with two shawls, a tattered feather boa and two cheap tiaras. No fingers, tongues or anything else unpleasant.

"Dress-up collection to pull out when kids need to be entertained or are determined to put on a show," she said.

"Seriously?"

She laughed at his expression. "Really. They're invaluable. In this case, I think that's all thrift store at best."

He put the lid back on and carried it to the designated thrift store pile.

She found a rock and mineral collection, which included some nice hunks of amethyst and other crystals as well as fossils she'd be able to sell. As heavy as it was, Erin had Sam drag it to a spot near the door. Valuing every specimen would be time-consuming, but worth it. Once she had time…

"I'll bet Toby would like some of those," Sam commented as he carried another tub to his card table.

"Of course he would," she mumbled. Now she'd feel guilty if she didn't choose some of the nicest pieces to go on a shelf in Toby's room.

At 9:30 p.m., she called a halt. She'd just finished digging through the contents of a tub and decided she needed better light to see whether some of the fabrics were salvageable when she realized it was her bedtime.

Sam looked surprised, then grinned crookedly. "Forgot about your alarm."

She wrinkled her nose. "I never dare to unless I want to sleepwalk through the next day."

Sam readily put back into place the lid he'd just peeled off, stood and turned his head, clearly evaluating the monumental task that lay ahead. He muttered something under his breath she didn't catch and didn't ask him to repeat.

"When I work out here, Toby likes to play hide-and-seek. He finds me right away, but *he* invariably finds new places to hide. Every time we move a few boxes or I pull furniture out and shift other things, voila! It's all new and different."

Amusement curved his mouth. "That might be fun."

A few minutes later, they turned out the lights and locked the garage door. *Moment of truth*, she thought.

"Um… I don't know what you want to do about sleeping, but, well, if you'd like to share my bed, that's okay."

"Was that an invitation?"

This time, she managed a simple, "Yes."

"Is Toby in his own room?"

"Yes, and he sleeps like a log. Besides, at his age he won't think a thing of it if he finds you in bed with me."

"Thank God." She hadn't known how still Sam had been,

until he crossed the kitchen and gathered her into his arms with a speed that left her dazzled.

SAM AWAKENED FROM an astonishing dream when the woman in his dream—no, in bed with him—eased away. He reached for her, but she evaded his hands.

"I hear Toby," she murmured.

Toby. Oh, man. Now Sam *really* didn't want to wake up.

"You can sleep a little longer if you want…"

He rubbed a hand over his face and opened his eyes. "Only if you'll come back to bed."

"Uh-huh. Sure." She laughed as she backed away.

A minute later, she left the room with a pile of clothes in hand, and he heard her and Toby talking briefly, then the sound of the shower. Yeah, he could use one of those. A neat pile of his clean clothes she'd deposited on her dresser meant he didn't have to squeeze in a trip home to restock his wardrobe. He momentarily felt a pang of guilt for the horses, but he'd called a neighbor boy yesterday who had his own horse and had cared for Sam's before.

After breakfast, he started work again in the garage while Erin got Toby settled with a coloring project at the kitchen table. She hadn't appeared yet when his phone rang with a call from an unfamiliar number.

He answered, identifying himself, and a woman said, "My name is Marsha Van Beek. I own the antique and collectibles mall where Erin Reid has a space. She gave me your number in case of a problem."

"What happened?"

The answer to his question was predictable: a break-in and burglary had occurred sometime during the night. Ms. Reed's space was one that had suffered some of the most attention and damage.

He assured her he'd tell Erin.

Yes, Ms. Van Beek had installed a burglar alarm, but wires had been cut to disable it. It was an old one, and she'd been thinking about replacing it. No, she hadn't called 9-1-1 yet. He asked her to do so and promised to be there within twenty minutes.

He pocketed his phone just as Erin appeared in the doorway to the garage.

"Toby will be happy for half an hour or so." She stopped. "Something's wrong." Then she shook her head. "More wrong."

When he gave her the latest news, she listened in silence. Finally, she said, "Do you think it was that guy who was so weird?"

"I do, but Ms. Van Beek says she should have some camera footage."

"I'd forgotten she had cameras. Thank goodness! But what about the security system?"

"Bypassed. Sounds like it was an antique. Pun intended."

"I need to go with you. Only—"

Sam shook his head. "You won't want Toby to see the damage. And remember, Patrick should be here shortly."

She waffled briefly over whether she should take her son to daycare, then said, "Yesterday was a long day for him. Maybe I can drop him off for a couple hours later today, just to see what needs to be done at the booth and how much I should plan to bring to fill gaps."

He stepped toward and held out his arms. "C'mere."

The way she melted into him, she needed the contact as much as he did. When at last she straightened away from him, he said, "I'll call when I know more. Don't open the door without being sure it's Patrick."

She promised. Sam stuck his head in the kitchen and admired Toby's artwork, kissed Erin lightly and let himself out.

When he parked in front of the antique mall, a marked sheriff's deputy car was already there. He rapped on the glass door, and a woman with improbably blue hair let him in.

"Detective McKeige?"

"Yes. You're Ms. Van Beek?"

"Marsha, please. There's a deputy here—"

"I saw. Show me what part of the business got hit." What he could see of the store near the entrance appeared fine; expansive windows and glass doors had offered some protection, since anyone inside—presumably using a flashlight—would have been too visible to any late passing traffic.

It was no surprise that Erin's double-space was at the center of the burglary and vandalism. He winced at the sight and spoke briefly to the deputy.

A dozen other spaces had also been hit. Some had been left alone; apparently the burglar hadn't been interested in antique tools, used vinyl records and books or textiles that seemed to include quilts, crocheted something—tablecloths? bedspreads?—and a basket filled to the brim with neatly pressed handkerchiefs. Did people still use those?

Focus.

Studying the carnage, he decided the burglar also hadn't been interested in furniture. Because it would be hard to resell? Or because he'd been alone, and hauling bigger pieces would have been beyond him?

This quarter of the mall was closest to the back entrance. The wires had been cut on a primitive security system on the back door.

He and Deputy Garvin joined to study the obvious gaps in merchandise—and the spiteful damage that had been the result of temper or done just for fun. China dishes were smashed, furniture thrown to the floor and in many cases broken, and shelving units pushed over. There were no marks of an ax. This looked, in fact, a lot like what he'd seen in the Snohomish antique dealer's garage and several other break-ins. That didn't mean the creep after Erin wasn't responsible, but Sam's gut said not now that he was at the scene.

The camera footage was lousy quality. He suspected those cameras were as old as the security system. Grainy or not, he was able to watch a man coming and going, carrying as much as he could to the propped-open doors in back. The camera out there had caught an SUV, parked at a slant so that the license plate couldn't be seen.

The guy had used his head. He knew he was on film and didn't care, because he showed his finger to the cameras a couple of times. He wore a black hooded sweatshirt over jeans and work boots. His face was covered.

Sam ran the tape forward and back, leaning in close. He'd swear that was a bandanna versus the ski mask worn by the man who attacked Jeremy Conyers at the storage facility. Sam made note of how high up the cameras were installed and guessed the burglar to be medium height, nowhere near as tall as Sam himself was.

"I want Erin to watch this footage," he told the mall owner. "I imagine she told you about the odd duck who approached her one of the last times she was here."

"Yes, she did. But with his face covered, he'll be hard to recognize." Marsha shook her head. "But of course I'll make sure she watches this."

Erin was going to be mad as hell, Sam thought, and out a lot of money. He discussed insurance coverage with Marsha Van Beek and wondered if Erin carried individual coverage on the merchandise she displayed here. He hoped so.

The deputy agreed to call for a fingerprint tech. Marsha would keep the closed sign up for today at least and start calling the other individuals whose spaces had been affected. Sam went out to his truck to call Erin.

Once she confirmed that Patrick had arrived, Sam described what he'd seen as well as he could. She asked about a few individual items, but he had to keep saying, "I don't know. It's a mess." He admitted not seeing a glass-fronted, locked case. In fact, broken glass had littered the floor in her space, and he felt sure the pricier pieces she'd locked up were gone.

He wasn't surprised to learn that she did maintain a careful inventory of what she took to the mall and what had sold. She also noted when she removed something herself because it wasn't selling.

"I think I have to take Toby to Mrs. Hall's after lunch whether he likes it or not. We all need to clean up our spaces and restock so that Marsha can reopen without having to answer a million questions. Which means I won't be able to keep searching here." Erin paused to consider her next words. "Would it be out of line if I get Patrick to help me load my truck?"

Sam laughed. "No. We'll call it his lunch hour."

He made the snap decision to join her, help her clean up and haul in new stock. He worked a lot more than forty hours a week, and he was doing his job in part when he was with Erin.

Sleeping with her... Well, that wasn't any of his lieutenant's business. And he wasn't prepared to analyze how involved he'd become with Erin and her cute kid.

Chapter Fifteen

Erin knew what she'd see—Sam had sent her a couple of photos on his phone—but when she arrived at the mall, she was shocked nonetheless. Shouldn't she be inured by this time, given everything that had already happened?

Standing behind her, Sam wrapped his hands around her upper arms and gently squeezed. Somehow, that was all she needed.

"What a creep," she said.

"That's one way to put it."

She squared her shoulders. "Let me see the other spaces he hit."

Two of the tenants had beaten her here and were beginning to clean up. They hadn't lost as much as she had, but only because she had a double space.

From her position on her knees as she picked through a pile of shattered glass and porcelain, Linda Bradford glanced up. "This stinks!"

"It does, but we're not alone," Erin said. "I know a couple of eBay sellers who have had break-ins at home. Oh, and an antique dealer, too."

Linda, a usually good-natured, middle-aged woman, grimaced. "Misery loves company, huh?" She smiled wryly. "Yell if you need a hand."

Erin thanked her and returned to her own space. She'd brought a broom and dustpan plus some empty cardboard boxes and black plastic bags.

Sam asked her to watch the surveillance video before she started work. The murky black-and-white images surprised her, although she blew out an angry breath the first time the burglar flipped her off. She sat in silence as it ran, then Sam restarted it so she could watch again.

Finally, she shook her head. "I don't think it's that weird guy. This looks more like...not a teenager, but close."

"I had the same impression. Something about the way he moves."

"But how is he going to sell the stuff he took?"

"Online?"

Erin mulled over his suggestion. "There's a thought. Maybe I should start searching for a few of the more distinctive pieces of jewelry I lost. Oh, and that occupied Japan vase!"

"That's a good idea. He may not be dumb enough to list them right away, but you never know."

"If this isn't the same guy who broke into my place, then it's just chance he blew through my space here."

"I'm afraid so." Sam gave her a side-arm hug. "What can I do to help?"

"Oh..." Resisting the temptation to just lean on him, she looked around. "Let's rescue anything that isn't broken first, then sweep up. Marsha says we can put everything in the dumpster out back. She'll order a second one if we need it."

There wasn't an awful lot that proved to be salvageable. One bookcase with cabinet doors on the bottom had escaped damage despite being toppled over. Erin was mad about the glass-fronted case. She could have replaced the glass, but the wood had split down one side, too. Sam hauled it out back.

It was depressing how quickly they *did* clean up and to

realize how much she'd lost. Marsha carried insurance that would cover some of the loss, once the tenants brought her lists of what had been stolen or broken and the value.

In the end, Erin looked around, made a mental list of what she should bring to start over again and gathered her cleaning supplies to go home for a first load.

SAM GAINED NEW respect for how hard she worked after assisting Erin that afternoon. Loading furniture into the back of her truck and his pickup, then unloading it and carrying it in at the other end was backbreaking word. Erin carried her half of the weight of each piece despite her fine-boned build. She had more muscle than showed.

This had to be done, so he didn't say a word about the sense of urgency riding him. He didn't remember ever having an investigation so tangled by what appeared to be unrelated crimes that just happened to *look* similar. Not only that, they were all occurring in a relatively rural, even peaceful part of the county.

If Erin hadn't found the box with the tongue and other less gruesome trophies, he might be speculating about whether the two sets of crimes were in fact related. As it was…he felt an itch every time he thought about the piles and piles of boxes and tubs filling Erin's two-car garage. There was more to be found, and this guy would be back soon.

He picked up burgers and fries for them all to eat for dinner, then got sucked into playing first a board game, then hide-and-seek out in the garage. Erin had been right—she was easy to find, but Toby, not so much. The kid could squirm into tiny spaces.

Every time, Sam couldn't help wondering if this tub or that one held more of a serial killer's goodies.

Given his dark thoughts, he almost decided to settle for cuddling Erin in bed that night, but seeing her slender, feminine body as she undressed changed his mind. Holding her after tender and then explosive lovemaking, he heard himself say, "It keeps getting better."

Her head bobbed where she rested it on his shoulder.

He didn't say, *I'm scared for you.* Or worse, *What if that scumbag got his hands on Toby, knowing you'd do anything to save your son?*

Sam hadn't ever gotten involved with a witness, victim or suspect in any investigation, and he didn't like the dread that hovered like a heavy raincloud whenever he wasn't with Erin *and* Toby. He was falling for both mother and child.

Strangely, the last thing he thought as he relaxed into sleep was, *I'm happy.*

Having so much at stake would only ratchet up his anxiety the next time he had to do his job and leave her to do hers.

Which happened a lot sooner than he expected.

AN ALARM OF some kind wrenched Sam out of a deep sleep. *What in...?* It took him longer than usual to surface enough to understand he was hearing his phone ringing.

While he groped for it, Erin mumbled as she struggled to untangle herself from the covers beside him.

His eyes found the digital numbers that read 4:17 a.m. The number calling him looked familiar but wasn't identified.

He cleared his throat and answered. "McKeige."

"Detective." The male voice was pitched barely above being a whisper. "This is Jeremy. Conyers. You know."

"What's going on?"

"I bedded down tonight at my uncle's house. I've been working on it, you know."

Sam knew.

"I'm hearing sounds in the garage. What should I do?"

"Stay where you are. Hide, if whoever is in the garage tries to enter the house. Is that door locked?"

"I...don't remember. It's just a push button."

"Okay. I'm on my way, and I'm calling for a deputy to back me up. We'll approach without sirens or lights but blast them when we pull into your driveway. Do you understand?"

"Yeah." The voice was even shakier. "I think he must know I'm here."

If Conyers had parked in the driveway himself, he was right. The intruder was either stupid, reckless...or enjoyed knowing the terror he caused when he broke into an occupied home.

Sam was reaching for his pants before he even ended the call.

Erin sat up, clutching the bedclothes to her. "Who was that?"

"Conyers. He's at his uncle's. Somebody is in the garage. I've got to go."

Sounding shaken, she said, "Be careful."

Thank God he had a Kevlar vest in his vehicle.

Conyer's uncle's place was less than half a mile from Erin's house. Idling a block away, Sam waited for backup. Unfortunately, the deputy radioed to let him know he'd been called to the scene of a shooting.

"Deputy Barker is a half hour out," the deputy told him, stress in his voice.

"Okay." This was the price they paid, policing a largely rural part of the state studded with small towns that in most cases contracted with the county for their law enforcement. "You take care."

"You, too."

Wishing he had full-body armor, Sam knew he had to go in. If a neighbor had called in the report of an intruder and Sam didn't know Jeremy Conyers was cowering in the house, he could have waited for backup. As it was, he didn't think twice. He accelerated toward the house mid-block, hitting lights and siren at the last second.

Then he slammed to a stop, blocking the driveway, and dove out to hunker behind the engine block, gun in his hands.

For an instant, nothing happened. Then a light appeared in a window a couple of houses away. Others came on. He gritted his teeth. Didn't people use their heads? Curiosity could kill someone compelled to step out on a porch—

A light above what was probably the neighbor's patio let him see the side door into Conyers's garage swing open. A dark shape appeared.

Sam yelled, "This is the police. Put down your weapon and lie on the ground with your arms outstretched!"

A bullet pinged off the fender of his SUV even before he heard the crack of a gunshot. Without hesitation, he returned fire.

Answering fire kept him pinned down. The moment it stopped, he ran for the corner of the garage, flattening his back before he peered into the narrow space. A thud and a squeak told him the scumbag had just thrown himself over a fence. Normally he'd have assumed someone fleeing would jump into that next-door neighbor's yard...but not when it had outdoor lighting.

Instead of going for the obvious, Sam sprinted through an open gate into Conyers's backyard. He was betting his quarry had gone over the fence at the back of the yard, but he was too far behind to catch him that way.

Seconds later, he threw himself behind the wheel of his county SUV, turned off the siren and lights and left off his headlights. He drove to the closest cross street, irritated to see that several neighbors had come out onto porches or front lawns to rubberneck.

The moment Sam eased around the corner, he switched on his headlights but caught no movement. He accelerated toward the next street, turned that corner and saw a flash of red brake lights as a big dark vehicle made a turn.

Now he hit his flashers and siren and accelerated in pursuit. He swore out loud. If only there'd been two of them here, they could have had this guy.

By the time he reached that corner, the vehicle, still driving without lights, had gained close to a block on him. It turned again. Sam followed but was losing ground. He was too aware that a dog might bolt out in front of him or a neighbor try to wave him down. There were reasons high-speed pursuits weren't a good idea, and in a packed neighborhood like this, any speed more than thirty miles an hour qualified.

Ten minutes later, he'd lost the guy.

He went on the radio to issue a BOLO, for what good that would do with only a couple of deputies working this part of the county and both possibly tied up with the shooting.

Jaw clenched, he turned off the flashers and siren and drove back to Conyers's house. When he rang, Jeremy came to the door, eyes wild, wearing jeans and a baggy Seattle Seahawks sweatshirt that might have been his uncle's.

"What happened?" He peered past Sam. "Did you get him?"

"Unfortunately not. He went over the back fence and was parked on that block. I caught a glimpse of the vehicle, but he was really booking, no headlights so he was hard to see, and I had to be more cautious." His jaw ached from frustration. "I'd like to get a look in the garage."

"Come in. I did what you said and stayed in the bedroom."

"That was smart," Sam assured him.

The interior of this standard-issue ranch-style house was

similar to Erin's, but more dated. Jeremy was going to have some work to do before he put this place on the market or moved in, if that was his intention.

The first glimpse into the garage startled Sam. Old metal file cabinets lined three sides and, as time went on, had been blocked by mountains of white banker's boxes that must hold files as well. A surprising number sat neatly in front of the garage door.

Closer to the interior door, heaps of paperwork had been tossed from boxes that were flung away. A few of the metal file cabinets lay on their sides, their contents adding to the heaps.

What riveted Sam was the red plastic two-gallon gas can sitting in the middle of the garage. No matches, but the would-be arsonist probably had those in his pocket.

"Son of a—" Jeremy muttered. "He was going to burn the place down."

"If he couldn't find what he was looking for. I'm half surprised he didn't—" Sam cut himself off. No point in scaring Jeremy more than he already had been.

But Jeremy understood. "If you'd had your siren on as you approached, he'd have had time to start a fire."

"That's not what I expected," Sam said grimly, "but you're right." He rubbed a hand over his scratchy jaw. "I assume you haven't found anything?"

"Nothing remotely current. I don't understand why Uncle Charles kept paperwork from decades ago. I mean, even when someone who was up-to-date on payments moves out, you might want to keep the records for a couple years in case there's an issue, but after that?"

"It probably just got away from him."

"Yeah." Jeremy's fear succumbed to depression. "But I can't throw anything away without looking at it first."

"What's the most recent date you've seen?"

He gave an unhappy laugh. "2009. That was in boxes at the front over where I started."

"Then I doubt you'll find anything relevant to the attack at your office. If you need to keep working on it, I suggest you do it in daylight with the garage door open and you staying aware. Otherwise, if you're not in any hurry to clear out the garage and house, you can lock up and stay away for now." Sam paused. "If you can afford it, I'd recommend you put a security system into place, or my bet is you'll have a mysterious house fire."

Jeremy groaned. "Yeah. Real estate prices are high enough these days, I sure don't want to lose the house. I haven't checked to find out what my uncle had it insured for, either."

"You'd better do that right away," Sam advised. "I'm going to put the gas can in the back of my SUV and get it checked for fingerprints."

"I sure don't want to leave it sitting here!"

Sam put on gloves, lifted the red can from the bottom to preserve any potential prints on the handle and carried it out the side door to his SUV.

Jeremy decided to lock up and drive home to shower and have breakfast before he opened the office at the storage facility.

"I take it you quit whatever job you had before your uncle died?" Sam asked.

"I moved back here to help out when Uncle Charles's health went downhill. He was my only family, since my parents are gone, and he and Aunt Marie didn't have kids. I haven't decided whether to sell the storage business and this house or stay. Either way, there's a lot of work ahead of me."

"I can see that." Two neighbors were advancing down the sidewalk toward them. Sam raised his voice. "Please go home. Mr. Conyers had a break-in, but the intruder is long gone."

Jeremy ignored them. "I'll lock up."

"I'll wait until you're ready to go." Fortunately, the curiosity seekers had reluctantly turned around and were shuffling in bathrobes and slippers back toward their own homes.

Jeremy was back in barely a couple of minutes. He'd left a light on inside the house, which Sam understood even if it wouldn't deter a man who'd broken into the garage with the full knowledge that someone was asleep in the house. That kind of boldness wasn't common, but they already knew this guy was fully prepared to commit violence directed at anyone who got in his way.

Sam suspected he might actively *want* to hurt or kill the homeowners who thwarted his need to find his lost treasures. The thought was enough to stir the hairs on the back of his neck. He needed to get back to Erin's.

SINCE THERE WAS no way she could go back to sleep, Erin got up, put on her fleece robe and checked on Toby before she put water on to boil. Sam wouldn't have left without locking behind himself, but she checked both the front door and the one into the garage. As expected, they were secure.

She decided on English breakfast tea instead of the usual herbal; Sam would undoubtedly be gone at least an hour, and Toby would bound out of bed, cheerful and energetic, any time after six. For now, she just sat, something she rarely did.

Relaxing was impossible, though, so she started making a mental list of what else she could put in her space at the mall with the least effort. Before she knew it, she'd drifted into worrying about Sam and what he'd found at Jeremy's uncle's house. It helped to know he'd called for backup, but that was no guarantee he wouldn't get shot or plunge into a fiery inferno to rescue Jeremy or... Oh, she could come up with plenty of possibilities.

Please keep him safe.

Her thoughts didn't wander far, because it had become instinctive to listen for any sound that didn't belong. Twice she heard cars passing out front. Neither even hesitated in front of her house. She kept an eye on her phone, which she'd set right in front of her on the table.

If there were any tubs she or Patrick or Sam hadn't gone through already here in the house, she'd have gone to work, if only to occupy her attention. But there was no way she was going into the garage by herself, leaving Toby alone in the house. She shivered at the idea of opening the door to the garage, knowing how easily someone could hide out there. Finally, she started scrolling through online news, reading a few articles that she'd probably forget the minute Sam called or came home.

Except this wasn't his home.

She had the unsettling feeling she'd just driven over a speed bump. She'd let herself feel too much for a man she'd known all along was here because his job demanded he both keep her safe and find anything in her house that would help him nail the black-masked killer who'd left Jeremy to die in that rage-fueled fire. The same man who'd searched her garage and tried to open the door into the house when she and Toby were alone here.

Not inviting Sam into her bed would have been smart, she thought, feeling cold despite the heat coming through the vents and her thick fuzzy robe. But it was too late to close that door, and she didn't want to, anyway. She told herself it was okay to let herself enjoy the connection between him and Toby, savor his touch and his smile and the passion in bed that was so new to her. As long as she gave herself a bitter-tasting dose of reality often enough that she didn't succumb entirely to fantasy.

She glanced at the stove. He'd been gone for more than an hour now. Didn't he know she'd be worried? If he'd just text...

At the sound of the key in the lock, Erin shot to her feet. That had to be him. Still, she hovered in the kitchen in case it *wasn't* him. She'd run to Toby's room and—

"Erin?" Sam said quietly, his eyes meeting hers before he closed and locked the door again.

She rushed to him, glad when his arms closed around her. The chillier air outside had come in with him. She hugged him and mumbled, "I was scared."

"Nothing to be scared about."

But something about his tone had her tilting her head back to see his face.

"You didn't catch him."

"No," he said shortly. His arms tightened. "My backup got diverted to another incident. I scared the guy out, we exchanged a few potshots, and he ran. He rocketed out of the neighborhood at speeds I couldn't match without risking an accident."

Her brain had stopped on the word *potshots*. "Wait. He *shot* at you?"

"Yeah. I have a couple of dents in my vehicle, and I think a bullet punched a hole in a window." His voice had lowered to a growl. "I'll have to report discharging my own firearm and go back in daylight to see if there are any traces of blood that would suggest I so much as winged him."

"So he's been carrying a gun." That hadn't occurred to her, although it should have.

Sam grunted. "That, or he picked one up recently."

"You could have been hurt." She wanted to feel numb but couldn't.

"Not likely. I have on a vest—"

That was why his already solid chest felt thicker.

"And most people aren't good shots. This guy is consumed by impulse and temper. I seriously doubt he's put in any time at a range."

"But all he had to do was point his gun in the right direction."

"At close range, that works. We were separated by twenty-five feet or more."

She'd believed Sam was invincible. Now she had to come to terms with the knowledge that she was in love with a man whose risk of being killed on the job had to be a lot higher than normal.

But surely violent crime wasn't common in eastern Snohomish County, she tried to persuade herself.

Someone had shot at him tonight.

She clenched her teeth to keep them from chattering and hugged him harder.

Chapter Sixteen

Sam wanted to hustle Erin back into her bedroom, strip off the robe and make love to her. The moment he set eyes on her, that was all he could think about. Unfortunately, a desperate glance at the clock told him it wasn't happening. Toby would be bouncing into the kitchen anytime.

Sam hoped she hadn't noticed his erection before she backed off, chattering about pouring him a cup of coffee and how she ought to get dressed.

He grimaced. She'd noticed, all right, or her cheeks wouldn't be pink. This was a drawback to getting involved with a woman who had a child.

How far he'd come, he thought in bemusement; two weeks ago, he wouldn't have considered doing any such thing, and not because a kid was an inconvenience. When was the last time he'd thought of Michael when he was with Toby? He couldn't call up the last instance. The boys were no more alike than Erin was like Ashley, thank God.

He hoped Erin was thinking the same way. It wasn't a good time to raise the subject, though. In fact, his priority had to be keeping mother and son safe.

No, he hadn't forgotten what mattered most.

Toby appeared soon enough, followed by the arrival of

the young deputy who had dived into what he might have considered a tedious job with seemingly genuine dedication.

Knapstad glanced at Sam. "Looks like your vehicle took some damage," he said in a low voice.

Sam grunted. "Unfortunately, that means I'll have to leave you two—three—on your own again while I get it looked at and fill out some reports." He briefly summed up the early-morning events and heard in return about the shooting, which had been a drive-by that left two victims hospitalized. Since witnesses saw the incident and one of them had had the rare presence of mind to memorize the license plate in question, two stoned guys in their early twenties were now behind bars.

Once they were up-to-date on news, Sam told Erin about his intentions, and she promised to stick close to home this morning. "I do have to take more stuff to the mall and mail some packages I have ready to go for eBay, but I can do that later in the afternoon."

He didn't want her near the mall but understood she needed to keep making a living. "If I'm back in time, I'll help you load and maybe go with you."

She opened her mouth, probably to argue that she usually did it on her own, but then closed it and clamped her lips together. She had to share his nervousness about the mall even though she agreed that the break-in and damage probably were separate from the obsession and violence that accompanied the killer who was sure to be back to her house.

"Keep your gun close," he ordered Knapstad before leaving.

He hadn't made it out to the highway before his phone rang. Deputy Knapstad.

Sam answered at once, identifying himself.

"I found something." The young deputy's voice shook.

"It's—uh, a hand. Mostly down to bone, but there's still polish on fingernails. It's, um, wearing a ring, too."

"I'm on my way back," Sam said, even as he gave a short burst of his siren, signaled and swung across the road to make a U-turn without slowing any more than he had to.

His heartbeat picked up. What else might be in the same container? How many more victims could they identify? Would they find something they could use to nail the killer?

Erin made sure Toby was occupied in his bedroom before she and Patrick hung over Sam as he donned latex gloves and picked through the contents of the tub that weren't materially different than those in the earlier one.

This was a killer who liked to collect the obviously feminine items worn by his victims. Oh, and their body parts, too.

In fact, a cardboard shoebox at the bottom revealed what had to be an ear complete with dangly sterling silver earring. The earring was tarnished, and the interior of the box splattered with rusty stains that turned her stomach. All their stomachs, maybe, since Patrick flinched and looked away, and Sam gently fit the lid back on the box.

She was surprised when he rotated the box to look at the end, until her gaze followed his. The box had held men's athletic shoes, size eleven and a half. The brand, model of shoe and store name were all emblazoned on the box.

Sam mumbled a few words he usually held back around her, then said, "Good work, both of you. I'll take this and start at the medical examiner's office."

She turned her head to look at the mountains of containers they had yet to search without any enthusiasm at all. Usually going through unseen items she'd won in storage unit auctions was like treasure hunting. Aside from the amazing contents of the one storage unit, mostly what she found was mundane—at best worth twenty or thirty dollars. But there was always the thread of excitement because a box might have stoneware hand-painted with animals that looked primitive but was highly collectible or Navajo squash-blossom jewelry or a nineteenth-century weathervane. People didn't always know what they had. She remembered fondly the campaign buttons for Harry Truman she'd sold for a significant amount, for example.

A queasy feeling in her stomach, she knew that excitement might always be tempered by the possibility that *this* plastic tub could contain something gruesome.

She walked Sam into the house and to the door just because she wanted to, but his grim expression and the knotted muscles in his jaw told her he felt much as she did, even if he also hoped for leads from the latest find.

She and Patrick worked steadily after Sam left, and she took the occasional break to entertain Toby. Sandwiches and cookies filled their stomachs at lunch. Her ear stayed tuned for her phone to ring, but Sam wasn't likely to learn anything until he had fingerprint matches and, eventually, a DNA match.

He did call midafternoon to let her know that he'd had to take the county-owned SUV in for body work, after which he'd catch a ride back to sheriff's headquarters and check out a replacement vehicle.

Sounding weary, he said, "I do have a name to go with the ear. When I saw it, something niggled at me. When I searched for female murder victims that had been dismembered in any way, I noted a woman who'd had an ear cut off. The earring matches what she was wearing."

"Who was she?" Erin felt compelled to know.

"Her name was Renee Legare. Twenty-four-year-old, newly-minted real estate agent in Coeur d'Alene, Idaho."

"I've been there. It's beautiful." Picturing the magnificent lake and expensive homes surrounding it now felt obscene.

"Yeah. We keep expanding his territory."

Sam didn't have to identify who *he* was.

"I don't think I'll make it back until close to five," he added. "Can you hold off the antique mall run until morning?"

"You can't follow me around everywhere I go. Don't you already have more threads you need to follow?"

"I'm waiting for a call back from the detective who investigated Ms. Legare's death," he admitted.

"I'll be careful. It should be a busy day at the mall. Usually I can get someone else to help me bring everything in."

"And walk you out," he said sternly.

"And walk me out." She didn't really have her fingers crossed behind her back, but she was envisioning them as if she did.

Patrick did his best to help her load, but given his walking cast, she felt guilty letting him lift anything. During the short drive, it was a struggle to smile and respond to Toby's chatter. The sickening knowledge of the latest finds hung over her, along with the fact that Sam's afternoon was partly busy with replacing his police vehicle because the one he'd been using was now *pocked by bullets*. Some must have come a lot closer to striking him than he'd admitted.

Surely this will be over soon, she thought. Or was it half prayer? Once forensic evidence produced a name, they'd also have photos, if only the dismal ones from driver's licenses, and then they could *look* for him. He was staying somewhere, buying groceries. People would have seen him. That he was faceless was possibly the creepiest part of all this.

After parking in back of the antique mall, she got lucky when two men who had a space exited together. They spotted her and walked over to offer to help her get everything in. She thanked them, grateful to have some extra time to arrange and rearrange her stock to be as appealing as possible.

When Toby got bored, she produced a handheld electronic game from her purse. He pounced on it, since she limited his time with it. The beeps seemed pitched to be annoying, if only to an adult ear.

She'd been right that this would be a busy day, which meant she chatted with browsers and took the name and number for a guy looking for a treadmill that she had in her garage. She kept meaning to list it on Craigslist, since it didn't quite fit here, and it wasn't the kind of thing you popped in the mail. Think how much space selling it would open up!

She took Marsha her list of stolen and damaged items and estimated value and was glad to hear that sales had risen steadily this year. One tenant who had suffered the most loss from the break-in had decided to give up her space. Marsha had a list of people who wanted in, but she offered it to Erin first.

The idea was tempting, but Erin didn't want to overextend herself. She worried about shortchanging Toby as it was. Since Jeremy Conyers hadn't come up with any information on the previous owners of the valuable contents of the storage unit, she ought to start work on photographing, describing and valuing everything.

And, of course, the days she'd spent searching everything she had piled up at home in search of a serial killer's precious collection had put her way behind.

Patrick called to let her know he hadn't found anything else and was heading home. He assured her he'd locked up.

It was almost five, and Toby, who hadn't had a nap, was

drooping. That set her to trying to think of a dinner she could produce quickly. She also wished that Sam would be there waiting for them.

THE FINGERPRINTS FROM this latest tub opened up half a dozen new avenues for Sam to explore. The prints on the plastic lid especially matched those on the other one, not surprisingly. Ditto those on some of the items inside, including the shoebox and a couple of items that best held prints. What might be as many as four victims were identified. Sam sat down to make calls.

Time got away from him once he connected with the first investigator, then received return calls from two others. They reacted much as the ones he'd spoken to after the first discoveries. Anger and determination infused their voices, but again the names of men they'd looked closely at didn't match those at other crimes scenes.

The third detective said, "This wasn't my case, you understand. The original investigator retired with the understanding I would try not to let this go cold. You know, we all have ones that get to us. I'm wondering if he had some thoughts that didn't make it into the record. If I can get in touch with him, do you mind if he calls you?"

"No, I'd be glad to mine him for whatever he knows." Every investigator considered possibilities they weren't able to pursue for one reason or another or crossed off because they seemed unlikely or reached a dead end.

At five o'clock, Sam left the desk he'd borrowed, took a last look to be sure he wasn't forgetting anything…and of course that was when his phone rang.

Rolling his shoulders to release some of the tension, he answered, "Detective McKeige."

A gruff voice said, "My name is Frank Billman. I'm the retired detective I hear you want to talk to."

"I do, indeed." Sam sat back down. He could talk on the drive back to Erin's house, but then his attention would be split between the conversation and traffic. This might not take long.

"This about Julia Keele?"

"Yes." Sam explained about Erin and the storage business, leading up to what had to be trophies collected by a killer—including from Ms. Keele. "I gather no body parts were taken from her—"

Billman made a sound of horror.

Sam hurried on, "But we found her fingerprint on a pendant in the latest box. As you know, I spoke to Detective Shanks, and he thought you might recall something that you hadn't included in your notes."

"Don't know for sure what I did note," the older man said slowly. "No, I thought I'd ruled out one fellow, so I might not have mentioned him."

"Him?"

"Name was... Let me think. Sawyer, I remember that because it's not a common first name. Sawyer Wilkins!" Billman sounded triumphant. "That's it. The guy made me real uneasy, but I didn't have enough cause to fingerprint him or even bring him in for an interview. I regretted for a while that I hadn't collected a fingerprint surreptitiously, but I knew the DA wouldn't act on it."

"There's still a lot of reluctance," Sam agreed.

"I guess Ms. Keele had taken a couple to look at a house—she was a real estate agent—and this fellow hovered out front. When she and the couple came back out, he asked if she could show *him* the house. She suggested he make an appointment with her for another time, since she was committed to showing the couple several more places. He took her card, that's what she told a friend, but hoped he didn't call."

"So he made her uneasy, too."

"Sounds like it. He'd given her his name, and I tracked him down, but Ms. Keele hadn't disappeared until a couple of days after that encounter. He said he went ahead and had another agent show him some houses instead of waiting."

"You confirmed he did."

"Yep. Like I say, I didn't have enough excuse to look hard at him."

"But you wanted an excuse."

"I did. Just a gut feeling."

Sam got those, too. "Nobody of that name came up in any of the investigations into the attacks and/or murders of other victims, but that doesn't mean anything. No one name came up twice with all the investigations put together."

"The friend who told me about this guy said Ms. Keele would have been willing to show him houses if he'd had a wife, but he seemed intense, and she didn't want to be alone with him."

Plenty of murderers came across as normal to their coworkers or neighbors. It was less common for people to say he gave them the creeps. But Sam couldn't help thinking about the man who'd waylaid Erin at the antique mall, his behavior distinctly *off* even before he'd grabbed her.

"I'll track down this Sawyer Wilkins," Sam said. "Thank you for calling. If you think of anything else…"

"I'll get on the horn," the retired detective assured him. "If something comes of this—"

"I'll let you know. I promise."

Sam hesitated after ending the call. He was already going to be later than he'd told Erin to expect him, but man, he wanted to do a search. It shouldn't take long, so he opened his laptop again and typed in the name. It popped up, and he prowled through multiple databases, scrutinizing the couple of images he found. Typical DMV, they weren't good, but he was willing to bet they were good enough for Erin to recognize if Wilkins had been the man at the mall. He printed them.

And then he straightened, as if electrified by what he saw on the screen. A Sawyer Wilkins had been a person of interest in a rape case in Spokane, Washington, not far from the Idaho border. Almost had to be the same guy, except... Sam frowned. If they'd taken him seriously, his fingerprints should be in the system. So maybe this was another dead end.

He couldn't leave it at that, though. Swearing, he dialed the number for the detective squad in Spokane. Probably too late in the day to get anyone, but even the distant possibility he'd found his perpetrator didn't let him put this call off until morning.

He was placed on hold, and while he waited, he checked with Deputy Knapstad. The rookie said he had let Erin know he was leaving her house locked up behind him. "She sounded fine, but she was running later than she expected."

Good. With luck, Erin wouldn't be too far ahead of him at her house.

A voice abruptly replaced elevator music. "This is Detective Throndsen. What can I do for you?"

Sam had the spiel down pat now.

Throndsen grunted. "Not my investigation, but let me take a look."

Sam waited, not so patiently, until the other man came back on.

"The detective who had that case thought he'd found his man. The victim didn't see a face—I guess he wore a mask of some kind—but we have fingerprints." He went quiet again for a couple of minutes. "The detective died suddenly from an aneurysm. His more active cases eventually got picked up by someone else, but this Wilkins had evidently done a bunk, so that one has gone cold."

"Were the fingerprints entered?"

Throndsen didn't sound happy—what investigator would have?—when he admitted, "It doesn't look like it. Can I follow up on this?"

"I'd appreciate it. I hope they haven't disappeared at the lab."

"Me, too." He took the info from Sam and ended the call as abruptly as he started it.

Sam was sometimes wrong when he felt this tingle between his shoulder blades, but not often.

ERIN COULDN'T REMEMBER the last name of the man who sold old tools in the booth near her—he didn't sell at a volume that required him to update his inventory anywhere near as often as she did—but nobody else seemed to be in the vicinity. In fact, the whole place was looking deserted, even though it stayed open until six.

She glanced at her phone to realize it was a lot later than she'd thought it was. Maybe she'd secretly hoped Sam would show up to walk her out to her car himself.

When she told James Whatever-his-name-was that she'd been having some trouble and asked if he'd walk her and Toby out, he agreed readily. "I heard about the mess here a couple of days ago. I don't blame you for being nervous."

She opened her mouth to explain that her problems went beyond the break-in, then closed it. Really, this wouldn't take him five minutes, so she just smiled and thanked him. Toby was tired enough that she swung him up to her hip, and James of the rusty tools fell in behind her as they headed to the back of the building. Did she dare let Toby nap this late in the day?

As she reached for the door handle, she heard a strange

sound behind her, a gasp, and then a thud. Erin had started to turn in alarm when a man's hands wrenched Toby from her hold.

"What are you—"

Oh God, oh God. He wore a black-knit face covering and had clamped a hand over Toby's mouth. Her little boy was waking up, beginning to struggle, but outmuscled.

"If you do anything to draw attention, you'll never see your kid again," the man who had control of her child snarled. "Do you hear me?"

The scream stayed trapped in her throat, and she bobbed her head.

"Give me your purse."

She'd already stuck her hand in to grab her phone but pulled it out and did as he'd asked.

He jerked his head to the door that she'd let close again. "Out."

What could she do but obey, even as she prayed there'd be other people here in back?

Except, now that she knew this killer was undoubtedly armed, would that be a good thing?

Chapter Seventeen

Once she had the heavy door open, he planted a hand on her back and shoved so hard she staggered. As she righted herself, she scanned the gravel parking lot, but only four vehicles were left. The one closest to the door was Marsha's.

"Straight ahead."

Out of the corner of her eye, she saw her own pickup truck, but of course he wouldn't want to take that. He had to be able to make a getaway after—

She couldn't let herself go there.

The big black SUV was right on the other side of her pickup, where it wouldn't catch the eye of anyone passing on the street.

It beeped as they approached. He opened the back door.

"Kid!" he snapped. "Lie down on the floor. You hear me? Your mom will be up with me. I'll hurt her if you try anything."

Toby whimpered. The last glimpse Erin had of his face showed it wet with tears as he was tossed forward, catching himself to curl up onto the floorboards. A hard hand on Erin's arm wrenched her forward.

"Quit whining! You help me find my stuff, and you might survive."

She knew the voice. This was the creepy man who'd

asked such weird questions that day. Which meant he was also a serial killer—and sick enough to cut off a victim's tongue, another one's ear and yet another woman's *hand*. And who knew what else they'd find in other tubs, if they had the chance to look?

If she'd thought she could throw herself out fast enough to also open the back door and grab Toby, she'd have done it. Instead, she sat. Her purse... He must have tossed it on the back seat, out of her reach. After a moment, she clicked the seat belt across herself.

"Mommy!" Toby cried.

"Shh," she said. She might have lied to reassure him, but their captor had climbed in behind the wheel and fired up the engine. He'd also pulled a handgun from somewhere and let it lie on his lap where she couldn't miss seeing it.

She'd never wanted a gun of her own, never fired one in her life, but right this minute, she knew she could and would shoot someone this close. Except, if she'd carried a gun, it would have been in her purse, as out of reach as her phone.

Gravel crunched under the tires as this brute drove forward and put on a signal before making the turn onto the road. In one of the holes in the mask, she could see his teeth, his lips drawn back from them.

I'm shaking, she realized and made herself stare straight ahead. *Sam will come.* Did this man know a cop had the key to her house and had been spending nights?

The drive was both too quick and felt as if it took forever.

Erin was careful not to turn her head as they approached her house, but her eyes darted down the side street and the block beyond her driveway. Sam still parked a distance away, so it wouldn't be obvious he was here.

Maybe it would be better if he *wasn't*. What if he came to greet them and met a bullet instead? He wouldn't be wearing a Kevlar vest when he was anticipating dinner instead of a confrontation. If he arrived later instead, he'd instantly know they shouldn't be in the garage. He might even hear a voice that shouldn't be here.

Her captor didn't park in the driveway, either, but he did pull to the curb less than half a block away. The better to load his treasures once she led him to them, Erin thought semi-hysterically. If only she had the slightest idea of the location of more of his boxes.

He turned off the engine, said, "Stay," and jumped out, coming around too quickly. He opened the back door first and lifted Toby out, then came to her door. Of course, he'd grabbed her purse, too. "Walk beside me." His voice was guttural. "If you see anyone you know, wave."

Her teeth chattered at a volume she hoped he didn't hear. She didn't know whether to be glad none of her near neighbors were out and about or not.

She tried to project comfort to Toby, but it was hard when his mouth was round with a silent wail and snot and tears both smeared his face.

The man stopped on the welcome mat. "Keys?"

"In my pocket." She'd gotten them out earlier so she didn't have to set down Toby to hunt for them.

He held out his hand for them, quickly picked out the house key and pushed open the door. He tossed the keys inside and pulled his gun, listening for a minute before easing inside, ready to fire.

Silence met them. No Sam.

Erin bit her lip until she tasted blood as she followed him inside.

He closed and locked the door, looked around and shook his head. "No wonder you can't find anything."

Oh, she wanted to protest the contempt in his voice but clamped her mouth shut. Should she tell him they had, in fact, found two tubs with his obscene collectibles in them?

No. As volatile as he'd seemed at her booth the first time, she thought he'd be so enraged she and Toby wouldn't survive until Sam got home.

"You must know how to find what I want." His eyes glittered at her through the holes in the mask.

"No. How can I? I don't even know if I *have* whatever it is you're looking for!"

His hand slid around Toby's throat.

She closed her eyes. "I...assume it's not furniture."

"No. Plastic tubs, like these." He nodded toward the piles that still filled too much of the living room.

"If you can tell me what's in them...or what color they are?"

He shrugged. "They're older ones. Blue or green, maybe? Not like these." He kicked a particularly sturdy, newer style in black accented by bright yellow.

"Um...how many did you have?"

"Four."

"I never would have bid on the contents of a storage unit that had so little in it."

"I had a key to—" the hesitation was almost infinitesimal, but she heard it "—a relative's unit." His anger had ratcheted. "Didn't know he was dead for long enough, that damned place sold everything!"

"Okay." She tried to keep her tone soothing. His hand had loosened from around Toby's throat. "I've looked through every tub inside the house. That pile—" she pointed "—is going to a thrift store. Those—" she signaled with her head "—have things I need to list online or will put in my space at the antique mall."

His eyes narrowed at her. "You've been looking for my things."

"Um, well, kind of, because the police told me you'd gone to the houses of some of the other people that bid on stuff in storage units. And....I assume that was you in my garage that night." She dampened her lips. "I could tell you if I'd found anything that might be yours if I knew what was in your boxes."

What she could see of his grin was so savage, she recoiled at the sight.

"You'd know if you'd found it."

Please, Sam.

"Oh, okay." She hated the tremor in her voice. "Well, then if I have anything of yours, it has to be in the garage."

His eyes narrowed to slits as he stared at her. "You'd better not be lying to me."

"I'm not." That came out steadier.

He dropped her purse and kicked it between piles, then strode to the door to the garage. His hand had left Toby's throat, but he gripped him hard, and weirdly, as if he was a strangely shaped parcel, not a small human being. He wouldn't feel a qualm about murdering a three-year-old.

If there was some way to remove Toby from the equation. *Please, God, let Toby stay quiet.*

She'd swear she heard the faint ring of her phone as the heavy steel door swung closed behind them.

"Where are they?" he demanded.

"I don't know. And that's the truth," she said hastily, when she saw his shoulders start to bunch in rage. "I...don't keep any kind of order. It doesn't matter to me which things came from what unit or garage sale or when I bought it." She bit her lip. "Although, it may help if you could tell me how long ago the unit your things were in might have been sold."

His lips curled back from his teeth. "Stolen from me, you mean."

"I... I can see why you'd see it that way."

"It might have been six or eight months ago."

Oh, boy. No wonder those tubs were scattered. It was a miracle they'd found any of them.

"Let's…just look for plastic tubs that *could* be yours. Oh, they wouldn't be over there. I just went through those." And found one of his, which suggested the remaining two might not be deeply buried.

When he glanced down at Toby, her heart constricted. The intruder had dropped him atop a couple of tubs. Toby's eyes met hers, and she shook her head silently.

"What about over here?" she said. After a moment of hesitation, he complied more than she anticipated, following her what might have been ten feet.

This might be as good as it got. She drew in a deep breath and yelled, "Hide, Toby! Go hide and seek!"

Her son uncurled.

The man started to lunge back toward him. Erin threw herself at him and hung from his arm. He tripped, they tangled…and Toby rocketed from his perch and vanished into the maze.

WHY WASN'T SHE ANSWERING?

Don't get paranoid, Sam told himself. She might be in the bathroom helping Toby wash his hands or had just left her phone in her purse and didn't hear the ring.

But he didn't like it. Two minutes later, he tried again. The third time she didn't answer, he hit his lights and sirens and sped down Highway 2 toward Monroe and beyond.

If she picked up the phone, she'd have to see the string of notifications and would call him. Would she really be so careless with her phone, given what was going on?

He didn't believe it.

Calculating to keep himself from panic, he tried to decide whether to enter by the front door or the new side door into the garage, to which he'd kept a key when he installed it. If she was there—if *he* was there with her—they'd be in the garage.

If this monster killed Toby or Erin, Sam didn't know if he had a damn thing left to live for.

He shook the thought off. He wouldn't believe he'd be too late. He couldn't function if he let himself grieve prematurely. Normally his goal would be to arrest a serial killer so he could be convicted in multiple jurisdictions and give closure to his many victims' families. Vivid images of killing that piece of scum himself raced through his head instead.

He could circle the house first. Crash through a window if he saw them.

No, it had to be the garage.

"YOU BITCH!"

The man slugged her so hard, her head snapped back. Darkness crept over her vision. *Toby.* She couldn't black out. She couldn't. But she did crash to the floor, and the back of her head bounced off the concrete.

Erin had to curl onto her side and breathe through the hammer blows of pain and the nausea that followed.

"Get up! If you don't get that kid back here, I'll shoot him when I do find him. You hear me?"

She tried to get to her hands and knees. "You don't need him. I know I can't fight back."

He kicked her hard enough to throw her back several feet. He'd connected with her hip, adding a stabbing pain. "Get up!"

She tried again. He grabbed her upper arm this time and yanked her to her feet.

"Find my boxes."

"Been trying," she mumbled.

"Do better."

"You should recognize them." She'd wanted to snap but it came out as another mumble.

The rage in his eyes would have terrified her if she hadn't somehow moved past that. *Endure.* Sam would come. She had to be alive for Sam. Even if he didn't love her, she knew what it would do to him if, after the crushing loss he'd suffered, he found her and Toby dead.

She swayed but took a step toward the piles of boxes she'd tried to direct this monster toward before. This time, he looked. When he didn't like the first tubs at the top, he threw them to one side so he could peel off the top of whatever one appeared familiar. Lids and contents flew. The crash of breaking glass and porcelain meant nothing right now.

His fingers bit hard into her arm as he dragged her on.

She wished she'd better seen which way Toby had gone. *Hide-and-seek.*

AFTER NOTING ERIN'S empty driveway, Sam locked onto the large black SUV immediately. He entered the license plate number in notes on his phone. No time to run it. He parked just out of sight around the corner, leaped out and closed the door with care so the sound wouldn't carry.

Vest... He didn't want to take time for that, either, but made himself. It might give him the chance to win a gunfight rather than go down immediately.

He'd already decided on the front door. He donned the Kevlar vest with awkward shrugs and dealt with the fastenings one-handed as he jogged the short distance, crossed the lawn and ascended the two porch steps. This was one occasion he'd have been glad of darkness, but daylight in the Northwest in early September still left long days.

Keys out. It only took him a fumbling second to find the right one... Insert it as carefully as if he were doing brain surgery... Turn it until he felt the click more than heard it... Gently turn the knob. The door opened. He hesitated, pushed it wide and entered with his weapon held in front of him.

The house was quiet. *Nobody here*, the quiet said. He eased in, placing his feet with care. Clear the kitchen and bedrooms first? His gut said no. Unless he was deluded, they had to be in the garage.

He laid his hand on the doorknob and turned it. It wasn't locked, and he didn't believe the young deputy would have left the house *without* locking even this interior door.

Sam eased it, too, open to the smallest of cracks. And that was when he heard an ugly string of obscenities followed by a thud and the sound of something shattering and knew he'd been right.

THE MASKED MAN was losing it, as wild as he'd been when she first set eyes on him in the storage facility office. Some distant part of Erin's brain wondered how he ever stalked his victims when he entirely lacked patience.

They worked their way along a serpentine gap between the next stacks. This wasn't one of Toby's favorite hiding places. By chance, half or more of the plastic tubs here were high quality, newer ones, which enraged the serial killer.

"But there are older ones here—"

"You're wasting my time!" He grabbed her and flung her into a pile of the boxes, which teetered. One at the top dropped down the other side.

Now her shoulder joined the chorus of pain. "We have to look here," she said again.

With no place to throw boxes in his way, he was driven to restacking them, the set of his face and the dark glitter in his eyes awakening fear that had almost vanished in numbness.

They reached the end. Erin hurried ahead back toward

the gorgeous furniture. *Get him past*, she told herself. If he threw a fit here—

He didn't even look at the furniture or the musical instruments in cases or the spectacular lamp that she had wanted to be a genuine Tiffany but probably wasn't.

They had reached the slightly more open space close to the garage door when the metal door into the house swung wide.

"Down on the floor!" Sam yelled.

The man crouched behind the barricade of boxes, locked his fingers around her ankle and pulled his gun from what had to be his waistband.

She couldn't move until he suddenly released her, stood and fired. *Pop, pop, pop.*

Frantic that Sam had been hit, she saw that he'd retreated behind the metal door. But now he emerged, coolly firing his own weapon.

She seized the chance to scuttle a few feet away and crouched. More bullets flew. That metal door would never look the same again.

Erin hunkered low, only feet from that gorgeous lamp. She remembered how heavy it was: solid bronze and the thick glass of an earlier era.

"Back off, or I'll kill her!"

She knew he wouldn't hesitate to do that, but he hadn't turned the gun her way, not yet.

When Sam emerged again, a sliver of him mostly shielded by the door, she lunged for the lamp, lifted it and swung as if she was still a star batter on her high school softball team. *He* was turning, that hateful man who'd hurt her, as she moved. He got off at least one shot. She was so focused on her swing, she didn't think of her peril.

The shade of the lamp smashed into his head, as if it were a jack-o-'lantern that could be pulverized. The sound was awful despite the thin knit mask. Seeing him collapse as if his strings had been cut, she dropped the lamp, turned her back and fell to her knees. Her stomach revolted, and she started to dry heave.

At first she couldn't make out what Sam was yelling, but finally heard, "Erin! Is he down?"

She lifted one hand and waved.

The next moment, Sam was on his knees beside her. He took in the sight of the bloody mess a few feet away, then used his foot to nudge the handgun that had fallen to the concrete floor and edged it well away from the fallen man. In case he came back from the dead and groped for it, she thought blearily. Sam lifted the mask enough to seek a pulse. She could tell he didn't find one.

Then he came back to her, wrapped his arm around her and, rough and tender at the same time, said, "Come on, sweetheart. Let's step away. Can you stand?"

Her head bobbed.

"Where's Toby?"

"Hide-and-seek," she whispered.

"Okay." He supported her as she stood, then steered her toward the chairs around the card table.

Sinking into one, she asked, "Is he dead? Are you sure?"

"Pretty sure." He cleared his throat. "I'd be congratulating myself for getting here in time, but it appears you didn't need me."

"I did." Unable to dissemble, she felt tears pool in her eyes and start to fall as she looked up at him. "I do."

"God." His face contorted. "I was so afraid."

"Me, too."

He cupped her face, using his thumbs to wash away tears. "I don't ever want to lose you."

Now she cried in earnest.

He laughed, groaned and straightened. "Let me go rescue Toby."

At least the dead man's face and head were covered, but... "Don't let him see..."

"Wouldn't think of it." Sam walked past the shattered lamp and the body, then raised his voice. "Olly olly oxen free! Come on out, Toby."

After a too-long moment of complete silence, which had Erin swiveling on the folding metal chair, a small voice sounded. "Sam?"

"Yup."

A minute later, Sam scooped up her small son and used his own big body to prevent Toby from seeing the fallen man.

The body. Because *she'd* killed him. Her stomach lurched again.

Somehow Sam convinced Erin to take Toby inside without him. By the time she reached the kitchen, she remembered how many places she hurt. But...no blood, as far as she could see. And Toby was intact, his body solid and wiry, his grip strong, his face blotchy from tears that no longer fell. He was fine.

She wanted to cry again but refused to allow herself. That would just scare him. Instead, she plopped him down on the raised seat on his chair at the table and said, "Thank goodness Sam got here, huh?"

"*Uh*-huh!" he agreed.

She heard the door open and close, and there was Sam walking toward them, his gaze never leaving hers. He must have made a call, since his phone was in his hand, and she envisioned what was to come: a dozen cops, flashing lights, an ambulance or two and EMTs who would peer at her and insist she go to the hospital for an MRI. There'd undoubtedly be questions, since she *had* killed a man, but she couldn't imagine anyone would really have trouble with it.

What came out of her mouth was, "How do I explain this to my landlord?"

Sam laughed. Really laughed.

Epilogue

Erin hadn't expected to sleep, but she had, since she opened her eyes to sunshine around the edges of the curtains. A new nurse was at her bedside, wanting a temperature and blood pressure, neither of which had anything to do with her injuries. She also heard footsteps in the hall that sounded like a man's.

The nurse was just brushing aside the curtain when Sam walked in.

"Oh, thank goodness!" Darn it, Erin's lips were still swollen on one side, so she didn't sound quite right. "You didn't bring Toby?"

"No, although I'm sure he's gotten the Hillyards up by now," he said drily. "I thought about stopping, but I wanted to talk to you first."

Oh, heavens—what now?

She'd deluded herself yesterday to think she'd remain at home for all the hubbub. The EMT decided she was concussed and should see a doctor and probably have an MRI. In fact, the EMT was right, but the doctor didn't think the concussion was serious and believed Erin could go home this morning.

Toby had been unhappy but okay when he realized he

couldn't go with her, but he then threw a rare fit because Sam wouldn't be able to stay with him, either. It was Erin who suggested Andrea Hillyard, the kind next-door neighbor Toby liked well. After all the gunshots fired in Erin's garage, Andrea and Darren wouldn't be surprised.

Now, she said cautiously, "Is this bad?"

"No." Creases deepened on Sam's forehead. "We have a name now. Sawyer Wilkins. And yes, he's the guy who got so pushy at the antique mall that day. His fingerprints matched the ones taken at multiple crime scenes. There are a lot of families who are going to be relieved to know he can't hurt anyone else."

"Because I killed him."

"If you hadn't, I'd have had to take him down. Don't feel any regret for a monster like him."

She bit her lip—*ow!*—and nodded. "Is that it?"

A glint of humor showed in Sam's brown eyes. "I don't know what you're thinking, unless you imagine the landlord has evicted you."

She wrinkled her nose. That was about the only part of her face that didn't hurt. "He might."

"Can I sit down?" Sam had been ignoring the chair, his eye on the bed, and she scooted over to give him room. He engulfed her hand in his much warmer one. The connection felt amazing. "Maybe it's time we told your landlord the truth," Sam suggested, then went entirely still, even his expression shutting down. Was he nervous? "I'm, ah, hoping you might want to shift your operation to my place, anyway. I have some empty outbuildings. Plenty of extra bedrooms. Horses, too."

"That's…kind of jumping ahead of yourself," she managed to say, although her heart had taken a giant leap.

"Yeah." Smiling as if he couldn't help himself, Sam bent

down and pressed a warm, soft kiss on her forehead. "But just so you know, I'm ready anytime you are. Everything that has happened stinks, except I met you two."

"And we met you," she had to say.

"So you did."

She searched his face. "Toby won't bring back bad memories?"

He shook his head. "Only good ones, and that's okay. Trying to forget didn't work. Like I told you, I've quit seeing Michael in Toby, anyway. I've...come to love him, too."

"Too?"

He still looked worn today, as if he'd aged yesterday when he must have feared he'd lose her...*and* Toby. Left with a body to explain, Sam wouldn't have gotten much sleep last night, either. He certainly hadn't shaved this morning, which was fine; she liked his stubble.

"I started falling for you from the beginning," he said, some extra grit in his voice. "I worked through my doubts faster than I would have expected to. There's nothing more I want than to marry you. I'd like to adopt Toby, too."

Without warning, tears blurred her vision.

He took her in his arms and murmured, "I'm sorry! I didn't mean to upset you. If you don't feel the same..."

Erin swiped her face against his clean T-shirt and looked up. "Of course I feel the same! I'm happy!"

When he gently kissed her swollen mouth, she felt the vibration of his chuckle.

From that first day when he'd strolled toward her where she sat on the asphalt hugging Toby, a possibility had unfurled in her. She hadn't consciously thought, *I could love this man*, but the fall hadn't been far.

He was right. A lot that happened had been terrifying, but she and Toby had found Sam.

And he'd found them.

* * * * *

HORSE RANCH HIDEOUT

TARA TAYLOR QUINN

To Rachel Reames Stoddard—you are who you need to be, I am honored to have raised you and I love you more than life.

Ma.

Chapter One

"Here you go, Nicole. It's official!" The clerk smiled as she slid some paperwork through the open bottom of the glass partition through which she spoke. "These tell you how to change your birth certificate, driver's license, and social security number..."

Blinking through her tears, Charlotte Duran... *NO*... *Nicole Compton*...glanced down at the sheet on the ledge in front of her, her gaze following the woman's blunt-tipped finger over a series of web addresses.

She continued to watch that hand as it reached out further, covering hers, giving her fingers a gentle squeeze. "Good luck," the woman said.

Charlotte—Nicole—nodded, then looked up and smiled. "Thank you," she said, meeting the woman's big brown eyes briefly...for just a second...before she took her paperwork and headed for the courthouse door. Back and shoulders straight, head high, she stepped outside into the warm spring air.

It was done.

She'd taken control of her life. Reclaimed the self that had been robbed from her. She couldn't remember the first year after her birth—the year she'd been Nicole—but she'd seen all the proof. Legal documents, photos that were a one hundred percent match for facial recognition when compared to Charlotte's year-old pictures, DNA.

Seeing pictures of the mother she'd always yearned to know holding her close, the look of love on the beautiful face she couldn't remember... Nicole swallowed at the thought. Blinked back more tears.

And Savannah...her somewhat intimidating and wonderful, loving, selfless older sister...she'd kept all the photos of Nicole's first year. A lot of which had included seven-year-old Savannah.

Sniffling, she climbed into the brand-new to her blue midsize American-made SUV. She wasn't a naturalized citizen, as she'd grown up thinking. She was American born. From American parents.

She had a heritage. A place where she belonged.

And a world to protect.

The thought brought her up short. She glanced in the rear-view mirror to see the tip of the suitcase visible in the far back of her new vehicle, and it strengthened her resolve.

She'd told Savannah she was going to a dude ranch in Colorado for a couple of weeks. That after three months of intense debriefing, biweekly meetings with the best of the best in the psychology arm of her sister's firm of experts, and her own exploration into possible futures for herself, she needed some downtime where no one knew anything about her. Where she could just be and let the dust settle.

She'd done the one thing she and Savannah had promised each other they would never do to each other. She'd lied.

Sort of.

Pulling onto the Phoenix bypass that would take her to the interstate leading north, Nicole gave verbal commands to set her global positioning system to an address outside Durango, Colorado, and took a deep breath. She *was* going to a ranch in Colorado. And a dude lived there.

As much as she adored her newfound older sister—and intended to stay close to her for the rest of her life—Nicole had to find her own place in the universe, too. No more living in a protected world where she felt safe and where she'd allowed herself to depend on another person to define her.

The only way she moved forward, became a person she could respect was to create a sense of independence.

Changing her name had been a huge step. One she hadn't yet shared with anyone but the court system. Savannah would be thrilled. At least Nicole figured she would be. Hoped she would be. Though maybe hurt that Nicole hadn't let her share the process.

But she was establishing a sense of self. And that was something she had to do alone.

Well...alone except for the help of a total stranger who she hoped to God she could convince to partner with her in her attempt to pay atonement. To obliterate a creation from her past.

To save others instead of herself.

Herself.

On the freeway headed north through the mountains toward Flagstaff, Nicole pulled off at the first scenic viewing point and parked in front of a vista that stretched as far as she could see. Showing mountains and valleys that were so much larger than her billion-dollar world had been.

With the strength of the mountains within her, she grabbed the paperwork from the seat beside her, setting it on her lap. Pulling out her phone, checking to ensure that she was close enough to towers to still have full service, she typed in the first website.

Only when all the websites had been visited, all of the official work was done did she let herself look up again.

She saw grace in the massive beauty, along with the

dangers inherent within the rugged slopes. Saw hope when once upon a time she'd had little conscious need of it.

Charlotte Duran and her privileged existence had just been legally and officially wiped off the face of the earth.

But the deeds she'd done, horrible crimes her innocent work for her father had contributed to...those were still living and breathing. Some of them hiding right there in that vastness, from what she'd been told. Illegal arms didn't hang out on popular highways, on display at roadside stands, waiting to be purchased. They switched hands under covers of darkness, even in broad daylight and in plain sight.

Like the trail she'd tracked through the Arizona mountains, up to Utah and over to Colorado. A trail with which Harcus Taylor was very familiar.

Eduardo Duran, the man whom Charlotte had grown up adoring as a father, the only family she'd ever known, was extinct. But a portion of his business lived on.

The one appendage that authorities hadn't found enough evidence to stop. Or prosecute.

Nicole had thought that watching the powerful billionaire and philanthropist be stripped of his identity and exposed as the criminal fraud he was would give her closure. That seeing him forced to face charges as ex–IRS paper pusher Hugh Gussman, the man he really was, the one who'd fathered her and faked his own death before kidnapping her as a baby, fleeing the country with millions stolen from the federal government, and lying to her about who she was, would put her past to rest. She'd been wrong.

She wasn't going to rest, establish legitimacy in her own mind or feel as though she belonged in her big sister's family until she knew that the damage she'd done had been eradicated as completely as the Duran family had been.

With resolve cemented by the certainty of that last

thought, Nicole put her new vehicle in Drive, and headed back onto the freeway.

Praying that Harcus Taylor was as driven as she was.

SEATED ON A fallen log, Harc Taylor sipped coffee still hot in his travel mug and surveyed the valley below him. Then the vastness of peaks in the distance.

"You know it all, don't you, sir?" He spoke aloud to the once-wild mustang bearing his saddle and currently munching on the forage Harc had stopped at for their afternoon snack. "All the secrets these hills keep?"

Imperial lifted his head long enough to snort in Harc's direction.

Nodding, he took the response as an affirmative and hoped that the regal horse had seen all the good the natural beauty that had been his home had to offer.

And little or none of the bad that Harcus imagined as he sat there.

Hoping, too, that one day he'd look out and believe in the peace that seemed to lay before him. To know its existence, not just view the mirage.

Someday he wanted to walk into his barn of once wild horses and consider himself worthy of their acceptance.

Wanted to trust himself enough to be able to assure them that he would never again be a man who'd compromise his ethics, who'd get so caught up in eliminating the wrongdoing he witnessed that he'd bend laws to the extreme in order to succeed.

He was done with shades of gray.

And, noticing the downward angle of the sun shining on the mountains, had to be done with his afternoon ride, too. Cutting the usual daily activity off an hour earlier than usual.

"We've got a visitor coming," he told Imperial. Grabbing the horse's reins, he lifted himself expertly into the saddle and turned the horse toward the small ranch they called home.

Nicole Compton.

She hadn't said why she wanted to see him. Had just asked for an appointment, an hour of his time.

He figured he knew, though. His horse-therapy program. People who were struggling, especially those with emotional issues, didn't always like to reveal their challenges to perfect strangers on the phone.

Whether Nicole had set the meeting for a matter concerning herself or on behalf of someone else, he was eager to meet the woman. Every single step he took to get his fledgling business off the ground was a step in the right direction.

The few successes he'd experienced had helped him get his big toe out of the dark world into which he'd sunk. But he had one hell of a long way to go before his full body emerged and he could stand tall and clean. Be proud of himself again.

He saw the unfamiliar blue SUV parked in the circular dirt drive in front of the house as he rode in from the back of the property. Figured his appointment had turned up a bit early—and instead of stabling Imperial, he rode the gelding past the barns and down the drive toward the house.

The white wood-sided two-story structure was almost fifty years old and a lot more than he needed, but it had come with the ranch—one of the few that was small enough for him to be able to afford. And kept him from view as he approached.

Whether Nicole was there as a potential client or on behalf of one, there was no better way to introduce her to Crimson Ranch than through Imperial.

He saw her first. Out of her car, Nicole had her back to the house, was facing the mowed green acres of front yard, separated from the road by nearly an acre of thirty-foot-tall oak trees.

His first impression—the woman wasn't dressed for horseback riding. So, maybe representing a potential client.

In a black skirt that ended just above mid-thigh and a form-fitting short-sleeved top, she might have fit in at a barn dance. If not for the footwear. Two-inch heels on leather sandals bearing an over-abundance of bling. Her hair, dark and silky looking in the sun, hung almost to her waist, completely uncontained. And yet...perfectly sculpted, too.

All about the haircut. He'd had enough experience with human disguises to have that one down pat.

The bag slung over her shoulder—thin strap, small, black—also bore bling.

She reeked money.

Yet the SUV, while a recent model and bearing temporary tags exposing it as a new purchase, was a mid-level vehicle from a common manufacturer. Not a high-end brand.

Imperial's clip-clopping gave them away before Harc was close enough to see the woman's expression clearly as she spun around.

But it wouldn't have mattered. He was down off his horse, facing away from the woman, walking Imperial to the barn before anyone had a chance to call out a greeting.

The woman on his property was not Nicole Compton. Nor was she welcome there. As soon as he had Imperial secure, he lifted his flannel shirt enough to pull out his Glock. Checked it for ammunition, though he knew full well the chamber was loaded. And with the weapon raised, headed back outside.

No way in hell was Charlotte Duran taking another thing from him.

The woman and her father had already cost him his soul.

SHE'D HEARD THE man was a tough one. Intimidating as they came. Nicole had not been prepared, in any way, to meet her host with a gun pointed straight between her eyes.

Raising her arms above her head, she realized, too late, that she had no idea if the gunman steadily approaching *was* Harcus Taylor. And quickly called out, "I'm Nicole Compton! I have an appointment with Mr. Taylor."

She was half an hour early.

The man obviously had tight security. Something she'd lived with her entire life.

And based on what she knew about Taylor, something he'd be wise to keep for the rest of his.

But while the gun boded well for her in a future association with the CIA agent, she couldn't take her eyes off the barrel as the dangerous-looking man approached.

"What's your business?" He barked the words as a challenge. As though if he didn't approve of her response, she'd be dead in seconds.

"I have an appointment with Mr. Taylor," she said again, pulling on the bravado Eduardo Duran had trained into her from her first memory of him.

As long as she didn't have a bullet between the eyes, she could hold her own with the best of them.

The man with the gun didn't lower his weapon. Nor did he slow his advance on her. At the moment, she was just thankful that the shakiness taking over her insides hadn't been apparent in her voice. The cliché Eduardo had been fond of came to mind. *Never let them see you sweat.*

She'd been through a lot in the past few months—too

much. She had been in critical danger. But she'd never in her life had a gun pointed at her.

She'd only ever seen them pointed at others as part of her protection.

And had never witnessed an actual shooting.

The threatening man stopped a few feet in front of her. "I'm asking you one last time to state your business," he said menacingly, speaking through gritted teeth.

She had nothing but the truth. Looking the man straight in his slitted dark eyes, she repeated, "My name is Nicole Compton. I have an appointment with Mr. Taylor."

Always speak with authority. Another one of Eduardo's oft-repeated life lessons came to her aid without forethought.

When the gun lowered slightly, Nicole's chin started to drop. She quickly shut her mouth. Duran had gone from pauper to billionaire. Of course he knew how to manipulate people to make things happen.

Thankful for the rules he'd taught her, even while she hated that they were a part of her, she continued to maintain eye contact with Taylor's watchdog.

"If you'd just let Mr. Taylor know I'm here," she said politely but in a tone she'd heard Eduardo use every time he was speaking to someone in his employ.

The gun was no longer pointing at head, but it drew Nicole's gaze as it moved to point at her chest, as accents to each word the man spoke. "Show me some ID."

Four words. Four distinct points of the pistol.

His hand was big. The knuckles worn. No mistaking the strength there. At such close range, and with her unarmed, the man didn't need to pull the trigger to kill her.

He could drop the gun and just do her in with his bare hands.

Bury her out there.

And no one would ever know.

Because she hadn't let a single soul know where she was going and why. Taking a note from her wise sister's playbook, she'd chosen not to involve her far-too-generous older sister, or Savannah's expert friends, in finding her absolution. Just as Savannah had set out to find Charlotte on her own just a few months before.

Rescuing her from the nightmare she hadn't known she'd been living in.

Savannah had used a cruise as her cover. Nicole's was a dude ranch.

Which meant she had to get past security and have her hour to ingratiate herself into ranch life. Leaving one hand up, she lowered the other, palm out, to the small clutch she wore everywhere, at all times.

"Don't move!" The voice was gravelly, and Nicole's gaze shot to her aggressor, seeing the gun aimed at her chest.

"You asked for my identification." Eduardo would be proud of the even tone.

Nicole hated that she was thankful for his tutelage.

"I know who you are, Charlotte Duran. And I'm giving you one more chance to state your purpose for trespassing on my ranch before I pull this trigger."

He wasn't going to shoot her. The impression hit as the man's voice faltered over those last words.

He knew who she was. The second fact hit and rocked her more.

And the third… "You're Harcus Taylor?"

He'd said *his* ranch.

And was clearly ready to order her off from it.

Not at all an auspicious start to what might be her only chance at success.

Chapter Two

"I am Nicole Compton." The woman's gaze didn't waver as she repeated, again, the lie she'd been telling.

Harc wanted her gone—but not until he'd figured out her game. He had a life load of unanswered questions where the Durans were concerned. There would be no more. Their ingestion ended there. Then.

Which was why when she reached for the inside of her purse a second time, he didn't shoot.

He'd have gone to the right of her left arm. A bullet intended to scare, not make contact with flesh. If he shot her, he could argue that he'd been defending himself—that she was a trespasser on his private property, threatening him—but there would be no more skating the lines between right and wrong.

If a weapon appeared from that shiny black leather all bets were off.

She didn't pull a gun. She pulled out an official court document. Handed it to him.

Nicole Gussman, also known as Natalie Willoughby, had legally changed her name to Nicole Compton.

"I was born Nicole Gussman," the woman said. As though that explained everything.

Raising his eyebrows, Harc shook his head. She was going to have to do better than that.

"My father is Hugh Gussman," she said then, her face losing all expression at the words.

Again, nothing. And Harc was out of patience. "Look, Charlotte, whatever you're after—just state your business so we both get out of this alive."

He didn't attempt to hide the threat in his voice. She was beneath contempt. To have the balls to invade his space, to disrupt the tiny piece of quiet he'd found inside himself...

Her gaze met his again. The emotion there...was unexpected. As were the words coming out of her mouth. "I need your help."

He turned his back. If she pulled a gun and shot him, then she did. His instincts told him she wouldn't. And he was done. He walked back down toward the barn where he'd left Imperial tied to a post. The part-time staff who helped him out had all left for the day.

He heard her steps behind him before he heard her cry. "Please!" He kept walking.

"You're in on it with him." Her words weren't loud. Or in accusation.

They seemed to be more like dawning awareness.

Which stopped him in his tracks. Spinning around, his nose flaring, his teeth clamped tightly together, he barely had enough time to reach out and keep her from walking into him. She'd been that close.

Her eyes, widened in fright, stared up at him. Glancing at his hands on her shoulders, feeling the tension in himself, he let go abruptly. Stepped back.

And saw her spin, running toward her car, darting to the right and left, as though she feared a bullet in back at any moment.

The sight struck him to the core. The fear. The helplessness.

It told him that he was missing critical pieces. He didn't want them. He'd left that world behind him. No going back. Period.

But what if it was coming after him and she'd come to warn him? "Wait!" he called, hurrying after the fleeing woman. A feat made a little less plausible for her based on the two-inch heels she was wearing. "Nicole," he called. "I'm sorry."

Always. Forever. For so much.

Most of all, for not having what it took to nail her father to his deathbed.

She'd almost reached her car. Could lock herself in and speed away.

He had her legal identity. Could find her. The photographic memory, or whatever helped him call up every detail, had served him well during his career and was still in fine working order. Even if his choices had become skewed.

She didn't get into the car. She turned to face him.

At which point, he slowed. Shoved the gun dangling from his hand into the waistband of his jeans where it belonged. Let his shirt fall back over it.

Figured the move was his at that point. "What did you need my help with?"

Her gaze tentative, she studied him. Shook her head. Reached for her door handle.

"I was told Duran was arrested," he said, the first thing that came to mind.

She frowned. "You were told? Of course you were told. You were a huge part of making that happen. If he'd gone to trial, you'd have been a star witness."

Her tone was off. All expression gone from her face again. So…what…she blamed him for her father's fate?

Or was she still considering the possibility that he was in with a conscienceless fiend like Eduardo Duran?

Because…he could have been. He'd gone where the FBI couldn't go. Had done things no one wanted to know about.

And…her words hit hard. "He's not going to trial?" He'd never felt the blood drain from his face before. Had heard of it happening to others. Stood there, feeling his skin get clammy, even as he tensed for battle.

Her frown of confusion confused him. "You had to have been told about the plea agreement," she said.

He relaxed some at the words. And shook his head. "I don't know what you've heard." He said the obvious. And then added, "I left the CIA six months ago. Other than a brief text on a burner phone that said, 'We got him but not on arms' I've had no contact with anyone connected to the Duran case since I walked away."

Her face paled. "You walked away? From the files I read you're the only one who…" She stopped, shook her head. Looked like she'd just lost her best friend.

Like she'd pinned some kind of hope on him. Which was ridiculous; he'd told so many lies he wasn't even sure he could believe himself anymore. He was most definitely friend to no one.

Except, he hoped, his stable of horses. He'd never lied to them.

She looked up at him again. "You didn't follow the case in the news?"

"Nope. News tends to be prevailingly bad, and I specifically don't avail myself of it." Couldn't risk getting riled up and thinking he had to get out there and do something about that over which he had no control.

He couldn't save the world.

Hell, he had moments when he wasn't even sure he could save himself.

Nicole… Charlotte Duran… Compton took a tentative-looking step forward. "Would you be willing to keep our meeting as planned?" she asked him. "It's important to me."

She'd said that last like he had a heart that could be swayed into letting sympathy guide his course.

The moist, almost lost look in her gaze got to him more. People could lie with their eyes, certainly. Actors did it all the time.

He'd made a career out of it.

But the brown-eyed gaze watching him wavered even as it held his. There was a depth to it he wasn't used to seeing. In others. Or in the mirror.

And...she might know something that he should be privy to, to protect his horses. Just because he'd walked away didn't mean that Duran's players had done the same.

Because he knew damned straight that there were some left.

That *some* had driven him to the verge of being just like them. One of them. Just playing for a different team.

Holding an arm toward the sweeping front porch on the house, the one place he'd spent money to dress completely, he said, "We can have a seat up here, if you'd like."

And was a bit shocked at the relief that flooded through him when she smiled.

CHARLOTTE DURAN WOULD have been halfway to the highway. Nicole wished she was as she followed the cantankerous and clearly dangerous man up the three steps to a lovely front porch. From the braided oval rug that covered nearly twenty feet in length to the table and padded chairs on one side and matching couch and rockers set on the other to the lovely red-flower-filled planters set around the space, the area screamed against a presence like that of the man who owned it.

Standing on the top step, she took another glance around,

finding beauty in the ugly moment. "This is nice," she said, not sure what to do next.

Did she claim the seat that appeared to be most advantageous to her, as Charlotte would do, or did she wait for him to lead the way?

"I saw it in a magazine," he said, shrugging as he headed over to the table. Pulled out a chair for her.

Not the one she'd have chosen. He was putting her back to the road. But she most definitely preferred the table over the couch or rockers.

She was there on business. With a very serious matter to discuss. Not lounging around having casual conversation.

As she sat, she thought about what he'd said. "You saw the furniture in a magazine?" she asked, more to be polite, to accept the second for them to regroup that he'd offered than because she cared who'd furnished his porch.

Sitting across from her, he kept a very clear eye on the yard, the drive, the front of the property. And she felt a little better about his choice of seating arrangement. She might not be able to have her own back, but if he had his, he'd have hers.

And he was armed.

"I saw the whole thing in a magazine," he told her. "Down to the planters."

Looking around again, she frowned. "And then you, what...called the magazine to find out where to get everything?"

With a sideways nod of his head, he said, "I'm a CIA agent. I didn't need some publisher to put me in touch with a photographer who'd put me in touch with the photo-shoot designer to get what I wanted."

Right. But... "You *were* a CIA agent." She repeated what she'd been told. Watching him.

Not trusting him.

But needing him.

"*Was*," he acknowledged. Sitting back, his hands folding on his stomach, drawing attention to the flatness of that part of his physique, he asked, "What's this meeting about?"

She'd rehearsed that exact moment during the many hours' drive she'd just taken from Phoenix to southwestern Colorado. Had her speech all planned out. Memorized to every pause she'd take.

But that was before she'd found out he hadn't seen the news.

"I'd like to give you some context, if you can humor me long enough to do so," she said, calling on her years as a guest lecturer at some of the most prestigious universities and private schools in California, speaking to packed auditoriums. She could be so many different people.

Was only just discovering how many guises her father had raised her to wear.

And was feeling like she was somehow marked with big red x's floating in a circle in the air around her.

Her normal had just been obliterated off the face of the earth. Or, more accurately, had simply evaporated into the ether.

Leaving…what…behind?

"You have an hour," the man finally said, after almost a minute spent silently studying her. "Use it however you think best."

An hour and not a second longer. The message in his words came through loud and clear.

She was good with that. Had grown up with clear expectation. Knew how to live within its boundaries.

Harcus Taylor might've been one tough dude.

For all but three months of Charlotte's lifetime, Eduardo Duran had been able to best all the Taylors who'd been after him. From multiple countries.

And in the end, for all the work the best investigative and enforcement agencies in the world had done, she and Savannah had been the ones who'd bested Eduardo. The two daughters he'd fathered and then betrayed had been his downfall.

There was irony in that, if nothing else.

"Until a little over three months ago, I believed I was born Charlotte Duran, in El Salvador. I believed my mother, an American, died giving birth to me and that she had no other family. Because my mother was American and had spent the months before my birth in America, I was able to apply for and receive American citizenship and did so, at my father's behest, when I was a teenager. I'd been aching to know more about myself and longed to be in America more than anything. At least that's how I remember it. I now know that he used me to get us back to the States under the assumed names he'd managed to obtain when he faked his own death and kidnapped me just after my first birthday."

She wouldn't bore him with all the details. Wouldn't waste the hour. But if she had a hope of convincing him to help her—a much steeper climb than she'd imagined now that she knew he'd walked away from the case before Eduardo had been caught—there were some things he had to understand about her.

"As of today, Charlotte Duran's fake identity has been permanently deleted."

"You said your father's name was Hugh Gussman."

He'd been paying attention. She took that as a positive. "It is." She swallowed, her throat dry in the dusty, seventy-degree early May air. And had to press on with what he'd missed in the news. "He was a supposedly happily married man, working for the IRS. A man of above-average intelligence who, in reality, was bored stiff at his job but couldn't leave it because he had a family to support and no other training."

"He'd grown up poor?"

Nicole blinked. Shrugged. "I have no idea how he grew up. I just know he was an only child whose parents died in a car accident when he was twenty. He'd just finished his last year of college and was already dating my mother." To her way of thinking, none of that mattered. And the hour was hers.

"He found a way to hack into various accounts and siphon money. At first he'd just done so to see if he could. To expose leaks. But had obviously found the thrill of succeeding far more heady than being a husband and father to two. He had almost two million put away when he figured out that someone was onto him. He came forward, said he'd hacked into a hacker. Said he knew who was taking the money and would testify as long as he and his family were protected because he was accusing a very powerful person. He was stepping up, putting himself at extreme risk to do the right thing. From what I've been told, my mother went to her grave believing in him one hundred percent. Loving him with her last breath. The day he was due to testify, he took me from my day care, then faked his own death, leaving in a deserted dirt field a body so badly burned that it was indistinguishable except for traces of epithelial found in the heel of a tennis shoe nearby. There was evidence of a body having been lying where the shoe was found. And a hole dug in the dirt that fit the heel of the shoe. The theory was that he'd been being tortured, had been moving his foot back and forth in pain, before they threw him on the fire... When really, he was living as Eduardo Duran."

She stopped. Feeling the cold sense of helpless fear creeping up on her again. A weakening sensation she hadn't known until the night she'd gone with FBI Agent Mike

Reynolds, known to her as her bodyguard Isaac Forrester to arrest her father.

"I was never seen again," she said then.

"And your mother and sister?"

"They were put in witness protection. And my missing person's report was as well, with DNA evidence to identify me if I was ever found. I became Natalie Willoughby, as far as the US government was concerned. At the same time, my father identified me as Charlotte Duran."

Her host had been watching the area behind her back as much as he'd had eyes on her. She kind of appreciated his lack of piercing attention while she, a person who'd grown up having her body—and information—guarded by professionals, laid herself bare.

She'd come with one thing to give Taylor, hoping that it would convince him to see through the job he'd started. She had time left in her hour to get there.

And wanted to get through everything that had to be said. Once done, she wasn't going to revisit the conversation again.

Ever.

"Is it true that you're just twenty-five and have three college degrees? Or is that just part of Charlotte's fake identity?" The question didn't carry a cruel tone.

Nicole felt the slap just the same. Her whole life had been a sham. How did someone ever find a person who was real in that?

"You did your homework on me," she said. She'd known he'd been privy to a particular program she'd written.

He shrugged. Waited.

"Yes, it's true. I imagine everything you found was true. Duran managed to amass billions in those twenty-four years he robbed from me. He had the wherewithal to make certain that there were no weak links." She stopped and then, looking over at him, said, "I'm as smart as, or smarter than, he was. He knew that there could be no falsities in my life or I'd find them."

"You owned the home the two of you lived in."

"He told me that the house went in my name for my protection. So that if anything ever happened to him, my home life wouldn't be interrupted. There wouldn't be probate or any question that the home went to me. He'd said that if he got in a car accident, for instance, and it was his fault and someone else in addition to him died, his estate could be sued. As long as I had the house, I could always sell it if I had to and be secure for the rest of my life."

The man had manipulated her down to the last speck of dust. "As Charlotte, I adored my father," she admitted then. "And because he was all I had, I worried a lot about being alone. I yearned for other family. His reasoning played right into that weakness."

Harcus Taylor nodded. Believing? Agreeing? Accepting?

Seeing how she'd been manipulated?

Realizing that she might never recover from that enough to have a normal existence or any kind of committed partner relationship? How could she ever trust another enough to be able to commingle emotionally again?

Or was he thinking the entire situation was too bizarre and she'd made the whole thing up?

"It sounds to me as though he loved you." Taylor's words cut through her. Sharply.

Unendingly.

She'd made a mistake coming to the man.

Had to find another way.

Even if she died in the attempt.

Her meeting with the ex–CIA agent hadn't gone in any way that she'd planned.

It had made one thing ever more clear to her, though.

She could change her name. She could love her newfound sister. She could yearn for a real life of her own.

But she was always going to be Eduardo Duran's daughter.

The woman who'd been conceived by—and then spent her entire life loving—a man who'd been committing heinous crimes since before she was born.

And she was done talking.

Chapter Three

Harc saw the change come over Nicole Compton.

Compton. Why?

He needed more, and based on the emotionless gaze, the straight face, and the sudden stillness about the woman, he sensed that his last question had lost him her interest. Which was what he'd been seeking, wholeheartedly and nonstop, since he'd first recognized Charlotte Duran on his property.

He'd wanted her, and anyone she might have brought with her, gone.

Right up until she'd started talking about her life.

Lifting the skinny strap of her thin black purse to her shoulder, the woman stood.

He couldn't let her leave. Not until he knew more.

Most particularly, knew what part she'd seen him playing in her day.

Taking a breath, Harc said "I'm sorry" for the second time in the few minutes he'd known the woman. Because he was.

And also because she'd given him another chance the first time he'd admitted to a mistake. Then, without forethought, he continued. "I can't imagine waking up one morning to find out my entire life has been a lie," he said. She deserved to be heard. To be understood.

Even if she was up to no good or intended to use him.

Whatever she was into, whatever she'd hoped to include him in aside—what had happened to her, the way she'd been raised was just not right.

She didn't pause in her retreat. Was almost at the stairs.

He remained seated. "I'm just saying…you were a kid who loved a parent who loved you. That was real." She'd given him the details for a reason.

He had to know what that was.

And it was clear that force wasn't going to do him a damned bit of good at the moment.

The fact that it had become his immediate reaction to getting things done was one of the reasons he'd walked away from the only career he'd ever wanted.

She turned. Holding her purse strap with both hands, she said, "I was driven to find more connection like I had with him. To find my mother's side of the family. Last year, without my father's knowledge, I entered my DNA into a family-finder database. But because we were so close, and I trusted him implicitly, I felt guilty and told him what I'd done. And unknown to me, he put an immediate watch on the company's databases."

Her tone held no inflection at all. Her face was turned toward him, but she seemed to be looking through him more than at him.

A well-played ruse? One of his fortes.

This didn't feel like that. But even if she was as good at acting as he'd become, he needed to know where she was leading him.

"My older sister, Savannah, has been looking for me my whole life," she said then. "She grew up in witness protection, believing that our father had been murdered by whoever he'd been about to testify against in his job with the IRS. And believing that I'd been kidnapped. She's a lawyer now, and partner, heading up the legal department, in a nationally renowned firm of experts. She'd spent her whole life worrying about me and entered her DNA, but not her contact information, into the same site as I did, allowing her to be notified if she had a match, but not notifying the other party. She knew of the danger, of which I was unaware. Her partners were unaware she'd ever had a different identity. But now in the know, they're in full protective mode."

The way she'd delivered that last statement, as though a warning, had his attention. He took note of the fact. He'd know all there was to know about the firm before he slept that night.

"But back to where I was, when Savannah came to California to find me, her partners didn't know that she was part of the witness protection program. Like me, she'd been forced into keeping secrets for twenty-four years. But she risked her own life, risked leaving protection, risked losing the partners who are her friends and only family to travel to California to make certain that I was okay. She thought I'd been adopted by a wealthy family and just wanted a glimpse of me, to know I was happy, and then she was just going to go. She had no idea who Eduardo was—criminally or biologically." She paused then. Shook her head. Clearly remembering things she wasn't saying. She just stood there like a statue, as though she wasn't real.

A sense of urgency washed over him. He waited for it to pass. But he couldn't let go of the fact that he needed Charlotte Duran… Nicole Compton…to stay a while longer.

If what she was saying was true…

Then what?

He was done.

Out.

But he had a stable full of horses—and the people they were being trained to help—to protect. If there was any chance his past life could bring evil to his doorstep, he had to know about it. To prevent it from happening.

"You mind sitting back down?" he asked her. "I'm getting a crick in my neck." More like he didn't want her swaying on her feet. He saw the woman's strength. Admired it.

But she looked like she'd had enough.

Maybe even too much.

She didn't immediately do his bidding. Seemed to be weighing pros and cons of whatever was on her mind.

He wasn't sure if it was a good thing or very bad when she finally took her seat.

He was going to find out why she was there. How she thought he was involved. But it had to be some pretty bad news to keep her from getting the hell away from him, when clearly that was what she most wanted to do.

He didn't blame her. He spent a lot of his time wishing he could get away from the man he'd become.

Nicole raised her gaze to his, and he saw life there again. And a boatload of regret. Something he'd seen in his mirror far too many times. "Eduardo was onto her," she said. "He put hitmen on her. Fortunately, the first bullet missed. After that, she knew to protect herself."

The firm of experts. Meant the sister was better than just good at her job. "You said she's a partner in this firm…and a lawyer what does she do, exactly?"

"She travels all over the country, taking on specialized cases. She has a team of lawyers who work with her as well, on a case-by-case basis depending on specialties."

Good to know. Or not.

Lawyers weren't at the top of his list of potential people he wanted getting close to his life. He'd always worked under direct orders. Was protected against prosecution.

The thought of jail time wasn't what bothered him.

It was the much larger judgment and form of justice—the opinion of society, largely shaped by lawyers—that was the problem.

"So she got her firm involved, and they brought Eduardo down?" He needed to get to the end of the tale. Her hour wasn't up yet. He felt like his time was.

When Nicole shook her head, Harc settled back. Wholly analytical again. For the moment.

"You know a guy named Mike Reynolds." Statement, not question. Still not a connection he was free to admit to.

"Why do you say that?"

"I first knew him as Isaac Forrester. My bodyguard."

Harc was privy to the information. Hadn't been sure she was.

Now she had his full attention. Would have had it an hour ago if she'd started there.

He'd done it, then? Mike had succeeded where Harc had failed? He'd be damned if he wasn't happy for the guy. He'd respected Mike. Had trusted the FBI agent more than anyone in his own agency.

"Mike had no idea about Savannah's relationship to me and wasn't sure how she was involved with Eduardo, but after she was shot at, he had her under FBI protection. Without her knowledge. She just thought he was a bodyguard helping her."

Harc knew the drill. Had been undercover in various forms since he'd graduated college. Was under guise right then, as he sat back as though just a rancher at the end of his day, listening to story. When, in fact, she had his full focus.

Critically.

He was filing pieces in places where they might or might not fit yet, but he wouldn't know unless he tried.

Puzzle building was what he did.

"She eventually told him that I was her sister. That I'd been kidnapped. She didn't tell him about being under witness protection, though, thinking she was protecting us all from whoever our father had been about to testify against."

But Mike wouldn't have told this Savannah woman who he was.

Yep. Been there, done that.

Mike had had a job to do. He'd been there to bring down Eduardo Duran. Not to reunite long lost sisters.

"I...unfortunately...chose then to rebel for the first time in my life and rigged security so that I could sneak out in the middle of the night just to have a day or two of alone time."

He almost sat up straight. Maintained his relaxed position through instinct borne of years of life and death training.

Right when her father was on the verge of being brought down—though she'd yet to tell him how her sister showing up had helped Mike get the job done—she suddenly decided to slip away?

Too much of a coincidence.

And he'd figured out how Savannah's presence had been the missing piece that had allowed Mike to bring down the guy that multiple US agencies, and international ones as well, had been after for two decades. Savannah had told him about her father's murder and sister's kidnapping, and Mike had put it all together with the ages and timeline of Eduardo's life as they knew it.

The FBI agent had detected another "too much of a coincidence" situation.

In another life, Harc and Mike might have made good work partners.

And none of what he was hearing was leading him to understand why Charlotte Duran had sought him out.

Unless...was Mike in some kind of trouble? Was someone holding him hostage? Or worse?

No way Harcus Taylor could turn his back on that one...

His thought was interrupted as Charlotte—he just couldn't stop thinking of her as such—said, "My disappearance put everyone in a panic, for very different reasons. Eduardo thought I'd been taken to get to him. Savannah thought she'd brought the past to my doorstep as well as her own. Mike thought Eduardo was behind my disappearance..."

He got the picture. Had heard enough of the blow by blow. Needed to know the end.

"In the end, Savannah and Mike worked together to find me. At an FBI safe house Savannah told me who she was—who I was."

Right. Too clean. "And you believed them?"

"Hell no!" The woman's tone, the look in her eye might have been part of the act. His gut told him it wasn't. "But once I was facing the DNA evidence my sister showed me...no," she shook her head. "Backing up... Savannah told me I'd been kidnapped... I knew I wasn't. When we first came to the States, I told Eduardo that I had to visit my mother's grave. When he told me that the cemetery had been vandalized and my mother's grave was no longer there, I freaked." She stopped, looking at Harc, this time as though she was really seeing *him*. Talking to *him*. As though him being the one listening to her made a difference. "I insisted that we get a DNA test. I had to know he was my real family. That I wasn't really alone in the world. And I took it one step further. I took things out of his bathroom for DNA samples and paid out of my own money to have my own independent test run, too, in addition to the one he had done for me."

She'd known. Some part of the girl had known that something wasn't right. She'd been fighting then.

Had finding out that Eduardo was really her parent—conceivably the only family she had in the world—turned her? Was that when she'd become his partner in business? Using her skills to help her father's illegal dealings remain invisible to authorities looking for proof to arrest and prosecute him?

Because he knew she'd done so.

No matter what she had to tell him, he'd seen the proof of her work himself.

"When I told Savannah and Mike that Eduardo was my biological father, all hell broke loose. Mostly within Savannah. She'd adored the father who'd been murdered when she was seven. Had spent her life grieving him. When it became apparent that not only were Savannah and I sisters but that our father had faked his own death and somehow become billionaire Eduardo Duran, I knew what I had to do," the woman continued, not batting an eye as she held his gaze. "While Isaac, Mike, and Savannah got in touch with Sierra's Web, my sister's firm, I called my father, told him how I rigged the technology to get out of the house on my own. I said that I was sorry, that I wanted to come home but would only do so if he'd quit trying to control my life so completely. He agreed immediately, and I was back home that night. With Sierra's Web's involvement, along with local police and the FBI, Eduardo was in custody by morning."

Wait. What? "You turned in Eduardo Duran? They let you go back in there, knowing the danger..."

She shrugged. "It's like I told Mike—I wasn't under arrest. I was a free agent. And if I chose to go to the home I owned, there was nothing anyone could do about it."

Harc's respect for the woman rose another notch. Even while he looked for the hook, the hole in her logic. And found it. "You made a deal..."

Mike had accepted Charlotte's help with an agreement that she wouldn't be prosecuted.

Harc would have done the same.

Watching the expressions flash quickly across the woman's face, there and gone, Harc didn't know what to think when, ultimately, she shrugged and said, "I don't blame you for thinking so, but no. I didn't know, at first, that I was a suspect in Eduardo's dealings, but quite frankly, I wouldn't have cared one way or the other. When you're faced with finding out that your entire life had been a lie, having people think wrong things about you seems like child's play. Of course, people aren't going to believe in you. You don't even have anything to believe about yourself."

You don't even have anything to believe about yourself.

Her words cut deep. Not aimed at him at all. But hitting him directly in the heart.

And Harc had to ask, one more time, "Why are you here?"

Then, before she could answer, he got up and walked away without looking back.

HE DIDN'T BELIEVE HER.

She didn't blame him.

But she was pretty sure he was going to help her. And after recounting her story, telling it aloud to a stranger who hadn't followed the case over the past three months, Nicole was more convinced than ever that she had to pursue the course she'd set.

It was her only hope for life ahead.

Using Mike's name had been a last resort. Something she'd promised herself she wouldn't need to do.

Something she didn't have his permission to do. Not that, technically, she needed his nod to tell her story, but if she hoped to be in his good graces in the future, she should have given him a heads up.

Same with Savannah and Sierra's Web.

But she wasn't changing her mind. She'd made her choice to put herself on the line, not them. The world wouldn't lose a whole lot without her. But without Sierra's Web and agents like Mike, a whole lot of people's lives would be one hell of a lot harder.

A couple of minutes passed before Harcus Taylor returned and sat. Saying nothing.

He'd asked why she was there. "I'm getting to my reason for seeking you out," she told him after running her self-check to make certain she was still happy with her previous decisions.

Finding a confidence she hadn't known was still within her, she rested her forearms along the chair in which she sat and said, "First, you should know that Hugh Gussman, my father, took a plea agreement. There's not going to be a trial."

The ex-agent's brow rose, his eyes widening. "The night that I went home, he agreed to turn over all his files, to testify to what he'd done in exchange for his right to life." He'd been a bit more verbose in the moment. He'd needed to know that Nicole could see him anytime she needed him. Wanted to see her. To see his grandchildren.

Fat chance of that.

She'd come to a different realization over the past few months. He'd known he was cooked. Wanted to spare himself the public humiliation of a trial. And had needed to make certain that he was not only going to escape any possibility of the death penalty, but he'd negotiated terms for what he'd determined were necessary to his safety in prison, too.

She hadn't stuck around to hear that list.

"He didn't want any more investigation into his endeavors," Taylor said aloud what Nicole—and she figured others—had determined. No one had mentioned it in her presence before.

Cocking her head, she said, "Case closed."

Except that it very much wasn't.

The tall-enough-to-be-intimidating, well-muscled, and in-perfect-shape man across from her raised an eyebrow as he said, "It's not closed, is it?"

He had his guard up. Which told her he didn't trust her motive for being there. And what she was going to have to tell him wouldn't give him reason to trust her.

But first, "Does the name Arnold Wagar mean anything to you?"

The single blink of his eyes gave her her answer. No matter what came out of his mouth. "Why are you asking?"

At least he hadn't sat there and lied to her. Not that she'd have held it against him if he had.

Taking a deep breath, she forged ahead with parts of the speech she'd originally planned to deliver upon arrival.

"The night of Eduardo's eventual arrest, Isaac… Mike… stayed close to me. But there was a period of time…minutes…when I was alone in the room where he'd set me up for any further interrogation or confirmation to information agents were gaining as, in another part of the house, various law enforcement heads were getting evidence from my father. As you can imagine, Eduardo didn't immediately capitulate. It took hours of mental manipulation and weeding through tidbits of truth to find the lies beneath before they had enough to arrest him…"

"...You were alone in the room," Harcus interrupted her.

Rescued her was more like it. The nightmare was always there. Showing itself to her. Over and over. Chronic remuneration.

She swallowed. Acknowledging that she'd been putting off the next part. Had tried on all kinds of ways to get what she needed from him without disclosing what she'd done. None had worked for her, and she knew, sitting there, that Taylor was only going to give her one shot.

"I hacked into Mike's computer files. I had to know the extent of what they had on my father. Of what he'd done. I saw a report that you'd written. About a year before Savannah came to find me you'd infiltrated an illegal arms dealing ring of a scope never seen before. You were certain Duran was the kingpin, and you'd infiltrated a sect that you thought was close to the top. You were due to..."

"...So, yes, the name Arnold Wagar does ring a bell." Harcus Taylor's interruption held rudeness, for sure. And irritation. But there was more. She couldn't read him as well as she'd learned to read most people—through Eduardo's tutelage, of course.

But she knew one thing. That look, the tone, the way the ex–CIA agent's nostrils were flaring...she had him.

He wasn't going to be able to walk away.

Chapter Four

He'd been due to cross another agency's agent. To risk a good man's life. To make his next move. Not to close a case. Or bring down an international illegal-arms ring. Just to get one step closer.

Not that Mike's report would have said as much. No, it would have read more in the lines of Harc being due to meet up with his contact.

The only way to get through that gate had been to prove his loyalty to the wrong crowd. By exposing one of his own.

He could run. He could hide.

The truth was there. Known not just by him but by others.

He'd done what he'd been ordered to do. Didn't matter that he'd managed to protect the other agent as well, that he'd saved the guy's life. That had been sheer luck.

And they'd ended up gaining nothing. The meet had been a setup.

He'd lost credibility with other agencies. But more importantly, that night he'd lost total credibility with himself. He'd done other questionable things. When he looked back, he could see how he'd compromised his ethics one little step at a time. Always justifying his actions with the knowledge that, ultimately, he was saving lives. But that last one…seeing the look in his compatriot's eyes when he'd outed him…it was a look he was never going to forget.

Charlotte Duran—most assuredly the woman sitting across from him, one who'd been setting him up since she'd arrived on his property, was a Duran through and through—watched him like a hawk eyeing her prey.

A hawk that was going to be very disappointed if she thought he'd walk one more step in shades of gray to save his own ass from being exposed by what she knew. If she thought she was going to blackmail him with the knowledge she'd illegally gained, she was in for a major letdown.

"So, what do you want?" he asked. Taking the initiative was almost always good. Spoke of confidence in his ability to handle the meeting. Of strength. Both of which he had plenty.

In his case, it also spoke of a lack of patience. Something he was running dangerously low on. He didn't like being played. Or put in a corner.

Didn't like that his six months out of the field had taken away some of his edge.

"You'd been following Arnold Wagar for six months before, by your admission, you walked away."

He crossed his arms. Gave one nod in her direction.

She continued. "I didn't see enough on Mike's computer to know your full connection to Wagar or Eduardo's criminal empire, didn't have a chance to read your full report, but the date of your first mentioning the new player on the field, Wagar—I'm certain of the date because it was my birthday—was the same day I told my father about having entered my DNA into that database."

Not a coincidence. She had his attention.

"And on the same day that Savannah got notice of our biological connection, Eduardo called me into his office and told me that Arnold Wagar had asked his permission to marry me and he'd granted it."

His sudden harsh intake of breath was unintentional. And got her attention.

After a visible swallow, she said, "Over the next week after my father told me I was engaged, his refusal to accept anything but my complete capitulation to his plans, in spite of the fact that I told him the man gives me the creeps, is what drove me to leave home that night."

Wagar was why she'd come to him.

He got that.

He saw an open door. And had no intention of walking through it. Wagar had been the man he'd been supposed to meet his last night on the job.

But...

Nicole—Charlotte—whoever he was dealing with leaned in toward him across the table—interrupting his thought before it could lead him astray. "Think about it, Harcus," she said.

And he held up his hand. He knew. Didn't want to think, much less hear about it. Didn't want to get sucked back in. "I go by Harc," he said inanely.

She didn't seem to hear him as she continued in the same tensely animated tone. "Everyone thinks, and all visible records show, that Wagar and Duran just connected over the past year. That Wagar was new to the scene. His family owns a portfolio of profitable, tax-paying companies, including a family-run winery that shipped expensive and very exclusive product all over the world. He was, ostensibly, in the US to expand the family business." She shook her head, and he heard what was coming. After the official account. Heard and didn't want to know.

He shook his head. Held up his hand.

She just continued anyway. "In his testimony that night

at the house, Duran admitted that he'd been shaken since hearing that I'd entered my DNA in that database. He'd begun looking for a way to secure my future. Wagar was it. He offered him a deal—marry me with a prenup that gave me half of the Wagar fortune if Wagar divorced me, and in exchange, Wagar's family got a partnership in Duran's legal entities. It all made perfect sense. Turns out, it was too perfect."

She wasn't going to stop. Was going to sit there and look him in the eye as she played her ace card. So he just said it, "They've been connected since the beginning." The words burned his throat. "And you finding your sister, her finding you was the one thing that could expose them."

"Savannah and I talked about Eduardo being so eager to marry me off to Wagar. And so urgently. They wanted me so tied to the situation that when they got rid of Savannah, I'd be forever one of them. It was Eduardo's biggest mistake. It drove me away from him for the first time ever. I left home. If not for Isaac... Mike..."

She let the rest of the sentence lay between them unsaid.

Didn't much matter. Harc could easily finish that sentence. What he couldn't do was let her talk him into getting into the fray again. Not even with the information he had stored in his photographic brain. Information that could help her.

Help her put away a lethal criminal?

Or help her help Wagar, by giving her the critical information that would let the two of them know what parts of their vast business holdings to destroy. It was possible that Duran had been successful, emotionally if not legally, in tying Charlotte to the plot. Perhaps she'd been clued in all along. Was only playing them all with the poor-lied-to-girl-in-distress act until she could join Wagar somewhere.

Had the old man taken the fall for his daughter and her partner in business?

Stranger things had happened.

Hugh Gussman had faked his own death, entered the world of crime in a hugely successful way—and he'd taken his year-old daughter with him. The fact was key in getting into the fiend's head. To understanding not only the choices he'd made but what had driven them, which would lead them to what might be happening in that very moment that they didn't yet see.

And not at all his concern.

Or his job.

Charlotte tapped the table. He looked up, met her gaze as she almost whispered, "He's still out there. Not only running what's suspected to be the world's largest illegal arms consortium, but who knows what other international branches of Duran's empire as well? We only know what Duran told us about his illegal dealings, which was far more than anyone apparently had on him."

We? Us?

A beginner manipulation tool to make him feel a part of things. Reeling him in.

No.

Or...

We, not *I*. *Us*, not *me*. Was Mike working with her? Had the agent sent her?

He sat up straight. Put his hands on the table. "What do you want from me?" Each word was distinct.

"I want you to help me stop him."

He almost laughed. She couldn't be serious.

"I'm sure your sister and her firm—and Mike, too, for that matter—would have a lot to say about that."

Her look was open and clear as she nodded. "That's why I haven't told them."

The woman might've been of above-average intelligence in some areas. Technology for one—he'd seen the results of her work, which was why she'd been on his radar once upon a time—but at the moment she sounded like an innocent, protected little kid who had no idea how the real world looked.

He trusted that version least of all.

"We have no credentials, no source of ongoing information, no team to back us up..." He started with the most obvious.

"...and that's why we might succeed where others fail," she interrupted. Then said, "Humor me just another minute."

She'd glanced at her watch. Which prompted him to look at his own.

Her hour had just ended. She'd known? Had she set some notification on her watch? Had it vibrated?

"I can't make a life or become...anybody I'd ever want to be, a decent human being...knowing that innocent people are being shot by illegally obtained guns. Whole communities are wiped out by them all over the world."

He didn't need the lecture. He knew way more than she ever would. Had seen one or two of those communities firsthand.

The women and children...

No.

He'd tried.

He'd failed.

And lost himself in the bargain.

Even if she was for real, being sincere, he had nothing to offer her.

HARCUS TAYLOR PUT his gun on the table. Sat back, arms crossed. "What you have is sheer coincidence."

She was losing him. Time to clone her father, put on pressure like she'd never done it before. She would not go to her grave having done nothing with her life but be her father's daughter.

The irony in her needing to become more like him to escape the life he'd trapped her in wasn't lost on her. It fueled her in a way she didn't really even understand.

Whatever it took. She had to stop Wagar.

"Those dates being exact aren't an accident. They link Wagar to Eduardo prior to the past year. Wagar first hit your radar the day that I told Duran about the database, Harc." She might have stumbled over the too familiar way to address him if she hadn't been all Duran in that moment. "What tipped you off to him that day?"

He looked upward. Not quite rolling his eyes, but close. "We knew that large shipments of arms were flowing out of El Salvador. In ways that couldn't happen without someone powerful paving the way. An informant led me to Wagar as the paver. Said that he'd been in touch with the kingpin. Seemed viable since he was Salvadoran. And then he was suddenly relocating to the US, to San Diego, where Duran was based. When they started hanging out together, we were certain we were getting close."

She frowned, then, as a wave of sheer panic shot through her. "Isaac knew this?"

Mike. Not Isaac. Isaac was the fake persona she'd trusted with her life. The man who'd saved her life. Mike was the FBI agent who was engaged to marry her older sister.

Oh, God. What if Mike was still playing them? Watching them?

Harc sat forward, arms on the table again, the back of his hand touching his gun. "No. The CIA isn't always big on interagency communication. In this case, my call. I was deep under. We didn't want to take the chance of communications being intercepted."

Her gaze on the flesh that was touching the gun barrel, she asked, "And?"

"It turned out in the end, after six months of undercover work, to be a false lead. And during the interim, while I was doing what I do, the agency did some checking of their own. They found nothing on Wagar or his family."

Well, that explained his attitude.

"What if I told you I don't think it was a dead end?"

He shrugged. Rolled his eyes. Shook his head.

"The first time I looked at your file, I was overwrought. I'd just found out...well, you know what I'd just found out. I saw that date that Wagar popped up on your radar, my birthday, knew it was the day I'd told Duran about the DNA database, and blanked on it. Just sat there, dead inside, until I heard Mike coming back and quickly backtracked so he wouldn't know anyone had been accessing his computer."

His eyebrows raised. As she'd expected them to do. "There was more than one time," he correctly guessed.

His fingers moved to the other side of his gun.

Ready to grab it?

At the moment, she wasn't the least bit fazed. She was so het up, she didn't care what he did with the damned thing. She needed his help.

And without it, she didn't have a life to go back to. He'd confirmed that he'd really just heard Wagar's name for the first time the very day she'd told her father about the database...that the lead had turned out false six months before Savannah had come to find her...

"Six months before Savannah found me was when Wagar started coming to the house," she said then. "Right after you dropped the case. Prior to that, Eduardo and I had seen him at social events. The two were acquainted, clearly, but he was never in our home those first six months."

Taylor sighed. "All coincidence, Charlotte. Nicole." He corrected, meeting her gaze for a second as he did so.

"Right, but this isn't. Your file mentioned a series of computer backstops that prevented file originality to be discovered."

He nodded. Seemingly bored. If she wasn't noticing the way his fingers were bouncing up and down on the table by his gun. And it hit her.

The weapon wasn't there to threaten her. It was there to calm him. As though having the thing close gave him some kind of comfort.

The possibility prompted her to lean in again. And her voice was softer as she said, "I can get to the origin."

His lips pursed.

He wasn't committing to anything, but he was no longer looking bored, either. His fingers on the table had stilled.

It was time.

"When everything was first happening, I was a mess," she told him. "Trying to stay calm and coherent to help put Eduardo away forever, to be there for my sister, to somehow grasp that I even had one...but as the weeks passed and things settled down, that date in your file kept bothering me. There'd been more there. Something I'd kind of recognized. Just a couple of symbols that were appropriately placed, but...that unread rest of the file kept playing with me. I couldn't let it go. What if, you know?"

Harcus's eyes widened. No other muscle on the man's body moved in any visible way.

"I offered to program both Mike and my sister's firm's computers with extra protection against hacking, giving them all a level of security nobody but us would know. I think they felt so sorry for what I was going through that they let me do it just to humor me. I'm damned good, but they've got an entire team of tech experts that have as much skill and experience as I do."

Harc's fingers started to thrum.

Watching them, she said, "I hacked into Mike's secure files again. Well, your file. And found what I was afraid was there. You mentioned the files with no obtainable sources…but those files you refer to, weren't ever produced."

With his chin jutting, his hands still, he said, "And you think you can find out the files' source?"

Finally. He was looking at her like she had something of worth to him. "I know I can."

"You expect me just to hand over highly classified material to *you*? That's assuming I even have access to it."

Emphasis on the *you* hurt. A lot. And yet she couldn't blame him a bit. That emphasis was exactly why she was never going to have a life if she couldn't right wrongs that she'd been a part of creating.

Whether anyone would ever believe that she hadn't had any knowledge that her programming skills were being used criminally, she couldn't say. Didn't even let herself hope that far ahead.

What she'd bet her last breath on was that he had those files. A guy like him…no way he'd walk away unless something so catastrophic had happened that he'd been at breaking point. And when you reached that point—you didn't turn your back without protecting it.

"I wrote the code that's stopping you from finding the source of those files when I was fourteen years old."

He went still. As in frozen. He didn't blink. He just sat there. His eyes on her, but almost unseeingly so.

"And not that I expect you to believe me, but I had no idea that my father had shared it with anyone or used it at all. And there's no telling what other of my stuff he's shared, or more likely sold to others..." She was rambling. Needing him to offer her the lifeline she'd come for.

Without so much as glancing her way, he got up, picked up his gun, and left her sitting there alone.

Again.

Chapter Five

He had her. One way or the other, the next little bit was going to show him why Charlotte Duran was at his ranch, ruining his day—and his mood, too.

Which was precarious at best on a good day.

Unless he got back to find her gone. He wanted to believe that was the best-case scenario.

As it was, after locking himself into the fire-safe secure room he entered through the newly laid floor in his kitchen, then unlocking the first of three safes, entering that one to head to a side wall before unlocking another safe, Harc reached into unplug one of the laptops stacked neatly in a wooden tray made specifically for the purpose of holding computers. A tray that fit into the specially made leather case for transporting them, too.

He didn't grab the case. Or the shelves. Just the one computer.

Locked the safe. Double-checked it. Let himself out of the walk-in safe, locked it behind him. Checked it. And then, verifying that the scope that would show him the kitchen was all clear, headed back up to daylight.

The security could be overkill.

It wasn't that he valued his life all that much. He just

wanted to know that he could save it if he had a mind to do so.

Mostly he was protecting the information that, in the wrong hands, could blow up the world. Or the equivalent thereof.

Things the agency had never known about.

And, God willing, never would.

What it said about him that he was trusting a known criminal's daughter more than he trusted the men and women who'd been on his own team, he didn't want to contemplate.

But he wasn't really trusting her.

Testing her was more like it.

He didn't welcome the slight lift of relief he felt when he saw her standing on his front porch, looking out over his property. Standing by the chair he'd assigned her. Not the stairs that would take her to her car and away from him.

She had guts.

Determination.

Whatever her reason for seeking him out—it was strong enough to be worth risking her life.

All qualities he'd have looked for in the past when assessing operatives.

She wasn't one.

And he wasn't assessing.

Old habits died hard.

His approach was silent. A talent he'd perfected.

She turned before he'd made it out of the house. Reclaimed her seat. Was positioned primly, gaze straight ahead, hands folded on the table in front of her when he joined her.

"Your shadow gave you away," she said conversationally when he pulled out the chair he'd vacated and sat.

"I didn't ask."

"You need to know who and what you're dealing with. What you can count on. Eduardo Duran had me convinced that, because of our wealth, I was a constant target and had to be aware of all things at all times. I went through my first training course at ten. Have repeated every year since. With harder challenges added each time. I can rappel. Stay alive in the wilderness for days. Swim for miles. Walk blindfolded out of a forest, relying on my other senses to avoid dangers planted there…"

He waited for her to take a breath before interrupting. "Too bad he didn't teach you how to keep yourself from rambling on when you're nervous."

She didn't flinch. He'd give her that. Holding his gaze steadily, she said, "I'm not nervous." And then glanced at the computer he'd carried out. "Fueled by determination, I'm overeager."

He filed away the piece of information. Whether true or false, the fact that she'd rather be seen one way than the other told him things about her.

Not that he needed to know except to get himself clear of her. Permanently.

Opening the computer, he left it off. Slid it over to her.

Held out a hand to it and said, "Do your thing."

He could have signed on, taken her right to the file that would show him if she'd been telling the truth about the code. Had actually planned to do just that when he'd walked out on her and during his journey back to her, too.

But the way she hung on…made him want to push her.

He wasn't proud of the fact. Didn't like it. But he accepted it. Right along with the rest of his unpleasant qualities. Denying his faults wasn't going to help a damned thing.

The idea was to try to correct them. To improve.

Which was another reason he had to get the woman out of there. She brought out the worst in him.

She flipped on the high-tech expensive laptop without looking for the switch. Just reached and clicked. For the next five minutes her fingers flew across the keys. He lost count of how many times her right-handed little finger hit Enter.

When the game had ceased to be fun and he was spending more time picturing the beer waiting for him in the fridge than keeping his guard up, he asked, "You ready for the password?"

The glance she gave over the top of the laptop was very clearly a query as to his sanity. Or intelligence. *As if*, it seemed to say.

And then she said, "I had that thirty seconds after you handed me the device. A combination of the most worn keys. Doesn't always work. I got lucky." She spoke slowly, as though her mind was elsewhere.

At the rate she'd been typing, with him sitting there assuming she'd been trying password attempts, she could've been anywhere on the device at that point.

He'd intended to take her right to the file that could prove truth or lie to her claims. But let her glean what she could from the laptop. There was nothing there that mattered to him. It was his gaming computer.

While he'd been undercover, he'd copied Wagar's impenetrable file into a new document. Had replaced everything he understood with made up information, leaving the code as it was. And then copied that file to his gaming drive.

He'd been working on decoding it ever since.

As a game. A puzzle. On the nights when the past tried to haunt him.

Another couple of minutes passed before the laptop

closed with a definitive click. Charlotte sat there, arms folded across her chest. Glaring at him.

"Very funny."

She wasn't leaving. But she looked like she wanted to.

What was keeping her there?

Her life quest, as she'd like to have him believe?

How could he ignore the possibility she was telling the truth? He was on a similar, and yet very different, journey of his own.

If what she said was true, she'd been unaware of the crimes in which she'd inadvertently been involved.

He'd made conscious choices to commit his less than stellar acts. With good motive, of course, he reminded himself.

The same thing he'd told himself every single time he crossed a line the man his parents had raised wouldn't have crossed.

The justification was true. But it had become little more than an excuse to allow him to press too far. And so, it fell far short of exonerating him in his own court.

"I can show you the file you might have wanted to see," he said, knowing that she'd found herself up against a plethora of complicated gaming code.

"I found the damned file, Taylor," she said, her tone anything but sweet. "And it traced right back to you. Very funny. Ha. Ha." She hadn't moved, though. Arms still tightly folded, she remained in her chair. Glaring at him. "I'm assuming I passed whatever test you just put me through. Now, you going to help me or not?"

She'd found the source of the implanted dummy document. Something he had not been able to do. Even knowing the source.

She'd surpassed the test. Not that he had any intention

of letting her in on that little tidbit. Not ever. He'd known she was good.

Had underestimated how good.

He wouldn't make that mistake a second time.

His gun was digging into his hip bone again. As it did when he sat with it shoved into his pants instead of its holster. Pulling it out, he set it back on the table. "Just for more grins, what is it exactly you're envisioning me doing to help you?"

"I was hoping you'd help me figure that out."

Uh-huh. Right. He stared her down.

Her gaze was dead serious.

"Come again?" he asked.

"If you've got copies of Wagar's files, which I suspect you do, I can get to the source. I can find where they originated from. How many various routes they traveled and maybe find specific players, too, but that last bit is less certain. From there, depending on what I find, I've got some ideas which I'm happy to run by you. I'm a women's studies lecturer, with a bachelor's degree in that as well as psychology and another in technology, who grew up playing with code to offset the boredom of being locked on a gorgeous estate with a parent who had me mastered in survival training. But I know bupkis about criminal minds or getting the better of them. From what I gathered from your file, you're a master at both."

He'd been, not he was.

She was offering him the one thing he'd needed to possibly bring down one of the world's most wanted men. Her father.

A better man than he had done that.

And he was thankful every day that Duran was done.

But was he?

The man was in prison. There for life without parole, he'd guess based on the scope of the fiend's crimes.

And if Charlotte... Nicole...was right, if Wagar had been involved from the beginning...they'd imprisoned a man. Slowed down his operation.

But they hadn't stopped it.

Putting a hand on his gun, he met the woman's gaze openly. Sincerely. "You need to get to Mike Reynolds," he said. "And Sierra's Web."

He'd heard of the firm. From multiple sources. Hadn't ever worked with them. But this one needed all hands on deck and if she had a familial in like she said...that was the time to use it.

"Today. Immediately. Tell them what you told me." His tone was growing more urgent with each word. He couldn't help it.

Couldn't pretend her missive didn't matter.

Or that the shaking of her head wasn't about to explode the top off from his.

No! No! No! She had him on board going in the wrong direction. Completely opposite to where and how she had to travel through the dangerous maze in front of her.

Quietly, eerily calmly resolved to leave, disappear, and handle things on her own, Nicole said, "I can't do that."

Just that. Nothing more.

His gaze burned with tension. "What do you mean you can't do that? You pull out your phone and dial."

She shook her head. "Let me rephrase. I refuse to do that. I'm doing this without them. And as I'm the only who can get into Wagar's records, that decision is mine to make. Either you're with me or you aren't. That's your choice here."

Hands on the strap of her bag, she prepared to stand. And go.

She'd played her cards.

If he folded, they were through.

There was no more discussion to be had.

He shook his head. Frowning as he said, "Why?"

She frowned right back at him. "*Why?*" There was irritation in the intonation of her delivery. She didn't bother to hide it. Not with him lobbing his own tension at her.

With his gun on the table, he leaned forward, forearms on either side of the weapon. Almost as though he was cradling it.

The odd posture softened her heart some, for no rational reason. She met his gaze and wanted to understand the man, not just the words, as he said, "Why are you doing this?"

"So I can live with myself. My work is being used to allow horrible people to debilitate good people, to finance criminal operations that ultimately destroy innocent lives..." She broke off at the continual shake of his head.

"Why are you forcing me to help you?"

She shook her head right back at him. Quickly. Continually, the touch of her hair moving around her a testimony that she was real. Alive. Awake. Not caught in a nightmare that just wouldn't end.

"I'm not forcing you," she told him as she stood. "I came to make a request. Period." Purse on her shoulder, she headed for the stairs.

"If you run away at every obstacle, you'll be dead before you get to the second one."

What the hell! More angry than anything, at that point, she spun around.

The man was watching her, his gaze clearly assessing. And she returned to her seat.

With his arms crossed, the gun alone on the table, he said, "Why *aren't* you seeking help from the authorities?"

"When officials get involved, things have to go through channels and protocols have to be followed."

He gave her a nod on that point.

"Gussman worked for the IRS. He managed to get away with more than two million dollars. He claims he worked on his own, but even I don't believe that one. Which tells me that there was, and maybe still is, someone high up, with an official position, involved. Maybe government officials. Maybe a mole in the FBI whose been quietly making personal investments all these years. Perhaps even someone who's being blackmailed and will continue to be until the entire operation—Wagar—is out of commission. We blindsided Gussman the night he was arrested. *I* blindsided him. I'd like to say it was because I was brave enough to face the possibility that he'd turn on me—claim that he had no idea what I'd been up to, blaming at least a lot of it on me—but that thought didn't cross my mind until weeks later…"

She paused. His gaze was softer as he waited. Not pushing her. Just…being there.

"Had he not made the deal to confess that night, others would have become involved. And I likely would have been indicted. It's also plausible that whoever had been paving his way would bury him to protect themselves. Regardless…we don't know who might be involved, so the less anyone knows about this, the better."

"The more likely you are to stay alive."

"If I don't stay alive, Wagar's illegal business ventures not only continue, they continue to grow." He wasn't going to come up with an argument strong enough to stop her course. Nor was he going to turn his back on her without consequences on the table.

He'd called her back.

The thought gave her hope. She pushed forward. "Because we don't know who else could be involved, if we go the official route, we risk someone tipping off Wagar. The more people who are involved, the more we run the risk that he finds out he's being investigated. He'll have all kinds of security protocols in place that would alert him."

"Which they'll do as soon as you start poking around."

She sat back. "Yep. That's the point. Difference is I wrote the code. I can manipulate it so that he can't figure out who's watching him."

"If he knows you wrote the code, he'll suspect you're behind it."

She nodded. She hadn't kidded herself about the risk involved in her undertaking.

"He gets to you before you get enough evidence against him, following however many trails you'll have to follow, figure your way through however many dead ends, then the whole thing is moot."

"That's where you come in."

"I thought you just wanted my files."

"I need your files most."

The man looked like he was playing a game of table tennis. He was finding sport in the conversation that was a matter of life and death to her. "Our best shot is to get him before he knows he's being looked at. Right now he's got to be feeling like he dodged a bullet. He's going to be looking for wolves at his back, yes, but also flourishing—with Eduardo gone, he has the profits all to himself."

The man just linked his fingers together and dropped them to his lap at that one.

"He knows Charlotte Duran," she told him. "He'll have a set of expectations where she's concerned. I'm no longer that woman."

His brows raised. "How do you mean?"

"I no longer have the confidence of being well established or well loved, which tends to make one feel secure and makes one soft. I have no illusions, nor am I still living under massive delusions. I don't have to keep up appearances or bite my tongue for Father's sake. To please him. Or to make him proud of me. I'm angry. And I have very little to lose."

Taylor leaned forward again, those arms around the weapon a second time. Something she believed to be a good sign. "You didn't have money of your own?"

He might've been good at assessing people. Watching the nuances. She was equally so. Him, to do his job and keep himself alive. Her, because she'd been bored a lot and had had nothing better to do than mentally dissect those around her. Different lives. Same result.

"I do have money," she told him. "I've sold a few computer programs that continue to pay me nicely."

"And your guest lecturing? I saw some pretty hefty stipends for those."

He hadn't just noticed her during his time investigating Wagar. He'd paid some pretty close attention. Rather than making her uncomfortable, the knowledge solidified her belief that he went over and above to notice everything in his effort to get the job done.

"I donated every dime," she told him. A couple of teaching gigs, with regular salaries, had grown one of her savings accounts, though.

"And Sierra's Web?" The question came at her like a slam at the tennis table. "Why aren't you going to them?"

She didn't even flinch. "Two reasons. One, I realize that I could be indicted, depending on how cleverly my code has been used. I had nothing to do with anything illegal, but it could look like I did, and while I'm willing to take the risk for myself—hoping that I'll be able to prove what is and is not my work—I will not risk my sister's livelihood, the firm, her friends' reputations by having them involved. In any way. And just so you know, Savannah made the same choice when she came to find me. She came alone. Her partners all thought she was on a cruise. Two, I will not put my sister in danger again. She's a lawyer, not a cop or a trained agent, but if she knows what I'm doing, she won't stay behind a desk."

So there. The thought was childish. Felt good anyway. She let out a deep breath for good measure.

"So that leaves Mike."

She held his gaze. "He's FBI, official. We aren't going that route."

The man's eyes narrowed.

"He doesn't know I hacked him, and I'd rather it stay that way," she admitted.

The intensity in the gaze pinning her didn't lessen even a little bit.

"And he's engaged to my sister, okay?" Information he could get for himself in less than a minute if he was half as good as he seemed. "I will not be responsible for bringing any more pain to her life or risk damaging his reputation for letting himself get hacked by his possibly criminal soon to be sister-in-law."

"And you don't want him to know he can't trust you."

The words were uttered softly. Making her feel emotions she'd promised herself were frozen. Making her weak, prone to manipulation.

Denying them made her more so. Looking Harcus Taylor straight in the eye, she said, "He *can* trust me. I did what I did to protect him."

And then, when the gaze coming at her didn't waver, added, "But I don't want him to think he can't."

The words earned her a slight nod. A softening in the looks coming at her.

And with that, she shut up.

Chapter Six

He couldn't do it. Could not let himself get sucked back in. He'd given himself his word. Any hope of trusting himself to do the right thing, trusting himself enough to allow others to trust him rested on him keeping that word.

And what about letting a determined, broken young woman venture out by herself to do something it had taken professionals around the globe years to even halfway do?

Was that right?

He could put in a call to Mike Reynolds himself. Tell him what Nicole had told him.

And possibly jeopardize the mission, and with it, the best chance they had at getting Wagar and everyone else involved.

Based on what he'd just seen Nicole do, she could feasibly not only expose Wagar's ways and means but every player in every channel connected to Wagar. Sellers. Buyers. Transporters.

Cartels.

If she had the time.

A plan to keep her safe.

And a way to draw the criminals out of the worldwide holes they were hiding in. What if he was able to not only know names—many of which would be aliases—but could convince people, in the flesh, to expose themselves?

No.

She wasn't going to seek other help. She'd forge ahead. Get herself killed. And Wagar would be full owner of the one thing that the world had to bring him down.

Unless Harcus Taylor went back to work. Albeit sans credentials. No agency backing. Without team support.

If they failed, he could end up in jail.

Worse than the prison in which he currently resided. He'd lose the fresh air. The freedom to come and go. Most importantly, he'd lose his horses.

And they, the wild and hurt, would lose him.

Unless he took them with him.

He shut the thought down before it could prosper. But not without having to acknowledge that his mind was already on the case.

He could turn down Nicole Compton/Charlotte Duran, but he'd go to bed at night and dream the case. Or worse, lie awake with it eating at him.

Because the opportunity was clearly there. Just waiting on him.

What kind of self-respect could he possibly hope to have, what kind of man could he ever be if he didn't try?

He looked up at her to see Charlotte's wise gaze watching him. The brilliant woman was old beyond her years.

Eleven years younger than him, and yet in some critical ways she'd been through so much more than he had.

Which—considering his career, the things he'd done, the drug and war zones he'd lived within—was saying a lot.

"If I do this..." He heard the words before he'd given them permission to be heard. Stopped midtrack, the sound of them ringing a warning in his ears. Loudly. Insistently.

She continued to watch him. As though his decision

didn't matter to her either way. A con? Or she'd just reached the point where she was okay within herself to go it alone?

"If I do this," he started again, consciously choosing his words second time around. "It's done my way. Other than what you do coding wise, I'm the boss. When I say *bark*, you bark like a dog. Got it?"

With raised brows—as if to ask, Who didn't know that?—she nodded.

He didn't like easy capitulations. More times than not, they bit you in the butt. "I'm serious, Nicole," he told her, his hand reaching for his gun.

To shove it back into the waistband of his jeans. "The first time you go against my bidding, I disappear."

Her mouth tightened. "Your bidding in terms of our safety and how we proceed in our efforts to get Wagar and anyone else involved," she stated in that tone that held no inflection whatsoever. But a hell of a lot of steel.

Getting her point, he held her gaze as she nodded. And then he said, "You have absolutely nothing to fear from me otherwise. I have never touched a woman without her consent, unless it was to catch a body that had been shot before it hit the ground."

A bit dramatic. But true nonetheless.

"Nor do I get off on ordering anyone around." He checked himself. Then added, "What you're proposing here could lead us into a situation where one second is the difference between life and death. There will be no time to think, to discuss. You act or you die."

She didn't even hesitate, nodding before he'd finished. And then said, "I understand."

That ready capitulation…just did not sit well with him. Assessing her, he was already second-guessing his decision to consider going back to work for one last case.

To finish his last case.

"I was raised by Eduardo Duran, Harc." Her tone was dry as she spoke to that which he'd been thinking but hadn't expressed. "I'm very well trained in doing what I'm told when I'm told in the name of my safety."

And with those words—with the seemingly privileged and so abusive life inherent within them—she had him.

FEELING AS THOUGH she had a train barreling down her back with every hour that Wagar was free to change anything he was doing before she had a chance to find him, Nicole suggested that Harc turn over access to his files immediately.

And the words she'd issued so confidently just moments before, agreeing to do his *bidding in terms of our safety and how we proceed in our efforts to get Wagar*...and... *I'm very well trained in doing what I'm told when I'm told in the name of my safety* came back to bite her.

Shaking his head, he stood and asked her to accompany him, leading her down the stairs and across the yard to one of the barns.

"We don't touch those files until I've got a plan in place to deal with whatever comes next. We need to be ready to act immediately, and we don't know to whom, what, or where they might lead us." He strode laconically toward the largest barn, the nicest-looking one, though they all had what looked to be fresh coats of brownish-red paint.

"We also have to be ready in case Wagar is alerted when you access whatever your code is keeping secret. He'll have protections in place—we have to count on that."

And while she hated the sense of standing at a precipice with the wind blowing and not being able to do a damned thing but wait before she could try to deal with the threat, he had her. On every level.

She'd given her word to him for good reason. And his explanations were spot on.

"I should get a hotel for tonight," she said then. She'd booked the dude-ranch vacation she'd told her sister she was taking. The place was only a couple of hours' drive north. She could still get there before dark if she left soon.

"It's best if you stay here."

There? Alone with him? The thought didn't alarm her nearly as much as it probably should have. To the contrary, the idea of remaining within his sphere felt better than not doing so.

"The court document you showed me, changing your identity—it's dated today."

She nodded. And noted his attention to detail, too.

"Who else knows?"

She shook her head, then looked over at him, striding beside her as she said, "No one. That's the point. I have to hit now. Charlotte is no more. And Nicole isn't yet in the global system. Everything's legally changed. Driver's license, credit cards. But it won't have registered anywhere yet. I'm told it could take a day or two and up to a couple of weeks. That's the time I have to act without being able to be traced in any way." She might not be a trained agent. But she was smart. Savvy.

And determined to succeed.

She was going to be an asset to him.

In spite of her privileged and very sheltered upbringing, her healthy bank account, she was not soft.

"I purchased the SUV last night from a private seller with a free and clear title signed over to Nicole Compton. Paid cash. Registered the tags online today."

"What about your sister?"

Feeling a sharp pang, she almost bumped into him as she shook her head again and said, "She knows I plan to change my name. She's expecting me to change it to Nicole *Willoughby*, the last name registered to my missing person's report through witness protection."

They were almost to the barn.

"As soon as I get to work on those files, I suspect Charlotte Duran could be on some dangerous radars. And for a short time, her identity will still pop up as valid."

"And when she doesn't, it could take some time before anyone figures out she became Nicole Compton," he added, pulling open the barn door, holding it for her.

His tone had changed. Almost as though he was humoring her. Or engaging in wishful thinking. She glanced at him as she passed by him to enter the tall wooden structure, and for a second there, it was though he was giving her something she'd yearned for her entire life.

Unconditional support.

ONCE ON THE JOB, Harc didn't turn off. Even in his sleep he was prepared, ready to jump into action instantly upon awaking. He also had never embarked on an operation without full intel, and...most importantly...a plan.

The lack of both hindered him. It wasn't going to stop him. Undercover, plans changed in seconds. Without notice.

His plan had just changed.

Nicole didn't ask why they were in the barn. She didn't say anything as she kept pace with him on the way to the post where he'd left Imperial tied up.

Her silence as she kept up with him won her some regard.

Other whinnies greeted them, though, and until his mind found some solid ground, he introduced her around. Making introductions at every one of the ten occupied stalls they passed. "This is Scarlet," he said, rubbing a hand down the older girl's nose as he passed. Carmine, Sangria, Fire, Mahogany were all in a row and received exactly the same attention.

"Over there are Vermillion, Burgundy, Ferrari, Salmon, and Brick," he told her as he stood in front of Mahogany's stall. All his horses were used to traversing rugged territory—and staying alive in it for days, too. Mahogany and Imperial were in the best shape.

"You ever do any riding?" he asked Nicole as he led the three-year-old mustang out of his stall and over by the post where Imperial stood grazing on hay.

She'd made her way to Imperial. Was rubbing a palm along the boy's flank. "As a kid in El Salvador," she told him. "The ocean estate wasn't intended for a barn or live animals."

She said the words as though repeating what she'd been told.

Probably as a kid. When Eduardo had used her citizenship to move them to the States. Maybe if the fiend had bought her a horse, she wouldn't have been so desperately lonely. Driven to entering her DNA into a family-finder database.

Harc entertained the thoughts as he pulled a saddle off the rail and lifted it to the gelding's back. Then tightened the cinch, and pulled his mind from places it had no reason to dwell. Charlotte Duran's upbringing being a key one.

He'd taken her on. From there, all that mattered was getting the job done. Her past, her future, her name, even, didn't matter.

Except where it helped them reach their goal.

Charlotte had disappeared off the face of the earth. He had to be sure to call her Nicole.

"Here, put these on." Reaching into a cupboard, grabbing a pile from the women's small cubby, he held out the denim and flannel to her, balanced on one palm. And when she took the clothes, he nodded toward a door that led to private restrooms. With doors that locked.

He could have had her duck into one of the empty stalls.

His instincts were tightly guiding him not to go casual with her, even for a second.

Maybe he didn't trust her.

Maybe it was something else.

He had no time to question that which didn't directly impact his next steps.

Imperial was re-saddled by the time Harc's guest reappeared. In jeans that were snug as today's fashions were more apt to be. She'd tucked in the hem of the flannel shirt. Let the rest flop over the waistband.

And the two-inch heels…

"There are boots in those cubbies over there," he told her, pointing to a corner several yards away. "And socks in the drawers underneath."

And when he caught himself watching her walk away, he swung around, filling with dread. Was he ready to work again? Did he have it in him to be part of a two-person team when the other person was not a suspect? Or was not believed to be attached to one?

The question gave birth to a thought that calmed him some. Nicole Compton was most definitely attached to a very bad person. More than one of them. Her father, of course. But she knew Arnold Wagar personally.

Only difference between the current case and ones from the past were that the attached person with whom he was working knew who he really was. Knew his goal.

And shared it.

Maybe, just maybe, he was going to get one last shot at redeeming himself in his own eyes by staying solidly within the boundaries of morality. Ethics. Legality.

And still closing the case that was haunting him.

IT HAD BEEN years since she'd been up on a horse, but Nicole figured out pretty quickly that, for her at least, riding a horse was like riding a bike. Once you'd learned, you knew how.

Her knees pulled in against Mahogany's sides as they started up a fairly steep slope and again as the strong horse trotted over uneven area at the top of the climb.

She had no idea where they were going. Or why. Just hoped it wouldn't be too far from the ranch. There was still another hour or so before sunset, but she did not relish being out in the mountains when that happened.

Had she been anywhere else, with anyone else, she'd have said so.

Instead, she rode. Left him to his silence. Until he broke it.

"Stirrups fitting okay?"

They'd been out twenty minutes. Had covered not one second of easy terrain since they'd set out. The question was coming a bit late.

She refrained from saying so. Just called out, "Fine."

Truth be known, the ride was treating her well. Being in the mountains, in the middle of nowhere, with no one watching her felt…a little like she imagined nirvana might feel.

Except, maybe, for the silence of her companion. And since he'd broken it, she asked, "Mahogany? Imperial? Vermillion, Burgundy, Ferrari, Salmon, Brick, Carmine, Sangria, Fire, Scarlet? And I saw a sign when I pulled in that said we're on the Crimson Ranch. You got a thing for the color red?"

His shrug was as visible from the back as the front, maybe more so with only the big broad shoulders visible in his upper back for distraction. "How do you know I didn't just purchase the ranch and horses already named?"

She'd done her research. That was how. But she said, "The ranch sign was new."

If she earned any points for observation, he didn't give any indication of that fact. If she was hoping to impress him, she'd better get herself in line damned quick.

There was nothing about what lay ahead that left room for any emotional blowback from her. That could come later. After they'd succeeded, and she was alone. They'd reached a flat land. Wide enough for them to ride side by side.

She wasn't upset when Harc slowed and waited for her to catch up with him. An evening ride to unwind was fine. If they didn't have a million pounds of work pressing down on them. Time to get to it. Even if just verbally.

"If you're going to call the shots, maybe you should get at it," she told him as she and Mahogany drew parallel to him and Imperial. The horses turned their heads toward each other, almost in greeting, and then their noses immediately pointed forward again.

He didn't even give her that brief of a glance as he responded to her comment with, "Why the last name Compton?"

None of his business. And no reason to make it an issue, either. "It's my sister's last name. Savannah Compton."

Let him make something of the choice. Poor little rich girl, still clinging to a need for family.

She glanced his way, daring him to think less of her, and watched as, with no change of expression, he just kept moving forward. Seeming to take in the expanse of miles all around them. And it dawned on her. "You knew."

Of course he had. The man would have done at least minimal checking during the couple of times they'd been apart.

If he hadn't already been familiar with the firm. She hadn't asked if he was. He hadn't said.

"You know who all of the partners are," she said, keeping her gaze on him.

His nod to the side could have been acknowledgment. Or simply a lack of caring to respond.

She got him calling the shots. He was the expert at field work. But there was no reason she couldn't be clued into some things. Like what he knew about her. Her life.

Whether or not he was even working on a plan, yet.

"Why all shades of red?" she asked him. Pushing him for no good reason. But feeling some better as she did so.

"No more shades of gray."

Succinct. Almost cryptic. But oddly enough, she got it.

Agreed a thousand percent.

And rode without further question, soaking in the moments of glorious, strength inducing natural peace he was treating her to, as they turned and headed back toward the ranch.

They'd returned to flat ground, the barns were in sight, when Harc rode up beside her again. "You're good in the saddle. You'll do fine."

What the hell? Do fine for what?

And the ride? It had been some kind of test.

Obviously he hadn't just been passing time, using it to enjoy a nightly ride before they dove into work mode.

Even knowing to be on her guard where taking him at face value was concerned, she'd underestimated him.

And wasn't sorry to find that out.

Or to be there, tackling the challenge of her life, with him by her side.

Even if he was a bit of a grouch.

Chapter Seven

It wasn't much of a plan. But Harc walked back to the ranch house beside Nicole with some first steps in mind.

He'd planned to tend to all of the horses alone, figuring her for heading back to the house on her own—giving her time to search whatever she could find in his home to show her that there was nothing of note. But she'd opted not only to brush, feed, and water Mahogany while he took care of Imperial but to help him check food and water for the nine other stalled horses as well.

To butter him up?

To thank him?

Or just because she was the kind of person who chipped in and helped wherever she could? One who didn't like to just sit around and do nothing?

She'd asked some about his daily routine the few times they'd passed in the barn—apparently assuming he took care of all the horses on his own, wondering why he had so many.

He'd told her about his part-time staff. A sentence about the fact that the horses were all wild mustang rescues of one kind or another. Leaving out the part about the dude-ranch weekends he was branching into with some of them.

And failing to mention the horse-therapy program that

was his lifeline at the moment. Literally. Not financially, but as a way to build a decent life for himself, contributing to the betterment of society without much chance of taking wrong turns.

"You have a lot of visitors?" she asked as they traversed the gravel drive.

The question seeming to come out of nowhere he said, "No." Then asked, "Why?"

Motioning toward her body in the dusk, she said, "The clothes. All sorted by size. Just something you inherited when you bought the place?"

He could leave it at that.

Except that it would be a lie, and he was done crossing the lines. He couldn't afford to bring any more gray areas into his life.

"I've got a couple of trained counselors bringing in people for horse therapy. Teenagers mostly. Many aren't ready to get on a horse, don't come prepared, so we keep the supplies here." Hearing himself spouting the words pissed him off even as he was saying them.

He'd just gone over the fact that he'd done well to keep his business to himself all evening. Maintaining personal distance between them.

And then he'd gone and spilled his closest beans all over himself.

He couldn't just tell her about the dude ranch? Visitors came without proper attire for that, too.

Bracing himself for a barrage of questions, he was surprised when all she said was "Who does the laundry?"

Not that it mattered, but "I do."

They'd reached the house. He wasn't sure if that was a good thing or bad. He was putting her in an upstairs bedroom. The one at the end of the hall furthest away from the staircase.

He'd be maintaining his usual position on the couch in the living area.

With the television on.

But before he could ship her off, they had to eat.

"Single-portion frozen dinners for supper," he told her as he held the kitchen door for her. Watching as she took in the old metal leg Formica topped kitchen table with four matching chairs. Something else he'd seen in a magazine. And paid too much for.

The rest of the kitchen was nothing to notice. Linoleum flooring that needed to be replaced, except that with its creases and cracks—some a product of laying separate squares, some of age and mis-care—completely hid the lines he'd cut in the floor for access when he'd had the basement re-dug five feet deeper than it had been.

Without a word, she walked to the old refrigerator, pulled open the small freezer compartment door on top. "There's nothing here."

There was, actually. Bags of ice.

He walked into the adjoining dining room, the hardwood floors that needed to be refinished completely bare but for the long freezer covering one wall.

Opening it, he was planning to just make the choices and take them out to the kitchen but heard her behind him.

Smelled her slightly flowery horsey scent.

Then felt her beside him, too.

"Wow" was all she said as she stared. "I don't think I've ever seen this many frozen dinners in one place. Not even a grocery store."

He was betting she hadn't been to all that many of those.

Duran would have had a huge household staff.

Still, she seemed game as she studied, then made a choice of Salisbury steak, mashed potatoes, green beans, and a small square of brownie.

He'd been expecting her to go for the rice-and-vegetable medley that he picked. Wednesday night was healthy-eating night. He had his rules. Didn't waver from them.

Just made living easier to know ahead what was coming.

"I had this for the first time a few weeks ago," she told him, smiling.

That momentary look transformed her. And shook him. Suddenly he was in his kitchen with a gorgeous, warm, happy-looking woman.

Instead of the beautiful but prickly genius who'd shown up on his doorstep to ensnare him.

And had been successful in doing so.

"Mike bought groceries—he's pretty much moved into Savannah's house with us—and he had had a couple of these. I was teasing him…he dared me to try one…and I've had three more since."

She was still grinning as she looked up at him. The expression faded immediately. A closed look covering her face.

She'd shown him someone she hadn't planned to share with him. Or anyone?

And he…for a second there…had he actually been jealous of the FBI agent?

A ludicrous thought if ever there was one.

Laying his dinner on the scarred countertop next to the oven, Harc turned the button to preheat the oven. Reached into the refrigerator for the beer he'd been thinking about earlier. Said, "Help yourself to whatever you want to drink." And pulled out his phone as he had a seat at the table.

He didn't look in her direction. What she chose to do was on her. He was working. Not babysitting.

Until he heard something drop hard onto the floor, and his gaze shot to where she'd been standing, leaning on the counter. Having *not* helped herself to anything to drink.

A phone lay on the floor. She was already bending over,

picking up the device, and as she righted herself, he caught a glimpse of skin that had gone completely white.

His chair scraped against the floor with a rough thud, as he shot up and over to her.

Looked over her shoulder to read what was on her screen. When she held it out to make his doing so easier, everything within him tightened.

A reminder that he was on the job.

Not entertaining a guest in his home who'd never had Salisbury steak as a child and had developed an affinity for it as an adult.

He was viewing a live newscast with closed caption.

Something about a cabin that had exploded that evening. He came to the words mid-sentence, but there was something about a gas buildup in a pipe…

No indication where the explosion had happened. Even what state.

"What is this?" he asked, reaching for the phone. She didn't try to maintain control over it. Let it slip away to him as though glad to have it gone.

"The dude ranch where I was meant to stay." Her voice wasn't weak. At all. But it wasn't anything he'd heard that day, either.

It was like she'd seen a ghost. One she recognized. Would fight against. But one she hadn't expected to see.

"I typed in a search for it, to see if I could do a late check-in online, just to make it looked like I was there…" Her voice weak, her words faded off.

With his thumb moving rapid-fire, he scrolled past the live video to read the article accompanying it. The explosion had happened a couple of hours earlier. Only the one cabin had been damaged. No one had been hurt.

And Nicole was still white as a sheet.

"I made the reservation in Charlotte's name. Because

I couldn't pay cash. I used Charlotte's credit card. I'd expected to stay there tonight. It should have been safe. No one knows I was contacting you. I made certain no one followed me out of Phoenix. I made the appointment with you from a library, borrowing a stranger's phone. No one would have any cause to know that I was contacting you or what I was telling you..."

Her words fell off there. She was looking at the device in his hand. Not him.

Not panicking.

Just looking more shaken than she had in the short time he'd known her. A hell of a lot more.

"There's no way anyone could have known I saw your file..."

In between watching her, he was still scrolling. Reading. "There's nothing here that indicates foul play," he finally told her. A gas line into the cabin had exploded. An insurance and public relations nightmare for the ranch owners, to be sure, far more than that if the cabin had been occupied, but still...

"It's cabin seventeen..."

And he knew. "You reserved cabin seventeen." He stopped, watching her, then when she looked at him, when he saw the disbelief in her gaze said, "Or rather, Charlotte did." The designation meant nothing to the facts.

But his instincts had told him clearly that it meant something critical to her.

So he said it again. Just to be clear. "Charlotte was targeted. Not you."

And sleeping arrangements had just changed.

They'd be spending the night together. In the basement.

TIME WAS OF the essence. And wasting.

Someone was out to silence her permanently. Harc and anyone else could think what they liked. She knew.

Had spent the past three months waiting for the other shoe to drop. The one with Duran written on it. Any Duran. And she was it.

With Eduardo in prison and all his interests frozen, those he'd talked into investing with him over the years were all out of luck.

She didn't blame any of them for thinking that her money should be theirs. Lawsuits had already been filed.

And there were those who wouldn't be content to wait for the legal system to play out. Those who didn't trust the system to work in their favor. And those who cared about what they were owed, not about the law. Or doing things legally.

In the event that assets from Eduardo's legal dealings were freed—which was to be expected—any monies left after paying investors could revert to Charlotte. Which would then legally process over to Nicole.

She'd already signed away her rights to it. She didn't want a cent from that man. If there was a way, she'd give him back the genes he'd given her, too.

These were all thoughts she kept to herself as she sat at the table alone and ate Salisbury steak. Swallowing wasn't easy. She did it anyway. She needed her strength.

Both mentally and physically. If she didn't feed her body, her mental faculties could suffer. And they were her only hope.

Harc leaned against the counter as he ate. Fork in one hand, phone in the other. At the rate his thumb was moving along the screen, he was doing nothing but scrolling. Whatever he was looking for appeared to be impossibly difficult for him to find.

He finally set his phone down to pick up his container of food and scoop up the last bite, and while his mouth was still filled with that bite, she said, "I need the files." He stopped chewing, and she sped forward. "The sooner

I get to work, the more chance I have of finding what we need before he finds me. From there, it's all yours. I'll turn over all I find, help you decipher whatever you need, go deeper, anything. And when you have no more need for my skills, I disappear."

She'd turned the planning over to him.

But her job had been clear from the start, and the idea that someone could be after her was no longer just theory. The sooner she got to work, the better chance that she'd be able to finish it in time.

She hadn't considered herself to be in danger until she'd hacked into Mike's computer and had read Harc's file on Wagar. And even then, the danger wasn't inherent until Wagar got notice of a breach on files protected by code she'd written.

"It's possible that there was just a gas leak that caused an explosion," she said aloud the thoughts that kept playing in her mind. She so wanted to believe the cabin being hers had been just a coincidence. "But we can't afford to ignore the possibility that it wasn't," she finished.

Charlotte was targeted, not you.

"And the thing that's off about that is that Wagar doesn't know that I'm onto him yet. No one does but you. So has he been watching for an opportunity to get me all along, without involving FBI agents and Sierra's Web experts—which would bring down a whole lot more heat on him—or is someone else out for me, too?"

"Who stands to benefit by you being gone?" he asked.

"Some women's shelters in San Diego. My assets are in a trust that goes to them. But they aren't privy to the information."

"Who else knows?"

"Just my sister. She's a lawyer. She set it up for me. And drew up the paperwork for me to waive any inheritance or insurance benefit I could receive from Duran, or monies he tries to gift me, if any of his legal assets are left intact. It all goes to the government to be dispersed among families who've lost members to illegal gunfire in this country."

She wished she had copies of it all on her phone. Should have thought to include them in the things she'd brought with her. She needed to know he trusted her legitimacy if she was going to fully trust him to try to keep her safe on the job.

And paranoia wasn't going to serve her or anyone else. She'd come to Harc Taylor. He wasn't out to get her.

Throwing his empty container into the trash, he reached for hers. "You done with that?"

It was cleaned out except for the brownie. She nodded. Pushed the disposable dish toward him. Watched as he took the brownie and finished it off in one bite.

Feeling a few seconds of relief, of anticipation as she looked toward finally getting her mind on the files she knew he had stored someplace, she watched from behind as he washed silverware and dropped it in a drying receptacle. Alongside what looked to be several days' worth of other utensils.

She managed to stave off a sense of looming oppression during the next minutes as Harc helped her bring in her things from the car. Even got distracted by the fact that she'd be spending the night in the same house with him.

The man was drop-dead gorgeous. If you liked the muscled, rugged type.

She never had.

But seemed to be developing a fondness for it. She took in his thick wavy blond hair, the light stubble along his jaw, and the blue eyes…which were pinning her as she stood just inside the front door with all her belongings at her feet.

The room was bare except for a couch and across the large room from there, a large flat screen television set.

A table of sorts sat at one end of the catch. It looked like an old travel trunk, positioned on its end.

Surprised at the bare-bone basics, she looked from the trunk to him.

"I found that up in the attic," he told her, as though his choice of side table was what she'd found odd.

"Your porch is gorgeous, almost to the point of elegant, but your house...has almost no furniture." And what there was looked ancient. As she said the words, the possible lack of a bed that night occurred to her. She glanced toward the stairs, leading up to what she assumed were bedrooms.

She'd just seen a partially burned cabin that she was supposed to have just checked into and she was worried about the ex–CIA agent's decor?

"I've been undercover most of my career. Rented a furnished place in DC during most of it," he said, as though that explained why he had almost state-of-the-art barns, filled with a small used clothing free store to boot, but hadn't bothered to furnish his home.

And as she stood there, waiting for his direction as to where she went with her things, she supposed the facts did explain the man somewhat. They gave her insight into what was important to him.

The realization settled a bit more of the tension inside her.

"I've spent my whole life in elegant mansions," she said aloud. A pampered, adored daughter who had only the control her criminal father allowed her. "I'd rather be here." The truth bore witness to her about herself. She was not only standing in Harc's living room of her own accord, she'd made every single choice that had brought her to that moment.

She was for real.

And…she had work to do.

Chapter Eight

The basic plan had formed. Telling her about it was next on the agenda. Right after he quit putting off getting to it.

Nicole was right. With the cabin explosion he couldn't waste any more time. Nor could he leave the woman standing in a pile of her things in his sad and bedraggled living room.

"I don't entertain," he said, almost a warning to her of what was to come. He wasn't prepared for house guests.

And until he knew more about what they were facing, the few dude-ranch cabins that were ready for guests were out of the question.

"I'm not here to be entertained." Her quiet words drew his gaze to her, and he got stuck there. In the truth pouring out toward him.

She really wanted to be where she was. Danger and all. Because the wealth she'd grown up with, some of which she obviously still had, meant nothing to her. Righting the wrongs she'd helped her father and others commit was all that mattered. He got the message.

It straightened his backbone. "That's good to know because you're going to be sleeping on an air mattress in the basement tonight," he told her. "With me on one down there, too."

"You sleep in the basement?"

He considered the response a good omen for what was to come. She was more interested in him choosing the basement for a bedroom than in the fact that they'd be sharing the space.

"No, I sleep on the couch. The basement has been altered. It's more of a bomb shelter. A bunker, if you will." Other than the company he'd hired to help him build the thing, no one in the world knew it was there.

And right beneath the house.

Her dark eyes widened. "A bunker?" Her delight reached him with such force he almost didn't hear the words. "This is perfect!"

Except that it wasn't.

But he'd get to that.

Not used to sharing full details of any of his work plans with anyone—by their very nature they'd had to be fluid and had changed on a dime—he had to take things one step at a time.

He reached for her suitcase. "The actual space is quite small," he warned her. "I'm single. Didn't figure I needed much."

"I'm good with the air mattress," she told him, picking up the rest of her stuff. A couple of cloth shoulder bags that nestled with the soft-sided briefcase she already had on.

And a steel forty-ounce cup. She'd sipped out of it the second she'd pulled it from her car.

The forty-count package of bottled water she'd insisted had to come in was all that was left on the floor by the door as they headed to the kitchen.

As he carried the thing down the stairs and then the ladder that led to the actual bunker, minutes later, he acknowledged to himself that he could have saved himself the trip simply by telling her what was coming next.

He'd chosen to lug water to save himself from conversation that was coming anyway.

Because he wasn't ready to present a plan he hadn't mentally vented enough? Or because he was still…what?

Fighting the fact that any of the present was even happening?

Was still harboring some notion that he was going to back out?

Because he knew that he was in as much danger being in partnership with the striking Duran heiress as any other force he'd ever faced in his life?

The woman's intelligence, her determination, her willingness to face whatever fear, whatever danger, whatever inconvenience and hardship necessary to undo wrongs… were captivating him.

Had he gotten soft?

Was a lack of total detachment going to prevent him from succeeding with their mission?

Where Wagar was concerned he couldn't remain impartial. He'd sold his soul proving that point. Was working with Duran's daughter going to permanently prevent him from buying it back?

Dropping the water by the wall along the ladder, Harc's attention went straight to the woman sitting on an air mattress he'd pointed out but hadn't yet taken out of the box when he'd left her alone down there. The second mattress, across the small space from the first, was in the process of receiving air from the pump that had come in the box.

"I have a better pump," he said inanely, looking to the closet door to the right of the ladder. The one she was using had clearly worked just fine.

Why did everything she did right, every unexpected move she made rile him so? At a time when it was critical that he be at the top of his game?

"I'm far more interested in what's behind that door," she said, nodding toward the thick metal structure down from where she'd placed his makeshift bed. "A freezer?"

"It's made kind of like a walk-in freezer in a restaurant," he gave a second less-than-stellar response. She just looked so…okay…sitting there.

In a place he'd never really pictured sharing with anyone.

Though he'd purchased two mattresses. Two chairs for the small table. Two sets of linens and towels.

And as it had turned out, the decision had been a good one. He'd made a commitment. Had lives counting on him being at his best. "It's a walk-in safe," he told her. And then added, "We'll get to that shortly."

Pulling out one of the two armless chairs pushed up to the wooden table, he turned it to face her and sat. Bent until his forearms were on his thighs and looked over at her.

"We aren't staying here."

Alarm filled her gaze. "What? Why? What's happened?"

Shaking his head he said, "My communication skills aren't the best. I don't do this. Don't work jobs with partners."

Her gaze was no less intense as she repeated "What's happened?"

"Nothing." With a quick self-check, he phrased, "Nothing that I know of. We're here for tonight. You aren't going to be working from here."

He paused, waiting for her emotional reaction, and sat up straight when none was forthcoming. She was still watching him, he seemed to have her complete attention. And so he said, "As soon as you start in on those files, we risk Wagar being onto us."

She nodded.

"We have no idea how long it's going to take you to find everything we're looking for. How many layers of your code we're going to need to get through to even find what else you might have to decode or hack into."

She nodded again.

"If we stay in one place and Wagar pinpoints the spot, our time will be very limited."

Her expression was concerned but open, too, and he felt his first sense of a possibility that he wasn't on a suicide mission. Or sending her on one.

And he wasn't completely dreading whatever came out of her mouth as she opened it to speak. "At first, I was thinking that him coming to us wouldn't be a bad thing. We'd catch him red-handed." She paused, then said, "But after the cabin explosion…even if it had nothing to do with Wagar…we could be dead before we know he's onto us."

In the bunker, *they'd* be safe. But there were other considerations. "Anyone who is working here or is on the ranch for therapy and all of the horses would be at risk."

He could shut the place down. Board the horses. Stay in the bunker and start over afterward. Had considered the option. But… "Considering that we have no idea how high up Duran's—and now Wagar's—contact is, assuming there is one—and in my expert opinion, there had to be someone, somewhere and likely still is—or Duran wouldn't have capitulated so easily or taken all of the blame himself…"

"He was protecting me."

"Maybe. Somewhat. But why not roll on someone else? Let them take the heat? He surely had enough people in high positions within his holdings to have passed the blame…"

Her eyes narrowed. "You think his guilty plea was to protect someone else. Someone with power over him?"

The consideration couldn't be ignored. But he kept going. "With that said, our best shot at ending this isn't just finding proof to bring Wagar down but…"

"Finding the guy my father's afraid of."

"If we can." He'd thought himself capable of anything. Which had driven him to do…anything. "The point is we don't just want Wagar. We need to draw out everyone."

She nodded. Her gaze steady as she sat on that sheetless mattress and asked, "How do we do that?"

How the woman gave off a sense of inner wealth as she capitulated to a stranger, he had no idea, but he was drawn to her.

And started to consider that with her help, he actually could do the good he'd set out to do when he'd taken on the Wagar case.

When he'd joined the agency to begin with.

"I've got satellite boxes here. A dozen of them. As long as we have the southern sky visible, we'll get internet through them. The service is paid for—an anonymous blanket policy put in place a few years ago…" He paused at the lie that rolled so easily off his tongue.

"You know how to hack into the service," she said.

At which he nodded. And then said, "I also have burner phones and all the supplies needed to survive for long periods of time."

The words, which showed him for a man who did not live above board, didn't seem to faze her. If anything, they appeared to give her strength.

She was sitting up straighter. Appearing fully focused on him. Seeming to accept it all. "These mountains have been holding secrets and those who don't want to be found since the beginning of time," he continued.

Her mouth dropped open before she said, "We're going to hide out in the mountains?"

He nodded. "Not just hide out. I'm hoping, with the change in locations, to lure enforcers out to find us. And we'll know, when they arrive, who they are," he told her.

"Enforcers?"

"Every government agency in the US is protected by enforcement officers. We see who shows up, we have the best chance of finding out who sent them."

"You have a suspicion, don't you?"

He wasn't sure. Didn't disclose his ideas until he was sure enough of what he was dealing with to risk the exposure.

"At this point, I think any number of entities could be involved." Singly, or in partnership. "And because of that cabin explosion, we don't know who might be after you. I want to leave here before daybreak. And we're taking Imperial and Mahogany with us. I plan to have the ranch continue business as usual. I have employees in place to handle every aspect of what goes on here in the event of my absence."

"You planned for the eventuality that you might have to vacate."

Clearly. "I've been involved with the worst of the worst. You don't take that on, live that way, without developing a sense of possible doom."

Her expression softened. "You get that same sense when you realize you grew up with the worst of the worst." Her words were uttered softly. And completely without self-pity.

She understood.

And that was the moment when the last of his doubts fled.

Until their mission was complete, he was all in.

THEY WERE TWO people who had no happily-ever-after waiting in their futures. That was what she took from the conversation with Harc right before they'd packed and turned in for an early night. To get the last bit of sleep on a proper mattress they might have for a while.

He'd loaded saddle bags. Enough for both horses. Had had her load her personal things in a backpack she'd be wearing. They'd worked silently.

She didn't see any computers going into his things. But then, he'd taken a backpack into his freezer safe, so she had no idea what he was bringing from there.

All she needed from him was a flash drive with files on them.

As she lay there in the dark, she understood why the ex-agent had only the basics of furnishings in his home. He didn't intend to spend time there. Or share it with anyone, fill it with family.

Ever.

The porch was where he spent whatever relaxation time he allowed himself.

She could be wrong, but her intuition was well-honed. It came from having to vet everything in her life in terms of how it would appear to her so protective father. From the few friends she had to the lectureships she'd accepted. Even the companies she'd chosen to sell her software to had had to stand up to Eduardo's scrutiny.

And there was no way she was ever going to just be a normal person who could have regular relationships. Not with the baggage she carried.

She'd erased Charlotte Duran's name from the records. She'd never be able to erase the woman from inside of her.

One day in Harc Taylor's company had shown her the truth.

No matter if she cleared her name or not, no matter how many amends she made, she wasn't *mom, dad, and the kids* material. She'd been shaped, from birth, by an international criminal.

And couldn't ask anyone else to sign on to that stigma.

Not that anyone was lining up to do so, she reminded

herself sleepily. Other than Arnold Wagar, she'd never been anywhere close to a proposal in her life. Something else Eduardo had seen to, she was sure. He'd teased a time or two that no one was good enough for his little girl.

Truth was he hadn't been good enough to allow anyone to get that close to her. As in, he'd had too much bad to hide.

"You still want to go ahead with this?" The voice came softly in the dark. She froze for a second, as though Harc could read her thoughts.

She'd thought him sound asleep, the way he'd talked about learning to sleep on the fly, to catch rest whenever and wherever he could—just before he'd headed into the tiny bathroom they were sharing after she'd done her own business there.

Debating whether she should just not answer, let him assume she was asleep, she considered the seriousness of his question.

And the fact that he *wasn't* asleep. "I do." Her tone was unequivocal. Not on purpose, but because that was how she felt.

"What's keeping you up?"

She almost laughed at that. Smiled a little. And said, "Other than the fact that I'm about to go on a dangerous mission with a CIA-trained agent in the hopes of bringing the wrath of hell to our hideout in the mountains so that I can attempt to repair some of the hellacious damage the man I grew up adoring has done?" She tried for levity.

Hardly made it to sarcasm.

"We aren't going to have a mountain hideout." He wasn't kidding. Not even a hint of humor coming at her.

He was awake because he was rethinking the plan? Or helping her altogether?

For a second, the idea of having an out brought relief.

But only for a second. He could quit. There was no out for her. "What's changed?"

She'd seen no more about the explosion, but she had to believe that someone was already after her. Had probably been watching her for a while. Searching her name, watching her credit card. The first time she'd been away from Sierra's Web protective reach, and the cabin she'd rented exploded? At a time she'd likely have been in it, if she'd driven straight there after leaving Phoenix. And even if there wasn't someone on her tail, she couldn't live with herself unless she did everything she could to stop Arnold Wagar.

The guy wasn't just a partner of her father's. He'd put his hands on her after she'd told him quite clearly not to touch. Just hands on her shoulders. An arm around her. But there'd been threat inherent in that touch.

He was a man who would not be told no.

And would make anyone who tried to thwart him, suffer.

It had only been a matter of time.

Shuddering, she lay flat on her back, eyes open, seeing images of shadows where she knew the ceiling to be. Harc hadn't answered her.

"What's changed?" she asked again.

"Nothing's changed. The plan was never to stay in one place. Hence multiple satellite dishes. We use one, leave it up and running, and move on."

She did smile then. "A trail of breadcrumbs," she said, picturing Wagar's face when the only report he got back was a photo of a small box. Or, better yet, saw it for himself.

Then he'd be as good as...her thought stopped midstream. She could not want to be with Harc Taylor because she believed he'd disregard all laws and kill the man they both hated.

"What happens at the end of the trail?" Her question held her fear. Tightly.

"Hopefully one hell of a celebration."

He hadn't known what she was asking. She purposefully hadn't made the query clear.

And in that moment, that lack bothered her most of all.

Chapter Nine

Imperial was used to predawn rides. Harc had taken a lot of them in the eight months he'd owned the place. And the horse. Imperial had been his first. Purchased the day he'd closed on the ranch.

The horse had worked his magic on Harc before he'd even heard of horse therapy. That lesson had come when he'd looked into filling his barn with more wild mustangs. Imperial had been up for auction. He'd acquired Mahogany that way, too. But the others had all come from a horse-rescue operation.

They were rehabilitated animals who'd been injured in the wild.

They knew what it was to be in pain. To suffer alone.

As he pulled to the first flat ground they came to after their initial climb to get up into the range, Harc waited for Mahogany to take the couple of steps to bring himself parallel to Imperial, and then said, "How you doing?"

"Fine." No hesitation in the response. And...maybe even a note of anticipation.

"The plan is to start out slow," he told her. "In terms of my part of things," he quickly clarified. "I want the first satellite base to be close enough to civilization that our trackers think we're underestimating them."

"Arnold would simply put it down to the weakness of a pampered, spoiled young woman," she said. "I don't think he's aware of all the rigorous training my father put me through."

The words carried a wealth of information. Enough so that he knew he needed it deciphered. "Why do you say that?"

"He was certain that he could manipulate me by force." She sounded nonchalant, was glancing toward the rising dawn on the horizon as she spoke, but Harc froze.

"How so?"

"Let's just say he let me know that he could do what he wanted and I couldn't do anything about it. And I let him think that."

Ah. He kept his approval to himself, but it was there. Full force. But he focused on what wasn't. "Did he force you...physically in some way?"

"Not like you mean. We were outside on the back grounds. Isaac... Mike was watching from an upstairs window."

"And your father had cameras all over the grounds." He'd gleaned that from some of the things she'd said the day before.

"Savannah was out in a boat on the water," she said then, her tone soft again. "Watching through binoculars." She was smiling as she turned toward Harc, and in that moment, her face was lovelier than the dawn. "That was before I even knew she existed."

There was a lot more to the story. He wanted it all.

And knew that he couldn't have it. He was on a case. And could only allow himself information, awareness that pertained to it. Lest emotion skew his instincts.

Again.

Whether or not the man they were after had physically

damaged her had been a need-to-know item. There could be residual post-trauma reaction showing up during the key showdown.

The rest was not pertinent to his getting the job done.

"By the way, I noticed my car was gone when we came out this morning. Where'd it go?"

He'd asked for the fob when she'd been getting in the shower. He'd been on his way up to check the grounds before he had her make the ascent.

"I had it driven up to the dude ranch you were supposed to be at, and then towed."

Eyes bugging, mouth dropped, she said, "You what?" There wasn't quite a yell in the voice, but it was close.

"If anyone gets on to you, as Nicole, they could trace it. It's best if someone finds it that they think your destination was where they expected you to be."

"You don't want them to know we're working together. That you're giving me access to Wagar's files."

He nodded.

And the subject just...dropped.

Once again, she'd surprised him.

THEY STOPPED MIDDAY. And while it had only been a few more than twenty-four hours since Nicole had left Phoenix, she felt as though she'd been away for weeks. Was already a different person.

What she was growing into remained to be seen.

They'd spent a good part of the morning crisscrossing back and forth across the same general area. Leaving plenty of evidence that someone had been there.

And that they'd gone back toward home as well.

Their stopping place had been accessed by pure rock, leaving no tracks. The area could be pinged, but the exact location would be difficult to pinpoint.

Harc knew the mountains like a lot of people knew their neighborhoods. He'd already mapped out their daily travels, streams for water collection and fishing, stopping points, her working hours, their sleep hours, and meals.

As they settled into the cave he'd chosen as the one to protect them overnight—more of a really deep indentation in the rockface than a structure that wound back into the mountain—he pulled things out of his packs one by one.

Two blow-up air mattresses like she and Savannah used to float in the pool. "While you work, I'm going to be taking care of all other life-sustaining details," he told her. "Including inflating and deflating as necessary. I'm also going to be fishing, but I'll be within earshot." He reached into his backpack then. "I want you to keep this with you at all times." He handed her a small black electrical device. "It's a walkie-talkie so we don't burn up internet or cell battery needlessly. From this point forward, even when we're riding, I want you to have this clipped to you at all times. It runs on good old-fashioned batteries, and I have a pocket full of them." He unzipped a small pouch inside his backpack to show her the supply. "I intend to stay within bandwidth reach at all times."

Nicole was impressed, feeling stronger and safer, more hopeful that they actually had a chance to succeed in bringing Wagar down, with each item Harc pulled out of his various compartments, but she was filled with nervous tension, too. Needing to get to the files he'd promised her.

Show-and-tell was great, and probably necessary, but every minute that passed without her having access to those files was another minute closer to danger finding them.

He pulled out a couple of handheld, lightweight solar charging packs, showed her how to use them. "We've got more of these, too," he said. "With only sunlight, it takes each one up to seven days to charge. They're all at full capacity right now. It's critical that we monitor them and keep them charging."

In the jeans she'd packed for a trip to the dude ranch, since Savannah had come into her room to chat while she filled her suitcase, and a lightweight long-sleeved shirt, with the riding boots Harc had given her bruising the sides of her thighs in her cross-legged position, Nicole stared over at the ex-agent. "You think we'll be out here more than seven days?"

He'd been reaching into one of the packs he'd hauled in, but stopped, with flannel-shirted arm still inside to look over at her. "I think being out here is our only reality until the job is done. We have no idea how long it's going to take, so we do what it takes to sustain ourselves long-term. We look to the case, every minute of every day, until it's done. We don't look toward where we go next."

He was teaching her. And she felt…honored. Ridiculous, probably, but true nonetheless. He knew who she was, what she'd come from, and he was giving her his respect, too.

The arm he'd shoved into a saddle pack came out, holding a couple of five-inch long cylinders with what looked like drinking lids on top. "These are our water filters. I'll boil water when I can, but when we can't these will work fine." He showed her how to attach them to containers that looked similar to water bottles. And how to easily clean the filters.

The next pack was filled with freeze-dried food. "Four and a half pounds and over seventy servings," Harc said, holding the pack open to show her the contents. "Just boil, let it sit for ten minutes, and you've got a meal."

She nodded. Getting a bit frustrated at the lengths he was going to stall giving her the files she needed. He'd said he was taking care of all the generalities while she worked.

He had water pouches, in the event that they were trapped

and couldn't collect their own. A first aid kit that contained things she'd only seen in the survival training Eduardo had insisted on. A folding shovel. A multipurpose tool.

As he pulled out the various pieces of the tool from its base, he told her what each one did. And she stopped him, nodding. "I'm fully versed in those," she told him. "Eduardo's training, remember?"

He stopped, looked over at her, blinked, as though remembering who she was and why they were there, and then, hands on the thighs of his jeans where he knelt, he nodded. "Sorry—I've taught a lot of these classes..." He handed her the utility tool and continued with, "And I'm always on my own when I'm actually on the job."

She understood, relaxed some. "You're good," she told him. "Continue on." She was humoring him but glad, suddenly to be doing it.

His next glance was all frown. "What are you going to do if I get hurt? Or fall over a cliff?"

Or was shot. His message hit her with a force far stronger than irritation, frustration, need to get to files, or anything else that had crossed her mind as she'd been sitting there.

He hadn't been holding a seminar. Wasting time. Or putting off getting her to work. He'd been protecting her life. Potentially saving it.

The things she'd taken for granted under Eduardo's care.

"I guess I *am* a bit of a spoiled socialite, huh?" she asked with a horrible taste in her mouth.

His gaze sharpened, and the couple of feet between them seemed to disappear as she was certain his warmth enveloped her through that glance even before he spoke. "You are nothing like that," he told her. "You're aware of those around you and of any residual you might be carrying from your past life. You care. And you have the courage and determination to do whatever it takes to repair, too."

He'd known her less than two days.

Still, some of what he'd said resonated deeply inside her. As truth.

And she knew that if she died trying to destroy Wagar's reign of terror, her life would end on a good note. Because she'd have given it up in an effort to right wrongs.

HE'D SAVED THE weapon pack for last. Nicole was clearly aware of the powerful sidearm he carried. He'd had it pretty much in her face the day before.

But he had a smaller, very powerful nine-millimeter for her, too. And plenty of ammunition. Pulling out a silencer, he loaded her gun, stood, and asked her to accompany him outside.

Untying Mahogany and Imperial from the tree he'd left them on, he walked them around the mountain a few yards, retied them, and came back. Handed her the weapon, gave her full tutelage. And when he was done, asked her, "You feel comfortable trying to shoot it?" he asked.

It was the last training session of the day. He'd planned them all the night before, while he'd lain beside her in his bunker, assimilating the job ahead. One he'd taken with no forewarning or briefing whatsoever.

The first one on which he'd have another human being, a noncriminal good person, with him at all times. A partner of sorts.

She'd nodded in response to his question, held out her hand for the weapon. He was waiting for her to look at him. For verbal assurance.

The glance she shot him was squinty-eyed, and not because of the sun—not only was she wearing sunglasses, but the sun was behind a cloud. "You feel comfortable?" he asked a second time.

"I do." She sounded like she was making a vow.

To him.

He shook his head, clearing his mind. And handed her the weapon. Pointed out to the left of them. Across a deep ravine. "See that tree over there? The one with the fallen branch hanging by the trunk? Aim for the leaves on that downed part."

With the gun in one hand, her other hand holding her gun wrist, she held the weapon down by her thighs, looking out. Her long hair was tied back, giving him a view of the slenderness of her neck. A sight that made her appear fragile.

What in the hell was he doing working with her? Taking on her quest?

Getting her killed?

The thought chilled him so much he turned to reach for the gun. Stopped instantly as she raised it. And shot.

Not at the leaves. At the small twig to which they were attached. The entire pile of them dropped down at least a hundred feet into the canyon below.

And he almost chucked. "Let me guess—not just survival training, but target shooting, too?"

She shook her head. "Oddly, no," she said softly, looking out toward her target. "He didn't want me anywhere near guns." Surprised, he cocked his head, was going to respond when she stopped him with "See the rock that looks like an *H*? Right below the two trees that are leaning together?"

Hands in his pockets, he nodded. Then said, "Yeah."

She pulled the trigger again. And within seconds he saw the glint as flying trajectile hit rock, causing sparks.

And he had to ask, "Where did you learn to shoot like that?"

"Through one of the domestic violence shelters that I support."

That she supported. Not just that she lectured for. Or donated to.

He took another note.

Every time he thought he had a handle on the woman, a fairly accurate profile, she surprised him yet again.

"Does Wagar know?" he asked. It could matter in how they played a showdown.

"Eduardo didn't, so no. I'm sure not." She sounded positive. And he remembered what she'd said about the man thinking he could physically force her to do his bidding.

In another lifetime, he'd have needed to know more about that incident. First and foremost, how many times had it repeated itself? And how far had it gone?

He didn't have another lifetime. And the one he did have was pretty much used up. At least in terms of any interpersonal human interaction.

In his current life, he reached for the nine-millimeter. Took off the silencer—used in case someone was already on their trail—put on the safety, and handed it back to her. "Keep this with you at all times as well," he said.

She blinked. Her brows raised. But she took the gun.

"What?" The question came even while he acknowledged that it wasn't a need-to-know thing. That pursuing was inappropriate.

She shook her head.

He turned back toward their makeshift lodging for the rest of the day and night. Letting it go. He thought. When she walked beside him, he turned his head as they stepped in unison. "You looked surprised."

She shrugged. Still said nothing.

Which, instead of shutting him up, drove him further. "Why would you be surprised that I'm arming you? I've made it pretty clear that you need to be able to take care of yourself out here in case you end up on your own." He'd thought he'd been quite clear on that one.

Needed to know that she was prepared for the eventuality.

"You'll trust me with a powerful weapon, yet you continue to stall the one thing I came for. Giving me access to the files that will lead me to Wagar."

He didn't like the *me* in that last bit but let it go. "It's not a matter of trust," he told her, impassioned and not caring if she knew it. "It's a matter of preparedness."

When she said nothing more, he stopped walking, and when she did as well, he turned to face her. "I need to know that you're fully prepared for what you're getting into here," he said. "The minute you access your code, break through it, our location becomes a potential target for some of the world's most dangerous people. Made more so by the fact that there's likely at least one high-up US government official or law enforcement agency mole involved."

She didn't break eye contact. Or even swallow hard. "I'm aware."

He peered down into her eyes. Boring into them. Needing to transmit the critical nature of what he was telling her. "Then how could you possibly want access to files without things firmly in place to withstand whatever attacks might come our way?"

"I wasn't planning to manipulate the code until we were set," she told him quietly. "And not even then, until I'm ready. I need to study the programming first. To get a feel for language used, like…the original coder's signature. I need to see how my own code has been successfully manipulated into files. And I'm hoping to be able to see how many levels deep I'm going to have to go to get to the root before I actually head in."

Right. He had some tech experience himself. Quite a lot of it.

And, once again, he'd sold her short. "You need to do

what I've been doing," he said then. And started walking again.

Relieved to find her moving along right beside him.

Chapter Ten

They'd taken the batteries out of their personal cell phones and left them in the bunker beneath Harc's house. His employees had been told he was called out of the country. He'd left the husband-and-wife team he'd hired to run the dude ranch in charge of his entire place. They'd be staying in one of the non-renovated cottages on the property until he returned.

Nicole hadn't thought about any of the hundred things he'd tended to since she'd descended on him the day before.

And realized another thing about herself she didn't like. Another residue left from her upbringing. Her world was too small.

Which meant her vision beyond herself was as well.

As intelligent as she was, as much as she knew, there was so much more that slipped past her awareness.

He'd shown her how to use the four-cup propane coffee maker to boil water for their packets of lunch. And while the water had been getting hot, he'd pulled the one-burner camping stove out of the bottom of his backpack.

She'd thought they'd be building fires for their cooking needs.

"We can't risk anyone seeing the smoke," he'd told her

when she'd said so. And she'd promised herself that would be the last time she had to ask in order to catch on.

In her old life, her responsibilities and the expectations others had of her had defined her days. Real life didn't come enclosed in those easily definable statistics. There was nothing controlling what might come at her.

As she sat down on the blown-up air mattress, pulling her computer out of her backpack to finally get to work on Thursday afternoon, Nicole realized that she'd had to get away from Savannah, even without the Wagar crisis eating her alive.

Because her sister had taken over where Eduardo had left off. Probably not meaning to. And likely because she'd been following Nicole's indications of what she needed. But her sister had been sheltering her. Limiting the demands on her.

And limiting her exposure to others as well. Or rather, others' exposure to her. The press. All the people she'd known in California, the high-society circle she'd traveled in through Eduardo, the scholars and shelter workers she'd befriended on her own. Sierra's Web had arranged for her privacy from all of them.

Giving her time to heal, Savannah had said. To acclimate.

Nicole didn't think she'd ever really do either. She could move on. Or not. Those were the choices before her.

She'd chosen to move on.

Which meant taking back control of something important that was stolen from her. Something she *could* reacquire. Preventing her work from being used for ill gain.

Harc had refilled the saddle bags with everything he'd removed. As soon as he was done with something, it went back into storage. And all the bags, other than her backpack, were by the cave's entrance. Ready to go at any moment.

He'd rolled large rocks over from two separate spaces

close to the cave's entrance. Had the unfolded shovel leaning against the wall. From what he'd said at lunch, he was planning to dig two separate bathroom holes. One for him, one for her. When it was time to go, the dirt would be swept back into the holes, rocks rolled back over them, to cover any sign of human activity.

Something else she hadn't given a lot of thought to the day before when she'd immediately agreed to head up into the mountains with a man she'd just met.

A man no one knew she was with.

She'd never peed in a hole before.

But she would. She had no doubt about that. The prospect was far better than holding it which was what she'd been doing since they'd left the ranch that morning.

Anticipation swirled through her as she turned on her fully charged laptop and signed into the satellite internet she'd just helped Harc set up.

He approached, his cowboy boots almost silent on the weathered rock face. She saw them, though, watched as they came closer. It was finally happening.

And she was scared out of her wits.

"It's all on here," he said. She didn't dare meet his gaze. Didn't want him to know about the fear sluicing through her. Glanced up to see the tiny, plastic-encased chip he was holding out to her.

She took it gently. Inserted it into her computer.

And focused on the screen.

Afraid. But not entertaining a single doubt. She was where she needed to be. Doing what she had to do.

And...the boots were still there.

She glanced up. All the way that time. Meeting Harc's gaze. "Last chance," he said. "You don't have to do this. Your father stole from you. And he's the one who passed on your programming."

The words made sense. Held truth. She felt the reality of both as she got locked into Harc's intense blue gaze.

Her resolve didn't waver. But she felt better. "Thank you," she nearly whispered and then clicked to open the drive he'd just handed her.

A PART OF him had hoped she'd change her mind. Back out. A very small part. One unfamiliar to him. All in all, he was still the guy who, once signed on, had to give everything he had to the job. To succeed.

And apparently, in spite of nine months of seeming recovery from the at-any-cost determination that had taken over him, he was still, at his core, the guy who couldn't walk away.

He just didn't think it was right that Nicole Compton should have to give up any more of her life—or lose it altogether—for having been born.

Didn't stop him from digging holes slightly smaller than the small boulders that would eventually be rolled back over to cover them. He fed and watered the horses, moving them into a shady area just yards from the cave's opening, with growth that allowed them to graze.

Kind of shaking his head as he did so. Imperial and Mahogany knew more about surviving in the Colorado mountains than he ever would. They'd been born there, wild and free.

And grown into adulthood there, too.

Before they'd been captured and domesticated due to over-population.

Which was one of the reasons he took Imperial out every chance he got. And was glad to get Mahogony back up on the mountain slopes as well.

Chores done, and not liking all the traits he'd seen in himself in the past twenty-four hours but accepting them just the same, Harc sat down between his horses, leaned up against the tree providing sun blockage for them, and opened a burner phone. One of the several he'd brought with him. A minute or two later he was signed on to the satellite internet and went to work himself.

He might not know deep-dive code, but he knew how to find out things. On the web. The dark web. And by hacking into places he shouldn't go, too.

In ways that would never be traced back to him.

And with permission as well. When he'd left the CIA, he'd been told, with no possibility of mistaken reference, that if, on his own, Wagar came to him or he had reason to believe that Wagar was coming after him, he should do what he needed to do.

He was just supposed to have contacted the director before doing so.

Unless, of course, he was in a position that made notification impossible.

He'd deemed his current circumstance one such situation.

Using several of his many aliases, in various ways, he worked until Nicole came out of their naturally provided rock campsite shortly before dinnertime.

When he saw her moving toward the hole he'd dug for her, he got up and walked in the opposite direction. Giving her time. Privacy.

Drawing a very clear boundary for himself between the job and personal time. There'd be none of the latter between them. Even in knowing how long she took in the bathroom.

As he had the thought, he had a flash of memory. The night before. Nicole coming out of the tiny lavatory in the bunker. At his suggestion she'd showered, before putting on the sweats, matching top and bottom, he'd brought from the barn's stash for her to sleep in. And she'd still only been ten minutes. So...too late to be spared one personal detail. She was quick with bathroom usage.

And he had far more important matters to contend with. Heading back toward the horses, he saw Nicole standing there, petting Mahogany, and picked up his pace.

"What'd you find?" he asked before he was even abreast of her.

As important, how exposed were they?

His own searches could have nudged a radar or two, but none that should put their lives in immediate danger.

If anything, he could have let a former trusted technical expert at the CIA know that he'd been online and put his own ethics in question.

A one-in-a-million chance, almost literally. The woman would have had to be searching a ten-year-old alias to spot his use of it to enter an official portal.

He didn't care a hell of a lot, either way.

"It's very clear that whoever created those files is hiding something," she said. "The levels of security and depth of walls to get to a source is intimidating. Or would be if you hadn't written the basis of the code."

He nodded. Watching her. Reading her facial expression, her body language as much as hearing her words.

She was onto something. She knew it.

And it concerned her.

"Can you break through it?"

"I can."

"Did you?"

"Not yet."

He wasn't sorry to hear that. And knew he should be. Someone who only wanted the job done, who wanted Wagar stopped and others exposed and brought to justice would be sorry.

Except that… "It's best if we find out all we can before we breach that final wall," he said aloud.

He thought he saw gratitude flash in the brown eyes that were steady on his. "I breached a basic security curtain," she said then. "It shouldn't raise any concerns, but it could. If someone was on the lookout for any hint of, say, me getting in."

He held eye contact as he said, "If Wagar has a team on the lookout for you accessing your code." He had to spell it right out. For both of their sakes.

Her nod was slow. But sure. Aware.

Adrenaline pumped through Harc. From a source he hadn't felt in a while. More than one of them. He was ready to jump from a plane without a parachute to get this guy. Could finally feel victory in his grasp.

And… God help him…he was attracted to the woman who was helping him. To her looks, absolutely. She was gorgeous, and he wasn't dead. But it was more than that. Her brain turned him on. Her ability to take a deep breath and do the hard job.

Her stamina and determination.

He'd spent almost all his undercover time with women in his sphere. Even in relationships with them when the situation required his going that far. Never, ever had the fact that they were helping him reach his goal attracted him to them.

Because they hadn't known the part they were playing in his schemes.

This one, Nicole Compton, did. But it wasn't that that was getting to him. He almost wished it was. To the contrary, it was the hint of vulnerability that had him wanting to throw the case to the wind and get her into protective custody.

To protect her himself. For more than just a day. Or a case.

As if he was a man a woman could ever trust to have her back outside of work. Thirty-six years and it had never happened. He could keep woman physically safe all day long.

Emotionally...he was just no good at that.

Not a welcome realization.

A fact to be aware of. To guard against.

All that was required to do that was to stay focused on work. Also pretty much a given for him. "Arnold Wagar left the country the afternoon before your father was arrested." He just blurted the news right out there.

"Someone was onto Isaac and Savannah. Or me. All of us."

He nodded. It was the logical assessment. Except, "You said, and by the account I read, your father was taken unaware when you arrived home that night."

They'd reached the edge of the cave. When Nicole ducked down to head inside and then straightened once there, he followed suit. The conversation was what mattered. Not where they held it.

She leaned against the wall, closed her eyes, and took a deep breath.

Her lips tight with tension.

Signs of stress. Of fear.

And he knew.

With the afternoon she'd spent and the news just imparted, she'd felt exposed outside.

Which he translated to mean that fear was taking hold. The enormity of the task she'd taken on, the danger involved was kicking in.

There was more that he needed to divulge. But it could wait long enough for her to catch a breath. To get on top of any panic the afternoon's work might be bringing down upon her.

And if fear won, if he needed to get her into protective

custody while he fought on without her, then he'd respect that choice, too.

Reaching for the pack that held their cellophane wrapped meals, he grabbed two, and the propane coffee maker, and headed toward the door. He'd be right there.

Not for the job, but because she seemed to need it.

They'd take a break from all that was bad. Concentrate on simple things. Comforting things. Like eating. And talking about horses. He'd amassed a lot of stories on that topic in the past eight months.

Above all, he was going to stay within her sights as she hid out.

Giving her a sense of security, even if ultimately it was a false one.

She had a job to do to buy her freedom. He knew what failing would cost her. So he would do everything he could to see that she succeeded.

To stop Wagar—absolutely, hands down, no doubt there. But his quest had taken on new purpose, too.

He was too late to buy back his own future, but he was going to help Charlotte Duran segue into the life Nicole Compton was trying to give her.

No matter what.

Chapter Eleven

He'd brought in the bed rolls hooked to the backs of their saddles while she'd been working. Hers sat on end by her backpack.

Shaking inside, feeling weak in ways she never had before, Nicole wouldn't let herself sink to the mattress. Or head out to Mahogany and ride off into the sunset.

Both options were tempting.

She'd always believed herself a strong person. Was only now realizing just how much Eduardo had shielded her from challenges that would have grown her strength.

That thought alone kept her standing.

She'd grow whatever she had to grow, cultivate with her last breath. She was not going to succumb to acceptance of the life her father had created for her. Had already started the battle three months before when she'd planned her own middle of the night escape and had successfully maneuvered hours of freedom for herself. Relying on the help of people with whom she'd become acquainted through her own efforts. People who'd never met her father.

And who Eduardo had not known.

So how did one of those people end up with a longer term Wagar association? She had to tell Harc. Just needed a minute to breathe before going down into the dark abyss with him.

He'd have questions, rapid-fire, which would require a clear mind and steady hands to go with all her resolve. To figure out how to more efficiently access the well of strength that had been boiling inside her for years.

To silence the fears.

Something she was now beginning to see Eduardo had also cultivated within her. From day one everything had always come down to one thing: Her safety. A trip. A school. A toy she wanted. The kind of lights on the Christmas tree. Even the bed—the room—she slept in.

She'd thought all of that showering of concern, the watching out for her at every turn had been a result of the great love he felt for her.

"He kept me weak, under his control, by making me afraid," she said aloud then, standing up straight as the light flashed inside her. All the studies she'd done, the work with domestic violence victims...mental manipulation was a huge part of that. She'd studied, lectured, she'd talked. She'd listened to women tell their stories to learn more, to be able to help others in their living reality. And she hadn't seen that she was one of them.

The fear that was threatening to suffocate her was in her mind as much as anything else. And something that she could fight. By not thinking about it. Dwelling. Remunerating.

She had to concentrate on the moment. The tasks directly in front of her. And let the future wait for her to affect it.

Approaching the opening of the cave and the back of the man kneeling over boiling water in a pot, she noticed how Harc Taylor's shoulders nearly spanned the width of the temporary abode, and took strength from them, too. She wasn't in the world alone, even if it felt that way.

She wasn't fighting her current battle alone.

He hadn't responded to her words. She wasn't sure he'd heard them. Or that he'd even needed to do so. But she made sure he heard what he had to know. "I've been having moments of panic for as long as I can remember. They always come *after* I get through whatever it is I'm doing. Never during. I long ago deemed it the *fall-apart aftermath*. And I also always work my way through those times. Thank you for the moment to do so."

He'd seen her at her worst. She was back.

He'd accept her or he wouldn't. He wasn't going to stop her.

Not that after her work that afternoon, she had the choice to give up and go home. She'd set retribution in motion.

"I find that focusing on menial tasks helps."

What? She stared at his back. He expected her to believe that... "You have panic attacks?"

The shoulder shrugged. "Probably not in the same way you're describing. I have doubts."

"Doubts that create negative feelings?"

He shrugged again. And then said, "Wagar flew into San Diego by private jet this morning."

Pulling out their camp forks and water filters, she attached the latter to the water bottles Harc had filled earlier. Didn't ask him how he'd gleaned his information. "Conveniently after the explosion last night," she said, warding off a shiver.

He turned, handing her the plastic bowl that held the prepared Alfredo with peas that had been little more than dried crunchy pieces vacuum packed into a pouch fifteen minutes before. He hadn't asked what she wanted for dinner.

Didn't much matter. He had what he had. Enough to feed them for over a week. More if he was able to catch any fish.

"I found a username today that is of note," she said

slowly as she chewed and swallowed. The pasta pieces were the right texture, the sauce palatable. She needed the nutrition. Focusing on dinner rather than the conversation staved off latent churning inside her.

Harc, who was seated on his blanketed mattress across from her, stopped chewing. Holding his bowl up by his chest, his spoon suspended in air not far from it, he looked at her.

And she looked back.

At the thick blond hair, the focus that was evident in his posture, his stiff expression as much as his eyes. She was on the right course.

The sensation brought by the thought wiped any hint of fear from her system as she said, "B M Megee, all lowercase. The email address of my mentor in college. A woman who has been instrumental in shaping my lectureship engagements, but more, one who I trusted explicitly."

Which was the most key point.

He put down his bowl. Stood. Walked to the edge of their enclosure, looked out, and then going back for his bowl, returned to the entrance and stood there sideways, looking between her and what she supposed was the horses. "What does she know that we wouldn't want Eduardo or Wagar to know?"

And a slice of fear returned, shooting through her before she shut it down. With a dose of anger toward those who thought it was okay to take control of lives that were not their own.

Okay to get rich by hurting people.

"Nothing that I can specifically recall," she told him. "I was always careful not to mention my father or home life. A choice instilled in from my earliest memory. And in college, I didn't talk about it because I'd developed a sense of guilt over how easy I'd had it all my life, while so many struggled just to put a roof over their heads. But with Barbie...in a low moment... I could have expressed feelings that others could use to manipulate me."

And there was the crux of the day's panic.

Along with, "The woman was everything I'd ever hoped to be. An acclaimed academic who gave her life to studying societal problems, with an emphasis on women in society and finding current-day, in-the-moment solutions where she could."

Another bite on the way to his mouth, Harc stopped it midway, nodded. Jutted his chin for a moment and asked, "Dedicated enough to take financial support for her causes? If, say, the father of one of her star students wanted to contribute but do so anonymously? So his daughter wouldn't find out?"

Of course she would have. The answer didn't have to be spoken. Its force swirled around the cave.

"And knowing Eduardo, once she'd accepted the assistance, she'd have been on his hook. He never gave something for nothing. He'd have studied her vulnerabilities and hit her where it would squeeze the hardest."

He scraped his bowl. Took the last half bite and held it and the spork as he said, "We have to assume she was reporting to him from the very beginning."

The culvert in her gut was telling her the same.

But she finished her dinner. Handed him the dish he'd wash along with their meager cutlery and got up to roll out her sleeping bag.

She'd made her bed and was going to have to lie—and maybe die—in it.

PIECES FLEW AROUND Harc's air space, sometimes moving into line to orbit there, sometimes all just randomly floating on their own. Wagar's timing on leaving and reentering the country had him greatly concerned.

It was like the guy had a psychic telling him when to come and when to go. Apart from that, how could he have known that Eduardo's capitulation was eminent when none of the players bringing him down knew? If the good guys didn't know, how could a mole among them have tipped him off?

And now the professor—he'd done his homework on her that night after dinner—and didn't like what he'd found.

A bankruptcy from years before. A cantankerous divorce. And a son with a jail record. All rife for making one vulnerable to what looked like easy money for doing nothing wrong.

Working as an unofficial, undercover bodyguard. Helping a wealthy man keep his only daughter safe while she ventured out into the world.

It could be more than that. The woman might have been an old lover of Eduardo's who'd been in his camp for years. Perhaps her husband had been doing business with Eduardo for years and the woman had been blackmailed.

Maybe she'd just needed money for her son and knowing how wealthy her mentee's father was, had sought out Eduardo for help.

And it could be less, too. Because Barbie MeGee had been Charlotte's mentor, it was possible that she'd just been on Eduardo and Wagar's radar just as someone to watch. The woman might've not even known.

As soon as he'd gleaned what he could quickly, he'd shut down the satellite signal that could potentially lead someone to their vicinity.

The goal he ultimately wanted.

To see who showed up, get them temporarily incapacitated, and turn them in.

Not in the middle of the night if he could avoid it.

The body's ability to regenerate was important.

Other than a few necessities—like the gun and ammo that never left his reach when he was working—all their supplies were packed in the saddlebags that were already attached to the two saddles on the ground just inside the door of their cave.

And in the backpacks that they'd put on when they arose before dawn to head out.

The packs would make saddling the horses a bit more awkward but much quicker, too. Time was of an essence.

As was the woman sleeping just a couple of yards away from him. Unless she was as good as deepfake as he was, the deep, even breathing told him she'd drifted off almost as soon as they'd laid down.

She'd made a soft comment. Something about the light of the moon shining into their space. He'd been spending the half hour since, trying to get his body to forget she was there, while his mind focused on keeping her alive and by his side until the job was through.

His body needed a good sleep, and he watched the display of randomly floating words behind his closed lids as he drifted off.

Imperial's hoof. Lifting. Lowering...

Harc sat straight up in his unzipped sleeping bag, gun in hand and cocked by the time he was fully awake. And heard the sound again. Imperial scraping the ground.

"Nicole. *Charlotte*," he hissed the name that was more likely to be recognizable to her unconscious mind as he slid into his waiting boots as he stood. She sat up. He heard the movement, saw it, too, out of the corner of his eye, on his way to the cave's entrance.

By the time he'd had a full screening of the land encompassing their little hideaway, she was right behind him, her sleeping roll under her arm.

Just as he'd described when he'd told her what to do if they had to leave in a hurry. She'd washed up before bed. He'd left her alone inside to do so. But he'd insisted that, like him, she sleep fully dressed.

She didn't ask questions. Just dropped the bag and went back for his. He heard a hiss as air left mattresses.

"Quickly," he said to her, fighting an urge to do it all himself, in order to keep his eye on the horizon. It was dark, and he knew what to look for.

"Gun loaded and in your waistband," he added.

And as soon as she appeared next to him a second time, he grabbed Mahogany's saddle. When he returned for Imperial's she'd already used the branch he'd left by the door to sweep the area of any random marking they might have left behind and was in her saddle, ready to go by the time his horse was saddled.

He shoved the two boulders, and within a minute, they'd left the space behind and were already heading upward, keeping cover in brush, behind tree clusters, as they rounded the mountain.

Other than some tamped-down grass where the horses had grazed the day before, there'd be no sign of any habitation at their campsite. And the grazing could have been done by numerous wild animals sharing the landscape with them.

Including mustangs just like Imperial and Mahogany.

Perhaps even biological relatives of theirs.

After several minutes of riding, they came to an area wide enough to ride side by side, and he slowed Imperial until Mahogany was abreast of him. Harc glanced over at Nicole. "You doing okay?" he asked.

They'd had an hour less sleep than he'd planned, but he'd

rested. And hoped she had, too. He couldn't tell much in the darkness.

"Other than needing to pee, yes," she told him, speaking as softly as he had.

Yeah, he had to go, too. Would have liked for them to get farther up the mountain from any potential ping to the satellite they'd been running but didn't relish dealing with wet trousers, either. He found a place to dismount, insisted that she do her business between the two horses while he moved behind a rock.

Privacy, modesty didn't matter a hell of lot when death was knocking.

Less than two minutes later, they were on the move again. And while Harc couldn't speak for Nicole, he didn't feel the least bit awkward for their stop.

The mission they were on, the lives they'd come from, the futures they were fighting for, and the powers trying to prevent them from reaching their goals had stripped away so much of what defined usual social conduct.

Or even the ability to be bothered by their lack.

He continued to keep close watch, to listen, and to pay attention to Imperial. The horse, who'd had nostrils flaring when Harc had exited the cave, seemed to have calmed down.

Which meant "We might be escaping a meandering bear. A mountain lion. Or pack of wolves, not necessarily a human predator," he told Nicole. Didn't really believe that to be the case. But hoped it was.

He felt fully confident in his ability to handle any encounter with mountain animal life.

He'd also been careful not to leave any trash or hint of food smell out, and unless they were cornered or rabid, most of the animals would steer clear of human scent.

"But we're escaping something," she said, her tone concerned but not betraying a hint of fear. More like a determined need to know.

"That's my belief."

"On what grounds?"

He glanced at her, looking for some sign of doubt in her posture. Her expression. The fading moon didn't help much. And dawn wasn't close enough to shine any light on the moment.

"You doubting me?" he asked. Didn't much matter to the case at hand. Except that he had to know that she wasn't going to question his authority the next time he said *Move*.

"Not at all. I'm just done being content with being kept in the dark regarding the dangers that lurk. I don't want protection. Or rather, I do, but I want informed protection. I need to be prepared to protect myself."

The woman was eleven years younger than him and yet continued to surprise him with her wisdom.

He'd been about to tell her exactly what tipped him off, but she spoke again. "I don't want to be told what I can't do so I don't get hurt. I need to know the risk and how best to handle it so that I don't get hurt."

He nodded. And said, "Horses have a hearing range of two miles. Sometimes a little more. They also sense heartbeats. When they're together in the wild, on open range, the herd will synchronize heartbeats to be warned of danger more quickly. They can actually hear a human heartbeat from four feet away."

He was going around the block with the explanation. But with what she'd just said, he felt compelled to tell her not only what had triggered him awake but why.

"Studies have shown that this happens with domesticated animals as well."

"Which is one reason why horse therapy works," she

said then, seemingly willing to travel along his tangent with him.

Perhaps not quite ready to know what he knew?

Buying herself time to process a sentence at a time?

"I'm guessing the horse can tell when the human is experiencing a surge of anxiety by accelerated heartrate," she continued.

"That's part of it," he told her. At least in his still very limited experience it was. And he then continued with, "Imperial and I have been working together, with the help of a trainer. When he senses danger, he's been trained not to whinny or make big moves. He scrapes his hooves against the ground. This calms him and keeps Mahogany calmer."

"You heard his hooves scraping," she guessed correctly.

"And I'm trained to wake up at the sound," he concluded, with an attempt at a hint of humor. Didn't quite pull it off.

Felt better for trying.

But knew he needed to include her more in his thoughts. "This is what we want. To draw him out here where we have a much better chance of identifying him. And capturing him. Even if 'him' is just hired hands."

He had ways of getting information out of underlings. His success rate had given him a reputation that was known through various agencies.

He chose not to share that part. Not unless he had to.

"And I need time to get the evidence to incriminate him," Nicole said. She'd tied back her hair when they'd stopped. Made seeing her expression a bit easier with the help of dawn creeping upon them.

He saw tension there.

"Exactly." There was more he could say, details he could give, agencies he'd have to call in when the timing was right, but for the moment, he left it at that.

Chapter Twelve

She'd read a lot about minimalist existence. Had thought she'd like to at least try a week or two of living that way, just to know how it felt.

Except for the constant threat of danger, Nicole wasn't hating the experience. Granted, she'd only been away from society, living with only the basics, for a little more than twenty-four hours.

And even if there were no danger and the gorgeous expanse of mountain glory eventually took on a sameness, being with Harc Taylor and his horses prevented any chance of boredom setting in.

Because it was imperative that she keep herself out of the pool of fear threatening to drown her, she was clinging to the source of good feeling in her immediate sphere.

The man whose every move caught her attention. Made more potent by his care for his horses. And his sharing them with her.

It was as though she had three soldiers marching in step with her as she fought her battle for freedom from a past she'd had little control over.

And if, while she was riding with the man, she got lost in the occasional fantasy about what it would be like to have his hands on her instead of his reins, his lips touching hers rather than sipping from the filter attached to his water bottle, who was she hurting?

To the contrary, she was helping...on a scope she could only imagine. By maintaining an emotional equilibrium that would allow her to focus and crack the code—keeping herself out of the panic mire—she'd be saving untold number of lives.

And maybe her own, too.

As she rode through dark to dawn and into full morning that Friday, Nicole became aware of another goal added to her list of things she had to accomplish out there.

Making certain that Harc Taylor made it back to his ranch. His horses.

Too late, she was seeing what she'd done to him, to the new life he'd created. She'd been so certain, based on what she'd read, that all he cared about was getting the bad guys, that, like Mike, he'd chosen to dedicate his life to making the world safer and had left his life's work due to major career fail.

Inadvertently because of her and her coding.

She'd thought by seeking him out, she was handing him what he most needed as well. The chance to succeed, to get his man. To quiet the demons with which he'd seemed to have ended his career. But after seeing him with Imperial and Mahogany, seeing the supplies in his barn, watching him in the mountains, an awareness was growing within her. Harc hadn't spent the past nine months pining for the life he'd been meant to live. He'd been finding it.

The thought spurred her to push herself, to focus more fully than ever, to block out everything except following where the code led.

They'd been riding for a few hours, climbing, then on flat ground, passing caves and laybys before climbing again—

with intermittent stops for stretching and snacks—when, on one such flat ground, Harc slowed to a stop.

"That cave," he said, pointing to a larger, deeper crevice than they'd been in the night before.

Glancing around, she liked the spot but was surprised by the stop. "It's only mid-morning."

"I don't want to bed down where the satellite signal has been used," he told her. Which made total sense. Most particularly with considering the hour early start to the day.

With her morning revelations driving her, Nicole grabbed her laptop, a satellite modem, and her water bottle and headed to the shade of a big tree, leaving Harc to take care of the horses and anything else that he deemed necessary.

Unlike the day before, she didn't hold back. Didn't go slowly, determining the lay of the land. She didn't hesitate out of fear of the fallback.

She dove hard and deep. Just as she'd been imagining she would before she'd acquired Harc Taylor's assistance. And became more acutely aware of the danger Eduardo Duran had been protecting her from all those years.

She'd wanted out of her gilded prison, and she'd most definitely accomplished the escape.

Trails led to trails. Not all of them connected to each other. But all connected, in one way or another, to the security code she'd written when she was fourteen.

Her heart pounded when she recognized Glob, too. A program she'd written specifically for her father to show all his monies in one place, while making invisible the accounts in which they sat.

"What?" Harc's voice brought her head up sharply. He was seated a few yards away, his phone in hand.

She shook her head. "I didn't say anything."

"You just hissed."

"I'm finding multiple different entities that have been

using a program I wrote specifically for Eduardo's business dealings, back when I thought they were legally held. It allows the user to set up a system by which he can see all his assets in one place, without disclosing where they came from or where they're currently sitting. It attached to his international accounts all over the world but would prevent anyone who was trying to hack him or who wanted to siphon off from him a little at a time from having access to them. He'd told me that he had separate accounting systems for every legal holding, rather than one global accounting firm, department, or entity, to prevent someone from getting greedy but more to protect them from being targets of blackmail."

It had made perfect sense to her at the time. Had made her admire and love her father more for his constant awareness of others and how being associated with him could put them at risk.

When, in truth, he'd been protecting himself from all the people, the countries, he'd been screwing over.

Harc was watching her. And while she allowed herself some of the warmth filling her at his gaze, she didn't get lost in the sensation. "What I'm finding here is frightening, Harc," she told him, business partner to business partner. "Glob is supposed to bring every interest together in one place. But in Wagar's files, I'm find multiple different global accounts. In other words..."

"We're either dealing with multiple Eduardo Durans around the world or Wagar is using the program on a different scale than your father did."

He could be right, though she didn't think so. "Dividing up his assets into categories," she went with his theory for a minute. "And having a separate Glob account for each category."

It wasn't how the program was designed to work. But

with all the levels of security and firewalls she'd been working her way around, she could definitely see Wagar being paranoid. And even more cautious than Eduardo had been.

"The program worked," she said then, not because it was one she'd written but because they had to face facts. "Eduardo was not caught because of his illegal business activities," she reminded. "None of you could breach his security protocols, largely because of Glob. He was only caught because of my entering my DNA in that database and my sister coming to find me."

The reminder mattered right then. "Wagar clearly was aware of the program's efficiency," she said then. "So why am I seeing it used on files that all seem to be pointing to separate identities?"

She saw the truth dawn as a darkening in Harc's eyes, a glint, and the sharpening of his features as they tensed. "Wagar's the kingpin, not Eduardo. Duran was just one of the man's many generals," he summed up.

It was beginning to look that way. She didn't speak the alarming fact aloud. Just nodded.

And watched Harc's back as he got up and walked away.

HARC STRODE STRAIGHT to his backpack. To the phone he'd taken out of the safe where he'd stored Wagar's files. And sent the encrypted message he hadn't expected to send.

Nicole would likely hate him.

She'd have to be alive to do that.

He'd take that as his win.

Her life over her affection.

If his source was still connected.

He couldn't just call in. Not only did he risk being pulled off the case since he was officially retired, but since he had no idea where a mole might be, he risked the entire operation he and Nicole had set in place.

And her possible cooperation. No one could compel her to work.

He waited five minutes. Ten. On guard over every conceivable, foreseeable danger that could have them in its sights.

He could get Nicole to a safe house. To a bunker. To a government building. All of which could be targeted and breached.

On the move, in the Colorado mountains—which were dense and rugged—lesser men than him had remained hidden for lifetimes. All he needed was the days, or weeks, it would take Nicole to get their evidence.

She had to have internet. His plan was still the best there was. Keep her moving. Burying used satellites in their sewage holes.

It just no longer included any attempt to lure the enemy to them.

Wagar as the kingpin was a complete game changer. Something he'd never even considered. The man was something of a boob. A privileged kid who'd grown into a man with too much power, certainly, one who thought himself above God, probably—but a kingpin?

Just didn't fit.

Arnold Wagar didn't have the ability to lead men. Or to command loyalty. He wasn't the richest man in the world. No matter how many hidden assets he held.

Harc would bet his life on that much.

So why was everything pointing to him?

Ten minutes passed in cyber silence. He and Mike Reynolds had once been two men of one mind. Where the Duran case was concerned, they'd shared a wavelength that had been unlike anything Harc had ever seen.

With Charlotte heading to a dude ranch for a week, one that Mike would have checked up on and would have seen the explosion…he'd only held out contacting the FBI agent about Nicole's name change, her coming to him, because he'd been confident that he could keep Nicole safe while they ended the last detail of the years' long case.

And because she'd only agreed to do the work no one else could do if he abided by her terms.

Her hacking of an FBI agent's computer, while a major infraction, wasn't the only reason she'd given for keeping her work secret. She'd refused to have her sister or Sierra's Web involved.

He'd truly believed—still did—that she'd stop her work, go completely off the grid, and finish it on her own someplace if she believed her terms had been compromised.

While he'd still been in sole possession of the files she'd needed, he'd had an upper hand. That was no longer the case.

And yeah, a part of him had been a bit too jazzed at the idea of riding out of the mountains with a bound and gagged Arnold Wagar hanging over the back of his horse.

Instead of being the hero, he'd just succeeded in proving to himself that he was as rogue as he'd been accused of being. Had lost the ability to properly measure risks involved, protocols, to make the smartest choices when in sight of getting the win.

Instead, he'd allowed a gorgeous, twenty-five-year-old genius, one he'd been studying for nearly a year, to get to him. To show him his weaknesses.

Except…they were on a cusp, like never before. If he could actually help end the Duran/Wagar reign of terror once and for all, he had to see things through. To walk away would disgust him worse than anything he did to see that particular job done.

He glanced over at the woman who'd gotten to him more than any other single person in his adult life. Hunched over her computer, her fingers flew on the keys, she studied, and they flew some more. Jealousy hit him.

Squinting, he focused on her more clearly. He was jealous of what? The computer keys? A screen?

The files on them?

Because they compelled such complete attention from her? Because she'd been willing to risk her life to get them?

Before his questions could lead to answers he didn't want, Harc felt the vibration against his palm. Stood behind Imperial, out of view of Nicole—not that she had attention on him—to see the message that had come in to his scrambled phone.

From the only other one that he'd open a message from on that line.

Encryption in place.

The code was their second level of security—letting him know, in the exact way the message had been composed, numbers of characters per word, even if the word itself couldn't be completed.

He finger typed to unscramble the message.

And took his first full breath since Nicole had told him what she'd just found.

A world of international generals was too big just for the two of them.

But with Mike off grid, having their backs—along with, Harc was sure, the entire Sierra's Web firm—and with the FBI agent's readiness to get several US federal protection agencies involved with a single symbol sent his way on the phone Harc held—or a twelve-hour lack of communication on same—Harc felt a whole lot better.

For his sake. And Nicole's.

Not that he ever expected her to see it that way.

HARC SEEMED DIFFERENT when he approached to let her know it was time to go. Nicole felt differently, too. Not only had they firmly entered the thick of things, but their enemy was more convoluted than they thought.

Not that she knew what Harc was thinking.

She was just glad that he was. Thinking. Focused.

They ate a quick meal—a mixture of scrambled eggs, pork, hashbrowns, and onions—that he'd boiled into edible form from their freeze-dried packs. She continued to work while she ate. He didn't demur.

She took care of personal business while he buried the satellite along with the manure the horses had deposited during the stop, and they were once again riding up. Over. And then downward, into a culvert on the opposite side of the peak from which they'd started.

Didn't matter how low they went as long they had an unobstructed view of the southern sky. He didn't have a lot to say as they rode, single file more than side by side, and she was glad for the time to assimilate all that she'd taken in during the time she'd had online. To mentally organize, categorize. To see patterns in what she knew.

To figure out the quickest way to get to what she didn't know.

Was she missing something she should already have picked up on? Or was more digging required.

Harc was counting on her. Many innocent people needed her.

She needed to make Savannah proud.

"You have any family?" she asked Harc as he slowed for Mahogany to reach Imperial's side. She was grasping, almost desperately, for conversation that would engage her. Resorting to focusing on him to revert her thoughts from places that would weaken her.

"Nope."

Just the one word. Neither the response nor the brevity of it surprised her. But it took her down a path of possible scenarios for his upbringing that distracted her from thoughts of things that would trigger panic within her.

"My folks were both military." His words fell into a full minute of silence. And she turned to see him looking out at the world around them. The mountains climbing up around them on all sides. "My father was one of the first America soldiers killed in Iraq after 9/11."

The words struck her deeply. On many levels. She'd thought they were similar—her and Harc. Islands in a world of societal acceptance. And maybe on some level they were. But he was, paternally, biologically, the complete antithesis of her.

Explained why Harc had decided on a life dedicated to protecting his country. To the exclusion of all else.

"And your mother?" she asked.

"She died on a skydiving training mission of all things. I barely remember her. I was raised by my father. And the people he hired to care for me when he deployed."

So they had some similarities. Not knowing their mothers. Having only paternal influence to guide them.

And people who were paid to care for them.

He moved, and through her peripheral vision, she could see his face turned in her direction. She pretended not to notice. Withstood the scrutiny through years of practice.

Taking an odd, and potentially dangerous, comfort from the part of their family disfunctions that they did share.

Not questioning why it mattered—that she and Harcus Taylor shared similarities—just going where she had to go mentally to maintain the emotional equilibrium that would allow her to be most productive.

"You mentioned Savannah," he said right then. Almost as though he'd read her thoughts and was challenging her choice to focus on him instead of the things that made her life seem like…a lie. Her sister welcoming her in, being a real loving family…as desperately as Nicole wanted it all, she was afraid to believe.

Didn't feel worthy.

Not yet. Not until she could get rid of the Charlotte Duran in her.

She hadn't responded to his comment. Was breathing a sigh of relief that he'd let it drop when he said, "You didn't mention your mother. Was she not as welcoming when you suddenly reappeared?"

What? Her head shot sideways, her gaze pinning him. "You think she'd shun me? The kidnapping wasn't my fault. I couldn't help what…"

She stopped. Seeing the soft look in his intense blue eyes. The slight nod of his chin.

He didn't say a word.

But she saw what he'd done.

He'd known. Not that it took a scientist, or even a trained psychologist, to figure out she had issues feeling good enough to live in her sister's world. But instead of talking sense to her, talking her through it all, he'd brought it out of her.

Truth from her own heart and soul.

"My mother passed away a couple of years ago after an extended illness," she said aloud, almost defensively.

But she wasn't taking offense due to what he'd said.

The walls were going up because in those last few moments of internal truth, her momentarily opened heart had taken a small bit of him inside.

Chapter Thirteen

Harc didn't hear back from Mike over the next couple of hours. Didn't know what, if anything, the agent knew about the explosion at the dude ranch.

He figured Mike would check up on his fiancée's little sister's whereabouts, even though she'd demanded time away without contact. Most particularly since Charlotte had been Isaac's charge for months prior to Savannah's appearance on the scene.

But their communication, only the scrambled symbols at that point, had to remain seemingly nonexistent.

At least until he knew more.

Had some inkling who in the upper echelon of US law enforcement or government was a mole. If there was one.

He had to assume there was. It was the only thing that made sense to him that would explain how Duran had pulled off his big disappearance and a new identity that included billions of dollars, all while raising a daughter from babyhood.

The second stop that day was as close to sea level as he could get and still be within the mountain range. He'd been to the area a couple of times since he'd bought his ranch.

A structure open in the front but deep, with a ceiling that served as the base of a thriving waterfall.

In the past, the spot had been a piece of heaven on earth to him. Breathtaking in its majesty. Which was saying a lot for a guy like him.

One more prone to shoot to kill than sit and ponder life's wonders.

"This is...phenomenal!" Nicole's smile fit right in with the rainbow shining in the water tumbling down beside her as she stood by the stream flowing swiftly away from them to places unknown.

She'd raised her voice some to be heard over the waterfall and he did as well as he responded with "We can't stay long. The horses won't be able to hear as well. But I need the signals to be scattered around various points of altitude and types of interests."

Truth be told, he'd wanted her to stand in the spot that had given him his first glimpse of possibility for redemption, for a future for himself, when he'd first landed outside of the life he'd thought he'd be in forever. He'd landed like a projectile. Dazed. Unsure of next steps.

Or even who he was.

He'd thought he'd found answers since then.

The past few days had shown him differently. And yet there he was, back at the place that had provided the first surge of inner power that was the start of what he'd thought would be a good journey.

As Nicole settled in to work, he hoped maybe he'd find another jolt of clarity there that day. One that would help him end the case that had ended him.

He unsaddled the horses long enough to brush them. Let them roam free for an hour. Filled water receptacles. Boiled water for another meal.

Handed one to Nicole—who'd barely glanced away from the screen as she uttered a barely discernible "Thanks"—then settled himself a distance away where he had the entire alcove in which she sat in sight. But could hear more from a distance, too.

With Imperial and Mahogany grazing close by him, their teeth nipping at weeds growing in the rocks on which they stood, Harc used a new burner phone to search every database he could access with various aliases to touch base with entities known to have been associated with Eduardo Duran and Arnold Wagar.

He'd been through them all. Ad nauseum. Was merely checking for updates.

And looked for more on the explosion at the dude-ranch cabin, too. It had been deemed an accident. The result of a minute gas leak.

He'd had to dig deep to find that much.

Because the minor blow had turned out not to be big news?

Or because it had been buried? Like so many of Duran's activities had been?

To an onlooker, he could be just another vacationer, a backpacker, enjoying the serenity on a peaceful Friday afternoon.

While every muscle in his body, every sense was on high alert. Undercover work at its core. Pretending to be one thing, while living another. Spending hours, days, weeks, months even, posing. Appearing to relax, to enjoy beers with friends, to sleep with his girlfriend, even plotting kill a compatriot, all in the name of making the world safer for those who had no idea about the underworld threatening them.

For their children.

And now for Nicole Compton, too. He checked on her most often. Just to see that she was still there, focused.

Two days on a horse in the mountains, and she still looked…elegant…to him. The long dark hair she'd left down glistened with health. And her demeanor, the way she held herself and her movements seemed to glide—there would always be a part of the wealthy atmosphere in which she'd grown up about her. In her.

A complete contrast to the simple life he and his father had shared, in a home without any hint of a woman's touch. Chairs to sit on. Beds to sleep in.

Clean. Put away.

No niceties.

As though knowing that he'd been thinking about her—and himself—in the same process, she suddenly exclaimed, "Oh my God!" and glanced up. Finding him.

Immediately on his feet as Nicole's words reached him, Harc flipped the safety off his gun as he glanced quickly in her direction and then, with the gun pointing the way, scanned the entire area around them.

With a glance at the horses, who were grazing contentedly, he hurried over to his temporary work partner. "What did you find?"

"Chats, Harc. There are a plethora of them. I'm just beginning to see the various chains. All different users. But not chatting with each other. The only commonality is the protocol being used and—" she met his gaze, communicating a fear that sliced into him "—one source that is the same."

"Wagar."

She nodded. "He's got these seemingly completely protected private chats going on with all these different people who don't seem to know about each other."

"What are they saying?"

She shook her head. "I haven't gotten that far yet. Everything's encrypted." Glancing from her screen back to him, she said, "But they're coming to his portal from all over the world."

He frowned. Glanced at the letters, figures, symbols on her screen, understanding none of it. "Including the US," he said, knowing it was true in spite of his ability to see for himself.

She nodded. "At least a dozen of them, from what I can see so far."

Chin tight, he asked, "Do you recognize any of the usernames?"

She was frowning—and shaking her head—as she looked at her screen again. "There's nothing as obvious as usernames. Everything is coded. I'll break it. I just haven't gotten that far yet."

He was sure she would, but not right then. The mission's scale was compounding in ways he hadn't expected. Or planned for. Any number of entities could be watching for signs of breach. "Time to go," he said, waiting for her nod before he went for the satellite, retrieved his shovel, and buried the unit in rocks deluged by the waterfall.

And while she took a second to pee, he quickly pulled out the scrambled device he and Mike had purchased—in double—together, typing cryptically, saddled Mahogany, and was saddling Imperial by the time she'd returned.

So much for his bizarre hope that Nicole would be able to absorb some supernatural healing power there.

She'd taken herself further into hell instead.

And he was paving the way for her to do it.

SHE'D WANTED AUTONOMY.

Even before she'd found out that her entire life was a big lie, she'd been busting at the seams for her freedom. Arnold Wagar being thrust upon her had just been the last straw.

And she hadn't been allowed a single life lesson upon which she could draw to give her strength. Her entire existence had been about weakness—multiple dangers surrounding her from which she needed constant protection.

Teaching her to rely on it being there.

Not how to be strong against the onslaught. Or how to endure hardship.

That was coming at her crash-course style. Her ability to pass the test remained to be seen.

"You can take me back if you'd like," she told Harc as they rode further into the dense Colorado mountains. The man had created a good life for himself. She was only just beginning to see how completely inappropriately invasive her descent upon him had been.

Spoiled little rich girl.

His gaze was searching as he looked sideways at her from atop Imperial. "You want to go back?"

She searched his expression, too. Couldn't tell what he wanted from her. Her entire life, she'd known what was expected of her. And gave him the truth. "I want to do what's best for you."

He shook his head. "That's not how life works," he told her. "Every situation, every person has a choice. You can only make your own."

She almost snorted at him. "I know that," she said. She'd been sheltered. She wasn't a child. "My choice is to regret having brought you into all of this."

"Without my files you wouldn't be in it."

Was the man deliberately trying to frustrate her? Irritate her?

Or was she egging him on? Because more than anything, she needed to engage with him. She couldn't explain it. No amount of higher education or intelligent quotient could make her reaction to him clear to her.

Other than a few glances at her, he was on constant surveillance of the area around them. As always. But he didn't seem a bit distracted from the conversation when he said, "So what do want to do?"

"I want to get these..." She broke off before the off-color remark escaped her lips. Surprising herself at the vehemence that had burst up from within her. "How about you?"

"Now more than ever." Not even a second passed for him to have considered the response. He was that certain.

So... "Tell me how to help you watch for danger," she said, then added, "I know to pay attention to Mahogany and Imperial. I've been doing that since this morning." When he'd told her why they'd left their beds so suddenly.

"It's more about keeping us from being seen," he said then. "If anyone is onto us, is out here searching, we can count on them having state-of-the-art equipment. High-powered binoculars. Optimum tracking devices. So we destroy the satellites ability to be tracked. And we keep ourselves in the shadows. Out of the sun's glint. Behind trees. The mountains in this state are known for being a great place to hide. For being a difficult place to find that which doesn't want to be found."

She took it all in. Verbatim. And asked, "What are you looking for when you scan the horizon?"

"Everything from movement or glints that could be indicative of lenses pointing in our direction, to weather conditions, sun's location, and landscape. Things that will affect how others stay hidden from us and how we hide."

Wisdom brought strength. She'd taught the concept to women who were learning to recognize signs of abuse, along with ways to escape the same.

And yet...she'd never recognized the extent of her own.

The thought brought her down another notch or two but didn't stop her from paying attention over the next couple of hours as they traveled, mostly in silence.

All four of them listening. Paying attention.

And she thought about the code she'd seen that day, too. Different scenarios were occurring to her, things that she could check offline. In the files themselves.

And that's where she found her strength. Inside her own mind. It was up to her to control where it dwelled. She'd studied psychology. She knew. Anxiety was a fear of the future. Of what could happen. A lot of times depression came from looking into the past. Her job was to stay focused only in the present. Where she was. Why. With whom.

With whom. As overwhelming as present moments appeared to be, there was one major factor that just felt good. With whom.

No past. No future. Only in the present.

The man with whom she shared a very unique set of circumstances—who they'd been, what they knew, and the skills they'd honed—to stop a major source of crime where no one else had.

A sound cracked in the distance. Echoing through the canyon yards to her left. Nicole barely registered the single blast before Mahogany reared up, her front hooves moving through the air.

Fear sliced through her, she slid backward and threw herself forward, clutching the saddle horn with one hand before throwing both arms around the horse's neck.

She had to stay on. Nothing else computed. Just staying on Mahogany's back.

"Whoa!" The deep voice, soft, but firm reached her as her feet twisted in the stirrups, and she squeezed her legs as hard as she could against the gelding's sides.

"Whoa."

Nicole clung to the sound, to the horse, and almost fell off when Mahogany's front hooves returned to earth and her neck lowered with them. Unbalancing Nicole, who's arms went down with the horse, while her boots, legs, and butt stayed in place.

Hands tangled in the reins, she held on. Grabbed frantically for the saddle horn. And felt hands on her hips, steadying her.

Then guiding her down to her feet.

Heart pounding, she stood on shaky legs, knees weak, and caught her breath as she looked up at Harc.

She'd managed to stay on.

Was still grateful for his steady hands at her waist. Wanted to thank him.

But got lost in the intensity shining at her from his blue eyes. As though under some kind of spell she couldn't look away.

"You okay?" his words broke through her to her.

She blinked. Stepped back. "Yes," she told him. Brushed herself off, went for Mahogany's reins. The whole thing had taken less than two minutes. And they had to go.

"Someone's shooting at us," she stated the obvious.

And was so busy getting ready to remount, she almost missed the shake of Harc's head. He was still there, his hand against Mahogany's neck. Calming the horse. "Not at us," he said then.

She climbed back up on the horse anyway. Took the reins. Running her palm against Mahogany's neck. If they'd been closer to the cliff edge... "How can you tell?" She stopped the fearful thought with conscious effort to focus on the moment.

"Came from the west, heading east. We're south."

She didn't ask how he knew. Let relief flow through her. And then said, "But it could be someone whose looking for us and thought they saw us."

His shrug gave a sense of unconcern, but he said, "Could be. Could also be a hunter."

"But it was definitely a gunshot."

Harc moved back to Imperial, who was pulling at weeds. "I can't say for sure. But it sounded like one to me."

He was back in the saddle and turned to look at her. "You okay to go on?"

Not completely. But she wasn't there to please herself. "Of course." She would make herself okay. If for no other reason right then, but to appear in a good light to the man who was beginning to mean way more to her than just a source of life-saving files.

Chapter Fourteen

He'd almost kissed her.

Absolutely not what he needed to be thinking about five minutes after a gun shot rang out. But Harc's gut was telling him that the shot hadn't been meant for them.

Someone whose operation was sophisticated enough to avoid international agencies with the best people on the case, wouldn't blow their presence—their cover—by shooting unless they were absolutely certain they had the target in sight.

And someone dealing in illegal arms would have a sniper rifle, which would not only bring the target clearly into focus but wouldn't sound like the crack of a twenty-two-caliber handgun.

Something else he kept from Nicole. Not to be cruel. Exactly the opposite. The next shot could be aimed at them, from a sniper's nest, and she could be dead. She still had time to get out. To go to the police. Get herself…where?

Without knowing who was working with Wagar, they had no idea where to put her to keep her safe. The man might have been willing to let her move about freely for the time being. Keeping an eye on her, but nothing else.

But not now that she'd breached at last some of his security walls. In a way that would have told him that she was the one doing it.

No one else could dismantle her code. Harc needed her aware of the danger. Constantly alert. It was the only way she'd have a chance of defending herself if the need arose.

Deliberately choosing a path that would keep them side by side, he said, "There's a peak not far ahead, an overhang, and, if I'm right, a decent-sized cave with a stream running in front of it. The flow rate is low, meaning not a lot of sound, but it's wide. You have to go through it to get to the cave."

She frowned. "So...the stream runs parallel to the mountain?"

He nodded. And she asked, "You're telling me we're going swimming?"

Her tone of voice, as though she was preparing herself to comply, not argue, almost brought a chuckle. Along with another dose of admiration. "No, Mahogany and Imperial will be able to walk through it. But no one will be able to get to us without alerting us they're there." Which was the key point he wanted her to know.

The danger was acute. But there was some inherent safety around, too.

"You've been there before?" she asked.

He shook his head. "I've been studying topographical maps of the area."

"Since you bought the ranch?"

He gave her a shrug that time, the flannel shirt sliding against his sides enough to raise the sudden acute desire he was finding himself fighting where she was concerned. "Just since you showed up on doorstep. Prior to that, I was content to do my own exploring."

Her glance was longer than he'd have liked before she

asked, "You know exactly where to take us after studying maps for less than two full days?"

She needed to be watching her surroundings at all times, not focusing that mesmerizing gaze on him.

Paying attention to everything. Like he was doing. Which included noticing her every move in his peripheral vision. "I have a photographic memory," he told her.

The information wasn't a secret. It was in his file someplace. Something Mike would have had access to.

"Now why doesn't that surprise me?" The question was clearly rhetorical, and he let it go. Or tried to. The tone of voice in which she'd said it kept reverberating as he pulled ahead of her to traverse the slope ahead.

Made him want to show her other, more physical, talents he had.

Something else he'd been known for undercover.

And another reason why he'd walked away.

NICOLE GOT TO work as soon as they'd made it to the cave where they'd be spending the night. Harc had insisted that the entire alcove be a no-internet zone, and she'd been in complete agreement. But only because she'd been mentally working through enough code-cracking ideas to keep her busy at the computer with the files she'd already downloaded.

She had some puzzles she had to solve before she dared move deeper into Wagar channels. If he knew she was there, he'd be scrambling to get new protocols in place. To prevent her from discovering a lot of what she needed to know. Was probably already doing so.

She was gambling on the fact that she was better than anyone else he could get to try to stop her. Otherwise, he wouldn't still be using fourteen-year-old Nicole's program.

Her goal was to get enough information to move on him

before he realized how deeply embedded she was. Which meant that she had to figure out how to be someone he chatted with without him knowing that she was posing as that someone.

Her personal dealings with the man had shown her the one thing she could use against him. He'd drastically underestimated her. Or overestimated himself.

Either way, having known him was going to work in her favor.

Even if the bullet earlier hadn't been meant for them—and the explosion in the dude-ranch cabin had just been an accident—even if Wagar didn't yet know she was fully onto him, he would know. There would be attacks. And bullets would be flying.

Nicole focused like Charlotte had never focused before. Every sense on high alert, she studied, typed, and tried again. Inching closer to understanding the chat encryptions. She'd chosen to focus on them first. Something was telling her that within those files, she would find what she needed to know to bring everything down. A name, something to get her started as she unraveled the many layers of protection, of hiding places within hiding places that she was finding herself up against.

It wasn't all brilliant. Some of it was downright sloppy. But that was its own protection. It was hard to decipher something that was filled with mistakes.

Harc inflated her air mattress. She moved into the cave to sit on it while she worked. At some point he brought food in. She ate without taking her eyes from the various windows she had open on screen.

Darkness started to invade the cave as the afternoon wore on. Light shone from outside, but the sun had moved behind her mountain cave, rather than shining over it. She was on the cusp of something. Could feel it. Was finding words hidden inside words. Translating symbol combinations into letters, finding words that coincided with other symbols.

She could be on the brink of success, or merely forming her own sets of formulas that matched various symbol placements. She had to think like someone who thought they were the best but might not be. Because it made sense to her that Wagar would have surrounded himself with likeminded soldiers.

Using her newest version of the multifaceted formula, she typed into the decoder she'd devised, hit Enter.

And stared.

What the hell? Mouth open, she read again. Then, with shaking fingers, entered more data, hit Enter, and read some more.

"What is it?" She heard Harc's voice from a distance before she became aware that he was approaching. Glanced out toward the stream. Saw him. The horses. Before her gaze returned like glue to her screen.

She didn't want him to see.

He had to see. Someone had to see.

With shaking fingers, she typed some more. There was nothing in front of her that was actionable. Nothing incriminating in terms of arrests.

"What's wrong?" He'd been on the other side of the stream. His feet sloshed as he hurried toward the cave's entrance.

She shook her head.

"You looked like you'd seen a ghost."

Staring up at him, all she could think about was wet socks and boots for a second, while her ears roared. He'd need his footwear to dry before they rode again.

We can manipulate her.

It's his mess. He'll clean it up.

We're keeping him safe. Minimum security. All the perks. His call.

He couldn't even get the damned proposal done. He's out.

We can manipulate her.

 Nicole typed. And read. Growing sicker, feeling weaker, by the minute.
 But couldn't stop. Driven beyond anything that affected her personally, she had to keep going.
 Not following any one conversation she just continued to put the random bits of coded messages she'd been using into the formula that was working. Taking what came.
 He couldn't even get the damned proposal done. He's out.
 Certain phrases kept interrupting her thoughts. Shouting at her as she attempted to move on.
 Harc was there. She smelled wetness. Saw the toes of his boots. Unless he sat down right next to her, back to the wall, he wouldn't be able to see her screen. Pulling more from one chat, she typed.

Watch her.

I'll take care of him.

She's too visible. Surrounded. Too risky.

Make a deal.

 Scrolling through code, she saw that the last, the deal part, came right before We can manipulate her. All one set of code.

It didn't show up that way. But with what she'd deciphered, she was beginning to piece together full pieces.

While she was falling into them.

The mattress dipped. Harc's weight.

"I'm in," she told him.

And closed her computer screen.

DREAD FILLED HIS gut as Harc watched Nicole. She'd had a shock. He could figure that much. Needed so much more.

But knew better than to push.

He was learning her.

She'd talk as soon as she had a moment to breathe. He pulled out his gun. Safety on. Set it on the mattress beside his right leg. Away from her. Kept his hand on it.

Listened for the horses tethered up just outside the cave.

Hoped to God that they had time assimilate, to act on whatever she'd found before they were acted upon.

"Arnold Wagar isn't the man we're after." Her first words fell baldly, no intonation. That was her shock?

It wasn't at all shocking to him. He didn't like the news. Meant he had no idea who he *was* after. Meant that all those months on Wagar had been a waste. But it made sense to instincts that had been leaning in that direction.

"Who is?" He went for the most key information.

"I don't know."

He nodded. Felt tension tighten his jaw.

"Other than some key points, a lot of what I've got here isn't even conversation between the same two people," she told him. "I've got about thirty sentences so far. Pulled from several chats. But one... I'd recognized something—CD and ED. It's what my father used to call us. In the chats, they were symbols, turned backward and interchanged, with other symbols between them—but I saw them in the midst of the coding and tried a formula that deleted the symbols in between them. Random symbols. Not the same ones. It was a long shot."

He was aware of the horses. Of the night that was on its way—due to throw them into darkness within the hour. But every sense was tuned to her.

The words she was saying. What she wasn't telling him yet.

Her eerie stillness.

Until she looked straight at him for the first time since he'd glanced up from across the stream and had seen her in shock, mouth open, in the distance.

He'd been setting barriers around the alcove, traps that would catch a toe, and make sound, if stepped upon. Fishing line, invisible at night, that would cause tripping. Falling.

And had nearly fallen himself as he tromped through the water to get to her.

Would have imparted any and all of it to her right then, had she not been looking at him as though she'd never seen him before.

She blinked. "I've got a lot of work to do," she said then, both hands clutching her laptop.

"Not until you tell me what's going on." That was not negotiable.

"I'm not sure yet," she started. Then, never looking away from him, she said, "I think I've been a pawn since I was a baby. A way to ensure my father's loyalty."

Harc coughed. "You're telling me Eduardo Duran—*Hugh Gussman*—is innocent?"

"Hell no. Just that I think he had such a superior opinion of himself that he refused to deny himself what he wanted. Which let them, whoever, know his weak spot." She shook her head. Frowned. Then said, "I don't really know that yet. But it makes sense. I'm just putting pieces together as they're coming to me. It seems pretty clear that his one mistake was bringing me with him. And somehow he thought marrying me off to Wagar was going to fix that?"

Opening her computer back up she tapped, typed, scrolled, and turned it so that he could see the screen.

Could read what she'd compiled.

And while there was nothing concrete in what he read in terms of their quest, their cause, the job he'd set for himself—he felt her shock.

Could only imagine the horror of knowing that her entire existence had been formed by a selfish man who chose to take what he wanted rather than leaving his daughter to have a normal life. And somewhere along the way she'd become a bargaining tool. Never being treated like a human being.

"As narcissistic as Gussman seems to be, as avaricious, it's also clear from this that, in his own way, the man valued you above all else."

"As a prized possession," she said, her tone flat. "I gave him legitimacy. Made him approachable. Seem warm. Even likeable."

"You adored him." He said what he knew had to be eating at her. Because it was eating at him, and he was as far an outsider as one could get. Then he finished with, "You adored who you believed he was." He told the more accurate truth.

And while he wanted to stay beside her in the cave, sit with her as she ached, he knew he couldn't. Feelings, other than gut instincts, didn't have a place on the job.

She hadn't found anything actionable yet, but she'd unearthed another game changer, and he had to get word to Mike.

NICOLE ABSORBED HARC'S WARMTH. Reminded herself that she lived in the moment. Not the future. Not the past.

And started to find her strength again. She couldn't help who she'd been born to. Nor what her father had done with her life. But she could completely shape every moment she resided in as she was there. By taking what she'd learned in the past—good and bad—and applying it to her present.

She had to get back to work.

Almost as though he'd read her thoughts, Harc stood up. "I'm going to take Imperial and do a more expansive perimeter check."

Her stomach tightened painfully, but she nodded. Understood. Wanted the reassurance of him knowing what was out there.

And she was scared to death of sitting in that cave in the mountains all alone. Except that the worst that could happen, her dying, wasn't as bad as being the weak, over-protected daughter of an international criminal. "I'm going to be sitting right here, working," she told him, paying more attention to her laptop than to him.

Being in her moment, not her fears.

"Where's your gun?"

The question sent another slither of fright through her. She reached into the backpack right beside her. Pulled out the weapon enough to show it to him.

"Get it out," he told her, still standing over her. "Have the safety off and by your right side, ready for you to grab in an instant."

She took the gun out with a shaking hand and said, "Scaring me is going to slow down production."

He didn't seem to move a muscle. "Not as much as having you incapacitated would do." There was no apology in his tone. Or compassion, either.

"Listen for Mahogany," he said as he headed for the cave's exit. "He'll let you know before anyone has a chance to get close enough to hurt you."

"Unless a sniper has a gun trained on me from farther than two miles away." She was being facetious. Didn't quite manage the smile to go with the words.

But looked up to see Harc shaking his head. "There's no straight shot into the cave," he told her. "Look around you—the only distance you can see is sky. Ten yards beyond that stream is down. Behind you there's up. And in here you're protected on both sides."

She nodded. Looked back at her computer, dismissing him to matters more important than comforting her.

But as he turned to go, took a couple of steps outside the cave, she called softly, "Harc?"

And when he turned, said, "Thank you."

The nod of his head brought the smile she'd been unable to find.

And a prayer that he'd return safely.

Chapter Fifteen

Sierra's Web had eyes on Arnold Wagar, in real time, electronically, and by watching those he was known to be connected to. Bodyguards.

Work-for-hire goons he was suspected to have had associations with in the past.

And a well-known problem eliminator with mob associations who'd just been released from prison after the first of the year.

All but that last bit had put Harc at ease as he'd ended the scrambled messaging communications he'd ridden down to receive. And then buried the satellite device he'd brought with him to ensure transmission.

Sierra's Web's vision was acute. The best there was. Mike had just assured Harc that not only would they be watching Wagar, they'd be doing a thorough deep dive on who could be pulling Wagar's strings.

And Mike had agreed with him, that Nicole's time frame to create the miracle they all needed was growing critically short. Sierra's Web tech expert, Hudson Warner, and his team had detected someone other than Nicole looking at Wagar's online security.

The FBI agent hadn't mentioned Savannah, and Harc hadn't asked about her. Since the woman was a partner in

Sierra's Web, it stood to reason that she was fully briefed, but the lawyer's skills weren't needed on the front line.

And Mike and Harc didn't ever cross that line.

Still, as he pushed Imperial to hightail it back to Nicole, as he considered all that he and Mike had discussed, he knew a growing sense of unease regarding the secret communication.

Which unsettled him far more than it should have.

He'd spent his entire adult life living two lives at once. The one those around him could see, and the one that worked in secret to solve heinous crimes.

Heart, emotion—soul, even—were sacrificed in order to succeed.

Which made it hard to explain why he felt almost lightheaded with relief as he and Imperial climbed the last half mile to the cave, careful to avoid the traps he'd set, and meandered across the stream toward Mahogany. And Harc could get eyes on the woman sitting up in the cave.

The gelding left behind was watching them, his long tail giving a wave, and Nicole...didn't even seem to look up. Engrossed in her computer screen, she was typing, then studying. Just as she'd been doing most of the afternoon.

Decrypting, he assumed.

Figuring that she hadn't moved since he'd left.

Until he got close enough to see the tamped-down marks in the patches of brush and dirt where Mahogany had been left to graze. Human-sized footprints that Harc hadn't made.

Watching the dark-haired head at work, Harc's heart gave a warm lurch new to him. Unsettling him. Changing him somehow.

When she didn't react to his return, he left her alone. But was aware of every move she made. Knew when she watched him fill the pot with water from the stream to make their last meal of the day. He was turned sideways and could see her with peripheral vision.

He was fine to pretend that his absence hadn't been a big deal, for either of them.

Liked it better that way.

Darkness was going to be fully upon them soon. And while they'd have some moonlight at the opening of the cave and the solar charges had enough juice to keep Nicole working, they needed to rest. He had a feeling the next day or two would not play out as the last two had.

The closer they got to Wagar, the more pressure the man felt, the higher the chance that he'd be sending hungry hounds trained to kill straight for them.

Harc was ready for them. He wasn't sure Nicole was.

Or even could be.

While she'd had survivalist training, and was freakishly smart, she didn't have the mindset of an agent. He'd seen the panic on her face. The way she had to fight to find her inner strength—formidable as he suspected it was.

Life hadn't prepared her to take on the evil that would be coming at them. Ironic, since her father had born and bred it, too.

He approached the cave just as the sun made its last dip. "Dinner's going to be ready in two, and then we need to get rest," he said, as though they were having just another day on a leisurely backpacking trip.

She nodded. "Shutting down will give my laptop time to charge." She closed the device as she was speaking. Set it aside.

He'd hoped for a bit of reading material to take him through dinner. And to prepare him, too. Had expected to be scrolling through random chat-room comments, akin to what she'd shown him earlier. Needed to see for himself, in case he recognized something she didn't. An alias. A code word.

She reached to her side, and he noticed the gun still lying there. Wondered if she'd taken it outside with her during her sojourn with Mahogany while he'd been gone. Didn't ask. The woman had spent her entire life with bodyguards watching her every move.

The hand by her gun reached out to him. "Here. I saved the day's work for you to have a copy, too."

He took the small plastic case containing a micro SD card. Nodded. Deposited the gift in his pocket. And while she rounded a boulder behind which he'd dug her personal hole, he gathered sporks and water bottles and had dinner waiting upon her return.

They were temporary partners. With different skills and responsibilities.

Not two people finding a kinship with each other.

WITH A BURNER phone offline, and plugged into a battery pack, Harc slid her micro SD card into a slot and read while they ate.

She'd expected him to get right on it. Just hadn't thought he'd do so while sitting two feet from her while she ate. With only the beam of a flashlight for her to see by.

Leaving her far too much space for the past to creep in on her. The things she'd discovered...about Wagar, proof that he was answering to someone who had ordered him back to the States to clean up his mess.

And before that...the reason he'd asked her to marry him.

There'd been more than she'd surmised, but she hadn't been completely off, either. The knowledge gave zero satisfaction.

Harc would be homing in on the more pertinent facts.

Wagar had another contact in the US who was calling shots. Someone other than Hugh Gussman.

And one in another country as well. She was thinking El Salvador, but until she could get back online, she couldn't verify much more than that.

She ate because she had to keep up her strength. The beef stroganoff wasn't gagging her, as she'd thought it might.

Partially because she was letting herself enjoy the view she had. Pure distraction. She knew it. Acknowledged that she was resorting to base humanity in an unbecoming way. But did it anyway. She'd found Harc attractive the first time she'd seen him.

Studying the rugged, very-different-from-anything-she-was-used-to masculinity wasn't hurting anyone.

Better that than let the darkness suffocate her, while the reality of having no life crushed her. Because she'd been fighting both possibilities since the first encryption that had included *CD. Charlotte Duran.* The initials had been the key to unlocking information that would hopefully end a quarter of a century of criminal activity.

They'd also deadened something inside her.

Had she really been holding on to hope that a man who'd stolen millions from the government while a trusted employee, who'd abandoned his wife and child, faked his own death, kidnapped his other child and fled the country, had been capable of loving her? Selflessly? Unconditionally? As a child should be loved.

As Savannah had been. As she'd have been had Hugh left her with the mother she'd so desperately needed growing up.

As her sister loved her still.

Because when Savannah looked at Nicole, she saw the baby she'd been. Savannah hadn't even known the woman Charlotte had become when she'd risked her life to save her.

Harc reached for his water bottle, a foot away from hers. His knuckles brushed against it. Knocked it over, and she caught it. Handing it to him.

And got caught by the glint she could see in his eyes as he focused on her. She wanted to stay there. Feeling... okay. To forget everything. The world she'd lived in. The one waiting that she wasn't sure she'd ever fit.

She wanted those slightly opened lips to touch hers. To wipe out thoughts. And replace fear with something better than that.

Then he took the bottle, sipped, and glanced back at his phone and she realized that he hadn't been caught in the sensual web with her.

She'd been there alone.

In a world that wasn't real.

Just as she'd been her entire life.

HARC NEEDED ANSWERS. He needed Nicole online, working her magic, getting more. He needed names. Places.

Account numbers.

He couldn't afford to bring a multinational, fully armed and trained devil to their door in the middle of the night with no backup.

But Nicole needed some sleep.

He was already asking more of her than she could easily manage. More than she'd been prepared to handle.

More than he'd have been able to handle as well as she was doing were their situations reversed.

While he hadn't yet read every communication verbatim, he had the gist of what she'd found. Proof without critical details.

There wasn't one kingpin. There were at least two.

Arnold Wagar was not one of them.

If the man didn't get rid of Charlotte Duran, permanently, in a way that couldn't point back at him, he was toast.

Judging by earlier chats, most of which had stopped three months before, Wagar used to have the ear of one of the kingpins. And ran some pretty powerful shows.

Neither man in charge appeared to be involved in the chats. Nor did they seem to be aware that they existed.

Wagar had recruited someone new. Someone he'd been lying to, but also filling in so he'd be up to speed. Which was how Nicole had managed to find out all that she had.

The chats alone were probably enough to give them Wagar.

But they'd be no closer to ending the reign of terror. Just as bringing in Hugh Gussman had not done so.

They were closer than ever. And as far away as they'd always been.

"If I hadn't put my DNA in that database, I'd still be living in a mansion, thinking I was adored by a generous, decent, extremely successful businessman." The words brought Harc's gaze from the screen he'd already ceased reading—had just been staring at—to the face of a goddess who appeared to be on the verge of being beaten.

Even as she sat upright and ate freeze-dried food to give her strength.

He hurt for her worse than he'd ever hurt for himself. Even as he knew he couldn't possibly know how she was feeling.

And he had to ask, "Would you want to go back there?"

"No." The response was immediate. Emphatic. And he hurt for her some more. Wanted to go back to staring at his phone, to escape from himself and his compelling desire to take her in his arms and let her feel what it was like to be loved.

Because…all he knew how to offer her was the physical stuff. He could bring joy, and experience it, in the moment—he was certain of that. Could give her a sense of being adored and cherished.

But only for the moment.

Which was no better than her father had done.

Instead, he cleared away the empty dishes. Took them outside to wash them, dumping the dirty water in his hole. Checked on the horses.

Put away everything he'd taken out of the packs. Had them ready by the cave's entrance.

Fully synced with the life his plan had created. Just like always. His chameleonlike skills had made him an excellent CIA agent. Not a great man.

But he had to try. She was sitting in the middle of her sleeping bag–covered mattress looking more lost than he'd ever felt. Which was saying something.

Bending over to secure the latch on the last pack, he said, "Maybe you sent your DNA in because you sensed that something was off. Inside, you knew. Which is why you were so desperate to find other family."

She shrugged.

"That act alone was the catalyst that brought down an entire portion of a bad empire," he reminded her. Because stuff like that mattered to him. Pulled him out of funks.

He glanced over as he stood. Saw her watching him in the beam from the flashlight. Decided they should have more water for the night. Reached for his bottle, filling it from the jug he'd carried in from the stream earlier. Glanced again, to see her...still watching. Seemingly following his every move.

And when she caught him watching her, she said, "Mike was there. He'd have found something eventually."

Maybe. Probably. But with no guarantee that it would have been enough to end Duran's reign.

She was still watching him, and he stood there, feeling like an idiot, loath to reach in for her water bottle, as she said, "Did you read the part about Wagar being ordered to marry me and then decide to return home to El Salvador permanently as a way to get me and Eduardo out of the country without looking like Eduardo was running away? Without raising suspicions? They wanted me out of reach of Savannah's search. And, if need be, once over there, they were going to keep me under lock and key, if I didn't comply with their wishes. They wanted me pregnant, with a child of my own, so I quit yearning for family, and they intended to put me to work creating more superior code. And to keep an eye on my previous work, to make certain that it wasn't being breached."

He hadn't read it all. But he'd had the gist of it. Felt useless as he nodded.

Held the jug on his lap as he sank down to his own mattress. Needing to be there for her. To find a way to help.

And feeling utterly helpless.

Not a familiar state for him. And not one he liked. At all.

"And because you refused to marry him, Arnold Wagar is now going to be on the run from the very powers he helped build." He said the words before he thought them through. Which was why he'd known he should back up and quit trying to be more than he was.

He saw the twist to her face as she said, "Unless he delivers me up." And felt the weight of his mistake.

Leaning forward, he reached for her water bottle. He'd fill it. Turn out the light. And hope to God she could find some respite in unconsciousness for a while.

But had to say, "That's not going to happen. I always get the job done, and right now, the job is protecting you." All bravado. Mixed with a dose of truth. He'd only ever failed on one case, and it was because he'd quit. As it turned out, that one failure had come back to give him a second chance.

The only way she was going to die was if he went first.

She stood as he was filling her bottle. Grabbed some things out of her pack, and flashlight in hand—pointed at the ground, not out, as he'd taught her—she headed just outside, behind her boulder. Getting ready for bed, thank God.

The sooner she found escape in sleep, the sooner he could hope to do the same. Even just for an hour or two. They'd have to be on the move before morning.

Even if they returned to the same camp at night, he had to move her elsewhere to get online. And had a better chance of doing that under the cover of darkness.

She could nap in the afternoon if need be.

Feeling more like himself as plans for the next twelve hours or so started to solidify, Harc put away the jug and grabbed a fresh filter to apply to Nicole's freshly filled water bottle.

Had just tightened the lid when she came back inside. Waiting while she repacked her things, he tried not to notice the freshly brushed hair or the lighter-colored jeans she'd donned with a black long-sleeved T-shirt that made her braless state more obvious than the looser shirt had the night before.

He didn't need to know that while she was sleeping in clothes as he'd said, she'd opted not to keep her chest bound up as well.

Either the previous night had been too uncomfortable for her or she'd quickly donned the bra while he'd been saddling the horses before dawn that morning.

As his body reacted to the thoughts he was trying to obliterate, Harc dropped to his own mattress, still holding Nicole's water. To have done otherwise would have meant getting closer to her as he handed it over, when what he needed was a trip out to bathe in the stream.

He was working.

On the job.

The reminders did little to help his current situation.

More times than not, undercover, he'd taken lovers as part of the job.

And beyond that, where Nicole was concerned, he'd already crossed the line between work and personal.

Even if he wasn't willing to accept the fact.

Chapter Sixteen

The nightmare wasn't ever going to end. Eduardo had stolen her life from her when she'd been just a baby. All the time he'd claimed to have been protecting her, he'd been caging her to protect himself. The more she dug, the more encompassing his deeds became.

She wasn't just the property of one criminal. Untold numbers, without names, were staking their claims on her. She knew too much.

And too little. She was in the race of her life, she got that loud and clear. Unless she figured out who they were before they found her, she was going to die.

But she wasn't going to go without reclaiming her life. She would not die as Eduardo had made her live.

Not ready for the one beam of light to go out, to leave her alone with the moon and the dark while her traveling companions got their rest, she took her time getting her toothbrush, paste, and body wipes neatly in their designated pocket inside her backpack. Her mind, her body were too fraught with the day's revelations, still reeling too much to allow sleep.

Shoving her folded dirty clothes in the plastic bag she'd packed in her suitcase in Phoenix for just that purpose, she placed it in the separate zippered portion at the bottom, thinking maybe she should just wash them and give them several hours of night air in which to dry. Except that would keep her companions up.

And then, with nothing else to do, she dropped from her knees to her butt on her mattress in the near dark and asked, "Do you know how horses sleep standing up?"

She did. And she knew why, too.

"Stay apparatus. A series of tendons, muscles, and joints that lock into place."

She nodded. There was more, but he'd summed up the gist of it. "And they do it because it takes them a bit of effort to stand from a lying position, which makes them vulnerable to prey."

She was babbling, engaging him in it and not feeling any more prone to sleep herself.

"They do lie down to sleep as well," he said, as though willing to engage in the inane with her. Shooting a smidgeon of warmth through her frozen soul. "In their stalls. And I've wondered if they ever did when they lived out here full time." He was slowly turning her water bottle around in his hands.

He glanced down as she watched him and held the drinking container out to her just as she reached to take it from him. Their fingers collided. The bottle dropped to the ground between them, and they both leaned in to rescue it.

Her fingers got to the bottle milliseconds before his did, and already in flight, his hand wrapped around hers.

Changed by the warmth of his touch, she didn't move except to look up at him. To hold on. It was as though, the day's frigidity melted away. Showing her that she was more than what her father had grown her into.

That she had choices yet to make that could define who she was.

That she was already making them.

Feelings more than actual thoughts, the impressions came at her as she held his gaze. Her eyes started to focus more in the moment. She saw the blue in his. The intensity.

The...wanting.

And she wanted.

To make her own choice. To indulge. To find forgetfulness. To feel good. To know him. All of him.

To be held by him.

Leaning in a little further, leaning on the water bottle she still held, Nicole brought her lips closer to Harc's. She didn't kiss him. Just closed in, her eyes still locking gazes with his. She wouldn't force anything.

He had to want it, too.

He moved closer, stopping with only a couple of inches between their faces. Giving her time?

She couldn't tear her gaze from his. Had to stay connected. Until he looked down at her lips. As though telling her what he wanted but wouldn't take without her permission.

As though asking if he could kiss them.

Her answer was just as silent as the question. She leaned in those two inches and pressed her lips to his.

MOLTEN DESIRE RACED through him, transporting him from rational thought to instinctive action. She'd touched him with an opened mouth, and his lips met hers fully ready to engage. He tongued her right out of the shoot. No finesse. No foreplay.

Just a hunger that had to be satiated.

There was nothing tentative about her lips. Or her intentions.

And he didn't intend to disappoint her. Leaning toward her, he wrapped an arm around her waist and lifted them both to her mattress, lying down with her in the softness of her sleeping bag. And kissed her. Again and again. Softly. Exploring. Tender. And hard and hungry, too. He couldn't stop. Couldn't get enough.

Half on top of her, he tangled his fingers in her hair. Got hotter by the way the silky strands seemed to restrain him. Chain him.

Right where he wanted to be.

Until she moaned. He slid to his side, his pelvis pressing against her thigh, his chest up against her ribs. Saw her eyes open, read the slumbrous heat there. "You okay?" he whispered.

"I've never been better." The words were a treasure. A gift.

A truth so stark that he felt as though he'd just heard from the depth of her heart. Heard it calling out for more.

As though he, the one who'd sold his own heart and soul, could help strengthen hers.

Harc had made mistakes. A lot of them. He had to get this one right. And she'd lived in that gilded cage.

"You've done this before?" he had to ask. Not to say he'd stop if she wanted to go on, but…he'd do some things… differently.

She nodded. Smiled again, seeming so mature and sexy that he had a hard time containing the explosion pressing for release. "I dated a med student," she told him. "We did it in the university lab." With another grin she said, "My bodyguard never entered classrooms with me."

The life she'd lived, the fact that she'd not only gotten herself out of it but was embracing a chance to be who she chose to be—someone who'd risk her life for others, to right wrongs—mesmerized him.

She traced a finger around his lips. "I've never felt like this though."

He wanted to nip at the finger. Restrained himself because it wasn't about him. "Like what?"

"Physically ignited. Not caring about anything beyond right now. Hungry."

"You want more?" he asked. She was in charge.

Completely.

"A lot more," she told him, looking him right in the eye. "I want to keep feeling like I feel right now. I want to want. And to get what I want. I want to be wanted. And to give until you cry for mercy." She stopped then. Blinked. As though she'd just shocked herself. And then smiled. "Yep, that's what I want," she said, her arms around his neck.

He kissed her then. Softly. Pulled back to look deeply into eyes partly in shadows with the flashlights dimming beam. Searching. Needing to know how best to make the next moments as perfect for her as possible.

"I want to be strong," she said then. "And...for a little while...just to be me. To forget what was. To let go of fear of what comes next. For some reason, you make all of that possible."

The declaration exploded in his chest as much as the feel of her was engorging him in other places. Harc lay there, awash in unfamiliar emotion that was swirling throughout the desire burning through him.

Nicole reached up to run her fingers along his brow. To touch his lips. "And I want to know what you want," she whispered, lifting her head to kiss him softly.

He had no words to give to such a moment. Came up blank. All he could do was gather her close. And show her.

He wanted her. More than just sex, he wanted to be something she would never forget. Something good.

The bridge from her old life, giving her an unforgettable, emotionally and physically mind-blowing passage into whatever her new life would be.

He wanted to hold on tight. To see her naked. Touch every part of her. Be touched by her. To know her completely.

To be the best she'd ever had.

Before he had to let her go.

MORNING WAS GOING to come. The fact drove Nicole higher. Sometimes faster, sometimes slower as she explored the most magnificent male form she'd ever imagined. Harc clothed had been rated-X fodder. His body without clothes was perfection.

Art.

Muscles that were big enough to proclaim powerful strength but not overbuilt and getting in the way. More, they were rock solid. All over his body. She explored every one of them. Head to toe. Prolonging the natural euphoria flowing through her. And she was pretty sure through him, too.

Every touch, every move, they were in sync. Pleasuring and being pleasured. The onslaught to her senses consumed her, driving her, until…finally, she had to climb onto him and have it all. Helping him with the condom he'd pulled out of the wallet in his pants pocket, she caressed his hardness. Sliding herself down onto him, she practically exploded just by the hungry, appreciative look in his eyes. By the fact that he was watching her, entering her and taking her in, too.

She wanted to take it slow, but their bodies were in control and did what they had to do. She moved, he did, and together they rode higher and higher until she couldn't help herself any longer. Convulsing around him, she closed her eyes, savoring wave after wave of exultation as he spasmed inside her.

Then…it was done.

Just as Harc had known that Nicole needed him, he got quite clearly that reality had returned when he came in from his hole a few minutes after the most incredible sex he'd ever had. Already inside her sleeping bag, Nicole was fully dressed. An assumption made by the lack of her clothes on the ground with his, and what he could see of the shirt covering her shoulders.

He didn't rush to dress, some perverse desire inside him driving him to take his time. Whether she was watching or not, she'd be aware. He was certain of that.

But when he buttoned the last button and picked up his gun, to place it by his hand as he lay down, he was all agent again.

Turned off the flashlight. Closed his eyes. And heard, "Thank you." Softly. Contentedly. And his chest flooded with warmth again.

His glib *Anytime, ma'am* turned into "You think you can sleep now?"

And when her "Mmm-hmm" reached him, he smiled.

For a minute. Maybe two. Until he heard even breathing coming from her direction and his mind flew to the danger he'd helped her walk into.

He should have known that things were bigger than just Duran and Wagar. All those months undercover in El Salvador, he should have uncovered more.

Self-conflagration came. And...went. Just...left.

No explanation.

Other than that, he had a job to do and couldn't waste time on that which couldn't be changed. Unless he wanted to continue to live amongst the mistakes.

Listening to the breathing of the young woman who'd come barreling into his life with such indistinguishable force, he knew she wasn't the only one who'd gained more than sex from their encounter that night.

From their acquaintance overall.

She'd come from something terrible. And had the courage, the determination to make the future different.

To *be* different in it.

She wouldn't let herself be wholly defined by who she'd been, but rather, was taking out of it what would suit her, and forging ahead one choice at a time, to be someone she could live with. He had to do at least that.

And more if he could.

He had to do whatever it took to see that she got the chance to make all the choices she had to make, to get to the future that promised to be everything she'd ever needed.

As young as she was, she was just getting started on carving out the rest of her life.

The eleven years between them sat heavily on him as he lay there, hands behind his head, listening...and coming into focus, too. His ranch was his life. He honestly wanted to get back to it. But not until he succeeded on his final mission.

Running through facts in his mind—those he'd known for more than year, and those just recently acquired—he looked beyond the shock, the emotions, the not knowing to pieces. Letting every piece of information floating around in his mind bump into each other. Trying to find what fit next to what. With what.

How it fit.

Looking for a mole, mostly. That was his ultimate key. Who knew Hugh Gussman back then? Who benefitted from the man's theft?

Who was sitting at the head of the empire?

How did they capture an unknown enemy? How did they stay alive when they didn't know who they were fighting?

So many agents had been through all the information at their disposal. Sierra's Web was getting a fresh look.

And the person was still undetected?
How could anyone be that good? For that long?
Pieces floated. They landed. They floated some more.
Harc drifted off. Woke up. Drifted off some more.
And then woke up.
Sat up.
Listening.

Chapter Seventeen

Harc's gaze shot to Nicole first. Her head was turned toward him, face seemed relaxed, as best he could tell. Her covers moved up and down regularly, evenly, with her breathing.

He immediately switched surveillance to the moonlight and shadows outside the cave. Picking out Imperial and Mahogany first. Both standing. Quietly.

Not on edge.

Nothing looked out of place. Even the stream flowed easily. The night, their small part of the world seemed peaceful.

He'd woken with a start.

And it hit him. A missing piece that was preventing him from putting together the puzzle.

Wasn't missing. They just hadn't seen it.

His subconscious had, though.

Hugh Gussman had been a regular guy. A husband. A father. He'd bowled in a league. And he'd been incredibly bright. Climbing up the ladder in the IRS, but bored with his job. To the point of trying to see if he could steal money in order to report the breach possibility and gain himself a larger promotion, sooner.

Instead, he'd been mesmerized by his ability to gain a

lot more money, a lot faster, by taking the darker route. After he'd amassed two million dollars, he'd reported his own work to the authorities, agreeing to name the perpetrator if he could be assured that he and his family would be safe. He'd been on his way to supposedly testify the day he'd turned up dead.

Except that he'd not only been alive and well, he'd had a one-year-old baby with him and managed to...disappear.

How?

Until three months ago, no one had even known Gussman had been alive. There'd been no "how" in existence.

And when he'd confessed, Gussman had written that he'd slipped over the border to Mexico and paid for new identities.

Lying back down, Harc let the facts flow in whatever fashion they would.

Wagar had been his main focus for the entire case—the reason Nicole had even sought him out—and because Wagar was the one with the most to lose if Nicole lived, the man's relationship with Duran kept resurfacing.

In Gussman's confession he'd said that he'd met Wagar the year before, at a black-tie charity function in Los Angeles. But that had clearly been a lie. Charlotte's security program written at fourteen had been in use in Wagar files for longer than that. Two years that he knew of so far. Could have been more. A lot more.

Arnold Wagar had been a kid living in El Salvador when Hugh Gussman was supposedly murdered. A teenager. Barely an adult. He'd grown up in wealth. Came from a well-respected family.

And his father had been a Salvadoran dignitary in the US at one point.

Which point?

Had anyone checked?

There'd been no reason to do so when they hadn't known about Duran and Gussman being one and the same. Gussman...who'd worked for the government.

Upright again, Harc itched to get a message to Mike. To have someone check for any associations from a quarter of century before held by Dignitary Wagar. And look to see if young Wagar and Hugh Gussman had ever crossed paths.

The conversations Nicole had found, decrypted... Wagar could have been talking about his own father—the elderly, well-respected patriarch of the family's century-old wine business—when he'd mentioned being toast if Charlotte Duran wasn't dealt with.

The elder Wagar was the CEO and president of a billion-dollar business that had well-and long-established international shipping capabilities.

Was it possible that the spoiled son wasn't the only one who'd gone rogue? Could Wagar's father be the kingpin?

A man with a private jet, with high clearance in the United States government, whose spoiled, weak son had befriended a genius with two million dollars...

The elder Wagar had had a lot to lose taking on Gussman. And for what? Two million was grocery money to a man of the elder Wagar's wealth.

Unless his wine business had been in trouble?

Or his son had been. Had Hugh rescued Arnold from some trouble in Washington when the family had traveled there with his father? And the elder Wagar had done him a favor for having aided his son? Helping him escape and then obtain new identities for his daughter and him?

Hugh could have lied to him, too. Told him that he'd been threatened. That he was a widower with a young child...

Or the Wagars could have been using their winery as a cover from the beginning. Could be a long-established criminal family. Even the head of a cartel.

Perhaps they'd recruited Gussman.

Heart pumping, Harc's mind continued to fly, his photographic memory showing him full documents he'd read, and he knew—with the certainty that had led him to close so many cases without loss of life—that he was onto something.

Maybe not cartel or even the elderly Wagar. But something.

When Charlotte told her father that she'd entered her DNA into that database, Duran had known that he could be exposed at any time. That not only Arnold Wagar, but perhaps an entire mob family in El Salvador, was also at risk.

Or someone else entirely. Someone closer to home.

Or further away.

But someone.

And it started with how Gussman got out of the country and became Eduardo Duran.

He'd lied about having just met Wagar the year before. Slipping over the border to Mexico could just as easily have been concocted.

Gussman had also claimed, in his confession, that the only reason he'd agreed when Wagar had asked for Charlotte's hand in marriage was because he'd simply wanted his daughter's future protected, with a prenup that gave her half of her husband's wealth were he to divorce her. In exchange, Wagar not only got a beautiful young wife with excellent skills he could use, but he got a sizeable chunk of Duran's legitimate business dealings as well.

Or would have.

If all had gone according to plan.

But from what Nicole had found the day before…that had all been a lie. The marriage had been designed to get him and Nicole out of the country legitimately. And to lock her away from Savannah. Or anything else she might want out of life that didn't include plans that had been put into place when she'd been an infant.

To the point of satisfying her need for more biological family, by providing her with children of her own. Through her marriage to Arnold Wagar.

Children of her own. The thought brought slamming back his time with Nicole hours before. The sex. The thought of Arnold Wagar having had his hands on that body…against Nicole's will…made him want to kill the man with his bare hands.

Glancing over at her again, he was shocked to see Nicole watching him. Eyes open, she hadn't moved. And wasn't smiling.

She deserved children of her own. With a man who would light up her world. Which most definitely left Harc out. Not that he'd considered being in. What they'd done… didn't even figure in to the moment that had yet to come.

Sex on the job was always that way.

Turning on the flashlight, he met her gaze, braced himself for what was quickly going to become her low opinion of him, and said, "We need to talk."

NICOLE SAT UP. Opened her mouth to assure Harc Taylor that he needn't worry that she was going to build the night before into anything more than it was, but sat with her mouth open as he got in first with, "I contacted Mike Reynolds."

The shock to her system was uncalled for. He'd never said he wouldn't contact the FBI agent. His agreement to help her after she'd laid down her stipulations had implied that he'd abide by them. At least to her that's what it had implied. He'd never actually said he'd respect her mandates.

Her mistake. Trusting someone she didn't even know.

A CIA agent.

Who'd quit his job.

Fear shot through her then, and reaching for her gun, she stood. If he was about to...

His hand clasped over her gun hand. Not hurting her, but holding tight. Keeping his grip steady, he rose to meet her face to face. "I'm sorry," he said, looking straight into her eyes. She wanted to lower her head, not look up at him—wanted to never look up to him again—but knew that she needed him.

And nodded.

As much as she hated having put herself in a position of having to do so.

She couldn't even think about what she'd done with him the night before. It hadn't been meant to be more than a way to get through the moment. And she had to let go of it.

Her chances of finding her way out of the mountains alone, without Harc's supplies, were negligible. And she wasn't ready to die.

"So Mike has known all along where we are? Where I am? What we're doing?" she asked as, heart in cold storage again, she focused on the tasks at hand.

Another skill she'd learned over the years of her growing up among her father's employees.

Harc's headshake surprised her. "I contacted him yesterday. We need his and Sierra's Web's help, Nicole..."

He'd contacted them before he'd had sex with her. Granted, she was the one who'd instigated the coupling. But had he complied, not out of a real desire for her or any emotional connection in the moment but because he was more like her father and Duran than she'd realized? Had he hoped, as Arnold Wagar had, to control her with the intensely emotional physical connection between them?

Had he been buying her cooperation in whatever he deemed came next?

The thought came. And went.

Even if he had been appeasing her, to what end? The one they both wanted. Obliterating everything Eduardo Duran had created, or been a part of. And if he gave her that, he gave her everything she'd come for.

Glad she'd held her tongue, she stood there, feeling betrayed by him anyway but knowing that her reasoning wasn't fair. She was falling for the guy. Not at all what he'd signed on for.

And not his fault that he hadn't slid a little bit in like with her, too.

Still. "You shouldn't have contacted him without letting me know," she said, her tone low, holding a smidgen of the anger she wanted to unleash.

On him, a little bit. But mostly her father. For playing her for the fool her entire life. Manipulating her to the point that she wasn't sure she'd ever be able to fully trust anyone.

Including herself.

"I weighed the risks," he told her, unblinking as he let go of her hand and stated facts as though in a courtroom. "I couldn't risk you knowing and going off the grid to do the work on your own, as you threatened to do. I understand why you didn't want Mike, your sister, or Sierra's Web involved. I've been at this gig a long time, Nicole, and I'm good at what I do, but I'm good because of the people who have my back when I'm in the field. Because of the information they can get for me, that I can't get myself without risking my cover."

The explanation was more than he'd had to give. She nodded again. And stepped away from him, reaching for the articles she'd take outside with her as she prepared for another day of work. Knowing that more was coming. He wouldn't have just confessed a day-old communication without reason.

He'd said they needed to talk. The line rarely boded well.

Setting her belongings in a pile on her mattress, she sat down and looked up at him, waiting.

"Knowing that your father isn't the kingpin, finding out that Wagar has been far more involved that we knew, he could be the head of a set of international generals. And I took that further—if not Wagar, someone else is—so we need more intel. I'm charged with keeping you safe. This entire thing might end up resting on what you find…it's bigger than who you fear putting in danger or someone losing a job, Nicole. With the head of this thing still out there, Sierra's Web is probably already in danger. You're public knowledge. People know you moved to Phoenix. Who you're related to. They have to assume that if you haven't already shared your expertise with the firm of experts, then you will."

She nodded. Stood. Toe to toe with him. Attempting to push back against the dread his words had instilled within her.

Savannah. Her firm…all that had been good in the three months since her life had literally imploded…stood to be hurt because of her.

Their little DNA match had become like a nuclear time bomb.

Because Charlotte had listened to her heart and reached out for family.

Harc's gaze seemed personal somehow as he looked her in the eye. "Just so you know," he said, "Mike and Sierra's Web were already delving into things. He'd been keeping tabs on you, as Charlotte, and they knew about the explosion at the dude ranch. They were already on high alert, not having been able to find any sign of life. Your license plate didn't show up on any traffic cams, your phone was off, you weren't using credit cards. Savannah was hugely relieved to know that you were okay. And with me."

Something else she should have figured—them checking up. Savannah had used the excuse of an exclusive vacation to disappear from her partners when she'd come to find Nicole. Nicole had just done the same. But Savannah had been a long-standing family member of the group she'd left. Nicole had only been around three months. And her father had been an international criminal. She could see how they'd think she needed watching over. And she probably would have too, if she'd ever had reason to think beyond her own small, protected world where she stayed cloistered, using her education and means to help strangers escape domestic abusers. The irony of that one wasn't lost on her.

Nor was another one. Sierra's Web hadn't been able to find her. "I was successful in putting Charlotte to death," she said. Not at all happy to know that she'd probably managed to accomplish the feat because of living with that international criminal all her life. "Which means that Wagar and whoever else will be having trouble finding me. It's like, whoever set that explosion, if it *was* purposeful, did us a favor. I could be dead."

Harc nodded. But then shook his head. "Anyone with means for a deeper investigation would be looking for a body—even if just a single piece of one that could prove DNA."

Hoping that the switch from nod to shake meant that he'd reconsidered the idea of just letting her believe the latter, to be wholly truthful with her, she said, "I hate that I didn't see the danger to Sierra's Web simply by their known association with me."

"Why would you have? We all thought that Wagar was a smaller fish in your father's pond. And the government had eyes on him."

He was right. And she appreciated the reminder. But he'd

still betrayed her trust. "Going forward, I am an equal in *this* partnership. You talk to me. I talk to you."

She expected to see his chest puff up at the very least. Or for him to glance away. Instead, he continued to hold her gaze and said simply, "Agreed."

The force of that one word gave her backbone some much-needed support.

He started to talk then, unloading on her so quickly, she had no time to feel. Only to focus. Follow along. Think.

She wholly agreed that the answer they were seeking led all the way back to Gussman's escape from the United States with a baby girl and gaining respectable new identities out of nowhere. Hated that she hadn't already reached the conclusion herself the day before.

As soon as she'd read Wagar's take on the wedding that was supposed to have happened between him and her, she should have known. Instead, she'd allowed herself to become overwhelmed by the proof that even in his supposed confession, Eduardo had lied. His written reasons for the wedding had been altruistic. To continue to protect her.

Had she really still been holding out some kind of hope that she had meant enough to him that he'd sacrifice anything for her? As she had so many times for him.

Was she really so desperate to be loved that she'd needed to know some of the closeness they'd supposedly shared had been real?

"Does Mike know that Wagar isn't the one running things?" she asked, when the ex-agent paused in his dissertation.

He nodded. "But I have to get with him as soon as possible. We need them all to do a deep dive on Gussman's past. To see if there was any chance Gussman and a young Wagar could have come in contact twenty-five years ago. And we need to know who else the Wagars, father or son, might have known then. This could be the source of our mole. Or could lead us to him."

"Or it could be the kingpin," she said, for want of a better word to describe the fiend who was still out there, running the show.

From what she'd gleaned, they'd thought, with Eduardo out of the picture, with his full confession, it would only be a matter of proof and then paperwork to take down Wagar and the rest of the operation.

She…through Harc…had been the source of the proof. It had all been so clear. And clean.

"Eduardo Duran was playing us all along," she said. "He lied about the reason for trying to force me to marry Wagar. And now that I've found my older code, we know he lied about just having met the man last year. The entire confession could be false. Every bit of it." Fear struck anew as she looked up at him.

Saw him nod as he said, "I reached the same conclusion about an hour ago. So say it's all false. To what end?"

Was the question rhetorical? Had he already figured out the end, too? Nicole told him what came to mind anyway. It could matter. She knew Eduardo better than anyone. "Maybe he's so well connected that he knows he's not long for prison. Whether there's a prison escape plan already in place or something working within the court system, he could be out and sitting in a country that doesn't extradite within hours. It's not like he hasn't successfully disappeared before."

With a baby who hadn't had a chance to know any better, let alone stop him.

Staring into Harc's blue eyes, still finding strength within them, she asked, "Do you really think it's possible he's that connected, that valuable?" Because she did. The one thing she'd always been able to count on was that Eduardo always got his way.

Until she'd entered her DNA in that database.

And had refused to marry Arnold Wagar.

Harc's shrug wasn't the instant denial she'd hoped for. But she wasn't surprised when he said, "Depends on what incriminating information he has on whom."

The words instilled renewed drive. Along with the time bomb they now had to assume was ticking at their backs. "I need to get online," she told him. "Since it's no longer just you and me needing to find and pull together all the pieces, I'll turn over the rest of the chat decoding to Sierra's Web. I've got to dive as deep as I can as quickly as I can with the code that only I know. Just tell me where and how we make that happen fast."

She thought, for a second, that his gaze warmed. In the dim light of the flashlight beam, she couldn't be sure.

But was positive she didn't want to know.

Either way.

Chapter Eighteen

If Hugh Gussman was still in the picture as largely as they were beginning to suspect, Nicole was in one hell of a lot more danger than Harc had ever imagined. No one knew her or could predict her thoughts, choices, and actions as well as her father could. The man had spent Nicole's entire life controlling, teaching, and manipulating her.

The thought was foremost on Harc's mind later that morning. They'd cleaned up and left camp to set up a very temporary base to get the satellite set up. Nicole sat beside Harc on a boulder by the horses, watching his screen right along with him as he passed scrambled messages back and forth between himself and Mike. First and foremost, Mike had obtained clearance for Harc to officially work the case.

He felt his partner in the wilderness stiffen. And then relax. Wanted to know what she was thinking, how she felt, and shook himself. Neither thing was pertinent to the moment.

And while he was glad to know that he had the authority to do what he had to do, he wasn't all that pleased to be back under protocols.

Not that they'd ever stopped him on a job in the past. He'd just vowed to be done with tightrope walking where right and wrong were concerned.

And yet his mind was swirling with facts, dangers, potential unknowns, and ideas when the next message came through.

He held out the burner, and he and Nicole read simultaneously. She turned to look at him, so close he could see the darker rim of brown around her iris as she said, "They want you to devise the plan."

She appeared to be pleased with the idea. But he needed to be sure. "This one is your call, Nicole. You put this whole process in motion. You're the one with the skills that have the capability of stopping this thing."

"You know Wagar," she told him without hesitation or even looking away. "You know the case. And your professional record for successful missions is exemplary. Which is why I'm out here with you right now."

He was the one breaking eye contact. To scan the horizon. And closer in, too. To keep a sharp eye on the horses. Assuring that they were remaining calm. "You're out here with me because you needed the files that I had," he reminded her.

"I had the files a couple of days ago." And she could have left at any point. It wasn't like he'd have shot her for doing so.

He was one of the good guys.

Mostly.

The thing they weren't talking about, the big elephant that had been on their table all morning, was like an invisible wall between them. He couldn't consider what they all were asking—that he take over an official case, take point—with walls he couldn't scale right in front of him. "This isn't because of last night, is it?" he asked.

Her expression stilled, blanked. Her shoulders dropped. "I resent the fact that you even had to ask. I'm trained in self defense, Harc, not combat. Or physical warfare. But

I'm far wiser than you give me credit for if you think, for one second, I would let the weight and scope of what we're facing, the lives of all of the potential innocents out there who have yet to be harmed, rest on an hour of sex."

Her disdain was as clear as his path forward.

But he didn't think he was ever going to forget the initial surge of very personal disappointment that had sliced through when he'd first heard the words.

THEY WERE STAYING in the mountains. Harc's initial plan to draw out the players in a quarter of a century long, very evil game, made the most sense to both of them. And ultimately to whatever small team Mike had had with him during their scrambled communications. She didn't ask if Savannah was there.

Couldn't allow herself to believe in the dream life her sister had promised over the past three months. She'd tried to let herself live it. To fit in.

But until she'd wiped their father from under her skin, until she could atone for the years she'd spent with him, she didn't belong there.

Law enforcement agencies from all over the world had been pursuing the crime organization that had made Eduardo Duran a billionaire. They'd thought they'd won, albeit only leaving Wagar's illegal arms branch, but from what Nicole had gleaned in the past couple of days, they hadn't stopped whoever was at the top. The kingpin had escaped pursuit yet again. And so they weren't going to chase him.

They were going to show him how dangerous they were to his operation. To force him to come to them to stop them.

And the rugged, dense mountains of Colorado were the perfect setup.

Trained experts would be dispatched on the ground, aware of Nicole and Harc's coordinates at all times. And twenty-four-hour satellite surveillance was already being put in place. With as few government and agency employees as possible aware of the moves. For op security purposes, much of the work would be put on Sierra's Web.

And while Nicole was thankful, hugely relieved, and moved by the support of her sister and the firm, she was also beset with an almost debilitating guilt, too.

She was sharp. Aware.

She should have seen. Or at least suspected.

"I spent the past five years becoming an expert in women's studies," she told Harc as, on horseback, they made their way quickly to the coordinates of the mountain alcove that Sierra's Web had determined, via satellite, was the best location to set up their operation. "I worked with victims of domestic violence, which almost always involves various forms of mental manipulation, and I never saw it happening to myself."

She felt like a fool. But more, she needed him to know her weakness. He'd need to be aware, to plan, in the event internal blinders prevented her from doing her job.

She was a potential risk.

He glanced over at her and then, with a quick nudge to Imperial's sides, hurried the horse up a short steep incline to flatter ground above. Slowing, while he watched her and Mahogany complete the climb behind him, he remained in the way of forward progress, bringing Mahogany to a stop as he said, "You were driven to hack Mike's computer. You then showed up and managed to convince a determined, retired CIA agent to turn over privileged files that only two men in the world knew existed, and to join you in risking your life to end your father's reign of terror."

She nodded. Not getting his point.

"So don't you ever doubt that you are the asset. That you will do anything it takes to right wrongs."

She opened her mouth to argue. To point out that if her mind was being played, she might unknowingly make wrong choices, but he held up a hand. Shook his head.

"Just by hacking Mike's computer, you'd already won the battle against your father, Nicole. You fought your way out. Don't give him any more power over you by allowing him to make you doubt yourself."

All well and good, but, "What if…"

He shook his head again. "No. Don't go there. Don't let him make you go there."

With a shift of the reins in his hands, he started Imperial—and thus Mahogany and Nicole—on their way. Leaving Nicole riding a horse in the mountains fighting with herself not to allow the doubt to win.

While she feared that she could get them all killed.

"We're all human," Harc turned to call back to her. And then, as they reached wider ground, stopped Imperial just long enough for Mahogany to pull alongside him. "We all make mistakes. Including you. If one is made here, by you, by me, by anyone who's just joined us in this fight, the rest of us adjust. Compensate. And continue pressing forward. That's how this life works."

This life. As a whole? Life in general? Or the dangerous and strangely compelling world of undercover work?

Nicole didn't figure a current definition of life mattered all that much.

But being there with Harc, working with him on that case did.

SATELLITE HAD SHOWN multiple other human occupations in their portion of the vast mountain range. Some of which would be legitimate backpackers. Most particularly at that time of year. But several were suspected as being already on the hunt for Nicole and Harc.

A pair of individuals had been tracked backward, through camera footage, to the first two sites where Harc had buried satellites. They were currently at the second, so a good day behind them. If they were lucky.

But those two might not be the only pair who'd been dispatched.

Satellite didn't penetrate rock walls, caves, or even see beneath thick underbrush.

Nor was it impenetrable. Depending on who they were after—say, someone with high government clearance—their hunters could be already tracking them, aware of every move they made.

Which was why Harc had determined that the next camp they set up would be permanent. As non-changing as things could be while undercover. He'd requested a location that contained rock overhang protection for the horses as well as a deep enough cave that he and Nicole would have a chance to go farther in, make some turns, if someone penetrated their location before they could escape.

Something they *would* do. Unless the ground crew already on its way to them were able to pick off the intruders first. Which was the plan.

He had to be prepared for every step of it to fail. If one did, he'd have another plan already in place to keep the op strong.

And heading toward success.

Reaching their desired upon location before mid-morning, he unmounted himself from Imperial's back with all senses on alert, studying every aspect of the area, designating the first step of the mission complete.

And a success.

Crossing it off his list and putting it behind him. Setting up camp was step two. Completed in better time than he'd expected with Nicole's help and their immediate attendance to the routines they'd set up for the past few days.

Her mattress was set up, with bedding rolled out, on the edge of the first turn into the mountain when he entered the cave. She was checking her gun.

"It's a weekend, so there will be more hikers out," he told her. "Not that I expect anyone to make it this far for an overnight jaunt—just want you to be aware..."

"I'm not going to shoot unless whoever I'm aiming at has a gun," she interrupted him. "And not then if you're there and have already drawn. I'm backup. Period."

He nodded. Smiled. Noticed that she'd blown up his mattress, too. And laid out his bedding.

Also by the turn. But separate from hers.

He'd had a thought or two about pushing them together.

So he could dive on top of her if he became aware of intruders at the last second in the night.

And maybe do other things. If she needed the escapism.

While he'd been standing there, wasting invaluable seconds, she seemed to have been completely unaware of him, pulling out her computer. Was already back against the wall with the thing on her lap.

Awareness of his brief lapse, of her lack of one, shot Harc into full focus and the next two hours passed in complete compliance with the plan. Never a waver.

The horses were set, both for their safety and for their ability to alert Harc while inside the cave. Holes were dug—Nicole's behind a boulder and up against the cave wall, providing her complete privacy but safety as well, since her ablution activity was the one instance when he didn't have eyes on her.

He set up traps around their perimeter, mapping each one to show to Nicole so she'd be aware and prepared.

The stream he'd insisted upon was only yards away from

the horses, and he caught, then cleaned lunch. Needing to give them both some real sustenance, even if just for mental-health purposes.

And while the fish was on a small camping cook pan, on the one small propane burner they had, he settled down to his own cognitive work. Delving into various files that occurred to him to seek out. Memorizing as he read. Trying to build a profile of the case from the new perspective they'd gained. Looking for connections.

Nicole opted to eat lunch inside while she worked, and he joined her. Asking for a rundown of her morning.

Her head shake wasn't encouraging, and he breathed back a hint of impatience. Not at her. At all. But at instincts that were screaming at him about the brigade coming for them. It wasn't far off. His best shot at keeping Nicole alive was if she found the masterfully hidden definitive proof they needed, accounts and names, before they were found.

"I'm in deep," she told him. "I've stumbled upon a couple of more sophisticated messaging protocols. But nothing that means much to me. Mostly just confirmations. Literally. Just says, Confirmed. Assuming I'm decrypting them correctly. I've made a list of dates and times, in case they correspond to any activities any of you are aware of that took place immediately prior to them."

Taking a bite of fish, he said, "Send it to Hudson Warner, and to me, please."

She nodded. Putting down her spork, she typed. And then said, "Done." Before turning her screen around.

Thinking she was showing him confirmation that she'd completed the task as requested, he barely glanced at it, until she said, "Here's the gist of what I've pulled out. I'm cutting and pasting like before. I just see nothing here except security protocols."

Setting his metal bowl on the mattress beside him, he

grabbed her device. Noticed battery level and reached for a new one. Then got up and went outside, checked the solar chargers. Both of which were almost at full capacity.

Which he'd already known. Of course he'd known. He'd set them up.

He'd just needed a second outside the cave. The wave of doubt he'd seen in Nicole's eyes as she'd taken one last glance at her screen before turning it to him...mirrored by what he'd heard in her voice...had sent such a flood of anger through him, he'd had to vacate. To breathe.

Eduardo Duran was a lucky man, being locked up in prison and not the one heading into the mountains to try to stop Charlotte Duran from exposing too much. Harc wasn't sure he wouldn't kill the man if they came face to face out there.

All the heinous crimes the man had committed over the years were enough to put him down. But the fact that he'd taken an innocent baby, stolen her life from her, to the point of the genius being unable to trust herself, stealing her confidence even when she was risking her life to do good...came close to unhinging him.

Something he'd never experienced before. Not on a case. Not ever.

With a glance at the horses, he took a deep breath and headed back inside. To the computer Nicole had left right where he'd set it.

Her bowl was empty.

As he sat down, she headed outside, behind her boulder.

And with both ears in full listen mode—a state he often slept in—he focused on the screen.

Traveled through the first page and halfway down the second—aware that Nicole was reentering the cave.

And froze.

Letters, some upside down, interspersed within various groupings of caps and lowercased code and symbols, jumped up at him.

Turning the screen as Nicole resumed her seat, he said, "What's this?"

She glanced, looked up at him. "It's garbage code. A series of parts of various security protocols that, as they're written, actually do nothing. Except confuse hackers."

Tense, he stared at her. "Are you certain? Exactly as they're written? These are all recognizable to you?"

She nodded. Then said, "All of the code is. And the series of letters, interspersed upright and upside down. They're placeholders in the event someone wanted to go in and put the protocol into place. They'd replace the nonsense with missing code to make it live. It's actually something I designed. Eduardo didn't need as many levels of security on some things and didn't want them to slow him down. I took them out of working order but left them in place in case something changed. Mostly, I was a kid being lazy and didn't want to delete it all only to have him ask me later to put it back."

His gaze sharpened. "You did this? In this file?"

She shook her head. Which eased the intensity tightening his jaw absolutely none. "No. I wrote this when he was having some employee complaints several years back. It was a way for leaders to keep him apprised of various activities without anyone else tapping into the conversation. But whoever used my code obviously didn't understand it. They just copied and pasted here."

He nodded. Chin jutting as he scrolled.

"Why? What did you find?" The worry in her tone cut into him. A feast for his own escalating concern.

"Because these letters, when you put them all together, spell a name I recognize."

Moving over to sit next to her, between her and the entrance to the cave—more as a protective move toward her than anything else—he pointed to the letters and characters he'd been referring to.

And spelled.

"Henry Villanosa," she said slowly, putting them all together. "Who's he?"

"An IRSCI—IRS criminal investigator." A man who'd been on the job for thirty years. Who—according to the Gussman case file Harc had read the day before—had been involved in the investigation of stolen funds case in which Hugh Gussman had been set to testify. Except the star witness had disappeared. And the money had never been found.

But Villanosa's name just had been. Hidden in stolen code in Wagar's files. Dated over a year ago. Just after Charlotte Duran had entered her DNA in the family-finder database.

He pulled out his phone.

Messaged Mike.

And had to physically restrain himself from taking Nicole into his arms. Shielding her from danger. As though any bullet that hit him couldn't just pass through him into her, too.

Sitting there knowing so much more, and still not enough, how could he possibly devise a failproof plan to keep her safe? To help set her free to find the life she deserved to have. If he could just do that—give a gifted and kind young woman the freedom to be whoever she wanted to be—maybe, just maybe, he'd find a piece of his soul again.

In that moment, in that cave, that *if* seemed larger than any obstacle Harc had ever faced.

For the first time in his life, he felt helpless.

At a time that was never going to matter more to him.

Chapter Nineteen

Henry Villanosa. She hadn't tried to unscramble the letters into a name. Had seen the old lazy code and had accepted it for what it was.

But as a team, she and Harc, with their different perspectives, had managed to find another piece to the seemingly impossible to unravel dynasty her father had been involved in.

And yet her one innocent act—sending in her DNA in the hopes of finding maternal family—was bringing wolves out of the woodwork. First Wagar. And then Villanosa.

She didn't waste time joining in Harc's communication with Mike. Agitated and driven, she went straight back to work. They were making strides. But were racing the clock to get enough.

Harc might've thought he and Sierra's Web, even the whole damned FBI, could keep her safe. She knew Eduardo's true power. And if he wasn't the kingpin and Wagar wasn't, that meant someone with even more connections was also after them.

Someone they didn't know. Couldn't guard against.

Someone who wanted her dead. As soon as he got to her, she would be.

She'd made a lot of progress that morning and typed fast. And then faster. Copying and pasting data as she went.

Within twenty minutes, she had confirmation that she'd been found out. They'd assumed, wanted it to happen, to draw out their enemies, but when she reached a wall of security that none of her tricks would breach, her heart started to pound. New protocols had been put in place the previous night. While she'd been having mindless sex with Harc Taylor.

The security code was good. Really good. She was better. Got through it in less than an hour. And then another. She'd made it through four completely different walls before she got back to information hidden behind them.

When actual accounts flashed onto her screen, she started to shake. To feel the snakelike fear ride up through her again. She didn't stop, though. Fully focused, she pushed forward. Copying and pasting as rapidly as possible, aware, every second, that she could be shut down again.

She didn't stop to access the information she was gathering. To read through it. There was no time. And reading was not what anyone needed from her. Harc had an entire firm and a team of agents to assess the information. Her job was to get it for them.

And then to somehow rest that night knowing that their campsite would be known to their aggressors.

She'd agreed to the plan.

Would find the strength to persevere as long as she had breath.

Scrolling from the page she'd just pasted to the next she needed to copy, Nicole froze. The words…they jumped off the screen at her. Almost literally. She stared.

And screamed, jumping so hard that her computer slid sideways off her lap, when Harc suddenly hurried into the cave. "I've been on with Mike," he said, his expression grim. His focus so intense on whatever was on his mind that he didn't even seem to have noticed her own bad moment.

Unless...he already knew.

She felt sick. Queasy. With butterflies turning to bees buzzing and stinging inside her abdomen.

"He had agents posing as you and me, chosen because of their physical resemblance to us, at the last site where you used the satellite yesterday. They were accosted an hour and a half ago..."

Her breath caught. She dragged in air past the tightness in her chest.

"The agents were able to take them down, to arrest them. They're refusing to talk, but Sierra's Web has already run backgrounds. They're both recent parolees, have been incarcerated for more than ten years. They're new hires, Nicole. And it's starting to look like that's part of the pattern. Has been all along. Which is why it's been so hard to break up the organization. While its fingers reach to the ends of the earth, it thrives due to a major outsourcing program that never uses the same people for more than a job or two, rather than relying on a loyal crew. The operation itself is likely quite small."

His words computed even as her skin grew tight. Hot. "You're saying it's going to be nearly impossible to get those we want to catch, to come to us. We've just got independent hitmen after us." Smart. Savvy.

And all Eduardo.

Staring up at Harc, aching everywhere, Nicole almost wished she was already dead.

IT ONLY TOOK a second, one look in Nicole's eyes to know that more was going on than the news he'd just brought in to her.

While they could figure that anyone who came after

them wasn't going to be able to give them the names and dates they'd need to convict whoever was involved at the top with Eduardo Duran, they'd just gleaned a very important piece of information. Had new lines of investigation they could now pursue. Someone would know some little thing that would tip the case.

If he and Nicole didn't succeed, that was.

Was that the problem? She was freaked out to learn that Wagar or whoever ruled him had sent thugs to get them? That their plan was working?

She'd spent her life looking at things on paper, from a very protected luxury fortress. Prior to coming to him, she'd been in the trenches for one day and one night in her entire life, running away from pressure to marry Wagar and then confronting her father. One day and one night when she'd believed herself the protected daughter of a well-respected decent living billionaire.

"You want to call it off?" he asked, standing there watching her right her computer. Adjust it on her lap. And do so again. "We can get a helicopter in here to pick you up right now."

He wasn't quitting. Walking away had been the worst thing he'd ever done. All the lines he'd skated, the tightropes he'd walked between right and wrong...he'd done for selfless reasons.

Walking away had been selfish. And weak. He'd been afraid that he wouldn't be able to keep himself in line.

He'd given in to the fear.

When Nicole finally raised her head to look up at him, he recognized some of that same fear. The kind he'd seen in the mirror. Fear of self.

Doubting your own mind.

Dropping down to his mattress, with the horses in full view, Harc pulled his gun from his waistband and set it beside him. Resting against his hand. "Talk to me." The words came of their own accord. Straight from his heart.

The look she shot him then was something he'd seen before. The day she'd come to meet with him. When he'd been acting like an ass.

Not at all what he'd been expecting.

Seconds passed, he withstood the look. It didn't change.

"Did you, while you were on a job, sleep with a woman solely to get closer to someone with whom she'd been acquainted?"

Everything stilled within him. And without. He was on high alert. Had agents in the mountains, risking their lives to protect Nicole as well as apprehend anyone connected to Arnold Wagar or Eduardo Duran. He had to know how she came upon the information. "Did you find further Wagar conversation? On top of what you sent to Sierra's Web?"

Her chin lifted. "You didn't answer my question." The look in her eyes...there might have been sadness there.

More, he felt as though he was looking at someone who was hiding something. Not a woman with whom he'd slept accusing him of being first rate scum.

And remembered more of their first meeting. The woman wasn't going to give until she got.

"I did," he said. And for complete clarity, but for no good reason that pertained to the job, he said, "More than once." Not liking how that sounded, and with the night before continuing to rear itself in his mind, he added, "I entered relationships with them. After they'd been vetted. And always used a condom."

He knew what that made him. Had known when he'd quit his job that the things he'd done precluded him from having a regular life in normalized society.

He'd broken all normal boundaries by which good guys were judged. Had proven himself impossible to trust.

When she'd come to him seeking his help, when he'd agreed to work with her, her trusting him hadn't even been on the table. Nor had he had a hell of a lot of trust in her, either, for that matter. She'd found him by hacking into his friend's computer.

And she was Eduardo Duran's daughter. Someone he'd been watching as a player in the man's criminal organization.

So why was it hitting him so hard to lose what he hadn't had to begin with?

She'd glanced down, farther than her screen. Almost bowing her head, but after taking a deep breath, met his gaze head on. "And did you turn on one of your own agents? Disclosing his cover to Wagar's people, in order to prove your own loyalty?"

His mind sharp, he ran through ramifications of what she knew. Considered how long she might have known. What it meant that they were having the conversation right then, with killers in the mountains, looking for them.

When she was supposed to be using the skills that only she had to find evidence no one else had to end the years-long reign of terror.

"I did," he said with a tilt of his head. Didn't bother to add that he'd also saved the man's life.

Her nod back hit him oddly, considering the topic of conversation. Almost as though she cared more about his response, than in the less than stellar actions she'd been grilling him about.

Because she'd known all along?

And the night before had changed things between them? Making his unsavory life choices matter more?

He'd given her what she'd wanted. Now it was his turn. "How long have you been waiting to ask me about those things?"

She shook her head.

"Have you known since you first came to see me?" He couldn't imagine Mike would have kept a dossier on him. She'd have had to thoroughly read multiple case reports. Which, based on how she'd described her hacking incident to him, she hadn't had time to do.

The stillness about her.

Almost a sense of defeat.

Acceptance laced with fear, he amended, remembering the way she'd yelled out and jumped when he'd first come in.

Fear...or guilt?

He almost felt as though in the time he'd been outside, she'd become someone else

"What's going on, Nicole?" He wanted to reach the woman he'd held the night before. His tone was all agent.

Lives were at stake.

And not just theirs.

"I think my father is talking to me."

Adrenaline raced through Harc. His right hand covered his gun. And though his mind told him he could have been living with the enemy the past few days, his instincts told him to offer help.

He just wasn't sure anymore if the instincts guiding him were work related—offer help as a means to find out all he could—or because he'd fallen for a woman he thought was incredible. No matter who she was or what she'd done.

HE'D PLACED HIS hand over his gun. Was ready to move with it.

But he hadn't aimed it at her.

Why she noticed, or why it mattered, Nicole wasn't sure. More, she was using that hand, the gun as a distraction from the harsher reality in front of her.

"I broke into a new system this morning. It allowed me

to view one bank account." She swallowed. Couldn't look back at the screen.

Was still fuzzy headed with ramifications. Trying to find her way out to focus, think clearly. To not let panic rob her of her ability to act wisely.

To protect herself. And others.

She'd get there. Was going to accept nothing less. She just had to find a way to speed up the process. Not get lost in minutia.

Like finding out that the man you'd slept with, the man you'd opened your whole heart to, slept with the women he got close to on the job.

And that he'd turned on one of his own. Could even have been Mike.

Or her, for that matter.

"Nicole?"

She heard Harc's voice through the fog. Left it out there.

Would her heart always lead her astray?

As it had with her father?

The thought, more than the voice, brought her upright. The man whose genes had given her life had robbed her of the life for which she'd always yearned. To be a normal kid in a regular family. To have a mother.

She hadn't even dared dream of a sibling.

Eduardo had stolen all that opportunity away from her. He'd robbed her of a chance to know and grow up loving and being loved by her mother.

He'd made her dependent solely on him. Giving her no chance to love anyone but him. Even her nannies...they'd come and gone on a regular basis.

He'd taught her to think like him.

But the blood in her veins was akin to Savannah, too. The big sister who'd risked everything, who'd nearly died, just to find Nicole. No strings attached.

Eduardo's entire empire had been run by him pulling the strings he'd injected into everyone around him. He'd been the master puppeteer.

No more.

"Nicole?"

"The account is mine." Or rather, "It has my name on it. Solely. With my—Charlotte Duran's—social security number and driver's license attached. The address is the post office box that I set up, and transferred all my accounts to, after moving to Phoenix."

"He doesn't know about Nicole."

The words weren't at all what she'd expected. They drew her gaze to the familiar intentness in Harc's blue eyes.

And yet...from a distance. They'd spent a few days in the mountains, as work partners. Had had sex. And if they survived the current situation, they'd go their individual ways. Never see or speak to each other again.

Thinking only about what he'd chosen to bring out of the hellacious mess she'd played right into, she said, "Or he does and he's just not yet ready to reveal the information," she said.

"How much money is in the account?"

Yeah, that was more to the point. "Over a billion dollars." And holy hell to that.

He didn't react. Just asked, "When was it established?"

Yeah, that, too. "Right after we moved to the States."

His gaze narrowed. She glanced over the several yard distance to their newest cave's entrance. Couldn't see much of the outside from her vantage point. Wasn't sure she wanted to do so.

"You're telling me you didn't know about the account?"

Hard to believe, right? She shook her head. "I knew of an account he set up for me, of course. I knew he made regular deposits to it, for my own security, he'd said. He had me pay the property taxes out of it, but otherwise the funds just sat there. Accruing. Three months ago, I emptied the money out, donated everything to women's shelters and a national domestic violence hotline number, and then closed the account."

He could believe her or not. She wouldn't blame him if he didn't. Didn't much matter.

She could hardly believe how naive she'd been. How she couldn't have known…because she knew him.

Better than anyone.

Chin up, she glanced right at him as she said, "This account is offshore." Watched his expression sharpen, his brows narrow.

"And it always held that much money?"

He was getting there. Maybe.

Could be she'd be the only one who ever would.

She shook her head. "He opened it with half a million."

"And deposited to it over the years?"

She nodded. "A quarter of a million a year."

Which didn't reach anywhere near a billion. Even for someone not great at math.

She and Harc were both top notch in that area.

"But it grew to a billion?"

She nodded.

"When?" The billion-dollar question.

Part of her was relieved that he got there so quickly, as she said, "The day I told him I put my DNA in that database." See, that had been her mistake.

Telling him.

She'd played her hand. Letting him know, by the admission, that he owned her. Played right into his. Had she not given him the heads up, he wouldn't have had a year to prepare. To notify Wagar. To get people on Savannah.

Her sister might have shown up, tipped off Mike—who

was already in residence and clever enough to have seen a stranger tracking his charge—and once they'd told her, she could have helped Mike infiltrate her father's dealings and end the entire nightmare right then and there.

There'd have been no Wagar proposal.

No running away.

No one shooting at Savannah.

But Eduardo would have had her.

He'd known it then.

And believed it, still.

That was how they were going to get him.

Even it meant taking her down with him.

Chapter Twenty

Nicole wasn't his lover. Or even his friend. She was no longer a work partner. Not because he deemed it that way, but her demeanor, her tone, everything about her spoke withdrawal from him.

He'd expected as much. He'd slept with her on the job. As he'd done with other women.

He'd ratted out a fellow agent to prove his cover's loyalty.

He'd come full circle. With a difference. He was no longer running away. He was back in. One-hundred percent.

Reaching for his computer, he held out his hand. And when she just looked at him, he asked, "Can I have the flash drive?" It was how she'd passed every bit of information on to him.

She shook her head. "I haven't put anything new on it."

Okay, he got it. She didn't trust him. Resented him, too. But the situation they were in went way beyond letting hurt feelings get in the way. The one thing they could count on with each other was their shared passion to bring down the entire empire that had made Eduardo Duran—and they had to assume others—very very rich.

"I need to see that account, Nicole." He didn't pretend to ask. Or talk like a friend, either. "I need to send it on to

Mike. They can trace account numbers, perhaps find out what bank it's sitting in, which opens a hell of a lot of doors."

When she didn't move, except to shake her head again, and didn't look away, either, he took a step back from the situation. Sat there assessing her.

Couldn't get a read.

She was her father's daughter.

And...he suspected that Gussman *was* the kingpin. With assistance, to be sure, but still...the man had managed to steal two million dollars from the United States government a quarter of a century before. Money that had never been found.

It wasn't that much of a stretch to realize that the genius had things over powerful people, keeping them loyal to him lest he expose the conceivably large portfolio he had. He'd already heard back that Villanosa was off the grid.

Because Gussman, Wagar, or someone else working with them was watching Nicole's progress online. The bad guys knew what they knew.

Villanosa was either in the wind, starting a new life under a new identity...

Or he was dead.

That was how people like Eduardo managed to flourish for decades.

It also meant that the organization was minus one powerful person. A man who'd had strong governmental influence—and classified intel, too.

Harc had to find a way to capitalize on the weakness.

Gussman was diabolically smart. A manipulator unlike anything Harc had seen before. He'd cold-bloodedly chosen to leave one daughter behind when he'd taken the other from their mother. Had even put a hit out on his firstborn when she got too close.

As Harc sat there, in visual battle with Nicole, pieces

started to fall into place one after another. Gussman's confession hadn't been for Charlotte's sake. It had been a preplanned move devised long before Charlotte and Mike had shown up at the mansion that night. Designed to manipulate everyone involved.

Which was what he'd been doing all along. Everywhere.

And was still doing? With Nicole?

The truth hit Harc like a punch in the gut. Delivered by a heavy-weight boxer. He stood up, taking his gun with him. Shoving it into his waistband, he said, "I need to see that file."

Her head shake, the raise of her brows was clear. Almost deliberate. "I've closed the chain," she told him. "You can take my laptop, have anyone you want analyze it—no one is going to find the information I had up on screen. And no one can compel me to show it to you, either. I'm not under arrest. And I know for a fact that you don't have anything on me to be able to arrest me."

He missed a breath or two. Couldn't believe that he'd been wrong about her over the past few days. Eduardo might have made her in his image.

Perhaps he'd taught her how to act in any situation.

But the man hadn't sent her to Harc. There'd been no reason to do so. Nothing for the man's empire to gain by exposing it to more scrutiny.

By exposing the lies in his confession.

But what about Nicole? Was she back under her father's control? Had she ever completely left it? She'd been devastated. Angry.

Didn't mean she didn't still love the man.

Staring her down, he said, "So does this mean you're done? We're through here?"

He wasn't. Not by a long shot. But there was no point in

being sitting ducks if they'd gained all they were going to in their current rendition.

The sudden widening of her eyes, before they narrowed in on him again caught his attention. Stuck.

Had she overplayed her hand? Did Eduardo need her to continue playing Harc, her sister, the FBI, Sierra's Web?

Or was something else going on? Something less easy to pinpoint. To understand.

Was she in trouble? More so than he, or anyone, knew?

As in, far more involved in Duran's operation than she wanted anyone to know? But then why seek him out? And more to the moment, why even tell him about the damned account she'd just supposedly discovered?

Because while she was somewhat in with Duran, he'd hidden too much from her for her to carry on without him?

She'd needed access to Wagar's files to find out what her father hadn't told her?

She hadn't answered his question. He wasn't backing away from it. "We done?" His tone held more threat than question.

Nicole raised her chin again. "No."

If he wasn't mistaken, there was a tremble in her chin, if not her voice.

Wishful thinking on his part?

"Then what? You continue to work, we all protect you while you do so, but you don't help us end this thing? You don't give us the information we need?"

At that, strange as hell, her face cleared. Setting aside her computer, she stood, eye to eye with him. "I swear to you, Harc. I will continue to share. I will give you everything you need. Just not information about that one account."

He held her gaze a long time. Delving deep. Mercilessly. She didn't even blink. And he believed what she'd just said.

Maybe he'd grown soft. His ability to do his job might have left him in the dust during his time away.

He didn't think so.

"Then let's get back to it," he said.

And walked out on her.

She had to do it. Nicole knew as well as she knew that she was no criminal, that she was the only one who could stop Eduardo Duran.

The only one who could think like he thought. The only possession he'd ever coveted and lost.

Standing alone in that cave, watching Harc's back as he headed toward the horses, she couldn't conceive of any way she'd succeed without his help. Mike and Sierra's Web—they were the icing on the mud she'd been served up. But Harc, he was her lifeline.

Her proof that no matter how much you'd lived in darkness, or consorted with thieves, you could still do good. Succeed.

Find love—even if only with animals who sensed a caring heart and didn't judge beyond it.

Would Mahogany and Imperial know that she'd crossed over? Even if only doing so undercover?

Harc no longer trusted her.

Which was for the best.

With that last thought, Nicole did some stretches and then sat back down. Opened her portal to the dark web, dove deep, and started to type.

Fearing that, even if she lived, she was going to lose herself for good.

She'd let Harc and Sierra's Web think that she was working toward finding them intel. She'd continue working on things she'd already accessed and downloaded that morning. Before the new portal had appeared on her screen.

She just couldn't be "seen" online poking into Wagar/Duran business.

Instead, she was going to accept the olive branch she knew her father had just offered her. Attempt to have him help her play both sides. And hope that she didn't get herself killed.

HARC MESSAGED WITH MIKE. Who immediately brought Savannah into the scrambled conversation. He was going forward with Nicole, no matter what the others thought, but he would not involve them unknowingly.

He wasn't all that surprised to have almost immediate confirmation that they were choosing to stay fully on board. With a note from Savannah to please watch her little sister's back more closely than ever.

And acknowledgment that, considering the brainwashing with which she'd grown up, they couldn't completely trust her.

He unscrambled the last bit with dread filling his gut.

They all knew they couldn't they let her go. Even if she'd been completely turned by Duran—or had never really left his camp—she was their best chance at getting the evidence they needed to bring down the rest of his empire.

Harc was in one hundred percent.

No matter who Nicole turned out to be—and great move to change her identity as a sign that she'd left Charlotte behind, to hide the fact that she hadn't—she hadn't been dealt a fair rap in the beginning. Being manipulated and brainwashed from the time you were a baby...just not right.

She was smart, though. Well educated and then some. And an adult. Fully aware of the fiend her father really was.

The choices she was currently making were on her.

He left her to whatever she was doing for another hour.

Until he got another message from Mike. Marked urgent.

In light of the information Harc had given them pursuant to the loaded offshore account in Charlotte's name, and at Harc's request, Mike had sent an agent in to have a discussion with Eduardo. Part of the man's plea agreement had included cooperation with authorities.

After which he'd always claimed to know nothing about whatever they'd brought him. Or took all blame on himself. He'd been in solitary confinement for weeks, giving him an opportunity to rethink his position.

Unscrambling took seconds. Comprehending what he was seeing, less than that. Shooting off an urgent reply to get more bodies in the mountains and watching the satellites for any and all movement, he spun on his heel and headed back to the cave that was beginning to feel more and more like a jail cell.

Nicole's. Not his.

He was the only guard.

NICOLE WAS STILL waiting for a response to pop up from Eduardo in the minimized window she'd kept open, and continued to check every few minutes. She needed him to see her there. Waiting. Picturing her pacing. Her face tight with worry. Needed him to get an immediate response from her when he did send her his acceptance of her own olive branch. She had to give him the relief and gratitude he'd expect from her.

Without going overboard.

In the meantime, she was doing her best to find anything she could in the morning's work that would gain her some traction—and trust—from Harc. And the others. Mike. Sierra's Web.

She couldn't let herself think about Savannah. Couldn't feel their connection. Not if she hoped to succeed at convincing Eduardo that meeting up with her sister had been a mistake. That they were nothing alike. That she didn't fit in with Savannah's world. That her sister was like their mother. She was Eduardo all the way. That he'd been right to leave them behind. And to pick her.

A series of numbers popped up in the decryption code she'd made up minutes before. Digits that, while different, mirrored the account number Eduardo had shown her earlier in the day.

And she knew...she'd just downloaded that information an hour before Eduardo's veiled message via a new portal exactly like the ones she'd been looking through—but with different encryption—had popped up. He'd set up security measures to have someone notified immediately if any accounts were breached.

There were no defining letters attaching. Nothing that she could see that identified the account owner. And she wouldn't expect there to be. The information would be hidden in another file. With different code.

Another part of a system she'd set up for her father. In her teens, she'd loved making up intricate codes for everything. Challenging him to decode them.

Even in the birthday cards she'd given him.

She shuddered at the thought of how much she'd adored the man. Was downloading the account information to the flash drive she'd pass on to Harc, when he came striding into the cave. His expression foreboding.

To say the least. Whatever was about to come at her... wasn't good.

She wanted to take it standing. Didn't trust herself to remain steady enough on her feet to pull off her ruse.

"What?" she asked, as though they were who they'd woken up as that morning. Or even who they'd been before they'd had sex the night before.

Either was far better than the stranger looking down at her as though he'd never seen her before in his life.

"Seriously, Harc. If you're going to shoot me, just do it. Or tell me that you're leaving and taking both horses with you." She wouldn't blame him for either.

And wouldn't stop what she'd started, either.

"Did you know?"

She blinked, shook her head. "About the account that seems to be lodged at the same bank as the one I found for myself this morning?" she asked, eyes open and honest as she met his stormy gaze. "I told you I would share with you everything I found." She pulled out the flash drive. "I just moved the information over for you. And you'll be able to see exactly when I accessed the information. And when I found the decryption that unlocked it for me."

Frowning, seeming almost lost for a second, he leaned over and took the flash drive. Then dropped to his butt on the edge of his mattress, knees up, his boots in the dirt between them, and with his arms on those knees, moved the drive from one hand to the next.

Then pocketed it. Pulling out his gun. Laying it down, with his right hand beside it.

Not touching it yet.

She took that to be a good sign.

"Did you know that your father was in solitary confinement?"

She frowned back at him. Seriously concerned for a moment that he was trying to make her as simple minded as her father had done. "Yeah, I knew," she told him. "Mike told Savannah he was refusing to cooperate—in his way, of course—meaning they couldn't do anything to prove it. Why? You think I purposely didn't tell you?"

"Stop!" His raised voice upset her. The note of pain she heard in it, almost unhinged her.

Blinking back tears, fearing he'd see them as the ploy they could have been had she been in Eduardo's clutches all along, she said, "Harc. I'm sorry I can't show you that account. Until this is through, I have to protect myself. I thought you'd understand that. If Eduardo has framed me, I can't be sitting in a jail cell right now. I've got to get this work done first. And with Mike and the FBI officially involved and you on protocol again, I can't take the chance that someone would have to arrest me." There was far more truth in the words than he'd ever believe, if he knew what she'd done.

He raised both arms to his knees again. Studied her. As a person communicating with a person. Not an agent on the job. "Why did you tell me about the damned thing, then?"

And she gave him the truth. "I didn't mean to. Didn't think I should. But… I couldn't keep it from you."

If Eduardo were monitoring the conversation, he'd be proud. As long as he couldn't see into Nicole's heart. Know how she really felt.

It hit her then that that was where Eduardo Duran had failed. Every time. He'd never understood that Charlotte wasn't exactly like him. That she didn't just live in her mind but was driven by a compassionate, caring heart that needed to love and be loved.

He'd seen her lectures, her philanthropy through his own critical lens. There was reason for everything he did. And every reason led to bolstering either his bank account or his stellar reputation.

Harc was still watching her. She wanted to crawl across the distance separating them and into his arms. To get lost there.

And never be found again.

But she had a role to play. Had to end things with her

father, once and for all. End them in the world. Not just her life.

"Why are you upset that I knew Duran was in solitary confinement and didn't tell you?" she asked then. Needing to find some place where they could share the same ground again. To be on the same team.

He shook his head, then dropped his chin to his chest. Looked up at her. Then lifted his head to meet her gaze as he said, "They went to bring him out of his cell for questioning this afternoon. He wasn't there."

Heart pounding, she felt the blood leave her face. Felt her head swim. Thought she was going to pass out. Forced herself to focus long enough to ask, "The cell was empty?"

The diabolical man could walk through walls? And still show up on body checks? And eat food and send the empty container out?

Harc shook his head. "There was an off-duty guard there. One who swears he knows nothing. Says he was bound and gagged and blindfolded, dragged there, and left."

"When?"

It mattered. More than anyone knew but her. More than they could know.

"Today. Mid-morning."

Right about the time she'd accessed that file.

Eduardo had had a plan.

And when she'd breached a certain predetermined point, someone on the top tier payroll with a whole lot of clout and ability to manipulate had set it in motion.

Eduardo. Even in a cement cage behind a locked steel door, the man had the ability to control his world. Whether he ruled those in power with intimidation, threat, or, more likely, huge amounts of money and promises of protection—twenty-five years of getting what he wanted proved he was a master at it.

Shaking, Nicole feared that she was never going to be free of him.

Or be able to stop him.

Chapter Twenty-One

She wouldn't share the account because he'd gone official on her and she was afraid it would incriminate her. Get her arrested before she could find the proof to end the empire her father had been involved with her entire life.

Harc wanted to believe her. He didn't...quite.

Outside making dinner, all senses on alert in spite of the many trained defenders on the ground surrounding him and Nicole, Harc believed that she hadn't meant to tell him about the account. But hadn't been able to keep the secret from him.

Mostly.

With the caveat that she was smart enough, savvy enough, had read him enough to have concocted the story to get back in his good graces. About why she wouldn't share the account. And about why she'd told him it existed.

The near tearful state—the same.

But the way the blood had drained from her face when she'd found out Eduardo was nowhere to be found—that hadn't been faked.

Even if she was in cahoots with him, she hadn't been happy to hear that he was likely free.

Because she feared him?

Or because he was leaving the country without her? And she feared her fate on her own?

He hated the not knowing.

After looking over the new information she'd downloaded to the flash drive, he believed that she'd just found the second bank account. Had already passed on the information to Mike. With any luck, they'd have the name of the bank soon.

Could begin digging from there.

He also believed that Nicole wanted to find evidence to eradicate the crime organization. Why else would she have come to him? He just wasn't positive she'd turn over the information to him once it was found.

Her father could have put her onto Mike and Harc. To get rid of evidence that only she could find.

She'd been shocked and hurt to find that second program she'd written. The one Wagar had been using. Meant even if she was working with Duran, he hadn't told her everything.

Perhaps just his way.

And it was possible the man wasn't sure he could trust her. She might be in the middle of a test of some sort. One which, if she failed, could get her killed.

Bottom line, some purpose with life-risking strength had driven Nicole Compton to breach Harc's privacy. He had to stick with her until that situation was resolved, one way or another.

The possibility that she could die in the process also weighed on him heavily.

He couldn't let personal thoughts get entangled with the facts or he'd lose focus.

A point he lost sight of when, two bites into dinner, Nicole—who was sitting on the ground nearer to the cave's entrance, facing the horses—said, "I'm finding myself less able to concentrate because I'm bothered by something."

He continued to eat. To maintain a semblance of calm. As all senses went on high alert. With a one shoulder shrug, he swallowed a bite and said, "You want to talk about it?"

Innocuous. No pressure. And an insult to her intelligence. Why else would she have brought it up? He took another bite of the stroganoff they were repeating for a second time.

"Not really, but I can't afford to be less than my best when every minute counts." She was eating, too, albeit more slowly than him. She was calmer than he liked, considering that she could be playing him.

All of them.

"The chatter I found this morning, between Wagar and... whoever...indicating that you slept with a woman close to Wagar when you were undercover..."

His gut dropped. He put down his bowl. Done eating. The utensil was nearly empty anyway. He'd seen bits of the messaging...had consumed everything she'd sent him. He'd only seen that he'd slept with a woman close to his subject while undercover. No specific mention of Arnold Wagar.

And nothing of note from the agents assigned to watch the man, either. Wagar was in the States. In California. Lying low.

But then, when the majority of your business took place on the computer, behind seemingly unending layers of encryption, you could be blowing up countries and who would know?

"I know I came on to you last night..."

Her words grabbed his full attention. His gaze shot over to her. Collided with hers. Was she looking for an apology?

Her eyes were clear, focused on his as she said, "I just need to know why you responded."

Really? He almost said the word aloud. Paused, not sure

what she was looking for. Some kind of reassurance that she was attractive?

In the midst of the intricate and hellacious situation they were engulfed with?

He shook his head without responding. The answer was too obvious. Didn't need saying. Yeah, she'd had the ability to get him off track. To consume him mind and body for a time.

He'd thought he was helping her through some rough moments. Helping them both.

Maybe he hadn't thought at all. Clearly, not enough.

And was getting hard again just thinking about that hour. One of the most pleasurable he could ever remember.

"When you're working, you sleep with a woman to get what you want from them," she said then. "To get them to confide in you, maybe give information that seems harmless to them but that you need for reasons of your own that you aren't disclosing to them. Or to get them to introduce you to someone."

And...boom. He got where the conversation was going.

Started to blurt the truth. Held his tongue while he considered the angles. What she might be seeking. If indeed her concentration was being affected by the not knowing. And he had a flash of her face the night before as she'd looked him in the eye.

There'd been no subterfuge. To the contrary, the lack of even a hint of walls between them had been completely new for him. No walls. Not from her. But not from him, either.

And that was when Harc knew that the job he was on had become personal. There was no way it couldn't be. No matter what he found out, he'd fallen for the woman.

And even if she was in trouble, he was going to do everything he could to see that she got out of it. Including killing the fiend who'd fathered her, if that was what it took to free her from him.

SHE SHOULDN'T HAVE ASKED. Nicole knew, most particularly in light of the duplicity she was practicing with her escaped father—a man who could be right there in the mountains with them ready to snatch her away again, that her sexual situation with Harc mattered not at all.

But twice since their pre-dinner conversation, she'd found herself staring at code instead of working to decipher it. While her mind was on Harc.

On duping him. Her chances of success there.

And on whether she could even pull it off. The man was different than anyone she'd ever met. Granted, she hadn't had a ton of experience in the dating field, but she'd been in the company of the male sex her entire life. If her father ever entertained women, it had been outside Charlotte's purview.

She'd been acting as his plus-one at charity and social events since she was a teenager.

She finished her dinner. Cleaned her own thin metal bowl. Took care of personal business. And as she headed toward the cave, saw Harc standing just outside it. Watching her approach.

Guarding her?

Or keeping an eye on the area in general?

She went to pass him, to head back in to work while there was still an hour of daylight, was choosing not look at him when she heard, "Nicole."

She wanted to be unaffected enough to ignore the soft, almost apologetic tone in his voice. She wasn't.

Stopping, she looked over at him. She didn't need his pity. She'd been desperate for escapism. Had known she could get it with him. She'd thrown herself at him.

She'd known the second she'd woken up that morning that she'd made that particular bed, and it was up to her to climb out of it.

"The women I've slept with while working—there were only three—the relationships were predetermined as part of the job. Not the sex...that only happened if it became obvious that I'd lose their interest if things didn't go to another level."

He was telling her something. His gaze said so. She still felt numb.

And hurt, too, which made no sense.

"Last night had nothing to do with this mission we're on. It was personal. Because you asked and I didn't want to reject you..." She paled. "...but also because I wasn't strong enough to find a noble high ground and deny myself the chance to share that with you."

Oh. For the first time since she'd awoken that morning Nicole felt warm. Inside and out.

She blinked. Look at him again. Didn't smile with her mouth but felt as though both of their gazes had shared a grin. Said, "Thank you." And, bowing her head, went back to work.

Spurred on by the possibility that the sooner she got through more layers of frustrating blocks—or heard from Hugh Gussman/Eduardo Duran—the sooner she'd have a chance to sink into some more incredible forgetfulness.

With a man she was never going to forget.

Even if he ended up hating her.

THE EVENING WAS too eerily quiet. Horses had grazed to their content. Harc brushed them, communing, and neither one of them gave him any cause for anything but calm.

As in before the storm?

Feeling like eyes were on his back, he couldn't help but concern himself with what was coming their way.

And how soon it would get there.

One thing he knew for certain, to his core, was that he had to sleep half-awake. And be at his most vigilant. Their campsite afforded more protection than most anywhere else they could be. Unless a chemical bomb landed in the middle of their small compound, they shouldn't be breached without warning. Every move they made outside the cave or the tarps he'd set up for personal business was being picked up by satellite.

As were the areas surrounding them.

And as one who found ways to get around procedures, he knew that nothing was foolproof. If he was on the other side of the barriers that had been set up, he'd find a way to get to that cave.

His task was to figure out how he'd best do so. And prepare for the eventualities.

Sourcing out the weakest spots, he set underground barriers to alert them in the eventuality of intruders. Littered the area with leaf covered TNT poppers set on hard ground or rocks.

His last messaging with Mike was frustrating in its lack of any hint of closure. Wagar remained in his California home. Eduardo hadn't shown up on any of the hundreds of traffic and other surveillance cameras Sierra's Web personnel had accessed, starting with the prison in California where he'd been held and expanding from there to Phoenix to southern Colorado and at all airports in between.

The BOLO had gone out to all agencies, both federal and local.

For all they knew, the man was holed up under the care of a plastic surgeon, changing his looks as he'd done in the past. With new identification papers already created.

He could also have been transported out of the country. Could be sitting on the beach somewhere without extradition, drinking mai tais on the beach.

That fact that Wagar was still in the States told Harc that Eduardo had remained in the country as well. An assumption with which Mike agreed. Believing as they did that the underground network of which the two were a part was small, and going with an agreed upon theory that Eduardo Duran was the kingpin, as they'd always assumed, everyone was on high alert, with multiple crews working round the clock, resting a lot of hope on Nicole's ability to get to the root of the operation before Duran got to her.

They'd traced the account number Nicole had given them to a bank in the Cayman Islands. But didn't get any further than that. Winchester Holmes, Sierra Web's financial partner and head of their entire financial team, was familiar with the bank. And with many who'd banked there. It was exclusive, refused to work with American authorities and was also known for their less-than-savory connections. He believed, based on the little he'd been able to determine from the finances Eduardo had turned over as his entire business portfolio upon confession, that the man had no go-to bank. But, rather, that he had a portfolio that appeared to be complete, while hiding any number of untold accounts in any number of untold locations.

The man was a genius.

So was his daughter.

And so were they—each in their own fields.

Mike sent the reminder at the tail end of the conversation.

Truth was, though, that Duran was just that good. Which was why he'd been eluding authorities for more than twenty-five years.

Harc was up against the case of his career, of his lifetime, one in which he'd developed a personal affiliation—and he didn't like, at all, how far away he was from closing it as he went inside the cave for his toiletries and fresh clothes before turning in for a while.

His rest would be intermittent. He'd lived that way for months at a time during various points of his career. That prospect didn't faze him. Sharing the small space with a woman who'd slipped by defenses he'd had up his entire career did.

Eyes wide, Nicole glanced up at Harc as soon he'd taken enough steps inside the cave to indicate that he was heading back her way. She just as quickly turned her gaze back toward her computer screen, stomach roiling. She'd heard back from Eduardo, just as she'd known she would.

Had information for Harc. Something that was going to hit him hard. If she delivered it, the teams backing Harc up would be all over it instantly, and Eduardo would know that. It would be her sign to him that she was working for him.

That the plea to come home, to be with the only person who really knew her, who loved her, to be where she'd always belonged was legitimate. She'd further strengthened that plea with a condition of her own—Wagar being permanently removed from anything to do with her.

She knew how to play Eduardo's game. Was making him choose, too.

The fact that the information she was staring at but hadn't yet downloaded to the flash drive Harc had returned to her earlier would also prove to Harc that she was on their side was part of what was stopping her.

The second she passed on Eduardo's information, Harc would never be able to trust her again.

Something he wouldn't know at first, of course, but from

that point on, she'd be counting the days and hours until he turned on her.

If her plan succeeded, he'd also have everything he'd wanted. Duran done. His organization demolished.

He reached for his toiletries. Would be heading out, leaving her to sit there in a battle she couldn't personally win, either way.

She had to be brave. Strong. To see the plan through. No matter the sacrifice to self.

And she couldn't afford to alert anyone else. First because no one knew how Eduardo was managing feats like a magician. Who was paving his way.

Or on his payroll.

Second because she wasn't sure she could pull the whole thing off if she wasn't on an island by herself. Eduardo knew her better than anyone. He'd know if she felt secure. She'd let some nuance slip. Something.

Let alone the fact that the more people who were brought in, the sooner Eduardo would figure out that she'd turned on him so completely.

She was on the hook. And so afraid that Eduardo would manage to slither through official protocols again.

And again.

Unless she stopped him.

"Harc?" She made the intonation rise on the last part of the syllable. Like she was just discovering something. Hit Save on the download so the timing of his file would verify the information had just appeared.

Rather than having been sitting there for more than half an hour as she'd vacillated with herself. Trying to figure out which of the horrible choices in front of her made her a better person. She went with the one she could live with. If she survived.

He turned at the entrance of the cave. Took a few steps toward her. "What's wrong?"

"I just found a whole series of conversations between Arnold Wagar and someone who was working for him," she said, shaking inside, her chest tightening like a vice over her lungs as she got close to the big reveal.

The one that had had her near tears and frozen on the one screen since she'd first read it.

Pulling out the flash drive, she reached it out to him. "They're with Clayton Abernathy," she said, her gaze meeting his as she delivered the name of the agent he'd double-crossed on his last assignment.

He'd taken the drive but froze as she said the name. Was staring in her direction. She wasn't sure he was seeing her, though. "You got word that Wagar needed you to prove your loyalty before being granted a meeting with him, right?"

"I wasn't sure it was Wagar," he said then, snapping into focus as his right hand rested against the gun jutting from the side of his shirt. "I was going to be meeting with him or a top lieutenant," he said, studying her. As though she'd been there. Had something to do with what had happened when she'd been busy lecturing and wishing she could live without *Isaac* at her heels every second of every day.

"Abernathy told Wagar that you were an undercover cop. CIA. The test of your loyalty was supposed to have ended your life. But you didn't act as they expected. You went for Abernathy, who you thought was in the range of fire, and escaped the bullet that was meant to have killed you." She held his gaze the entire time she delivered the news. Willing him to not only believe her. But to know that she felt his pain.

That she cared.

Personally.

He seemed to get the message. He held on to her gaze,

too. His eyes glistening with intensity. He nodded. And his "Thank you" was more of a caress than mere words before he said, "I'm going to message Mike," and walked out.

Nicole wanted to follow him. To be with him, a hand at his back, as he delivered the newest detail to Mike. Her knees were so weak, she hadn't been sure she could stand.

But she'd be ready for him when he returned. Inviting him in again, consoling him as he'd consoled her the night before. Filling her soul before it went completely dark.

Loving him for the short time left before he found out she wasn't to be trusted.

Because she knew, with the same certainty that dictated Eduardo's successes, that Harc was going to find her out. Like Hugh Gussman, Harc was just that good.

Exhausted, she shut down her computer, readied herself for bed, and was lying awake in her sleeping bed with a small flashlight putting a soft glow over the darkness that had fallen by the time Harc returned to her.

She didn't ask how his scrambled message conversation had transpired. The answer was pretty much a given. Mike and the agencies and firm involved with the investigation would be arresting the CIA agent and bringing him in for questioning.

At which time he'd deny knowing anything about which they were speaking. But this time, with what she'd downloaded and given Harc, the authorities would have proof to make the claims stick.

The double agent would be prosecuted. Sent to jail.

And unless she did her job right, he'd end up disappearing from his cell, too. And given a new life someplace of his choosing...

She needed Harc. To feel his touch. To lose herself in him until everything but thoughts of him were obliterated long enough for her to breathe.

Almost as though he'd read her mind, he pulled his mattress over and dropped it next to hers. Shoving it up against hers with his foot. And then dropping down to it.

Desire ignited inside her, swam through her veins as she watched him settle his gun under the top corner of the mattress. Thinking of how much more accessible and comfortable things were going to be with twice the space—on fire even more for him having thought of it—she reached out a hand to him.

Felt it flounder in dead air as he lay just out of reach, on his side on the edge of his mattress, his back turned toward her.

And she realized he hadn't moved the mattress over for pleasure. He'd done so to put himself between her and the cave's opening.

He was doing his job.

He wasn't going to be doing her.

Chapter Twenty-Two

Harc came to with a start, fully aware of the direction from which the pop had come. Gun in hand, he stood, heard Nicole rustle, and put his left hand behind him, signaling for her to stay back.

He couldn't hear the horses. His gut tightened.

"Get your gun," he whispered. "And stay put as long as you know where I am and am still standing. I shoot from behind as quickly as I do forward."

Something he'd already told her. And bore repeating. She hadn't seemed to take it to heart at the time.

He took another step forward, heard her take the safety off her pistol—a Glock—smaller than his, but powerful. He stepped soundlessly, quickly, to the side of the cave's opening.

Sliding outside, he kept himself covered, by rock overhang above, brush around him, keeping his back to the mountain—just as he'd planned. Got close enough to the horse's cover to see that they were both there.

Lying down as they did when they slept in their stalls. Relief was brief. He wanted to believe that Imperial and Mahogany had taken to their new shelter as they had to the nice roomy stalls he'd had built for them at the ranch.

He knew better.

Nor did he think that someone had gotten close to them. Imperial would have given the loud sniff with which he'd been trained to alert Harc.

Usually when Harc's tension was escalating, but any time the horse sensed danger. No way the former wild animal would have lain down to sleep in the former mountains that had been his home.

Had it been him, he'd have dropped a treat for the mustangs from above—something light like pieces of banana—that had been shot with something to make them sleep. Quiet. Inobtrusive. Nothing that would alert them or wake him.

Something for which he hadn't planned.

But looking up, he saw exactly where the culprit would have been to successfully complete the feat. Knew, too, that in the amount of time it would have taken the horses to eat and then lie down to sleep, the fiend could be right there with them.

Watching. Waiting.

He had no idea how many were out there. Or how close Mike's agents and Sierra's Web's protectors might be.

Counted on the perp or perps not being visible by satellite.

Something much easier to accomplish in the dark. Based on the moon there was another couple of hours before dawn.

If Harc could hold the enemy off until then, he'd have all the help he needed. Coming at the intruders from behind.

Frozen in place, he kept watch. Ready to shoot at any movement around the entrance to the cave. Waiting to hear more pops. Watching the two locations he'd also scouted for best ways into the camp.

One involved climbing up the mountain from over a mile below.

The other, going up half a mile and scaling down. Either

would require skill and equipment. Something a professional would already know and have prepared for.

And would require arrival one at a time.

Giving him one chance to take each one down before the next appeared.

Unless they came from both locations at once.

Temperatures had dropped from the balmy seventy during the day to the thirties that were expected for late spring. Sweating, he welcomed the chill.

Couldn't shun his awareness of the so-special woman in the cave just yards away. Trusting him to keep her safe.

Needing him to keep her safe, even if she didn't trust him.

Attack was imminent. His gut, his soul, and his mind were all clear on that.

As he told himself that he could single-handedly take down anything that came at him in however many numbers. That he was fully prepared.

That good at what he did.

And prayed that help was there, guarding his back.

EDUARDO DURAN.

Picturing the man behind his desk in the home in which she'd grown up, the completely confident and self-assured look on his face as he dealt with one irritant and another—getting rid of them without raising his voice or losing his charming smile—Nicole shuddered. Adjusted the gun in her suddenly sweating palm.

She'd known he'd act quickly. That her clock had been ticking. She hadn't expected him to pounce within hours of the making of their deal.

As she stood against the wall of the cave, near the entrance so she could keep Harc in sight, realization hit.

Harc had messaged Mike.

Authorities had moved in on Abernathy immediately.

And that had been Eduardo's cue.

Every move a preplanned piece on the chess board of life.

With such forethought and precise planning that checkmate was inevitable. The man was only going to die when his physical organs grew so old they could no longer be revived.

And he was coming for her.

He'd had his proof that she was working for him.

And he had her.

But not without a fight.

He was the kingpin. She had no doubts there anymore.

The lack of information she'd been able to find, other than what Wagar had been using for his own deeds—none of which had led to Eduardo Duran directly—told her that there *was* no one else. There'd have been a virtual connection someplace.

Or a clear lack of one. A void.

She'd found no void. Just dead ends when it came to actually getting to the money. Most of what Eduardo had done wasn't on paper.

Or spoken about over modern technology, either.

Which is what had made him so successful.

He'd been word of mouth. Fistfuls of cash for those who were willing to keep their mouths shut, to make one thing happen quietly, low risk, in order to get rich fast.

He'd been the brains. Millions of successful plans carried to completion. No two exactly alike. That would have bored him.

Days of staring at her own misused code, living in her father's head, and seeing the end of her life in sight, brought clarity.

A strange kind of peace.

She knew.

No more doubts.

There'd be no proof. Not without finding every tiny dealer out there who'd been touched by Duran money once or twice. And was willing to talk. But even then, the deed would be too small on its own, the evidence nowhere near enough to bring down an empire.

Duran knew that. He'd styled his business that way from the beginning.

And when he'd needed bigger help, he'd chosen well. A CIA agent. An IRSCI. The spoiled, avaricious son of a foreign dignitary.

There could be more.

While Nicole stood there, gun aimed and ready to shoot at any movement that wasn't Harc, her senses focused so completely on those yards of land before the drop-off and around both cliffs to the sides of them. She knew that when the case was over, when the mountains were clear of Eduardo's men and Harc went home to his ranch, Eduardo's world would be unchanged.

He'd probably move.

Maybe not. Maybe he'd fight the court battle, to prove that he wasn't guilty of convictable crimes. His confession had already been shown as false. She'd proven that.

The financial details he'd given would be bogus, too. She had no doubt of that.

He'd say he was protecting her.

She was his scapegoat.

The realization was new. And yet...felt like she'd known forever. Everything that he'd ever done could be explained by his need to care for his baby girl.

On some level.

He was a fiend. A murderer. A thief and an abuser. And smart enough to have come up with the perfect crime.

Which he'd repeated countless times in the twenty-five years she'd been alive. Right under her nose.

Using her technological creations to transfer funds and then make the tracking of such impossible. He hadn't just used them. He'd manipulated them in such a way that even he wouldn't know how to trace them. It was all random.

Except for the Wagar part.

He'd be next, after Harc and Nicole. She was sure of that, too. The man's cry for help the other day...maybe that had been directed at her, too.

Wagar had failed to keep Nicole in line, to romance her and give her and Eduardo a legal and clearly understood passage out of the country when Nicole screwed up and entered her DNA in the database.

The man would do better, surrendering himself to the police.

Nicole started to shake. From standing frozen in one position, but also with the thought that struck. Keeping her senses tuned outward, she kept her gun in hand as she retrieved her computer. Dove into Wagar's private channel and told him to go to the police.

Told him that Duran's plan was in motion and he wouldn't live out the night if he didn't get protection immediately. Banking on the selfish man's weakness, his desire for life over death to prompt him to make the call.

If he saw the message in time.

And so he'd know it was her, she repeated, in an offhand fashion, something he'd said to her months ago when he'd tried to force her to kiss him on the back grounds of her father's mansion.

He'd said that she would be his. And she'd like it.

I'll never be yours. And I never liked you, she typed.

Then punched in the code to send through the security protocols.

Gun in hand, she left her computer on the ground. Took up her previous position, standing guard.

Heard a shot ring out.

And knew her time had come.

HARC GOT THE one whose head popped up to ground level from down below a single second before the arm bearing a revolver appeared. Got him before the guy's shot went off.

He spun in the next second, saw no movement slithering down from above. But heard the land as another one of his TNT pops went off. He shot behind a boulder that protected him from the second attacker, at least for a few seconds. And saw the second head coming up over the edge of the cliff, was ready for the gun to appear, aimed right at him.

"Stop!" The voice was female. He hardly recognized it. Didn't turn. Couldn't take his focus off the head. "I go willingly, as long as Harc Taylor is left alone. The second he is harmed, I shoot myself, and the program I wrote and have set to go live will do so as planned."

What in the hell was she doing?

He took his gaze off the man hanging onto the side of the cliff—gun in hand but not currently aimed—long enough to confirm that Nicole was standing in the middle of their encampment with a gun pointed at her head.

He scanned for the dropper. Saw no one.

Glanced at his known shooter again. The gun still lay on the ground, within the grasp of the hands and arms hanging on.

"Daddy?" the woman called, her tone unrecognizable to him. "You're here, aren't you? You wouldn't leave me out in the night to do this all alone."

Harc didn't breathe. Waiting. Neither of the horses had moved. He prayed the drugs kept them down a little while longer.

"I need to see you, Daddy. I've missed you so much."

Harc heard the familiar sound of tears in the voice. Recognition hit him like bricks in the gut.

And he knew. She wasn't crying for the man who'd robbed his daughter of her right to a life of her own. She was crying for what she'd almost had.

What she'd wanted—that for which she'd started to grow a tiny bit of hope.

No one had moved. Which was Harc's clue that she was right. The hired thugs knew what Nicole did—that Eduardo was there. The man's one weakness had always been the child he'd mistakenly thought he owned. Because she'd been from his seed. His daughter.

Hugh Gussman wasn't going to let this one go down without him.

Even if, ultimately, she had to die.

"I answered the second I saw your message, Daddy," she continued to stand there, gun to her head, calling out in an almost childlike tone. "I did as you asked. I'm so sorry I didn't want to marry Wagar. And that I entered my DNA into that database. I was just lonely, Daddy. I'm so, so sorry." She started to cry then.

It took everything Harc had to leave her standing there, alone, with her sobs.

But she'd just given him clues as to what she was doing. Playing out a scenario she'd kept from him, from everyone. Eduardo had contacted her.

And she'd gone back to him. In cyberspace.

Leading to the horror playing out before him.

He had to trust her. To let her show him the way.

Unless...had Duran manipulated her into getting herself killed?

Or even killing herself?

Some kind of sick version of Munchausen syndrome?

He had to trust her. And keep his focus on saving her life, too.

"Daddy? I'm sorry! Please come get me."

Harc saw the head on the ground move slightly. In the direction from which he'd heard the most recent pop. Just as a voice came from trees above it. "Taylor, drop the gun, and my daughter lives. Don't, and you both die."

Harc set his gun on the ground at his feet.

HE HAD A smaller pistol in an ankle holder. Nicole had seen Harc strap it on that morning. When they'd barely been speaking. Both pretending that they hadn't spent part of the night naked together.

She held on to the thought, letting it feed the tears that were her only chance at getting Harc out of there alive. As much as her father saw her as a possession, one he'd likely kill if he felt justified in doing so, he also prided himself on lavishing her with fulfilled wishes. And being able to console every pain she'd ever felt.

Thinking of Harc kept her purpose strong and the tears coming. Eduardo didn't like her tears. They panicked him. She'd learned young to suck them back. Her inability to do so would knock him some.

The shaking was not part of the plan. Not that it had been all that intricate to begin with.

Saving Harc. Exposing Eduardo. Perhaps dying in the process. She'd just known that it had to end.

And that she could make it happen.

Her father knew full well she could have put a program in motion. He'd want to keep her from letting it go live.

He couldn't be sure what all she knew. She'd lived with him a long time.

Eduardo's voice had come from above. The ensuing silence told her that he was either aiming for a big final moment. Or on his way down to her.

She braced for either.

The man at the cliff, athletic build, several inches shorter than the CIA agent she'd fallen in love with, had climbed all the way up and stood, gun aimed toward Harc. She prayed he had his little pistol in hand and would get the first shot off if the man moved to shoot.

In daylight, she'd put her money on him every time. But in the dark…discernment of a small muscle move could prove impossible.

Still, it was clear that he was waiting further instruction. Her father was still at the helm.

But his ship had definite leaks in it.

Wagar was a wild card.

And two of Duran's powerhouses had been exposed.

He was a pro at taking hits and making them appear as bonuses. New ways to conquer. To win. But he'd taken a lot of them recently. One after another.

He had to be aware of the chinks hitting his armor.

He'd have known that if Harc Taylor or any other authorities had enough on him to convict him without a confession, they'd never have accepted the plea deal.

Or at least figure them for being smarter than that.

And her deep dive into his protocols would have told him that they were still looking for that evidence.

There had to be something there he didn't want her to find. The thought filtered down through her very deliberate continued show of weakness. Almost wiping the tears from her face.

Not much. She was certain she'd been right about any lack of findable proof. For the most part. But something that would end him.

"I found it, Daddy," she called. "It's in the program I

wrote tonight. It will go live unless I stop it." She hiccupped. Caught a whiff of his cologne. Dropped her gun arm from up by her head down to her thigh. Then, in a weaker tone, said, "And I'm so sorry about that, too."

Truth seeped into her despair.

He'd arrived.

And she *was* sorry.

Because the last piece of her own puzzle had just come to her.

As much as she hated Hugh Gussman and Eduardo Duran, she loved him, too.

Chapter Twenty-Three

She'd been communicating with Duran. Behind his back. Shock and disappointment hung in the air Harc was breathing. Mixed with more.

She'd made provisions for him to live.

He had no time for feelings. Processed all information as it came at him. Fully focused. Nicole was using the strongest weapon she had—her mind.

She might've been working with her father. But she wasn't working against Harc.

Filling in the blanks from there, Harc saw what was coming. Weighed options.

"Daddy..." Running to the man as he appeared around the corner, Nicole wrapped her arms around his neck, hugging him close. When the older man's arms circled his daughter with equal fervor, Harc's emotions went into deep freeze. He calculated.

Came up with several responses, all equally valid, depending on circumstance.

Duran was impressive in person. Even in darkness illuminated only by the moonlight. Tall, lithe, athletic, the man commanded respect in the middle of the night after rappelling down a mountain side.

He was also armed. Harc noted the bulge in the man's

jeans beneath the hooded sweatshirt Duran wore. Suspected there was an equal one in his waistband.

He could relate. Figured a third gun on the man's ankle and a knife slid into a sock on the other leg. He knew the drill.

Lived it. Even on the ranch. Some habits didn't die.

The goon at the cliff still had his gun trained on Harc. Second hired man still hadn't shown himself. That one worried Harc some. He didn't like not knowing.

No sound from the horses.

Nor any sign of agents on the ground.

The hug ended. Hugh Gussman's arm remained around his daughter's back. Claiming ownership. The man never glanced in Harc's direction. He took a step.

Nicole did not.

"Not yet, Daddy. Harcus Taylor goes first. As soon as I know he's safely with authorities, I'm yours."

"We don't have time to play games, Char," the man said. "I give you my word he won't be touched."

The man was good. Too good. Forcing Nicole to trust him. Or admit that she didn't.

Go. He willed her. His mind clicking, crossing off scenarios, bringing others up to play. He could take the guy at the cliff. Didn't know how many others there'd be.

"You gave me your word by coming down here," she told him. "I need to know I can trust you to do as you say, Daddy. I'm not a little girl anymore. It has to work both ways."

He wasn't going to kill her right then and there. She seemed to know that.

Harc was beginning to suspect the man wasn't going to kill his daughter at all. He really thought he had enough control over her to be able to keep her. His prized possession.

He wasn't as sure that Nicole had fallen back under his spell.

She was fighting too hard for Harc. But requiring the show of trust was a good call.

About ready to pop out of his skin with his need to do more than just stand and watch the woman put her life on the line, Harc took her cue. Kept his place in the game. A pawn. Standing on the same square. Untouched.

"How do you know I wouldn't have him shot the second he's out of ear range? Or quietly captured before he's ten feet away?"

"Because I'm trusting you." Four words. Said so softly Harc barely heard them. Lined with love. There was no mistaking that. Then, more loudly, she added, "And because that program is going to publish in the portal, like I said, but the information is also going to be hitting key inboxes if he doesn't make it back to safety. You taught me well, Daddy. Respect has to work both ways. I let you down. But you betrayed me, too."

She was good. Impressive. And hadn't looked at Harc once.

He could hardly believe it when Eduardo bowed his head. More than a nod. Clearly a sign of acquiescence. Whether genuine or not, Harc had no idea. Couldn't take a chance on thinking that it was.

He saw the man give a nod toward the man at the cliff. Was already reaching for the gun he'd dropped to the ground when he heard...movement. But no shot. Glancing up he saw cliff guy holster his gun.

"Get your gun and go," Eduardo's voice aimed at Harc was filled with authority. And warning, too.

Harc was only going to be given one chance. Gun in hand, he held it tight. Took note of the fact that any bullet he'd shoot at the older man would hit his daughter as well. Eduardo, still holding on to Nicole, had put himself between her and Harc.

Not just a defensive move to save his daughter. Harc got the message. Eduardo would always be the wall between Harcus Taylor and Nicole Compton.

He was also going to let Harc walk out of there. Whatever Nicole had found on him was a game changer.

And she hadn't shared it with him.

The thing they'd come to the mountains to find—something that could end the kingpin's twenty-five-year reign, close down his organization permanently—and she'd found it. But hadn't turned it over to authorities.

"How do I report in when I'm safe?" he asked. "What number do I call?"

"You call me." Nicole's voice. Not her father's. "On the phone you supplied."

They were the last words he heard her say.

OF ALL THE ways she'd envisioned herself heading out of the mountain—including in a body bag—on foot with her father hadn't been one. The enforcer at the cliff fell in right behind them, making good on Eduardo's choice to let Harc go. When a second man appeared as they rounded the cliff and led the way in front of them, Nicole took a breath filled with relief.

They were really going to let Harc go.

She'd saved his life.

And if that's all she did, she'd die on a good note. A decent person. Who'd been born to the wrong man and had to pay for his sins.

She'd been eerily calm since her father had appeared. No panic. No shaking.

She didn't want to die. Wasn't giving up.

To the contrary, the burst of success filled her with more

strength than she'd ever known. She didn't try to break free of her father's arm around her waist. To the contrary, she wrapped him with her own. Allowing herself those moments in the woods to think about reasons why she'd loved him.

"You never missed a Christmas," she said aloud. "No matter where you were or had to be, you either took me with you or you made it home." They'd walked off the way she and Harc had come in. And were taking things carefully.

Eduardo gave her side a gentle squeeze—a hug, not a hold—and said, "You're my princess."

He didn't sound right to her. There was a lack of something...confidence? Or maybe it was the presence of something. Worry.

She'd never heard him with a tone of doubt underlying anything he said.

And it wasn't that either, she realized as she replayed his words and realized they'd been laced with sadness.

Because the easy days were over?

Or because she was?

"I'm assuming we're leaving the country," she said then, talking softly enough that those behind and in front of them couldn't hear.

"A car is waiting to take us to a helicopter that will land us on a yacht. From there we take another helicopter to a private air strip. And on to Morocco."

Morocco. Not El Salvador.

She didn't ask about Arnold Wagar. Didn't want to know.

What mattered to her was the man would not be touching her again. She'd die first.

Die. Death. The words, the concept...it was like they were guiding her. As though she had some kind of wish to end her life.

She stumbled. Her father caught her, steadied her. And

it hit her. He'd protected her. But he'd never let her have her own identity. She'd been raised in his image. But she wasn't him. Wasn't even all that much like him.

The past three months, the past days, she'd been defining herself. She knew what was worth living for.

And what was worth dying for, too.

Choices made from the depths of a soul that had been smothering for most of her life.

She didn't want her life to end. It was just beginning. But if she had to die, she was right with herself. A concept she'd never even considered before.

And should have. Long before.

As the strip they were walking along narrowed into a climb, Hugh Gussman fell into step behind her, a hand at her back as needed. She slid some, clawed some, made her way upward. And wondered if her father felt right about the life he'd lived.

She didn't ask. Nor did she question him further about their plans. How long were they going to hike without sustenance? Would they make it out of the mountains yet that day? On foot?

Just like their escape from the country, he'd have it all planned.

Unless he chose to kill her as soon as she deadened the cyber messaging she'd told him she had scheduled to publish. She wasn't going to make that easy on him. He'd taken her gun, but he'd seen to it that she had one hell of a lot of self-defense training, and she'd use every single aspect of it in a fight for her life.

She'd stay calm. Use her mind. The one weapon she had that just might be more powerful than his. It wasn't less—she believed that much.

And if he intended to let her live, to start a new life with him, she might go. Just long enough to nail him.

She had other family.

A vision of Savannah smiling at her from her raft in the pool in her big sister's backyard flashed into Nicole's mind. Followed by others. One in the middle of the night. Just a head above the covers, eyes wide and filled with love, as Nicole lay with her head on the next pillow, trying to comprehend that her entire life had been a lie.

Savannah—whose only family were her partners. They'd welcomed Nicole into the fold, and Nicole wanted to be a contributing part of it.

She also had a heart that had just done a speed course on falling in love. She'd always been a quick learner.

Giving herself a mental shake, she shied away from any other thoughts of Harc. Every step was working toward his freedom from harm. With agents on the ground in the mountains, she expected a call from him within the hour.

Half of that had already passed.

She hoped they weren't trying to come after her. Eduardo would have men posted every step of the way. He didn't follow protocols other than his own. He played dirty. And he'd spare no expense, stop at nothing to get what he wanted.

She had to pee.

And was going to need water.

Dawn would be breaking, and then what? Satellite vision would increase tenfold. No way was Eduardo unaware of that possibility. Nor would he allow himself to be caught in such a basic way.

He had to keep her alive, though. Until he could be certain that she hadn't found the one thing that made him vulnerable. On and off as they hiked, she'd been trying to figure out what it was. Had been taking a huge risk threatening him with it when she hadn't known for sure that it existed. Just, knowing him, it made sense to her that it did.

He'd already be out of the country otherwise.

Ordering whatever hits he wanted made.

They'd come to a clearing. A flat area in between towering mountain peaks. As soon as she stepped onto it, uniformed guards appeared, rifles pointed.

Her heart started to pound. Until, in the darkness, she made out the helicopter.

With a US Army seal.

The guns weren't protecting Eduardo. They were pointed at him.

She started to shake. And to cry.

Harc had saved her.

EDUARDO'S ENTOURAGE HAD WON. They'd made it to the clearing before Mike's teams had. Tearing up inside, Harc moved stealthily down the tree trunk, taking in every aspect of the flat ground he'd had in view from his branch for the past fifteen minutes. Dim view.

Cursing at himself for the night binoculars in his pack and not on him, he counted a dozen bodies with rifles. Falling with precision into two lines forming a pathway to the opened door of the copter.

A stolen vessel. Made possible with the equally pilfered credentials of one double agent, Clayton Abernathy, who'd been found dead sometime after midnight.

Duran had used him one last time. Served him up to Nicole and then had him murdered. Leaving no forensic evidence behind.

And if Nicole got on that helicopter, there'd be no trace of her for Harc to find.

Mike, multiple agencies, and Sierra's Web had been online with him since the second he'd walked free of the encampment. Agents in the area had been following intruders since before Harc came out of the cave.

The ones who'd drugged the horses had already been apprehended with paraphernalia found on them.

Over a mile away.

That arrest had just happened when Harc first called in.

Imperial and Mahogany were still out but alive and breathing steadily, he'd been told.

Somehow he had to provide the same fate for Nicole. Alive and breathing steadily.

Him against a dozen armed hitmen.

Nicole had just arrived at the door of the helicopter. Was being helped up. Harc's phone buzzed. Agents were two minutes away.

He didn't have that much time. Harc aimed his gun. The machine's props were already turning. Ready to lift off. Once Eduardo was on board, the thing would be in the air.

The criminal mastermind lifted both hands up to the opening in the copter.

And Harc pulled his trigger.

THE BLAST DEAFENED HER. Falling from the bench she'd just perched upon to the floor, Nicole shoved her body underneath the seat as far as she could. Shaking hard, she remained frozen to the spot, listening to the shouting, both inside and outside the aircraft.

Followed by a barrage of gunfire.

Booted feet passed in front of her. A door slammed. Covering her ears, she braced for a bullet. And prayed that Harc had made it to safety.

He hadn't called.

And Eduardo was leaving her there to die. If she didn't explode in the helicopter, he'd make sure she got caught in the gunfire.

He'd bested her after all.

She'd known the possibility was there.

Tears dripped from her eyes down her cheeks. An awakening of sorts.

She wasn't going to die while hiding in fear.

As the gunfire continued to rage outside, though with less secession and maybe fewer guns, she slid out from under the bench and saw one of her father's go bags.

The helicopter...it had been his.

She'd climbed aboard thinking she'd been saved—because Harc had been. Instead, she'd been on her way to meet her fate.

The go bag.

It held at least one gun. Always. Less than a minute later, armed, she made her way toward the side door of the helicopter. Keeping herself hidden inside, she took a quick look outward.

Her breath caught, her heart pounded through her lungs, as she saw Harc, gun raised and pointed at one of the men she recognized from the trek through the woods. But Eduardo was coming up behind Harc, armed and aimed.

"No!" The scream ripped out of her. Renting the air.

Guns went off. Hers. Others.

And she fell to the edge of the door, shaking, watching as though in slow motion as bodies fell.

Eduardo's. The guards'.

And Harc's.

WINDED, HARC LAY on the ground for the couple of seconds it took him to realize that it was over. And then his gaze focused on his gun where it had fallen when he'd been hit. He started to reach for it.

Had to get to Nicole.

"Harc!" He heard her scream in the midst of the fray, over voices calling orders, feet rushing. And closed his eyes in gratitude for a brief second.

She was alive.
They'd done it.

NICOLE HEARD ALL about how Harc had saved her life. His shot at the cockpit, disabling the instrument panel, had been dangerous. A few inches either way could have blown up the aircraft. Instead, he'd given agents on the way to the clearing time to arrive.

And how her scream had alerted an FBI agent she'd never heard of to Eduardo's approach on Harc, resulting in the agent killing her father.

Harc's gun had taken down the last of Eduardo's newly hired henchmen. Just as the bullet from Eduardo's gun had gone off, missing Harc's chest due to the FBI agent's bullet hitting him.

She listened while everyone talked around her. Both in the helicopter ride out of the mountain carrying an unconscious Harc with a tourniquet tied around his leg, and in the private waiting room she'd been shown to upon arrival at the hospital in Denver.

The bullet had hit an artery. And while an agent on-site had managed to stem the flow, Harc had lost a lot of blood.

Was in surgery.

And she was...numb.

Couldn't feel a thing. Except a lack of air. She could draw breath. Just couldn't seem to get enough of it to relax. Every muscle in her body taut, she sat there. She heard. She comprehended. She even nodded where appropriate. Shook her head.

Said thanks once.

She was a robot. The body leftover from the woman she'd been.

If Harc died...

"Nicole!" A jolt rent through her as she heard Savannah's voice. She'd been told Mike and her sister were on their way. On an hours-long flight.

Had she imagined the sound?

Forcing herself to respond, to look toward the voice, she caught only a glimpse of the tears in her sister's eyes before she was caught up in Savannah's arms, her sister's head next to hers. Holding hers.

Sobs rent her body. Horrible, ugly wracking sounds that hurt her from the inside out. And she held on. Tightly.

Feeling Savannah's body start to rock slowly. Side to side. Taking Nicole's with it. In a rhythm that felt...familiar to her. Not in a memory type of way.

In an instinctive one.

Closing her eyes, she gave herself up to the soft motion. While tears continued to roll slowly past her shut lids, the sobs let go of their hold on her body.

And when she was ready, she pulled away. "I'm so sorry," she told her sister. "So sorry." She shook her head. "I'm sorry."

Savannah's head shook softly as her soft fingers pushed the tangled hair away from Nicole's face. "You have nothing to be sorry for, sweetie," she said. And then more firmly, with a wide open almost steely look in her eyes: "Nothing."

She knew that wasn't true. "Harc..."

"Your scream saved his life."

The words struck a chord within her. She stared at her sister. Seeing the scene again. The body's going down. Shuddered. Saw possibility.

"He saved mine," she said then. Putting pieces together. What she'd known. What she'd heard. "If he hadn't shot the cockpit, I'd have been in the air when agents arrived."

Whisking away to God knew where with the man who'd fathered her.

"He's dead," she said then. No antecedent to the pronoun.

Savannah didn't seem to need one. She nodded. Touched her forehead to Nicole's. "I know."

Looking in her big sister's eyes she said, "I loved him."

Savannah didn't look disappointed as she nodded.

And Nicole said, "And I hated him so much."

Savannah's smile denoted no happiness but a curious, comforting understanding as she said, "Me, too." And followed it with, "For both."

They talked softly then, just the two of them. Savannah told Nicole how her dad had been her hero her entire life. Before he'd "died" and afterward, as she'd believed he'd given his life to right egregious wrongs.

And Nicole told her sister, again, about Eduardo never missing a Christmas with her. There'd be more. Sometime.

In bits and pieces as Nicole healed. As they both did.

Savannah's sudden smile, lighting her face, brought a hint of hope for the future to Nicole as her sister said, "And by the way... Nicole! You chose the name Mom gave you!" Then, more softly, "And Compton..." Savannah's lips tightened, her chin clenched, and her eyes filled with tears again. "That's me."

"It's us," Nicole told her. "Sisters. Family."

Savannah opened her mouth, but Nicole didn't get to hear whatever her sister's response would be. The door opened and Mike was standing there.

She hadn't even thought about the fact that he hadn't come in with Savannah.

Standing, Nicole studied his face. "What?" she asked. She'd lived with the man as her constant companion—except in the bed and bathrooms—for months. She knew that look. He had something to tell her.

"Harc's out of surgery. Awake. And asking for yo..."

She missed the end of the last word as she ran from the room.

HARC HATED HOSPITALS. Hospital beds. And everything about being confined. He'd been told he'd be free to leave in the morning as long as there were no complications. And he agreed to abide by doctor's orders.

He'd already broken those. Was propped in the chair in his room, his left, very bandaged leg extended and braced with the footrest. The feat had cost him some sweat. No tears.

No way he was going to say goodbye to Nicole lying in some damned bed like a helpless, injured soul.

He'd barely gotten his leg settled before the door opened and she was there.

Still in the shirt he'd seen her walk into the cave in after changing the night before. The same jeans. Her hair hadn't been brushed.

She'd been crying. A lot.

Eduardo was dead.

Other than the blood loss, Harc hadn't been in any real danger. Bodily at any rate. The fact that he'd been shot in the back of thigh was going to play with him for a while.

Undercover agents never turned their backs on their enemies.

He'd just been surrounded by them...

Nicole had stopped just inside the door. Her big brown eyes filling with tears. He saw her draw breath. Straighten her shoulders.

Prepared himself to get through the next moments.

And then home to Imperial and Mahogany who, Mike had just told him, were back in their stalls, having been checked by his vet and were expected to be just fine. Both had eaten.

She took a step closer. Then another. Each one bringing them nearer to the goodbye. He had no right to make it difficult for her. Or prolong it. She was finally free. A young woman who'd been robbed of a past, with her entire future stretching freshly ahead of her.

He just had to know one thing. "What did you find on your father?" They'd been searching for years. He needed the closure.

"Nothing." She looked him straight in the eye as she said so. Coming closer all the while. He'd have backed up if his chair wasn't already against the wall.

When she reached him, she...didn't stop coming at him. She ran her fingers through his hair. Touched his face. Smiling. And crying, too.

"I had to think like him," she said softly. "And as scary as it was to find out, I was pretty good at it."

The tone of voice...he'd heard it the night they'd made love...it broke down some barriers inside him. Enough to say, "You did good. Better than good. You impressed the hell out me. And got the job done."

She deserved to know all of that. But no more. The fact that he'd never met a woman like her, was certain he never would again, would be kept to himself.

He was a semi-retired CIA agent who'd made some morally questionable decisions, with a ranch to run. Not a young man with his entire future stretching out before him.

Kneeling down, she folded her arms over his good thigh. Making it nearly impossible for him to keep his hands to himself. "I know it's way too soon and that I have no idea what any kind of regular life even looks like, let alone how good I'll be at it, but..." She stopped. Looked up at him. With a hint of arrogance that kind of turned him on. Even in his newly out of anesthetic, but painkiller-less, state. "Actually, that's not quite right. I know a lot," she said. "I've experienced horrors unlike people in regular life feel. I've got three degrees. And most importantly, I know what I want to live for. And what I'm willing to die for, too."

He smiled. Couldn't help himself. The woman was...just that intriguing. Beguiling. Inspiring. Admirable... "What do want to live for?"

"Another night naked with you."

He coughed. With some spit attached. Not at all cool. Or even a hint of sexy. More like a guy in a hospital gown drooling all over himself.

Or the partially broken man that he was. Recently zipped up bullet hole notwithstanding.

With one thumb, she wiped his lower lip. "Why aren't you in bed?"

He wasn't going to answer that. And so he said, "What are you willing to die for?"

She nodded, as though to say, *Okay*. As though he'd just issued a challenge and she was willing to take it on.

"Another night naked with you."

There was nothing sexy in the vulnerable look in her eyes or the soft, almost pleading tone of her voice. He couldn't look away. Or gently remove her arms from his thigh. He should. He had to.

He couldn't. "You have no idea what being with me would mean."

"I think I do," she said, sounding more like herself. Assured. Confident. "I've just spent days sharing caves with you, Harc. Voiding into holes. Eating freeze-dried food. On the verge of death. And talking about things that matter. Riding horses in a gorgeous mountain range and experiencing the most incredible lovemaking I'm ever going to know. I invaded your home. Made you defensive. Angry. If I find out you sniffle instead of using a tissue, throw your dirty clothes on the floor, or listen to acid rock...it's just not going to matter."

He was sinking. Had to stop her. "You don't like acid

rock?" he asked, as though the dislike would be a mortal sin.

"No. Do you?"

She had him. "No."

With a nod, Nicole sat back. On her butt. On the floor. No hands on him. He felt bereft. Put it down to the anesthesia.

"Here's the thing," she said then. "You've spent over a decade living fake lives. Getting so completely into them that you slept with fake partners..."

Now she was getting it. He felt the truth slice clean through him but had known all along where the conversation had to lead.

To end.

"I've lived an entire fake life, Harc. Yet when you look at me, you see...me. Not Charlotte Duran or Nicole Compton. You just see...a person."

He nodded. She was right. He did.

"When nothing else seems real, you are."

He swallowed. Hard.

"You don't judge by a straight line of right and wrong. Or by action alone. You judge by motive. By heart. You don't trust what you see. Or hear. You need more. And because of that, you understand that I'm not always going to trust. And you can live with that."

"How do you know that?" She could be wrong. He'd rather lose her right away, then down the road.

"Because you were at the clearing this afternoon. You shot the helicopter. And you asked for me when you came out of surgery. I didn't trust you enough in the end," she said. "Eduardo had contacted me through a portal I'd hacked, and I didn't tell you that. Nor did I share my plan with you to play him at his own game. I went double agent on you, and...you still shot the helicopter."

"I'm eleven years older than you."

"I'm eleven years younger than you."

"I live on a ranch."

"I can't think of anything I'd like more. Lord knows, I need the therapy."

Finally, he found his out. "I was actually thinking about going back to work. In some fashion. Not undercover. But I'm good at what I do. I know things. I can help."

She smiled then. "I've already told Savannah that I want to stay on with Sierra's Web. I was thinking maybe, down the road, there could be a house in Phoenix and the ranch waiting for us when we need a break or have time off."

"Like at Christmas." The words came out of his mouth before he could stop them.

With tears in her eyes, Nicole climbed back up on his good leg. "I love you, Harcus Taylor. I'm a piece of work. Life with me won't be easy. But I'm going to love you until the day I die and after that, too."

Harc felt moisture prick his eyes. Not tears. Something more than that. Stronger. His heart melting, if such a thing were possible. He had no more fight in him.

"You can let yourself accept love, Harc." The whispered words slid inside him.

Without allowing another second to pass, he leaned over. Put hands under both of her arms and lifted her up to his good thigh, wrapped his arms around her, and held on. "I love you, Nicole," he said with his face in her neck. "I don't trust this entire situation between us, but I can't fight it. I love you. The Charlotte part, the Nicole part, and the parts that are yet to reveal themselves."

His chest lightened with every word.

And his instincts laid back, grinning.
There'd be challenges ahead. Problems, even.
But he'd finally found the man he'd always wanted to be.
He'd been inside him all along.
Driving him.
It had just taken seeing himself in Nicole's eyes for him to understand.

* * * * *

COMING SOON!

We really hope you enjoyed reading this book.
If you're looking for more romance
be sure to head to the shops when
new books are available on

Thursday 28th August

To see which titles are coming soon, please visit
millsandboon.co.uk/nextmonth

MILLS & BOON

FOUR BRAND NEW BOOKS FROM
MILLS & BOON MODERN

The same great stories you love, a stylish new look!

OUT NOW

Eight Modern stories published every month, find them all at:

millsandboon.co.uk

Afterglow Books is a trend-led, trope-filled list of books with diverse, authentic and relatable characters, a wide array of voices and representations, plus real world trials and tribulations. Featuring all the tropes you could possibly want (think small-town settings, fake relationships, grumpy vs sunshine, enemies to lovers) and all with a generous dose of spice in every story.

@millsandboonuk
@millsandboonuk
afterglowbooks.co.uk
#AfterglowBooks

For all the latest book news, exclusive content and giveaways scan the QR code below to sign up to the Afterglow newsletter:

LET'S TALK
Romance

For exclusive extracts, competitions and special offers, find us online:

- **f** MillsandBoon
- **X** @MillsandBoon
- **◉** @MillsandBoonUK
- **♪** @MillsandBoonUK

Get in touch on 01413 063 232

For all the latest titles coming soon, visit
millsandboon.co.uk/nextmonth